SWIFT NICK OF THE YORK ROAD

By

GEORGE EDGAR

AUTHOR OF "THE BLUE BIRD'S-EYE," ETC.

MILLS & BOON, LIMITED

49 RUPERT STREET

LONDON, W.

SWIFT NICK OF THE YORK ROAD

CHAPTER I

ISAACS, the Jew, rubbed his hands. His club, in part hotel and in part gaming house, was prospering.

The prosperity of this feature of the night life of Covent Garden depended on the rooms being full of men with money to burn and of other men capable of exciting the heat which brings about financial combustion. On this night, a Monday, in the January of 1670, the rooms were full.

Isaacs' place in Covent Garden was a night house when night houses were notorious. The proprietor was in no sense a particular man. And, indeed, why should he have been particular in his methods ? In a warm period he was considered " hot, devilishly hot ! " and the nicest term of endearment bestowed on him implied that he was a " demned deep old blade," or " a precious rascal." The most that can be said for Isaacs was that he fitted his day and generation. The town was alive with birds of prey, from the dangerous hawk who brought down and killed the victim to the less dangerous but perhaps more abominable vultures who assembled to fight over the discarded carrion. Isaacs was of the vulture class, and when he went over the carcass he made a precious good job of it, picking clean and fine and leaving nothing for any other bird with watering beak beyond the bare white bones.

One pride Isaacs had in life. His house in Covent Garden was select. You might wine there and get roaring drunk, or dice there and come out skinned of your last guinea. You might quarrel there and even fight, using the language of a chairman or a postboy. But in these things you had to have address and to go through with them in a manner.

The word select was a term misused by Isaacs, as it is in our own day. During the reign of Isaacs, in Covent Garden, a flowered waistcoat covered a multitude of social sins. A perruque might curl upon a head hatching the plots of a devil ; a gentlemanly and well-turned leg did not necessarily avoid all the mud about a very dirty town. Isaacs' patrons were select in that their daily habit was impressive to the point of courtliness ; but neither the Jew proprietor, nor any other man, could guarantee the quality of manliness gilded by a studied show of outward finery.

I do not suppose Isaacs cared one of his brass buttons for the quality of character behind the brave war-paint. The manner rather than the matter of the man was of more importance. Isaacs himself, fat, hooked-nosed, pot-bellied, was too grasping to buy gilt lace for his faded habit, and remained consistently snuff-coloured in a garb that served him as livery. He was indeed too mean to wear the ostentatious linen of his day, or silken hose, and was content with wristbands, not too clean, and worsted stockings, showing that he had the tradesman's habit of mind, for all his select surroundings.

Figure this man Isaacs and his rooms for yourself. He occupied a house in Covent Garden which might have been taken for a private dwelling only it had divided doors, always open at night, and the windows of every floor were lighted until the sun struggled out each morning.

At night, Isaacs' rooms were illuminated by many candles within, while torches blazed without. Round the doors swarmed chairmen, linkboys, vendors of foodstuffs, runners, and seedy idlers. They quarrelled amongst themselves on the lighted causeway, or hurled unspeakable badinage at painted women walking by, who accepted verbal insolence with fixed hard smiles—the last tragic sign of their degradation. Strange, restless, and nomadic people floated through the night about Covent Garden and swirled away into the roystering Strand, where excited gentlemen battled with drunken chairmen, for fun; or turned, for completer enjoyment, to an attack on the decrepit, beshawled old men who formed the watch.

In entering these Covent Garden rooms you

would have been subjected to a polite scrutiny : ten chances to one by the vigilant Jew himself. The select character of the patrons was maintained by a polite fiction. In theory, new-comers needed some introduction. In practice, Isaacs found the way out for all who promised to have pockets lined with guineas. Familiar patrons passed into the lighted hall and up the heavy oak stairs, the fawning Jew bowing before them like a dancing master. With such a party we might ascend the lighted staircase, though the hour is five o'clock in the morning and frequenters of Isaacs' are beginning to leave the night haunt for the purpose of heralding the coming day in more reputable quarters.

In an anteroom, of the nature of a hall, panelled and lit by candles guttering in their brackets, three men were standing, and these were joined almost immediately by Isaacs, inclined to unbend a little after the long night. The rooms were still busy. One could hear the clatter of plates, the noise caused by the footsteps of people moving about the upper rooms, traces of song of the convivial order, and now and again bursts of drunken laughter.

One of the three men was Buck Dowling, a gentleman of standing, though little was known of his family. The other was a verdant youth from the country, young Squire Drew. Drew was a pigeon who had fluttered some fine feathers since he came into his father's broad acres in Yorkshire. Now, he was growing wiser through experience and more rookish in his outlook as his feathers diminished through a ceaseless process of plucking.

Both were young men, and stood in the ante-room, hatted, booted, cloaked for the outside. They were evidently on the point of taking their departure. They stood clinking glasses with a third man, whom they called Captain Ralph. Captain Ralph Barclay was tall, magnificently dressed, and startlingly sober for such an hour and in such surroundings.

He stood a full six feet in stature, but his height was accentuated by an elaborate black perruque. He wore a coat of shining black silk, fitting close to the body and long in the skirts ; the whole being elaborately braided and buttoned. The sleeves were slashed to show the fine linen of the shirt underneath, the laces of which were caught up with ribbons and fell in folds over the white, jewelled hands. The black silk stockings, starting with a roll over the breeches at the knees, were gartered with precious stones, and silver buckles flashed on the pointed shoes. A dress sword, with a jewelled hilt, hung from the waist.

Though drinking with the two men of the town, he was sober and his interest in them was obviously forced. When they laughed as they clinked glasses, Captain Ralph laughed with them, but mirthlessly, and there was a metallic quality about every note that rang as cold as steel. He had heavily marked brows, bold dark eyes which roved ceaselessly with the appraising restlessness of a courtesan's, and a mouth that in repose was closed tight and represented a thin, long line. When he laughed, and the lips opened, firm white teeth showed, glistening, in a

I*

manner that made one think of a lean and hungry dog. Most of all one noticed his nose—large, curved, with a high bridge, and ending in thin and sensitive nostrils. The hawk-like shape of this pronounced feature gave to the dark face, sallow through long hours, a suggestion of implacable, almost cruel alertness.

As Squire Drew held up his glass, that gallant's knees sagged a little and he reeled as he spoke, while his speech was not free from the tell-tale hiccough.

" Here's to you, Buck, and to you, Captain Ralph, and, damn me, as this is a stirrup cup, I'll take in Isaacs, too. I ought to be moving soon; I must have a clear head before breakfast, for I have to meet one of those lawyer sharks at eleven."

" More of the broad acres going ? " asked Buck Dowling, with a laugh, in which Captain Ralph joined as they clinked glasses.

" God's luck or the devil's—yes. Sir George and you have put a monkey on at least a hundred acres by to-night's play. I have the devil's own luck when I play with Captain Ralph, though I did stick it into Nevinson, earlier in the night."

Captain Ralph Barclay, flicking a speck of dust from his silken hose, smiled coldly.

" One must play up to the luck while it lasts," he said, with acid geniality. " Your turn will come. Everything comes to the man who plays the waiting game."

" And meanwhile the acres go," said Drew, with the doleful self-pity of the drunken man.

"What's the odds?" said Isaacs, sidling closer. "A man is only young once and must have his fling. A gallant of spirit will forget his losses and think only of his revenge."

"Yes," said Buck Dowling, slapping Drew on his cloaked back. "Everything is possible to a man of spirit. And remember, to-morrow no one will be happier to give you revenge than Captain Ralph and myself. To-morrow the luck may turn and we may be seeing our lawyers the day after that—eh, Captain Ralph?"

"Odds, yes," Captain Ralph rejoined, and his laugh was a sneer. "To-night the devil was in the cards. You are sure to have your turn with the jade Fortune. Here's to to-morrow. Isaacs! more mulled wine for a third stirrup cup. The morning air is raw outside and we must be careful of our young friend."

As Isaacs turned to order an attendant, a great noise came from the apartment to which the ante-room led. It was a mingled uproar. One heard something like a cheer, much laughter, the tramp of feet, and the thud of falling furniture. In the midst of the uproar the door opened. A man, laughing aloud, came out and, banging the door behind him, reeled unsteadily forward. When he neared the group he lurched towards an ottoman and sat there, laughing almost hysterically, until his fat, drunken face, grown purple, shook like a blancmange.

The new-comer was a well-known habitué, Sir Christopher Pike. A stout, blond man, his perruque was askew on his head, his ruffles were working to the back of his neck, and his dress was soiled and dishevelled. He looked what he was, an easy-going, extravagant, and somewhat foolish bon-vivant.

Sir Christopher, laughing in drunken glee, was not exactly a pretty spectacle.

" You are pleased to be amused," said Captain Barclay, and his alert eye swept over the shaking, grotesque figure on the ottoman with a faint suggestion of contempt.

" In faith, I am," the stout man replied. " I am vastly entertained. I have never laughed so much since I drove my grey mare into a Roundhead barber's shop window. Laugh! by the Lord, what a game ! "

Captain Barclay's attention was excited to an acute pitch of interest by the word game. The sound of the very word seemed to stimulate him, acting like a whiff of powder on a war horse.

" What game ? " he asked, curtly. " I thought the play was over."

" Yes, what is the game ? " Buck Dowling added. " Out with it, man, and don't sit there hiccoughing laughter like a child with the growing pain."

" Tell, us, Sir Christopher," Drew urged. " No gentleman should be a spoil-sport. If there be a game afoot, we ought to know."

" See for yourself," said Sir Christopher, finding himself pressed all round. " I call it a demned, amusing entertainment. It proves what I say, that life is a screaming puppet show. It discovers the fact that I have a demned nice sense of humour and appreciate the odds of a situation fit for play actors!" Again Sir Christopher leaned back on the seat he occupied and his body shook once more, as he passed from one peal of laughter to another.

" In the Lord's name, Christopher, tell us what excites your idea of humour. You fat men, in wine, become as hysterical as a lot of silly old women, calling over the water of Holland. Out with it, man," urged Captain Barclay.

" By my sacred heart of fire," the laughing figure returned, " it is the new fool from the country— that Nevinson. Sir Ladbroke Drake has plied him with port so freely that he is like to a mad bull. He has let his courage run away with his discretion."

" He has been losing heavily all the week here," said Isaacs, reflectively. " He dropped five hundred in these rooms last night."

" That I well know," answered Captain Ralph Barclay. " I had half of them and found the coins of the best." He spoke the words with a cold grin that was almost malignant.

" Well, you won't have many more," said Sir Christopher Pike. " What he's lost this week is nothing to what he's losing now. He has been losing all night at cards, and now he has lost his head and is throwing Sir Ladbroke Drake, high or low, for fifty guineas a throw. And the more he loses, the more he wants to play. And the more he plays, the more like a bull he gets. He looks as if he were charging into an all-sorts shop."

Captain Ralph Barclay made a move towards the door. When gamblers lost their heads, it was his mission in life to be present. If the young fool, Nevinson, were throwing for foolish amounts in the assembly room, with his mind whipped up to the work by wine, he, Captain Ralph, was wasting golden minutes by gossiping in the anteroom. Even as he thought the words, the loud noises in the next room ceased, and the unusual silence, caused by the sudden cessation of laughter, gave Isaacs' rooms, blasé already after a hot night, an eerie atmosphere, which made its proprietor uneasy and started him off for the same door to which Captain Ralph Barclay was moving. They reached it together, followed by the two cloaked and booted men, who under the new excitement had changed their minds about going home. The Jew threw open the door and a strange sight met the eyes of the party as they entered.

The room was big and dark, panelled in oak that was nearly black. The lighted candles did not dissipate the gloom, but served rather to accentuate it. About the apartment were tables for every kind of hazard. In a big, open grate a fire was burning low. The carpeted floor was littered with used and scattered playing-cards. There were empty bottles everywhere, some lying on the deserted tables, where their contents had dribbled away on to the green baize ; others, broken, were strewn about the floor. On these tables were spent candles, guttering out in their sticks, while others flamed in brackets, dripped their wax and burnt low. The atmosphere was hot and heavy with the fumes of wine and tobacco and vitiated with the presence of many people, breathing and rebreathing the air of a confined space, made all the worse because the windows were closed and the curtains drawn. The room was charged with the high note of passion, sometimes described as electric.

About twenty men were in the room, garmented in every colour. All wore the perruque of the period, which curled over their shoulders and made them look taller and more dignified than they were They sported the long coats, fitting closely to tne body, in various hues, and the waistcoats reaching to the knees and held by interminable buttons of different metals ; they displayed, in cravats at their throats and by the slashes in their sleeves, the volume of linen that marked the gentleman of Charles's day. After a long sitting their finery was somewhat dishevelled. The nice turn of a cravat had gone ; laces and linen were soiled ; some of their bows had fallen out of place ; here and there a brightly coloured waistcoat was stained with wine.

There was every imaginable type of face present, from the lean, bold, cynical countenance of the hawk, to the broad, round, good-humoured jowl of some simple gentleman, there to see life as it was known in his day. Some of the faces were coldly calculating and impassively sober ; others were red and flushed with wine ; a few were vacant of any suggestion of comprehension, the eyes stupefied and glazed with drink, the lips hanging loose and the heads sometimes lolling under the burden of approaching insensibility. Indeed, one gaudily dressed youngster, sporting a claret-coloured coat, lay full length on the floor, his wigged head hidden by the table. He had fallen there over his wine, and in the excitement had been left to his drunken sleep. His snoring gave a gross touch of common humanity to the strained silence of the room.

The whole of the men present had deserted their tables and were grouped round one near to the fire. As the three new-comers entered the room, no one looked towards them. Attention was riveted on two men, who were throwing against each other with the dice. First one took the box and rattled it, tumbling the marked ivory cubes on the felt top of the table. As the gamblers bent to count the throw, the men about them craned forward. Then the second player took the box and shook it.

He was a young man. It was evident he was not of the town, for his clothes were a little more sober in cut than those about him. His habit was however very good and extremely neat, setting off a youthful, tall, and well-set-up figure. He had been drinking slightly. His cheeks were red and his eyes were glowing ; as he shook the box he did so with a recklessness in marked contrast to the careful manner of the man who had just made his throw. He was a handsome lad, in the early twenties, a trifle rakish and dissipated in appearance, and displaying no signs of unsophistication. He wore a dark-blue velvet coat with braided buttons, and underneath a dull grey vesture of silk, held together by many tiny buttons of polished brass or gold. His sleeves were not slashed, and beyond them his linen, good but plain, showed only its laced edging. He looked very handsome, standing there in the wavering light of the guttering candles.

" Low—it is," the other man said. " You lose again." The throw had been for fifty guineas, and the coins staked were swept up by the younger man's opponent, while the still tongues of those about the table began to babble again.

The older man was Sir Ladbroke Drake, who had served King Charles and had come back from France when the second Charles returned from his refuge abroad. He was a middle-aged man, handsome in a sinister fashion, cool and collected, with the nice, quick, assured movements of the habitual gambler. The sinister note in his make-up was a subtle suggestion of craftiness, expressed by the somewhat uneasy and furtive sweep of his eye, his fixed attention on the game, and his clear-headed, guarded control of himself, in a place where most of the people present were far away from a standard of sobriety making for sound judgment.

In habit, he was well dressed to the point of being a dandy. It was a sign of the temperament of the man that his attire was as correct in its ordered neatness as if he had just stepped from his dressing-room and out of the hands of his valet. His dress was much the same in form as his opponent's, but richer in texture and more varied in colour. His coat and breeches were of a ribbed, salmon-coloured silk, and the long vest reaching to his knees was of gold brocade, around which a silk sash was tied. His linen was the whitest and the finest in the room.

At his left side peeped the jewelled hilt of a long sword, worn under the skirt of his ample coat, a few inches of the scabbard showing at his heels.

The younger man, Nicholas Nevinson, laughed recklessly as Sir Ladbroke Drake caught up the dice on the table and dropped them one by one in the cup. As he did so, he looked with cynical coolness on Nevinson.

The wine was in the young man's blood.

"Rip me," he said; "I'm at the end of my tether. I'll throw you for all I have left. Damn me, the luck must turn. Did ever the ivories run so deadly against a man? You've thrown high every time you have called."

Nevinson took out a leather bag from his waistcoat pocket and emptied the contents on the table. From it poured a little stream of gold—in all, thirty guineas.

"The last of the patrimony," he said, with a reckless laugh. "I'll call you for that; the man who shows the highest wins in one throw."

Sir Ladbroke Drake took the box. His face was grimly intent as he rattled the cubes. The crowd round the tables drew nearer as the dice were thrown on the green cloth.

The silence was broken by the sight of the cubes. They lay there close together—two sixes. As he counted them, a crafty smile played round the firm mouth of the gamester. He picked up the cubes, replaced them in the cup, and handed it to Nevinson.

"You have a chance of throwing the twelve to save your money," he said.

Nevinson took the cup and rattled it vigorously. The sound of the dice was the only noise in the room.

For the last time he threw the ivory cubes upon the table. Those who craned their necks saw that he had thrown a two and a one.

"My game," said Sir Ladbroke, tersely, and glanced an inquiry at his opponent.

"I am satisfied," said Nevinson, slightly pale, and sobering rapidly.

As he spoke he fingered the dice on the table.

"To-morrow, I will give you your revenge," suggested Sir Ladbroke, with grim courtesy.

Nevinson rolled the cube with his finger, absently.

"To-morrow—well, who knows," he began, vaguely. His eyes were fixed on the dice he had been fingering, and suddenly a strange fire lit them. Almost as his expression changed, his opponent, watchful as ever, thrust out his hand to pick them up. Nevinson caught the outstretched fingers in a grip of steel. They faced each other, almost unnoticed, for the company had turned away to talk of this gambling duel and the excitement of the evening.

"Stop!" said Nevinson. "Drop those dice."

"What do you mean?" Sir Ladbroke shouted, his grey face turning a shade paler as he attempted to drag away his hand.

"Drop those dice," Nevinson repeated, sternly. He gave the hand a twist and the two cubes fell upon the table. He rolled the pair by flicking them with his hand, and each time they stopped, low.   At once he picked up the cup, placed the dice in it, shook them and threw again.

They settled down and totalled three—the number he had last thrown.

As he did so the company were attracted by his action and again drew nearer the table, their attention fixed on Nevinson's unusual action.

"Blackleg! these are not the dice you threw. These are loaded," Nevinson said, looking straight at Drake.

Though his face was grey Sir Ladbroke did not flinch.   Indeed, a grim smile played round his thin lips.

"Zounds, you forget yourself," he said; "you are drunk with your losses and know not what you say."

"Gentlemen, gentlemen. The hour is late," Isaacs' purring voice interrupted. His instinct told him of the beginning of a scene.

"I'm neither drunk with wine nor with my losses," said Nevinson. "I say it soberly, and call you cheat to your face. Gentlemen, I invite you to test these dice. They are loaded."

Before he could speak another word Sir Ladbroke, whose eye had been searching the company and had rested for a moment, with complete understanding, on the watching face of Captain Ralph Barclay, sprang towards Nevinson, apparently white-hot with indignation.

The two men closed and began to wrestle in the centre of the room. The other players, in an excited hubbub, rushed towards them and tried to tear the men apart. Every one seemed to lose his head. In the *mêlée* Nevinson was borne down by Drake, and fell with his head against the table leg, the pair of dice flying from his hands.

One man only seemed to see them—Captain Ralph Barclay. Unobserved in the *mêlée* he picked them up, and as he did so dropped another pair on the floor. It took but a moment to do this. Almost as soon as it was done, both combatants were on their feet and were being tightly held by their friends.

Drake's furtive eyes searched the room as he stood up. They met Captain Ralph's keen glance, and the eyes of the other professional gambler reassured him with an almost imperceptible sign. His desire to renew the scene seemed to vanish; a frigid air of dignity gave place to his former white anger.

" By God, sir! this is an insult," he said, sternly.

Nevinson, held back by several friends, struggled to free himself.

" The dice, gentlemen—test the dice," he cried.

" You shall answer for this," hissed Sir Ladbroke.

" I will, and heartily too," Nevinson shouted. " If the dice are not loaded, I'll give you all the satisfaction you need."

Isaacs, looking about, saw the dice on the floor, and pounced on them.

" Here they are," he said; " let's end this uproar. It is a simple matter to test them."

" I leave it to any gentleman in the room," Nevinson urged, angrily.

" Permit me," Captain Ralph Barclay suggested,

holding out his hand for the pair of suspected dice.

" I shall be perfectly satisfied with your verdict," Nevinson answered.

" Captain Ralph will suit me admirably," sneered Drake.

The group of excited men stood round Captain Ralph Barclay. That gentleman slipped the dice into the cup. He shook and threw—five and a three. Again he threw—two sixes. A third time he threw —six and five.

He looked, slowly, at the company, with a half-smile on his hawk-like face.

" The dice are right," he said. " They throw a fair hazard."

Nevinson was dumbfounded.

" I would have sworn by the Book they threw low," he said.

" You would have given false evidence," Captain Ralph replied, grimly.

A gentleman pulled Nevinson's elbow and whispered earnestly in his ear.

" Come away; apologise and get out," he urged. " Sir Ladbroke Drake is the finest swordsman in Europe."

A hush fell upon the company. Sir Ladbroke Drake stood alone, his face pale but determined, a vicious gleam in his sinister eye.

" Well ? " he asked, peremptorily.

" As you please, Captain Ralph," Nevinson answered, promptly. " I cannot make good my assertion. I leave the matter in your hands."

"An accusation of cheating cannot be withdrawn with an apology," Sir Ladbroke said, speaking the words slowly and distinctly.

"No," answered his accuser. "I hold myself at your service, and am prepared to give you the only satisfaction one gentleman may offer to another."

"I choose swords," Sir Ladbroke answered. "We might meet at daybreak—that will be within two hours—in the Green Park. Captain Ralph Barclay will act as my second."

Nevinson bowed to his opponent.

"The Honourable George Taunton will serve for me and wait upon Captain Ralph," he said, a smile upon his reckless face.

A burst of laughter greeted the naming of Nevinson's second. The man he had selected was the young blood, in the claret-coloured coat, who had been lying, drunk and asleep, underneath the table.

Taunton was struggling to a sitting posture and stretching himself like a man wakening from a long sleep.

"I am at your service, Nevinson ; and begad, I'm always glad to perform any little kindness for a friend. Captain Ralph and I will meet and settle the preliminaries at once."

The company again roared their laughter at his ready response.

"Upon my honour, Nevinson, why two hot-headed fools want to cross swords so early on a January morning is more than any fellow can understand," Taunton grumbled, as, a trifle unsteadily, he turned to leave the room with Captain Ralph.

CHAPTER II

An hour later, Nicholas Nevinson was sitting alone in his rooms, a suite in a dingy, evil-smelling apartment house in Drury Lane.

They were poor rooms indeed for a gentleman of quality, sparsely furnished and badly lighted. A candle, the flame of which wavered as it caught the draught, stood on the table in the centre of the room, and that oasis of illumination only served to place the rest of the apartment in deeper shadows. On the same table, Nevinson's sword, unsheathed, lay shining in the fitful light.

Nevinson had reached his quarters after a brief walk from Covent Garden. Entering the room he took off his perruque and his long-skirted coat for greater ease, and perhaps the better to protect those articles of attire.

Then he picked up the sword, and his keen grey eye glanced shrewdly along the polished blade. He made one or two passes at the candles, the steel swishing through the air and glittering as if it were flashing lightning. After testing the weapon by pressing its point upon the floor and finding it strong in its steely spring, Nevinson placed the sword on the table again and threw himself into a high-backed chair standing in front of the empty fireplace.

No one other than Nevinson was astir in the grim house, in Old Drury. The domestics were still abed, and had not yet awakened to the calls of duty. The place was uncanny in its quietness. The only sounds, indeed, were caused by Nevinson's movements or the pattering and scratching of mice in the wainscoting. As Nevinson sat on the high-backed chair the silence without was broken. Shuffling footsteps told that some one was turning into the street.

Nevinson stirred as he heard the sound, went to the window, and threw open one of the leaded panes.

He looked out into a dismal, blank darkness. The fog of a frosty morning streamed into the room, its cold breath on Nevinson's hot face refreshing and bracing him. Nothing was visible outside but the wan, unsteady light given off by an approaching lantern. As the figure carrying it came nearer, Nevinson made out the round, caped, shawled figure of the watchman.

" Six o'clock, good people all," the shambling functionary called, in a voice hoarse with the rigours of the night. " Six o'clock and a fine frosty morning. A cold and frosty morning. Six o'clock."

The voice boomed hoarsely as it drew nearer and repeated the message, doling it out as if it were a chant. The man with the caped and shawled shoulders stood clearly outlined for a moment, and then passed on his ghostly progress, until, afar off, he gave no sign, and was indicated only by the waning light of the unsteady lantern.

Nevinson closed the window with a snap, and again threw himself into the high-backed chair, shivering slightly as he looked into the empty fireplace.

"Ugh! six o'clock," he muttered. "The day will be breaking within the hour, and a devilish cold day it will be. A pleasant morning on which to meet a fire-eater like Drake. I've the jaundice in my marrow and a frozen stomach to boot. But I'll go on the chance of letting some of Drake's blood, for as sure as God gave me eyes, those dice were loaded."

He sat on, idly pursuing these speculations for perhaps five minutes, when his attention was arrested by footsteps once again sounding in the street. The tread of the new-comer was quick and confident; the sound indicated youthful and well-shod movement. The steps came nearer, very quickly, and betokened a definite object. When the advancing man reached Nevinson's apartment house, he stopped and instantly hammered on the outer door.

"So ho! there comes my second, George Taunton, if I never breakfast again," Nevinson said. Rising and seizing the candlestick, he went out into the hall and threw open the door.

"God's life, Nevinson, there you are!" said the voice of Taunton. He was cloaked to the ears, and his slouched hat was pulled down over his eyes. As he followed Nevinson's lighted candle he took off the hat and loosened the folds of his cloak, revealing the fact that he was attired as Nevinson had seen him at Isaacs.'

"Damn the morning," he said, filling up the silences in the quiet house with his bright rattle. "And damn all the breed of hot-headed bloods who quarrel over their wine. I give you my sacred word of honour, it's an ill thing to start a frosty day with a duel. Only the best of friendship would call me out on such a morning to be a spectator to such Tom Fool blood letting."

"I am sure you oblige me vastly," Nevinson answered with a smile, leading his caller to the inner room.

"I do," replied Taunton, who, once in the room, threw himself down in the big chair. "My cursed perruque is as stiff as an icicle. It shows my warm heart for friendship when I don't chill off and disappear out of a game like this. But there—what's the odds?"

Taunton, sitting there, put jollity into the dark room. He was an irrepressible Irishman, a gentleman of fortune, who existed no one knew how. He had bright eyes audacious in their challenge; his face was round and red, despite his over-night debauch; a perpetual smile hovered about his lips. Most of all, he had youth, confidence, and that high mettlesome manner men call courage. Sitting there, he looked critically on his host before speaking again.

"Well," he said, at length, "how goes it?"

"I am frost-bitten to my heart's core," Nevinson answered. "If he bloods me, my veins will run ice."

Taunton got up and stood by the side of his friend.

" Rip me, but I believe you are hipped," he said.

" I am," Nevinson answered.

" Sink me, too, if you are not showing the white feather," Taunton added audaciously, and with intent. The effect of his words at once became apparent, for Nevinson stiffened and his grey eyes blazed.

" I'll ask you for satisfaction, my man, for that, immediately I am free of my obligation to Sir Ladbroke," he replied, coldly.

Taunton, half playfully, turned Nevinson round, until he stood in the small zone of feeble light.

" Zounds ; what a fire-eater ! That's the way to talk," he said, with a gay, reckless laugh. " It's better to fight than to watch on a cold morning. But there—let's have a look at you."

He gazed at Nevinson for a minute and then rattled on.

" You look the stuff, and you've got a glint in your bonnie eye that will put the come-hither on that blackleg, Drake. I know your sort. There's a bit of the Lancashire breed about you. And you are all right—by the Lord Harry, yes. I've seen you do some fool things since I knew you, but I've never seen you show the white feather. My apologies. But you looked hipped, my good chap —as if you were going to a hanging instead of a bonnie fight."

His eyes met the empty grate.

" Why—of course," he said, aloud. " No damned fire. Like your addle-pated notion of things. The pluckiest men find their spirits at zero when their feet are cold. A blaze on a frosty morning cheers the eye, warms the feet, steadies the heart, improves the temper, and adds ten to one to your chances of carving a hole in the amiable carcass of Drake. Trust me, I know. I have been out on frosty mornings before, and, curse me, I lay it down as an axiom of sound conduct in affairs of honour, that the warmer you keep your man the more chance he has of coming back to breakfast without being carved up like a round of beef."

Taunton talked on, and Nevinson sat in the stiff-backed chair, listening. Something like half an hour sped by, and then Taunton went to the window and looked out. The darkness outside was giving place to a greying atmosphere indicating daybreak. By seven o'clock the morning would be quite light. As he observed this fact, Taunton's manner changed. More soberly he turned to his principal.

"Damme," he said, at length. "I like you, lad, although you have only been on the town a few months. I admire your spirit in meeting a man with Drake's reputation, vastly."

"A season is a long time, and in that short period I have had ample opportunity of making a fool of myself," Nevinson replied, speaking his thoughts aloud.

"Well—I admit it is folly for a raw youth to challenge a swordsman of Sir Ladbroke's calibre," Taunton said, his eyes fixed on Nevinson.

Nevinson laughed lightly.

"My heart does not beat more rapidly for that. My meeting with Sir Ladbroke is the least of my preoccupations," Nevinson answered.

" It ought to be your greatest. As your second, I'm in duty bound to tell you Drake is the best swordsman in London, if not in Europe. He is merciless, too, in his play with the blade." Taunton eyed his man as he spoke, but the statement did not disturb Nevinson.

" I know, I know," Nevinson answered, bitterly. " But what is my poor carcass worth, if he make mincemeat of it. As for swordsmanship, I have learnt mine from men who would be his master to-day, and at the worst Drake will only pink me. My folly lies in the fact that I'm at the end of my tether. Even if Sir Ladbroke does not. kill me, I shall have to make my exit from town. I am sporting my last five guineas now. The only regret I have is that I am spending my last day by going out on a demned cold morning to give the satisfaction of a gentleman to a man I know in my heart to be a vulgar cheat. Those dice were loaded."

" That I know better than you do," Taunton said ; " but it is too late to prove anything now. Those two bullies will act together, and the probabilities of the story are with them. All the same, as I lay dreaming on the floor, I saw what others missed. Captain Ralph Barclay, as black a rook as Drake, picked up the dice that slipped from your hand and laid down two others—the two that were found and tested."

" The devil, he did ? " Nevinson ejaculated.

" No ; the devil was Barclay," Taunton answered. " I was too stupid to take it in at the time, and now it is too late to challenge them. You could make my information an excuse for not meeting Drake, if you chose."

Nevinson's eyes glittered.

"Why harp on excuse? I want to meet him," he said. "The pleasure of spitting Drake is the only satisfaction I shall have for the outlay of my whole fortune."

"The deuce!" Taunton ejaculated. "You mean that?"

"Yes," Nevinson answered; "I am ruined. The most of the last hundred of the portion, some ten thousand pounds in all, was pouched by Sir Ladbroke with the last two throws. You may rest assured, crossing swords with him does not worry me. I look upon the chance of spitting him as a pleasure."

The second's eyes brightened, and he held out his hand to Nevinson.

"Well—damme! That's the right spirit," he said, "and if you are going to have the pleasure and to give me my share, we had better be starting now. The day is within an ace of breaking. Rip me, I admire your attitude. It justifies my self-sacrifice in being abroad on a withering morning, instead of being comfortably abed."

The two young men warmly attired themselves for their journey. Nevinson, with the instincts of a dandy, performed an elaborate toilet. He carefully readjusted his perruque and cravat, and reassumed his coat with as much precision as if he were going to a ball. Quietly taking up his sword, he ran his eye lovingly along the shining blade and replaced it in the scabbard. Then wrapping himself in a long grey cloak, and pulling down the brim of a soft felt hat, he bowed to his second.

"I am at your service," he said, throwing the cloak round his shoulders.

"And I am at yours," said Taunton, with a bow still more profound, and commencing to lead the way down the passage to the door.

Together they left the grim house in Drury Lane and hurriedly walked through the grey and misty streets in the direction of the park. Neither man spoke very much on that journey. Nevinson was busy with his own thoughts, and they were bitter enough. He was reviewing, one by one, the follies of his brief season in town, the crowning item of which was the altercation that had set him on the errand of meeting Sir Ladbroke Drake.

Almost on the stroke of seven they were entering the Green Park. So deserted was it at that time, they might have been in the heart of the country. For some minutes they were the only visible living people. They began to parade rapidly up and down a patch of turf beneath an archway of trees, to counteract the shrewd bite in the morning air. They had promenaded for some five minutes, almost in silence, when men began to straggle towards them in twos and threes. The new-comers were mostly frequenters of Isaacs' rooms who, having seen the quarrel begin, desired to be in at the end, and had relinquished the prospect of bed for the purpose. A dishevelled crew, they chaffed and laughed as they renewed acquaintance with each other and secretly made bets on the prospects of the combatants.

Their greetings had scarcely been completed when two figures known to most of them slowly entered the park and came towards the assembly. One was Sir Ladbroke Drake and the other his second, Captain Ralph Barclay.

Sir Ladbroke, heavily cloaked, walked forward with the mincing manner of a dandy bored to distraction. His second, the massive and dour Captain Ralph Barclay, swaggered with the blustering manner of a soldier who has seen much service.

When the two men came up with the party already assembled Sir Ladbroke saluted them, and then languidly leaned against a tree, smiling at the badinage of some of his intimates. He carried his studied, nonchalant manner to the length of yawning, as though the outcome of the matter were one of complete indifference to him.

Captain Ralph returned from a consultation with the Honourable George Taunton, and a whispered conversation took place between him and his principal.

" I understand there is no apology," Drake said, looking grimly at Nevinson.

" None," said Nevinson. " I await your pleasure."

" Then the sooner we get a demned unpleasant business over the better. I'll spit this loosed-tongued hawbuck in five minutes," he added with a sneer, speaking to the company generally.

2

Nevinson, standing, still cloaked, bowed at the suggestion with superb confidence, and for the first time Sir Ladbroke looked annoyed. He had hoped to see his studied manner produce some irritation in the attitude of his opponent.

Slowly, Sir Ladbroke began to divert himself of his outer clothing; first the cloak, then the long-skirted coat and the sleeved waistcoat. At length he stood prepared and shivering slightly as he faced the world in his breeches and fine linen. He had disrobed very deliberately and with cool composure, for Sir Ladbroke knew the value of manner in influencing the minds of men. To his surprise, Nevinson had been equally deliberate, and instead of preparing hastily, in the manner of youth, and remaining to wait and fret while experience dallied nonchalantly with the details, he took some seconds longer than his opponent. As Sir Ladbroke waited, his pale, sinister face flushed slightly with annoyance.

The two men came forward and measured their blades against each other. Squire Drew, who acted as Master of Ceremonies, stood with drawn sword, to strike up the blades if the rules of the duel were not observed. He looked at both parties to the quarrel and then stepped back.

" On guard," he said, briefly, and at once Nevinson adopted the tactics of defence.

Sir Ladbroke Drake was a great swordsman, in a day when gentlemen were early schooled to the use of the blade. His manner was that of a man who had no doubt of the issue ; his attack was impetuous and overpowering. The gleam in his sinister eye showed that his intention was to maim his man, vitally. A successful duel, ending even fatally, would only add to his reputation in the hot-headed society in which he moved. So confident was he, that after a few swift passes, countered dexterously, he lunged vigorously at his opponent. His blade flashed in the grey morning air, but another blade met his, so strongly handled that the lunge not only missed its mark but seemed to break itself on a guarding wall of steel. When Sir Ladbroke looked into the eyes of his opponent, surprised that his lunge had not been effective, he almost started. Though Nevinson's face was firmly set, there was a mocking gleam in his quiet grey eyes, almost amounting to laughter. Drake's temper grew at once more calculating. For the first time, in that chilly morning encounter, doubt of its outcome flashed through his mind. The blades crossed and recrossed; lunge and parry followed rapidly; the steel rang in the cool morning air. Suddenly it was borne in upon the spectators that a meeting which was to have been mere aimless butchery, in view of Sir Ladbroke's well-known proficiency, was rapidly turning into the fight of his life.

During an interval Sir Ladbroke returned to his second.

"Why don't you spit the damned little whelp?" Captain Barclay asked, irritably.

Drake's breath was coming and going in short, gasping spasms after the exertion.

"God's life! the hawbuck knows the sword," he said, tensely. "His defence is as stubborn as a wall, and he has a wrist like iron."

"Slit him through the throat and make an end of it," Captain Ralph advised, and the two men again stood opposite to each other and were on guard.

In the second rally a change came over the spirit of this sword play. Amid deep silence, Sir Ladbroke went into the engagement determined to take his second's advice. His attack was almost irresistible; but all the time he met the same firm, sure, impenetrable defence as the two blades clashed, and each time he looked the lurking laughter in Nevinson's eyes maddened him.

After the repeated failure of his favourite lunge, a trick of the sword taught him in Paris that only had one masterstroke, he met Nevinson's grey eyes lit with the mockery that never seemed to leave them. Drake lost his temper, and tried the lunge again. By all the rules of the game, as he knew it, his sword should have pierced his opponent's heart. The thrust, however, was arrested in the only way known to Sir Ladbroke. His opponent's quivering blade seemed to be twining round his own. The force of the lunge came to a dead stop. There was a shock, a clash, a grim second in which strength of nerve, muscle, and steel was tested, and then Sir Ladbroke's sword spun through the air, out of his right hand, and Nevinson's blade, freed from the barrier, ran him straight through the right shoulder. A vivid red stain dyed the white linen as Sir Ladbroke fell back.

Nevinson, with the same gleam of subdued laughter lurking in his quiet eyes, picked up the blade and offered it to his opponent.

Sir Ladbroke Drake stood to receive it, ashen of face, anger in his eyes, and seething in his mind, so that he scarcely felt the pain of his wound.

He took the sword, offered with quiet dignity by his opponent, and his face had lost all its calm and was now fiercely malignant.

" A trick ; a lucky hit.   Honour is not satisfied," he screamed.   " Let us go on.   I'll fight you to the death."

" On guard," was Nevinson's only reply, and the two blades crossed again.

But this time their rally was not even prolonged. Drake was almost blind with anger.   His mouth set in a vicious line, his temper urging him on, he tried his favourite lunge.   Again it met the firm defiance of a resolute blade.   Again Sir Ladbroke's blade flew out of his hand and was tossed a dozen yards in the air.   And once again Nevinson's sword was sheathed, this time through Drake's right arm, the shirt sleeve turning crimson as the sword passed through the flesh.

" My man cannot go on," said Captain Barclay, who saw the disadvantage of his principal.

" Surely," said Squire Drew, " the matter has been sufficiently well adjusted ? "

" Adjusted be damned ! " Sir Ladbroke shouted, his anger rising higher with this second humiliation. " I can go on and will.   I'll fight him with my left hand, as long as I've a drop of blood in my body."

Nevinson stood there, brave and gallant, in the clearing light of the early morning.   His grey eyes were flashing with the resolute glitter of his own blade. His frigid calmness was impressive when contrasted with the anger of his opponent.

"I refuse to continue," he said, sternly.

"I call you coward," Drake shouted, fuming.

"You may call me what you like," Nevinson said, contemptuously. "Twice I have disarmed you, and twice I have run you through. If we continue, the next time I shall drive my blade through your black heart."

"Do it—by God, do it!" Sir Ladbroke urged, every vestige of self-control gone.

"No," answered Nevinson, with frigid calm. "I do not want to take a dog's life. I have given you the satisfaction of a gentleman, and have proved my right to refuse to fight a scoundrel and a blackleg. I repeat now, what I said last night—the dice were loaded. Captain Ralph Barclay picked them up. The dice he tested were not the same."

The dismay in the face of the two gamblers was apparent, and the tide of opinion from the lookers-on was setting against them.

"By God, sir, I shall call you to account for this, myself," said Captain Ralph, blusteringly.

"Wherever and whenever you like," answered Nevinson. "Now—if you choose. Mr. Taunton will serve me again, as my second."

"With all the pleasure in life," the Honourable George replied, and his gay manner showed how much he was enjoying himself.

Squire Drew brought the strange situation to an end.

"The duel is abortive," he said. "Nevinson

has proved himself a man of courage, capable of defending his own honour.   He repeats the accusation of cheating.   The affair has now become a matter for inquiry at Isaacs' rooms.   Gentlemen, I see no use in continuing this altercation."

"I am still prepared to give Captain Barclay all the satisfaction he desires," Nevinson suggested, the gleam of laughter in his eyes growing more pronounced than ever.

The Captain scowled, but his manner was not convincing.   He knew by comparison with Sir Ladbroke's swordsmanship the chances of his own.

"After the inquiry," he said, attempting, and not successfully, to retain his dignified poise, "I will raise the matter with you again."

"Before or after, as you please," said Nevinson, "it is immaterial to me."

"I have my principal to consider," urged the Captain weakly.

"It is the duty of one blackleg to attend to another, just as it is a gentleman's right," Nevinson answered.   Then, with restrained laughter still present in every line of his youthful face, he added, audaciously: "Look after him well, Captain Barclay.   I absolve you of any necessity of defending your own honour until we meet at Isaacs'."

The gambler scowled, but his discretion was the better part of his valour.

Nevinson turned gaily to his second.

"Come, Taunton," he said.   "We have had a merry morning.   My swordsmanship is—what? Shall we say, fair to middling—eh?"

" Amazing," Taunton answered, enthusiastically. " You spitted him like a cook trussing a fowl."

" Then do me the honour of breakfasting with me, out of my last five guineas," Nevinson suggested. " We should celebrate the achievement."

" With all the pleasure in the world," Taunton replied, helping his friend to attire himself. " On a morning such as this is, the idea of breakfast shows you are a man of sense as well as a damned game bird of courage."

CHAPTER III

NICHOLAS NEVINSON had breakfasted with his second, the Honourable George Taunton. From the scene of the duel the two friends had repaired to a tavern off Wych Street, frequented largely by men who seemed to have been abroad all night, and there they had spent a merry brace of hours. Already the duel was town talk, and every rattle in London who had presumptions to being looked upon as a man of fashion was gossiping intimately about the spitting of Sir Ladbroke Drake. Town tattle, never kind to a person who had had a fall, was perhaps in this case not more unjust than the subject warranted. That Drake's humiliation was popular amongst the bravoes of the day, at this early morning breakfasting house, was obvious, nor was the reason of it far to seek. The grim gambler of fashion, swordsman of reputation, under his studied dandyism had, through his prestige as a deadly antagonist, ruled the little army of sharps and rooks forming the night life of London with a high hand. They gloried in his fall.

Nevinson had to face the joyous congratulations of such of his friends as were about. He comported himself with more modesty than was usually displayed under the same circumstances. He was young enough to enjoy the popularity following his action and the deference paid to a man who had proved his courage so conspicuously. In the most extravagant spirits he made the most of his brief popularity, and, as he entertained his friend, basked in the smiles of the world of the town. The hour of eleven o'clock had turned before Nevinson's breakfast ended. By the time they rose to go, Nevinson had lavishly dissipated one of his last five guineas, a fact that rudely called him to his senses and the needs of the situation. With many protestations of affection and esteem he parted with his friend Taunton, and set out for his meagre rooms in Drury Lane.

Noon was passed before he awoke from a brief sleep and performed an elaborate toilet, giving to it the time and circumstance the occasion demanded. His velvet frippery of the night before gave place to a coat of simpler habit, a beautiful example of the tailoring of the period. Of a cloth of vivid green, the coat hung closely to the figure, and widened out at the skirts. Though simple in its effect, the garment was turned back elaborately at the collar, and the front was edged with buttons embroidered with silver thread and heavily tasselled, set an inch or so apart; the corresponding holes being braided heavily with the same material. The sleeves were rolled back into a gauntlet and served to show the linen without the elaborate slashes of the period. Although less pretentious, the coat gave Nevinson a more rakish appearance than he had presented at Isaacs' rooms amongst the men of fashion assembled there. As part of his attire, he retained the long grey waistcoat, with its opening at the neck for an elaborate cravat. The garment fell so far below the waist that it reached to the blue silk hose rolled high above the breeches. A square-toed, short-gaitered boot with high red heels and flashing buckles completed his raiment for the day.

Thus we again find him in the bay window of the oak-panelled room, pluming the feather in a green felt hat. He looked what he was, a handsome man, less dissipated than the gentlemen of his time, though the pallor and languor of his manner suggested that nature was demanding payment for the excitements of the immediate past in the reactions of the present.

Nevinson assumed his lace handkerchief, and finally adjusted his sword. When he took up the slenderly lined purse from the table, it held his attention for a minute. He clinked the contents in his hand, thoughtfully.

" Four guineas and some small change," he said aloud, with something like a groan. " Was ever a man of fortune so hipped and compromised by his necessities. Four guineas and a sword do not form the best equipment for a bright but frosty world," he added. " But sink me, the sword has served me well enough to-day. I am richer in repute by it, if not in coin, and even four guineas are mighty good so long as one owns them intact, with their four pictures of Good King Charles upon them." He shrugged his shoulders and went on

with his soliloquy. " A man may do well enough
for a day on four guineas, if he keep away from the
gaming table. To-morrow———"

He stopped at the word and began to whistle,
gloomily. A minute he spent in this manner ; then
his face brightened.

" Hang to-morrow," he said, answering his own
doubts. " I am out o' spirits—and what's the
odds ! Surely it is enough that I am alive to-day.
Besides, if I saunter, I may see the lovely Lady
Peggy."

As he spoke the conclusion of these simple philo-
sophical speculations aloud, a servant came into
the room—a dowdy, half-dressed girl, with hair
awry, a smudge upon her nose, and her unfastened
bodice showing glimpses of a bare brown neck.

" If you please, my gentleman," she said, " the
laundress. A crown for your shirts, she asks, and
will not be gainsaid."

Nevinson's spirits were dashed to zero again.

" The devil take her," he said, irritably. " Tell
her I am a man of fashion and will not be dunned."

" I told her so yesterday, sir," the girl answered.
" She said she would dun you until she got her money
if you were King Charles himself."

" The round-headed leech," Nevinson ejaculated,
as he threw a coin on to the table. " Take it and
be gone. Pay this blood-sucker, Marie, and see
she leaves my linen. So long as one has a clean
shirt one may still seem to be a gentleman."

He smiled as he spoke the grim jest, and the waiting
girl withdrew. In three minutes she was back again.

Nevinson looked at her, with suspicions in his bright grey eyes.

"A pest on you; what now—eh?" he asked. "The bootman is it, or the hosier? One or more of these huckstering tradesmen, I'll wager."

"No, sir; please, sir," the girl answered. "It is a letter," she went on to explain, holding out a sealed and scented *billet-doux*.

"A dun—on my oath, a dun," Nevinson said, in mock agony of spirit and taking but little notice.

"It has scent upon it," the servant girl said, turning it over. "It's addressed in a fashionable hand. I'll warrant the maid who brought it was in West End service where they give you all you want to eat. I should judge so by the ribbons in the saucy hussy's hair."

As she spoke, Nevinson seized the letter and tore open the seal. After briefly glancing at the contents, he kissed the paper gaily and commenced to caper madly about the room, exaggerating some of the movements of the minuet, and kissing his hand to Marie, whose astonishment was apparent on her smudged face.

"May all the race of duns be damned!" he called gaily. "I am rich! rich, I tell you, if Peggy only smile on me."

He plunged his hand into his low waistcoat pocket, and fumbled with some small change.

"Here, herald of the morning, angel of light—go wash thy face," he said to Marie, gaily. "There is money for a ribbon to tie up your hair. Then you may stand at the door this evening and smile on some blade in Drury Lane and make him as light o' heart as the note you have carried has made me."

Marie left the room, convinced that the light-hearted occupant of the chamber had gone mad. But Nevinson's madness was no more than comes from the extravagance of the youthful lover. His difficulties had fallen away from him like a mantle. The jibing crowd of duns he had mentally pictured, lean and hungry for the last of his few guineas, was forgotten. Peggy Sheldon had given him a rendezvous—a voluntary one—for the first time. The sun was in his heaven, and, as if by magic, all had become right with his world.

The *billet-doux*, which bore an address in Bloomsbury, seemed bare enough of protestations to damp the spirit of the most ardent lover; but the summons of the message was enough to set Nevinson's volatile spirit on fire. Scrawled in a feminine hand, the note read: " My uncle and guardian having gone on a journey, I am venturing to the pavilion in Marylebone Gardens for tea. From our frequent meetings, I know you to be a gentleman of spirit. As I have something to confide in you, I count on you being there at the hour of four, to the great obligation of——"

" Yours, Peggy Sheldon," the young man said, ecstatically. " May she count on me? By the Lord, I will be there, if I have to carve my way through a regiment of Sir Ladbroke Drakes."

He completed his toilet slowly and carefully. " A pleasant errand," he said to himself; " and anyway it will take me out of this and the army of duns. If I remain indoors I shall have all the leeches in London barking at my heels, for poverty travels swiftly, like ill news. Well, I'll spend the afternoon with the fair Peggy and the duns can go to the devil. Then, by midnight I shall still have a guinea to drink a health to a ruined gambler's exit.''

Be sure that Nevinson was at the Marylebone Gardens by the hour appointed. These grounds, in the centre of which was an old manor house and a variety of pavilions, were used by the people of West London, chiefly as a summer pleasure resort, where masques were held, and a variety of out-door entertainments of the day. In winter they were almost deserted, but in the evenings there was always a certain amount of patronage for the assembly rooms, where games of hazard—piquet, faro, and the like—were played. By day the gardens served lovers who planned assignations there, and their part in the development of matches in the life of London town, legitimate and otherwise, was no inconsiderable one.

Nevinson, sauntering at the main entrance, had not to wait very long before a family coach drove up with a rattle. It was a cumbrous vehicle, the box mounted on the front axle, the coach itself balanced on heavy straps. The panels of the coach were vividly red, with a variety of coloured orna-mentation upon them and a florid coat-of-arms on the centre of each.

A girl's face glanced out of the high windows as

the coachman pulled up with a flourish, bringing the mettlesome horses almost on to their haunches as he did so. Her face lighted with pleasure as she saw the waiting gallant, who hastily opened the door, lowered the steps, and helped her to alight.

"La! Mr. Nevinson," she said. "You keep your appointments well."

"I do not often have the pleasure of such gracious company," he replied. "Your presence gave me wings."

She smiled again appreciatively, and offered her arm, which he took.

"I must not stay more than an hour," she began, speaking rapidly and eagerly. "I ought to be back long before my guardian arrives at six o'clock. Take me to the quietest room, and order me a dish of tea. I am very tired after being jolted over these country roads."

She did not look tired, but her pleasant affectation served as a reason for leaning heavily on Nevinson's arm, and he thrilled with the contact of the dainty burden hanging upon him.

Peggy Sheldon was typical of her day. The daughter of a wealthy merchant, orphaned for many years, with an ample fortune in her own right, she was living in the charge of her guardian and uncle, a stern, purse-proud trader, apparently loyal, though of the Puritan habit, at his mansion in Tavistock Place. John Sheldon was the last person in the world to have the guardianship of a tricksy, high-spirited girl, as this narrative will show, and their enforced association was not a happy one. The girl's evident high spirits arose, in part out of her adventure ; but much of her gaiety was due to the reaction of being away from the gloomy old house in Bloomsbury and the still more depressing observation of her sombre uncle.

She was a tall girl, standing very straight. The beauty of her carriage, the youthful roundness of her figure, could not be hidden by the monstrous eccentricities of the feminine attire of her day. To Peggy's credit, and to her better appearance, she had simplified the prevailing mode, and her winsomeness was accentuated by the contrast. She wore a dress of flowered silk, embroidered, with the prevailing stomacher giving an exaggerated length to the waist. Her skirts were full, distended slightly by the farthingale. About her high, round shoulders, and draping most of her figure, was a long blue cloak, lined with fur, caught at the throat, but now thrown back. Upon her wealth of natural hair, which fell in bunches of ringlets behind, was a wide-brimmed hat of furred felt, plumed boldly with a great dyed feather.

Most of all, men were arrested by her face. Powdered a little, the colour a trifle heightened by rouge, the eyebrows sharply lined with pencil, despite the accepted artificialities hers was a rounded, youthful face. Peggy Sheldon was of the dark, oval-faced type of beauty. Her eyes, set far apart, glowed with health and spirit. The nose was full and round, though delicately shaped, and gave some indication of her buoyant temperament. When Peggy Sheldon smiled the full lips parted and showed regular teeth, as fine as polished ivory. Her manner was a strange combination of youthful gaiety, irrepressible spirits, dignity, and confidence born of self-control. Her voice was low in key, round with a velvety richness, and strange possibilities of depth of feeling lurked in her lightest word.

Nicholas had met Peggy Sheldon many times during his season in town. As a man just come into his portion, living in a way of life that indicated eligibility, he had not been discouraged. But the talk of the town had been busy with Nevinson's whirling life of pleasure; his ruin had been a matter of certainty to shrewd observers; and, as a consequence, John Sheldon had, during the later days, put obstacles in the way of an intercourse rapidly drifting to intimacy. No declarations of love had passed between the two, but Nevinson had laid court to the smiles of a winning girl, and in many ways Peggy had shown preference for his attentions.

In the fading light of the afternoon Nevinson sat looking at Peggy Sheldon, as she chatted, poising her dish of tea at a table near one of the windows in the deserted room. This casement overlooked an ill-kept lawn, neglected since the last summer, upon which a few of autumn's leaves, crisp with the frost, tumbled as the wind stirred them.

The agreeable rattle of their first greetings was over. There had been the usual badinage. They had talked of balls and routs, of the latest card-parties, and, it must be admitted, of the current scandal of a malicious society. And when they had exhausted the topics of the day, a silence fell

between them as if the glamour of the wintry
twilight, softening the aspect outside and throwing
the room into deep shadows, had thrown a mantle
between them. The girl looked absently out of
the window, and followed the fluttering leaves as
the wind stirred them; the man, with a moody
light in his bold grey eyes, fixed his glance upon
Peggy's oval face.

"A penny for them," she said, using the language of lovers the world over, her eyes drifting
back to his face.

A dull flush reddened Nevinson's cheeks, in
startling contrast to his former pallor.

"A penny is all they are worth," he answered,
readily, and lightly enough.

"And who is to be the judge of that?" Peggy
answered.

"The man who sits in judgment on himself," he
replied, enjoying his own grim humour. "God's
life!" he exclaimed, urgently; "I look upon your
face, and it cries shame upon the follies of my past."

"It judges no one," she answered, a tender light
in her hazel eyes. "If I know my own face, it
judges no one—least of all you. Rather it might
speak of the future, if it speak at all, and I would
have it so."

"With a past like mine there is no future,"
Nevinson said, glumly enough, and in sharp contrast with his former spirits.

Now, while she was near him, her face dimpling
with pleasure as she listened to his words, her voice
almost caressing in its tenderness, the scent of her

presence drifting a subtle charm that bound him
to her, Nevinson was impelled to tell the girl what
he had no right to utter. All he was—a foolish
gambler, ruined by his own headlong follies—and the
courses leading to his downfall, swam in a set of
accusing pictures through his mind, holding him
silent.

" Have you been so very foolish, Mr. Nevinson ? " Peggy asked.

" Surely you know," he answered. " I am the
gossip of the town, and they have picked me bare
enough with their tongues. They get mighty
fine fun when they talk of Nick Nevinson, mad as
a March hare, who, of his small fortune, has now
barely two gold guineas to rub together."

" So bad as that ? " she asked, her voice, vibrant
and sympathetic, urging him on.

" So bad that it is past the mending," he said,
sadly. " I would like to have looked in your eyes
and told you what is in my heart. Peggy, I am
going away."

" Going away ? " she faltered. " Where would
you go, and why need you go ? I have asked you
to come here because I wanted you."

" Where do I go ? " he replied, bitterly. " Who
knows or cares, but the devil who drives the likes
of me onwards to their own ruin ? "

" I care," Peggy said, and her eyes were warm, and
swimming with sympathy.

" A few short months ago that would have made
me happy," Nevinson replied. " To-day the knowledge but adds to my burden. Forget me, and

forget that I might have offered you love, and asked for that precious gift from you. I must go away. The town is too hot to hold me. The ghosts of all my debts rise up in duns. The people who have plucked me wait upon my appearance for the last feather. North, south, east, or west— it does not matter. If there be fortune any way, there I go. Only "—he stopped as he spoke the word.

" Yes—only, mad Nick Nevinson ? " she said, softly. " Tell me the part unsaid ; I have a right to know."

" Only if fortune lie either way and my quest lead to it, I shall come back—to you."

Peggy blushed as he spoke the words, significant of much she had wished to hear.

They sat in the darkening room, together, silent. So still was she, he could hear her breathing, and the faint tender rustle each single breath drew from her silken gown.

" God protect you in your quest," she said, at last ; " and if you ride back, God send you reach me in time."

Nicholas looked into the girl's troubled face as he heard her words, at once full of sweet confession and foreboding.

" What mean you by that ? " he asked, arrested by her manner.

He rose as he spoke and paced the quiet apartment.

Peggy seemed to make up her mind to speak her thoughts.

"I have need of friends," she said; "and the friend who could help me might have been my lover. I am proud you have shown me your heart, and I will show you mine. You know Sir Ladbroke Drake?"

A grim smile swept across Nevinson's face.

"In faith—yes," he said. "I had the honour of running my blade through his shoulder this morning. It is one of the few honours that have come to me that I have enjoyed."

"You fought him?" she asked, breathlessly; and Peggy's eyes sparkled.

"Yes, and to some purpose," he said, speaking rapidly. "I could have slain him like a dog, but I blooded him mildly like a gentleman. He will be abed these three or four days as a consequence of my morning greeting."

She laughed, almost happy in her lover's skill.

"A great man with the sword is Sir Ladbroke Drake, the town says," she commented. "He intimidates all about him. Do you know, I fear that man?"

"Why?" he asked. "Why should you fear him?"

"I cannot tell you," she answered. "My uncle is curious in his manner of late. He is mixed up in many matters. Strange people come and go from our house, and one of these is Sir Ladbroke Drake. He and my uncle have some enterprise together, and Sir Ladbroke has some ascendancy over my guardian. I have seen this for some weeks now, and he is using his power to play for my hand. Sir Ladbroke has hinted of this often of late, but yesterday he half made the proposal. I refused to hear him," she ended, proudly.

" And then ? " Nicholas asked.

" The discussion broke off there, with a threat," she added. " Sir Ladbroke suggested that when the time came my uncle dare not cross him. My guardian is a dour man, misguided in much that he does, but tenacious, and if Sir Ladbroke is right, and he is in the man's power, he might use force."

" You think that ? " Nicholas asked, urgently.

" I fear that," she said, simply. " Strange incidents are occurring in our house, and Sir Ladbroke's manner has been so ugly that a display of force would not be stranger than much occurring now."

" By the Lord, that must not be," Nevinson said, springing to her side. " You will not consent; say you will not consent."

" I will never consent," she said, clearly and decisively. " I may exaggerate, but I fear that man, and my fear makes me desire to be served by friends, if occasion demand their help, and if, as he has hinted, he can bring pressure to bear on my uncle."

Peggy rose as she spoke and began to pull the blue, fur-lined cloak about her, indicating an intention to depart.

Standing by her side, Nevinson suddenly took her hands. He held them firmly, and Peggy did not seek to free herself, but rather drew closer to him, so that she remained standing in a half-embrace.

" Hear me," he said, his voice husky with emotion. " I am your friend. If I were worth your while, I would be more to you than friend. Listen to me and let me say it, asking nothing but the right to serve you. I love you—you only; your dear face, your dear voice, your dear body, and your dearer soul. When you have cause to be afraid of this man, command me. I do not fear him. This morning I held his life at the point of my sword. Wherever I go I will let you know where I am, and if his wishes annoy you, or give you a moment's unrest, ask me to come back. I have nothing to offer but my service. Command me when you need it, for it is yours without return."

Peggy's manner suddenly lightened. There was an odd feminine gleam of laughter in her eyes. A smile played about her lips, which were so subtly tender.

"Dear, mad Nick Nevinson," she said, softly; "your very simplicity makes all the evil in you an innocent cloak; but it is bravely spoken of you all the same. I called you to me for that promise to-day, and from now I shall hold you to it as a pledge. I wanted to hear you speak the words I knew were in your heart. Now see me to my carriage. You have made me very happy."

Nevinson helped Peggy with her wraps, and together they went, slowly, dallying in the manner of lovers, towards the waiting coach. Peggy ascended first and looked down on Nevinson.

"Come, I will drive you back," she said; and her invitation was in itself a caress. There was a gay light in his eyes as he climbed up into the heavy vehicle and took a seat beside his mistress.

As the coach rumbled away, a tall man came from

the assembly rooms and stood glancing down the road after the vanishing conveyance. Clad in a sombre, black mantle and a looped hat that flaunted no feather, standing there in the deserted country road, he looked what he was, an evil, sinister bird of prey. The man who watched Peggy's carriage disappear was Captain Ralph Barclay, the associate of Sir Ladbroke Drake.

CHAPTER IV

THE happenings at Isaacs' the night after the duel may be explained in the light of certain incidents that occurred during the day.

Sir Ladbroke Drake retired from Hyde Park, wounded slightly in two places. The attentions of a surgeon proved that the sword thrusts in the right shoulder and arm were only superficial. The wounds, when dressed, scarcely inconvenienced Sir Ladbroke, but he kept his room during that day and for a week following. Truth to tell, Nevinson had wounded the gambler's pride more than he had hurt him physically. It was no small matter for a gentleman of fashion to be treated in such a cavalier manner. Sir Ladbroke was not only a gentleman of fashion, but he was a man who had to push his fortunes by habitual attendance at the gaming tables. Such a method of raising the wind made it necessary for Sir Ladbroke to skate over a vast expanse of thin ice, and this he had done, for many years, dexterously. His honour, that delicate social quality, was intact.

Imputations cast upon Sir Ladbroke's tarnished reputation had to be substantiated at the point of the sword. In affairs of honour he had more than held his own. Of duels in which he had killed his man, there were several, while a long list of affairs less tragic in their results had allowed him to emerge successfully and rehabilitated. A knowledge of these was woven into the history of the town of his day. He depended for protection on his sinister reputation of being a dangerous man to affront, and habitually used it as a means of furbishing up a very doubtful character. Men who had been cheated by him in manner heartless and barefaced remained silent. A reason for Sir Ladbroke Drake's domination of the turbulent forces of the town was his power to maintain the impression that a still tongue was better than an early morning encounter with his sword point.

The hour was midday on the morning of the duel. Sir Ladbroke was sitting in his living room, part of a grim set of chambers in Craven Street, Strand. His wounds had been dressed and he had breakfasted. Clad in a loose dressing gown, he looked an older man than people assumed him to be who only saw him by night. With his perruque laid aside, Sir Ladbroke proved slightly bald. His repose of manner, part of a studied habit, did not go with him into privacy. One saw him as a man who showed traces of a wearing life. In the strong light of early morning his colour was bad. He was neither rubicund nor pale, and yet he was both at the same time. The result was a drawn, lean, angular face, yellow in its pallor where the skin was not inflamed. Looking on this face at such an hour, one did not think of generous impulses, honest emotions, or manly actions. Every line seemed foreign to a square deal, in the light of day. The real character of the man showed up, warningly, away from his favourite haunts. He had about him the elusive, furtive atmosphere that sets the mind thinking of night, crowded rooms and artificial light, heat and excitement, the mad hazard and the midnight follies of men.

To him came his familiar, Captain Barclay, at the hour of noon. A younger man, bigger of feature, more prone to self-indulgence, he was a less dangerous rogue.

The room he entered was a gloomy apartment in the front of a house in Craven Street. The window gave one the grim prospect of looking upon a row of similar houses opposite, whose living rooms seemed as cheerless as those occupied by the gamester.

Sir Ladbroke was propped up in a big arm-chair, and a man who did not know him might have assumed that he was dozing. But as soon as Barclay entered and seated himself, he sat bolt upright and scrutinised the new-comer carefully.

"Well?" he asked, peremptorily. "Tell me the gossip of the day."

The other man remained silent. His attitude irritated Sir Ladbroke, who impatiently flicked his fingers, as if he were spurring on his guest to talk.

"Out with it, man—out with it," he began, harshly enough. "They say—what do they say? Blood of my heart, I'm no chicken. Half of what they say I know. I have not scoured the town for a quarter of a century without knowing what the gossips make of a fall such as mine has been."

Still Captain Barclay remained silent.

"They praise this upstart popinjay because he pinked me—eh?" Drake went on, his irritation increasing. "And perhaps they say—damme, I know them well—that he did not turn the trick neatly enough, or he would have slit my heart—eh? And they say that it's a fall, and a mighty bad fall, for a man of fashion who has ruffled it with the best of them—eh? All this is said by those who talk of other people's humiliations."

Captain Barclay slowly nodded his head, and his loose cheeks quivered assent.

"They say exactly that and more," he answered.

"More—yes; there will be more," Sir Ladbroke agreed, with rising anger. "More, with a nod of the head, a wink, and a leer. More, with an 'I told you so'; or, going farther, with an 'I could tell you more, if I chose.' And there'll be the man who adds, 'I dare say there was something in what this mad, young Nevinson said.' I expect they find cause for merriment because I have not silenced this painted image of a gallant at the point of the sword. Hell take them—let them say. I have not done with this young rip yet; I'll make every cobble-stone in London red-hot to his feet when he walks."

"There is the inquiry at Isaacs'," Captain Barclay pointed out, speaking slowly and evidently disturbed in his mind.

"An inquiry at Isaacs'?" Sir Ladbroke almost

screamed. "What in the name of God have we to do with an inquiry?"

"But we have to do with it," Barclay answered. "It is going to be held. I'm leaving town this afternoon."

Sir Ladbroke Drake stiffened in the chair and the inflamed parts of his face went an ugly purple with anger.

"You'll leave town?" he said. "You'll leave me in the lurch when I can't play my hand? You will do nothing of the sort. You'll stay, or I'll whisper things about you that will make you unable to get back."

The other man's face flushed.

"What good will my staying do?" he asked, surlily.

"You are in this, up to the hilt," Drake said, grimly. "Neither you nor I can afford to have this sort of thing said about us at the inquiry. You'll stay and face your share of the music, and see that full justice is done to mine."

"Well, then, there's no good in getting hysterical about it, like a player's wench with the vapours. I'll stay if you say so," Barclay answered, surlily. "But, damme! what I am to do at the inquiry I don't know."

"But I do," Sir Ladbroke said. "You will lie, and keep on lying. My depositions will lie, and Isaacs will lie or I'll bring the town about his ears and scatter his night house to the four winds. Yes, and we can pack the committee. There is Squire Drew; I'll press my claims on his estate if he does not come in. If Buck Dowling acts against us, I'll call him out. That ass, Pike—he'll be on the committee and with us, or I'll know the reason why. I have a pull on him, and I'll make him dance to our tune. I'll make a list and you shall see Isaacs. We'll pack the committee, and instead of a verdict against us for cheating, there will be one against this madman, Nevinson. You follow me?"

Captain Barclay listened, and his hawklike face brightened as he did so. They remained in earnest conversation, and Sir Ladbroke sketched his plot. It grew more convincing as he dwelt upon the details. By one o'clock, when Captain Barclay went off to see Isaacs, where he took a midday chop, the proposed inquiry was as likely to reach the truth as many other inquiries are. When that panderer to the follies of his world, Isaacs, had been alternately threatened and cajoled by the astute and slippery Barclay, Nevinson's chance of getting justice done to his attack on Drake's honour was as good as the chance of a Puritan getting political justice in that day.

At eleven o'clock that evening there was a new note in Isaacs' rooms. Men were playing only in a perfunctory manner, or not at all. Habitual visitors there were, more prone to gossip in groups about the fireplaces and in the long corridors. Sounds of conviviality were not so marked. Indeed, though the place was quieter, more members had turned up than usually gathered together on an ordinary night. A man with a shrewd knowledge of the place would have been able to tell interesting details of the personalities of most of the well-dressed men who swaggered about the corridors, or plumed themselves as they gossiped by candlelight in the close and stuffy rooms. Truth to tell, Captain Barclay, at the instigation of Sir Ladbroke, had not only packed the committee, but had also packed the club. He had not found it difficult to make many birds of one feather flock together, and within the four walls of Isaacs' he had brought under one roof as nice a collection of gentlemanly blacklegs as could have been assembled anywhere in London. Isaacs himself, more servile than ever, was here, there, and everywhere. He fawned and bowed, smiled and gossiped, and fluttered uneasily from one group to another, as if he had been galvanised to an excess of geniality. He had a word, a joke, a nod and a bow, a recognition and a greeting for every one. But Isaacs was uneasy, for though his cunning Jewish face was smiling, his flabby cheeks were yellow, and his sly eyes, furtive in their anxiety, belied every effort he made to seem more than his cheerful self.

Downstairs men were standing about, drinking and gossiping. Upstairs a committee of six was sitting, the men lounging in stiff high-backed chairs around a long table, on which was a row of lighted candles. They included, besides Lord Bleakmoor, the chairman, young Squire Drew, the dissipated Buck Dowling, and Sir Christopher Pike.

When Nevinson entered the rooms, instinctively he felt the changed atmosphere of the place. Isaacs' big liveried servants eyed him curiously, and he noted they were in full force and very watchful. The Jew keeper of the gambling hell failed to smile on him, or hurry forward with a greeting. His bow, barely observable, was frigid and non-committal. Rakish men about town, who had hailed him uproariously, night after night, as possible plunder, stood away. A few gentlemen he had known came up and warmly congratulated him on the successful outcome of the duel and the punishment of a suspected man, whom they chose to believe had been unmasked.

Noting this change, Nevinson slowly walked up to Isaacs, a dozen gallants in the corridor watching him as he did so. Perhaps that is why Nevinson, frank and youthful, his courage indicated by his flashing eyes and firm set lips, walked with more studied deportment and with a slight ostentation of manner that seemed to convey a challenge.

"This inquiry, Isaacs; where is it to be held, and when?" he asked.

The Jew's restless manner suddenly altered. He changed: visibly stiffening and bristling as a man will do who has to go through an unpleasant task.

"They are sitting now in the faro room," he said, furtively meeting Nevinson's steady glance.

"The devil they are," Nevinson answered. "And without me?"

"They are examining the Honourable George Taunton. You may enter if you choose. Yours is the only evidence they lack. The committee have examined every one who was present."

3

"Behind my back," Nevinson said, his anger rising. "Zounds, this is an insult!"

Isaacs rubbed his hands, nervously.

"It is my inquiry, not yours. We follow the usual practice, I believe," he answered, and underneath his servility was something like a sneer.

"And a damned comfortable 'usual' practice it is," Nevinson said, his voice rising angrily as several members began to edge closer and listen more carefully to the altercation.

"The usual thing, I say," Isaacs insisted, and glanced at an attendant, as if to call his attention to the possibility of an immediate scene.

Nevinson noted Isaacs' imperceptible sign. His grey, determined eyes flashed, and his mouth shut firmly. By a strong effort of self-control he resumed his studied ease of manner.

"Very good, Isaacs," he said, with a careless nod. "I'll go up and see who compose this committee who hold inquiry behind my back and what they are doing."

Without further parley he went upstairs. The door to the faro room was opened by a liveried attendant. His appearance as he entered for a moment compelled the attention of the members round the table, but none greeted him. George Taunton, sitting in a chair alone at the far end of the table, stood up and recognised Nevinson with boyish pleasure.

"Ah, Nick! I'm bearding the lions," he said, waving his hand in the direction of the committee, as Nevinson acknowledged the greeting.

Lord Bleakmoor, a man of the town, and Isaacs' ground landlord, rapped on the table.

"Attend to the questions, please," he said.

Squire Drew was examining George Taunton, who had just repeated the story of what he had seen while lying under the table.

"You know Sir Ladbroke Drake denies this in his written statement?"

"Yes," answered Taunton.

"Also that Captain Barclay has denied the truth of the incident?"

"Yes," Taunton said, firmly.

"You were lying under the table," Drew suggested. "You were, not to put too fine a point on it, er——"

"Oh, say it! say it!" Taunton said, with half a laugh. "I had consumed four bottles of port, and I am but a three-bottle man at best. I was drunk."

Nevinson smiled, but no answering gleam flickered on any of the set faces of the committee.

"However amiable you may be after four bottles," suggested the chairman, acidly, "you will admit your condition did not lend itself to clear judgment."

"I would like to say——" began Taunton.

"I think that is all, sir," the chairman interrupted, looking round on his colleagues as if the matter had been prearranged.

"It is by no means all," said the irrepressible Irishman. "I had been the worse for wine, but I had also been asleep. When I woke up I was

as clear-headed as any gentleman here. I saw
what I say happened, and Sir Ladbroke Drake knows
that it did happen."

" I think you may leave the matter now and
withdraw," the chairman replied, coolly dismissing
him.

The committee and Nevinson remained alone
in the room after Taunton's swaggering exit.

The chairman motioned Nevinson to the seat left
vacant by the last witness.

" We have heard all the evidence," he said, speaking slowly. " I assume you reiterate your charges
that the dice were loaded ? "

" I do," Nevinson answered.

" They were tested after the accusation and were
not loaded," the chairman suggested.

" They were not the same dice," Nevinson answered, quickly.

" How do you prove that ? " asked the chairman.

" Taunton's statement proves it," he replied.

" The evidence of a man confessedly the worse
for drink," the chairman commented. " The accusation of cheating rests on your bare word."

" It does not," Nevinson replied. " Taunton's
evidence supports it."

" As you choose. We are here to inquire into the
matter. Nothing is gained by arguing about the
facts. I suppose you have no other evidence."

" None," Nevinson answered.

" Thank you for attending," Lord Bleakmoor
said, with a formal bow. " That is as far as we can
go, and we may now turn to consider our conclusion."

As Nevinson stepped out of the room occupied by the committee, he came face to face with Captain Barclay in the corridor. The gambler was lingering with a few of his friends, and his furtive eyes barely concealed their malicious gleam as Nevinson passed. For a moment he seemed about to utter the taunt trembling for expression on his lips, but discretion, or second thoughts, kept him silent. Nevinson, with a glance of disdain, cut the man dead and walked, with a faint swaggering suggestion meant to convey offence, past him and out of the room.

Barclay's face flushed an angry red before this studied insult. He looked as if about to start after Nevinson, but with a great effort of self-control he passed the incident off with a laugh, and remained in earnest conversation with his friends.

Outside, in one of the anterooms, Nevinson joined Taunton, and the two talked over the incidents of the evening in the company of a few friends. Having decided on the outcome of the inquiry, they fixed upon a plan of action. During the half-hour in which the committee deliberated both Nevinson and Taunton began to circulate quietly amongst their friends.

A very shrewd observer would have noted that, as the moments dragged away, the company of men gossiping about the rooms began to separate into unusual groupings. Isaacs, who knew his book as well as any one, was quick to observe a departure from the ordinary routine. At once he grew more nervously excited, and redoubled his amiable attempts to stimulate the good-humour of all around him. He bustled about every part of the house, for he knew the signs, and they were not good in his eyes. His best patrons, men of social position and untarnished honour, the backbone of his business, were clustered together in separate groups. When a professional gamester joined one of these groups it split up and reformed again without him. The better element in the house were annoyed, and in their annoyance automatically separated from men who were suspect.

It was nearing midnight when the company were invited into the room where the committee was still sitting. The men comprising it were still about the table, and looked a trifle self-conscious, as all the patrons of the house, some fifty in number, trooped in.

As the frequenters of this gaming house entered in twos and threes and took up their position in a crowd at the bottom of the table, there was some natural disorder and disturbance, but the new-comers to the room quickly settled down. Faces were stern, temper was running high ; there were signs of a gathering storm in the unusual silence.

Lord Bleakmoor may have noticed the influences at work, for his manner was nervous. Settling his wig and playing irritably with the edges of his long cravat, he rose slowly and faced the company. In a thin voice he rasped out the decision of the inquiry.

" We have duly considered all the available

evidence, in the interest of the patrons of these rooms. We find——"

He paused a moment and looked round carefully. Isaacs, whose restless glance flitted from one face to another, wet his hot, dry lips with the tip of his tongue.

"Go on; go on," said a tall, lean aristocrat, Sir Charles Digby, breaking the tense silence of the room.

"We find that Mr. Nevinson's accusation is not proved, and is indeed unsupported by any reliable evidence," continued Lord Bleakmoor, his words sounding like pistol shots in the still room.

"That comes of lying under the table," Taunton said, and his comment raised a guffaw that instantly died away.

"Mr. Nevinson, having given Sir Ladbroke Drake satisfaction, ought as a gentleman to tender him an apology. That is our unanimous decision."

"Suppose Mr. Nevinson refuses to apologise—what then?" Nicholas asked, with a sneer.

"Then we recommend his exclusion from these rooms," Lord Bleakmoor answered, his glance wavering as he noted how all present waited upon his words.

There was another long, nervous pause. Then, a slight murmur of dissent. The murmur died away, and again the room became quiet—uneasily quiet—and men involuntarily turned pale and bit their lips.

Nevinson, slightly excited, a red spot flaming a warning on either cheek, advanced to the end of the table and thumped its surface with his knuckles.

" Here and now," he shouted, " I tell this committee to its face, and every gentleman in this room, I will not apologise to a damned blackleg. What I said was true, and I have accounted for my accusation at the point of the sword. I go farther, since you deserve it, gentlemen. I impeach the personal honour of every member of this committee. It has been packed by a Jew pimp, in the interests of a cheat, Sir Ladbroke Drake, and a liar, Captain Ralph Barclay."

That gentleman sprang forward, drawing his sword. He could not stand so public an affront, though his cool mind was not easy about the outcome, after the early morning's work.

" I'll call you to account for this—by God, I will ! " he shouted.

" Here and now if you choose," Nevinson answered, striking him over the face with the back of his hand. " I have already offered you the privilege once to-day."

" House, house ! " shouted Isaacs, and his liveried attendants leaped forward and seized Nicholas from behind.

Struggling, he repeated his accusation. " A blackguard committee defending a pair of blackguard members—that is what I say. There is not an honest gentleman in this room who does not know the truth. There is not a man of honour assenting to this monstrous decision whose reputation is not tarnished by his own silence. Unhand me there, you hired bullies," he cried, struggling to free himself from the servants of the gambling den.

Isaacs stepped forward, his one idea being to pour oil on a rising storm of angry passion.

" Put this man out," he said to his attendants, turning white as he spoke. " My rooms are notoriously select, and in the interests of all the gentlemen present I insist on order being maintained. I ask every member to support me in this matter."

" It's a damned, wicked shame !" Taunton yelled, the devil dancing in his Irish eyes. " I'm not going to see an honest game bird shamed before the town by such a committee. I'm with Nevinson, whom I know has been basely used. I'm with Nevinson—blade and all," he added, drawing his sword as he spoke.

" And I'm with Nevinson, too," Sir Charles Digby said, speaking slowly and with emotionless dignity. He drew his blade with a flourish and moved with Taunton towards Nevinson.

His action was a lighted match to a train of gunpowder. A dozen, a score, thirty blades were drawn, the stark threat of steel gleaming wickedly in the candlelight. Instinctively the assembled crowd divided into two parties, as they had divided below. The men of undoubted integrity found themselves confronting a larger gang of night hawks, led by Captain Barclay, who had brought them together. Taunton prodded Isaacs about his worsted stockinged legs until the Jew screamed. The same attention bestowed on the gaming house keeper's hired men caused them to bellow and run, leaving Nicholas free.

3*

Instinctively he turned and faced the leader of the little blackleg army, Captain Barclay.

" You need satisfaction, and, by God, you shall have it. On guard, sir," he shouted.

Their swords crossed, and the two lines of steel, glittering danger as they twined about each other, set all the hearts in the room racing with passion.

" Gentlemen, gentlemen," Isaacs shouted. " Think of me—of my select rooms, of my property," he moaned.

He was thrust aside by both parties to the quarrel, a foolish man no longer effective, having unloosed a whirlwind which had paralysed his control with the first indications of its power.

Nicholas lunged at Barclay and drew him. He met the Captain's thrust with the parry he had used on Drake in the early morning. When Barclay felt the pressure of the steel driven by the iron wrist, his eyes wavered. His blade yielded instantly, flew into the air, and fell on Isaacs, laying his forehead open. Nicholas leapt forward, but the Captain swiftly retreated. The room by now was a whirl of mingled furies. A dozen duels were going on at once. Blade clashed against blade, men swore and stamped, chairs and tables were overturned, while one by one the candles fell and were trodden out, leaving the room in darkness.

The men, fighting in the gloom, made for the corridors. Outside the attendants were putting out the lights. The whole place was now in darkness. The orgy degenerated into a bloodthirsty *mêlée*. A mad stampede followed. The *mêlée* ended in a wrestle for the staircase and the exits. Swearing and shouting, man closed on man, and the whole company, using fists and feet, fought their way out of the hot, dark rooms into the hall, and so flooded into Covent Garden, where the moonlight flashed a cold, pale blue on the drawn swords, showing men who were their adversaries and where they stood. Thus they engaged in a running free fight in the open air, to the joy of the street rabble, until their anger cooled before the coming of a strong patrol of armed watchmen. That night, for once in its fast life, Isaacs' establishment was in darkness by twelve o'clock. The Jew retired to his bedroom and locked himself in. The shock was so great that for three days he remained there, drinking hot brandy day and night. Indeed, three nights passed before he had the courage to take up his pimpish burden and again set blazing the lights that drew the gay, careless moths of the town into his dangerous web.

CHAPTER V

WHEN Isaacs' rooms, in a midnight frenzy, vomited forth scores of fighting men, Nevinson found himself on the pavement of Covent Garden, opposite Lord Bleakmoor. That nobleman stood with drawn sword in his hand, badly dishevelled and greatly excited after disentangling himself from Nevinson's vigorous embrace.

During the scramble. for the stairs they had come together in the dark corridor. They had wrestled, pulled, and hauled away at each other with vigorous ill-will, on the pull-devil, pull-baker plan. Pressed from behind and still struggling, they had staggered out of the crowded night house into the cooler air of Covent Garden. There, on the pavement, amid linkboys, chairmen, women of the night, and more noisome human jackals nosing about the gutters for mean plunder, they had separated and recognised each other. At once their manner grew more frigid and dignified.

"I did not realise who was doing me the honour to attempt to gouge my eyes out," Nicholas said, irritably.

"You have inflicted a most ungentlemanly abrasion on my shin bone," said his lordship of Bleakmoor.

" Perhaps you would desire to continue on more correct lines," suggested Nicholas, oblivious of the crowd.

" With all the pleasure in the world," Lord Bleakmoor answered. " I am at your service."

Nicholas again put himself on guard for the third time that day. A grim smile flickered across his bold features. He was evidently thinking of the turbulent passage he had had through town, since the breaking of the morning. His grey eyes were fixed intently on his opponent's movements, and without any great effort he easily held Lord Bleakmoor off. The third encounter did not last many moments. Lord Bleakmoor was no swordsman. Before they had been engaged a minute he lunged carelessly, and Nicholas tore the sword out of the peer's hand with his favourite counter. Fuming and disarmed, he stood before Nevinson, who offered him his weapon with a bow that scarcely concealed his sense of triumph. A hugely delighted street crowd closed firmly about the two men, evidently desiring more.

" The Virgin preserve the lad ; did you see that ? " a bird of the night said, speaking to those about him.

" As likely a job of meat carving as ever I hope to see," answered a thick-set man in uniform— evidently a chairman. " Go on, gentlemen, I beseech you, for the love of glory. It is not often the likes of us see the quality fight."

" Have at him again, my young fancy lad," a dirty linkman shouted. " I'll light him home if he can walk when you've finished with him." He, too, was enjoying the turn-up in the street.

Lord Bleakmoor's temper was rapidly cooling. He neither liked the attentions of Nicholas nor those of the crowd. Drawing himself up with as much dignity as he could summon, he sheathed his sword.

" This is neither the time nor the place for a satisfactory adjustment of our affairs," he said, at length.

" My time is at your disposal," Nicholas answered, readily. " Any place you may choose will suit me."

An attendant pushed his way into the centre of the crowd with a cloak, which Lord Bleakmoor slowly resumed. Several of the gamblers, having settled their personal quarrels, came closer to the scene of the altercation. Nicholas noted that amongst those approaching was Captain Barclay and a group of his hired bravoes. The knowledge of this was not hidden from Lord Bleakmoor, whose manner showed a return of confidence.

" The question of time and place is a matter I can leave," he said, with a sneer. " A man who brings false accusations of cheating against gentlemen is not in a position to be nice about points of honour."

Nevinson found his choler rising, and would have retorted in kind, but many of Lord Bleakmoor's friends were appearing, and he deemed it wiser to withdraw than to be mixed up in a disorderly street fight, with several not very scrupulous gentlemen attacking him at once.

" I shall raise the matter again," he said, sternly ;

"perhaps at a more opportune moment. The verdict of your packed committee does not give you the right to insult me."

"That we shall see in good time," Lord Bleakmoor answered, icily. As he spoke he turned on his heel and walked in the direction of his friends.

Nicholas secured his cloak from one of the attendants and crossed Covent Garden alone. He had not gone very far when he overtook the Honourable George Taunton, who, with the aid of an old watchman, was ruefully looking over a rent in his coat.

The two friends fell to talking of the incidents of the night, and congratulated each other on getting out of the gaming house alive.

A notorious night house stood with invitingly open doors almost at their elbows. It was well known to all the turbulent members of fashion who frequented Covent Garden as "The Finish." "The Finish" was a small tavern, with three rooms upon the ground floor, badly lit, which attracted some of the best company in London, and some of the worst. The best people entered the narrow passage leading to the hot, badly ventilated rooms out of sheer curiosity. The worst, many of whom were regulars, found it a suitable rendezvous, and drifted in out of the surge of life swirling about the doors. Into this house Nicholas and his friend entered for the purpose of examining the havoc played on their apparel by the recent *mêlée*, and setting it to rights, so that they could continue on their round of the available pleasures of the night.

A needle and thread plied by the landlady, sundry brushings, a pull here and there on the cravats, and much shooting of linen, soon set our two gallants aright. From the private room which they first entered, they walked into the narrow passage. Ordering glasses of hot brandy, they stood there, clinking the tumblers and laughing as they consumed the spirit.

"Well—here's to our next merry meeting," Taunton said, gaily.

They bowed to each other as the glasses clashed together.

"Our day is not over yet, surely," Nevinson replied gaily. "The night is young and the town is still alive."

"What are you up to?" Taunton asked. "I'm game for anything, from a raid on the faro tables to pinning a Charlie in his box."

"I am going to take a last glimpse of polite society," Nevinson returned, recklessly. "I am a sort of Cinderella at the feast. I still possess two guineas more, and that will give me two further hours of joy. Then, exit mad Nick Nevinson."

"You mean that, Nevinson, on your sacred word of honour?" Taunton said, earnestly. "I'm in luck to-day. I could loan you twenty guineas, and, damme, we are good enough friends for you to say the word that will make me do it."

"No, Taunton," Nicholas replied, "it's devilish good of you, but I won't borrow; I am at the end of my tether, and borrowing will only keep me dancing on a loose string. To-night, after the last of my guineas has gone, I take the plunge."

"And what are you going to plunge into?" Taunton asked, curiously.

"Into the first highway," Nevinson answered. "I'll follow my nose out of London along the road that best fills my eye, and leave chance to bespeak adventure. Enough of this," he added, slapping his friend on the back. "Potman, more hot brandy. My troubles ill suit a merry evening."

Again the two men drank—this time to Nevinson's adventure. As Nicholas drained his glass he began to pull his cloak closer about him.

"Now, let's be out and about," he said. "I must make the most of my golden hours. I'm for the Aigyle Rooms at once. I would have pleasant thoughts of my last hours as a gentleman of fortune. I will have life and the best of society; fashion and its more social follies; red wine, pretty women, music and the dance. And if you join me, no one will be a gayer rogue than Nicholas Nevinson, I promise you."

Taunton turned towards the door, and Nicholas was about to follow him when he was arrested by a man plucking on his shoulder.

"A moment in your ear, my gay gallant," the new-comer said, huskily.

Nicholas was impelled by his first impression to shake off the stranger as a needy adventurer. But looking into the face of the man he changed his mind and manner.

"Wait one minute for me," he called to Taunton, who stood clicking his heels on the flags at the entrance. Then he turned to the fellow who had arrested his progress.

He was a man whose personality would have held the attention of any one. A big, bold, swarthy man, with a round face and three rolls of red chin to balance it—he was getting well into middle age. Particularly compelling about him were his bright eyes, set far apart, in which mingled slyness and uncertain geniality seemed to frolic together. He wore a hard shovel-hat, very much weatherbeaten and set at an angle on his head. From beneath it hung his long, black hair, a thick, greasy lock of this falling over his forehead. He had a trick of sweeping it away from his eyes with the back of a heavy, brown, ungloved hand. His nose was big, curved jovially, and made one think of a great jug handle. His face was pitted with traces of the small-pox. His heavy jowl, clean shaven, had the mark of an old scar across it on the right side. He was dressed in a country manner that suggested the open road, horses and coaches, or wagons. A great coat of a thick, blue material, with many capes about the shoulders and a huge collar, covered his burly figure and reached down to his heavy top boots. One sleeve of the coat flapped as he moved, and was obviously empty. He had lost his left arm.

" A word in your ear, young gallant," this strange person said, in a husky, throaty voice that suggested a lifetime of exposure. " I heard a part of your talk just now, and I had the pleasure of seeing you fling the sword out of the elderly buck's hand in

Covent Garden. I say to myself when I see that and hear what you say, 'Here's a gentleman of spirit what wants a-looking after.' Rip me, you put him with his back to the wall in double quick time.''

The stout stranger nodded wisely, and his convivial face shone with a huge geniality.

"You are hopping the twig, I hear," he went on; "you are going on the road. Now, what I don't know about the road ain't no manner of use to no man. You come to me." He tapped his big nose with the forefinger of his one hand.

"It's devilish kind," Nicholas said, much amused by the manner of the man. "Do you intend to adopt me?"

"What are you going to do on the road, d'ye think?" the other man asked. "Is it the High Toby—the stand-and-deliver game and all the rest of it—eh?"

"God's life, man, no! I have never thought of that," Nicholas answered, half in anger.

The stout, one-armed man looked disappointed.

"No man ever does think of it, when he's flush of coin and the weather is fair. What's the matter with it, anyway? You've come out of Isaacs' rooms, haven't you? I know him and his crew. He's the damnedest old pimp in good King Charles's London. Well, if you've only got a couple of Old Rowley's blessed images in gold, you've been plucked by Isaacs and his gang, I'll warrant. Go on the road and levy toll on them and their class. They skin you in town and you wait for them and skin them in the country. It's fair, young master, ain't it ? "

Nevinson laughed in the man's face, oddly earnest and quaintly genial as it was. He found it impossible to be angry with the stranger. He shook his head decisively and began to move to the door, where Taunton was showing signs of impatience.

" Here—one minute, sir," the stout man cried, holding Nicholas by the cloaked elbow. " They're fair game and good game. Every one of these town-bred dandies would cheat the devil himself at cards. You come to me if you think over what I've said. I can show you some tricks of the road and put you on to a life as merry as a girl's first fairing ; and, mind you this, never a day without lashons of drink and a pocket full of bright red guineas. Say the word, my buck ; say the word and be a soldier of fortune."

Nevinson, still laughing, again made for the door.

" Not on your life," he said, decisively. " Unhand me ; there's a good fellow. My friend is waiting."

" Well, one more word," the other man said, speaking earnestly. " If you think it over and are in a difficulty and want help, you come to me. I keep the Lantern Tavern, just after you leave Barnet on the North Road. We get fine company at the Lantern, and if you pass that way think of old Steve Randall and drop in. I can give you a mulled wine that will make your hair curl. You're a bonnie gallant, and you take my old eyes better than any fancy man I've seen since Du Vall stopped coming along the road."

Nevinson, by dint of using actual force, broke away from Steve Randall, and with a high-spirited laugh set out to join his friend.

"All right, my covey," he said, waving his hand gaily as he went out; "I'll call in as I pass. There's no more harm in mulled wine than a headache," he added; "and one never knows how good mulled wine is until one gets out on the North Road. Goodnight to you, Master Steve Randall."

"And good-night to you, my brave buck," old Steve called in his rusty, throaty voice. "You are sure to come my way along the old North Road."

Nicholas and Taunton disappeared from the doorway, and Steve Randall shuffled along to a snuggery, where, heavily coated as he was, he sat close to the fire and ordered in a bowl of hot brandy.

Although the house was noisy and merry and haunted with the uproarious laughter of the frequenters of taverns, the snuggery was quiet.

Steve Randall stirred the fire with the heel of his top boot. Then he lounged back in a heavy settle, filled a glass from the bowl, held it up to the firelight, winked through it at the flame, and tossed off the reeking fluid as if it were so much water.

Smacking his lips reflectively, he communed with himself.

"A mighty good lad," he said, striking his knee with his one heavy hand. "A mettlesome bird, if I know a game cock: a bird who will fly along the North Road or I'm a damned Dutchman."

He sat there following his own thoughts.

" Somehow you can tell the men who will play old Harry on the highway," he went on. " It's in their blood, bones, and marrow. It's in the way they stand up and swagger when they walk; it's in the very cock of their eyes. If I know the High Toby, the fly-by-night spirit is in the eye of that game bird or my name is not Steve Randall, and may I never house another ruffler or take my share of the swag for putting him close to the great game."

He sat there weaving his own fancies into the future, his face growing more rubicund under the influence of the hot spirit.

In a room opposite, a group of men were drinking and carousing. They were heavily booted and spurred; they were warmly coated, and arms hung in their belts. All were drinking greedily and noisily; their intoxicated laughter rang through the house and seemed to set it rocking and vibrating.

" Order, order for the song," said one. " Galloping Tom Simpson will oblige you, gentlemen. He will sing ' The Golden Farmer's Last Farewell.' "

They stood up in a body, raised their glasses and clinked them together.

" Here's a health to the Golden Farmer," cried a roysterer, a lean man who made one think of a dissipated greyhound. " A good sort and a rare Old Toby man, the Golden Farmer—God rest his bones wherever they lie rotting."

With noisy glee they settled for their song, and a rollicking voice began to throw off sinister lines to the dirge-like melody loved by the hawkers of broad streets.

> "A gang of robbers then
> Myself did entertain ;
> Notorious, hardy highwaymen
> Who did like ruffians reign.
> We'd rob, we'd laugh and joke,
> And revel night and day ;
> But now the lot of us is broke,
> 'Tis I that leads the way."

The verse rounded off with a chorus which they all roared lustily, banging their pots upon the oaken table.

The grisly song had a dozen verses, and the half-drunken tippler trolled them off slowly, one by one. It tailed off into the usual moralising of these ballads on the ends of lives that were short and merry.

> "Long have I lived, you see,
> By this unlawful trade,
> And at the length am brought to be
> A just example made.
> God grant my sins forgive,
> Whose laws I did offend,
> For here I may no longer live,
> My life is at an end."

To this dirge-like last verse they sang the chorus with more gusto than ever, and when, in a variety of foolish noises, the ballad ended and comparative silence followed, the lean man stood up and banged his pot lustily on the table to secure the further attention of his comrades.

"Here's a health to the song," he said, uproariously, " and a good song, too. And all upstanding, gentlemen, drink deep and hearty to the Golden Farmer. A good 'un and a rare Old Tobyman—damn his dead eyes—and God rest his poor old bones wherever they are rotting, as I said before."

The company, some six or eight men, stood up, looked with drunken solemnity into each other's eyes, raised their mugs and glasses, and set them down, empty and with a flourish, roaring for more drink at the end of this startling ceremony.

Old Steve Randall listened to their revelling with a contemptuous leer on his round face.

" A pest upon such rascals—vermin and scum of the road," he said, half aloud. " I have always said a Tobyman should be a gentleman. No gentleman would brawl about the profession in a tavern within the shadow of Bow Street. They deserve to rot, and all their like, with the bones of the Golden Farmer."

So saying, and crossing himself as he mentioned the Golden Farmer, he drank off another brandy, hitched his many capes closer about him, and went with a roll and a waddle into the shadows of Covent Garden.

CHAPTER VI

As Steve Randall sat weaving a net into the future, Nicholas Nevinson and George Taunton arrived at the Argyle Rooms. In common with many places of public resort of that day, the Argyle Rooms were privately owned, but they differed from the most in being administered by a committee of patrons, and a mighty exclusive affair the members made of their control.

The Argyle Rooms were situate in Regent Street, sufficiently near to the Haymarket to catch some of the riotous contagion of the heart of the West End, and sufficiently far away to escape contact with some of its more obvious corruption. They served as a place of assembly for all that was brightest and gayest in London's social life and all that was of good repute—the sweetest part of which was not very far advanced. To these rooms came extravagantly attired gentlemen of the town, their costumed dames and marriageable daughters, with a sprinkling of younger men of fashion, scions of great houses, and men of substance who followed in the train of the latter, encouraged by many a matron with a keen eye for a good match.

The rooms were on the small side, but luxuriously

furnished. The walls were tapestried, and sometimes enriched with gilt ornamentations; the floors
were thickly carpeted, excepting the dancing saloon;
the rooms were lit by many candles. There one
might dance, if young enough in mind or body;
the place was a famous resort for supper; there
were corners for the *tête-à-tête* if approved by alert-
minded mothers and chaperons; the card-rooms,
in which play ruled high, but not notoriously so,
amongst men and women, were always busy, though
the gaming was conducted with stately decorum and
formal dignity. The right of entry to the Argyle
Rooms was jealously guarded, and could only be
secured by introduction and through a heavy sub-
scription. The committee had the power to expel
accepted guests who did not conform to its reading
of the social usages, amenities and accepted stan-
dards of honour.

As Nevinson entered the rooms, both he and
Taunton were soon greeted by many friends, who
comported themselves with fine manners, somewhat
grotesque when set side by side with the prevailing
note of light-hearted badinage. Amongst so many
friends, the two men quietly separated.

The outstanding personality in these rooms was
Beau Morris, who, under a manner that was almost
foolishly egregious and suave to the point of servility, applied a social rule with an iron hand and
an inflexible mind. Beau Morris was a sort of
permanent Master of Ceremonies. He had the
largest proprietary interest in the rooms, and his
success in life was due to his power to interest the

socially eminent and keep their sanction and patronage as a cloak of exclusiveness for his business
operations. He was a little man, corpulent and
florid, yet brisk in action. In movement, he had
the agility of a dancing master. No one could
bow with such a precise grace, or give an arm to
a lady, or bend to listen to the querulous complaint
of some dowager, whose great name and high breeding did not always control an irritable temper. No
one could dig a snuff-box into the ribs of the great
with more confident familiarity, or tell, with smile
and leer, the piquant story that sets the table in
a roar after dinner, or starts a merry round of similar
conceits when the hour is late and men forgather
alone. No one could walk with more mincing step,
prinking with a pleasure feminine to the point of
sickliness in a man. And, last, no one had a longer
memory for faces and personalities and the tact to
make the instant advance with the right turn of a
phrase—a power that gave him unchallenged
intimacy with the great.

Such a man he was, ubiquitous, as he marched
about the rooms he ruled with abject respect for
the wishes of his committee. A bow here, an
elaborate handshake there ; a hand at piquet in
the card-room followed by a few minutes of dalliance
in the ball-room ; an ear for a complaint, a repartee
for a grinning buck, a laughing phrase of raillery
for the demure, self-conscious maiden, an almost
abject desire to please the matrons, were parts of
his social armoury and gave him uncontested sway
at the Argyle Rooms.

In a day when dress was extravagant, he was more than extravagantly dressed. No one had a wig more crisply curled. His salmon-coloured coat was richly embroidered with threads of gold, the skirts being distended by artificial stiffenings that gave him a grotesquely fussy appearance. His cravats were works of art and miracles of arrangement ; his linen was tied and bowed, knotted with many laces, and fell from his turned-back sleeves in prodigal folds. His waistcoats were at once the admiration and inspiration of social London, and one of his triumphs, which looked at first sight like a vest of chain-mail of solid gold, but was in reality a closely woven brocade from the French looms, adorned his short, round body, falling almost to his knees.

When Nicholas entered the rooms, Beau Morris was prinking, smiling, and bowing his way through the hall. In the ordinary course of routine, during Nevinson's life in the town, he had always stepped aside for a jest in passing, a bow, and a politely extravagant inquiry after the young man's health. To-night, he was preoccupied and missed noting Nevinson's arrival.

"Odd—damned odd!" Nevinson said, absently to himself. "The old buck usually has an eye for every one as true as a gimlet, even in a crowd."

He did not pursue his train of thought, but plunged into the gaiety about him. If that were to be his last night he would make the most of it, He had discovered a partner, and was leading a pert, young debutante to the pleasures of London towards the corridor giving access to the dancing saloon, when, to his astonishment and delight, he saw Peggy Sheldon advancing towards him on the arm of her uncle, John Sheldon.

Sheldon was a sour, ill-favoured man, clad in a black habit, rich but severe, that suggested the Puritan at heart, and gave the man a clerkly note in a setting which produced such gaudy butterflies as Beau Morris. His very cravat was tight, pinched, and severe in its elegance.

John Sheldon was of the lean, long, and lank type. His small head was set on narrow shoulders which were slightly bent. His lean body ended in spidery legs. He wore a close, mean dress wig ; his narrow forehead was prominent ; his eyebrows were heavy and met over sunk, crafty, piglike eyes ; his nose was long and slightly bent, as if in its day it had been broken.

The ugliest feature of John Sheldon's face was the mouth, a big one. The lips of it puckered grimly and hung loosely at the corners, giving a last definite suggestion to the general impression his whole personality conveyed—that he was a man of craft and cunning, constantly hatching schemes to satisfy his own avaricious nature.

Nevinson did not like the man, but he was Peggy's guardian. He advanced eagerly and even cordially towards Sheldon, who walked with the girl upon his arm. His joy at seeing Peggy once again quickly faded from Nevinson's face. To his astonishment John Sheldon stalked forward, without showing the slightest sign of recognition, and passed on, de-

liberately giving the young man the cut direct.
Nevinson, seeing his intent, looked his pain and
surprise in the direction of Peggy. The ardent girl,
who had been so charming in her reliance upon
his affection and courage that afternoon, glanced
away. Nicholas could see the cost of the effort
of doing so. Her eyes were suspiciously bright; the
girl's face was flushed; her bosom was heaving.
There was unusual fire in the glance she averted
from her lover's gaze.

"La, Mr. Nevinson!" said the lady on his arm,
"they do not seem mighty pleased to meet you."

He did not answer, but fumed within himself.
Perturbed, uneasy in his mind, Nicholas proved
a dull partner in the following round dance. In
the crowded room, lit by hundreds of candles, alive
with colour, heavy with the odour of scents, gay
with light-hearted laughter and noisy with the ring
of buckled shoes and the trip of painted slippers,
Nevinson danced mechanically. He fancied, too,
that acquaintances he met in the intricacies of the
dance did not meet his glance with the usual signs
of pleasure. Growing upon him as a conviction
was the thought that people were looking upon him
curiously, as if he were the subject of town talk.
He saw Peggy dancing, at the far end of the room,
with a youthful partner, who smiled at her inanely,
his fatuous face inflamed by the reflection from a
plum-coloured waistcoat. Once, as he whirled his
partner round in the rally, he saw John Sheldon
standing at one of the curtained entrances with
two other men. One was Lord Bleakmoor and the

other Beau Morris. Bleakmoor was speaking; Sheldon, frowning, was listening; the gorgeous Master of Ceremonies maintained a running series of emphatic, servile nods of assent, until every curl in his perruque danced again.

Nicholas grew still more absent-minded. It was evident his pretty partner had had enough of him, and thought his conduct tiresome, before the dance had ended. When the company on the floor dispersed, Nevinson led her back to her chaperon with the usual commonplaces of small talk. He turned slowly away, but not before he had heard a significant conversation, which lingered in his mind like the shadow of a coming event.

"Heaven save us," said the stout matron to the demure girl; "what an awkward baggage you are! Here I just turn my back for a second to talk to Lady Hadling and you run off to dance with that coxcomb, Nevinson. And to-night of all nights, too," she added, bridling.

"La, mamma, there is no pleasing you!" the girl added, gently enough. "I found him monstrously dull, but I have not heard before that you object to him. Why should I not dance with him to-night as well as last week or the week before?"

"People are talking of him," Nevinson heard the stout matron say. "The whole town is ringing with his infamy. They say——"

Nevinson had passed out of earshot, and did not discover what "they" were saying, but he had learnt enough. He had always been the subject of gossip —it was the natural outcome of his recklessness.

In his gay world he was about to commit the enormous sin of being poor. But that ranked as social awkwardness rather than infamy. He could not help but jump to the conclusion, thoughtless as he was, that the news of the inquiry and fracas in Covent Garden had travelled fast, and that as fast as the facts moved they were being distorted by the way. He argued that for these attentions he had to thank Lord Bleakmoor, and perhaps Captain Barclay.

Nevinson's manner stiffened, and a fixed purpose began to gather in the rigid lines of his gay, dare-devil face. He knew his last hour had come, for financially he could not continue. But gambler and adventurer as he was at heart, he wanted to round off his brief innings as a butterfly of fortune with a brave show, and make his exit in the manner of the well-graced player. He decided to seek Mistress Peggy Sheldon for some explanation of the slight put upon him by herself and uncle.

Events moved rapidly. For Peggy, he had not to search very long. The girl was looking for him, unostentatiously, through the crowded rooms. As the next dance progressed, they met face to face in a corridor, leading from the ball-room out into a retiring room, used largely by the younger bucks and eligible maidens for the lighter purposes of flirtation.

Peggy laid her hand upon Nevinson's coat sleeve and led him with gentle command into the quiet room near them. There was only a liveried attendant there, passing through. When he had travelled out of distance, she checked the impatient torrent of protest rising to his lips with a gesture of her slim, white hand. Her manner was serious and urgent.

"Nicholas," she said, "don't let us play at cross purposes and waste precious time. Do as I bid you, and leave at once."

"Why?" he asked, sternly.

She spoke rapidly and with a feverish desire to get her message delivered, as if she were talking against time.

"Your enemies are here—and in force," Peggy exclaimed quickly. "My uncle has seen Captain Barclay—sent by Sir Ladbroke Drake. He discovered us at the Marylebone Gardens. Apparently Barclay told Sir Ladbroke, and was ordered by him to come on here and tell my uncle. I was told, as my uncle forced me to come to the rooms, that I must not even recognise you, on pain of his displeasure. That I am risking now."

Peggy paused a moment in her breathless narrative.

"But, by the Lord, Mistress Peggy, what is that to make you pale or distraught, or afraid for me? Surely I do not wither before a foolish old man's displeasure," Nevinson said.

"That is not the worst—I would it were," she answered, taking up the narrative again as hurriedly as before. "Lord Bleakmoor comes from Covent Garden, strongly incensed. He has reported infamous conduct against you, unworthy of a gentleman. He is backed by Captain Barclay and half a score of others, and they have laid their complaint before Beau Morris, who is with them, urged on by uncle. Already the committee has sat and decided

4

against you, and gossip that should make your ears burn is going from hand to mouth with the fierceness of a roaring blaze."

" Do you believe this devilish tittle-tattle ? " he asked, looking into her eyes and almost trembling.

" Zounds, no," Peggy said, superb trust vibrating in her young, full voice. " Follies, yes, and by the peck or bushel, I believe of you, but infamous conduct—no. That is neither here nor there, so far as I am concerned. I must go back to the ladies under whose charge I am. But before I go, promise me two things."

She looked at him appealingly, in a manner that made his heart beat faster.

" I promise you, readily, anything," he answered.

" Reckless to the end," Peggy answered, brightening. " I'll remember that and perhaps ask you for the moon one day. But now you must promise to keep me advised of your movements. I may need your help."

" Right willingly," he said, intense conviction in his voice and manner.

" And you will go away from these rooms—now," Peggy pleaded, urgently.

Nevinson stiffened under this suggestion, as if he had been offered a blow. His jaws set firmly and a light Peggy had never seen flamed in the grey eyes so often bright with lurking good-humour.

" You ask much of me," he said. " I do not like to fade away, a beaten mongrel with tail down. I do not fear one living soul of all the wretched pack. I'll be hunter, not hunted, and I'll stand my ground. No ill have I done to any man other than myself—unless it be letting the fresh, morning air into Drake's ugly carcass. What can they do?"

"Hush, Nicholas, and listen to what I say," Peggy said, abruptly. "I must not be found here, and some one is coming. What can they do, you ask. What they are going to do, that will they do —affront you before every one here and expel you ignominiously. Go now and save yourself this deadly insult and—adieu. God save you in your next adventures, and send you better fortune. And, I pray you, keep me in your heart, as I have your image printed in mine."

Peggy left him without a further word, dropping a hasty curtsey as she went tripping along the waxed flooring of the corridor. Nevinson would have followed her, on first impulses. Then, so greatly had her urgent words affected him, he stood still and swiftly deliberated. He even started to the door to obey her command, repugnant as it was, and as he did so George Taunton came hastily forward, concern written on his good-humoured face.

"Nevinson, for the love of God, hasten and get out. Surely you have heard?" he said.

"Damme, the air is too thick with dire omens and threatening portents for me to miss them. They fall like flakes of snow," Nevinson said.

"Well, flee before the storm," Taunton urged, "and save yourself a cruel affront."

"I hate to fly," Nevinson answered. "I'd sooner face the pack with my sword, and one by one I'd carve out all the sores upon their easily wounded honour."

"Oh, damn courage!" Taunton said, his manner agitated. "There will be no swords. There'll just be an insolent command from Beau Morris ordering you to get out as if you were a mangy dog, or a faro cheat, or a bleating Roundhead; and if you do not go, they'll cast you forth like a filthy beggar whose disorder has offended them."

Taunton's concern was so sincere that Nevinson was about to yield to his request which coincided so closely with Peggy Sheldon's command.

"I'll go," he said, slowly; "out of love for a lady and good-will for an excellent friend."

Taunton's Irish face showed its relief, and he turned to hasten Nevinson's departure.

They were too late. As the two men turned towards the door, they were met by a group of gentlemen. There was Beau Morris, his ruddy face still more aflame, and lit by an indignation not wholly righteous. He had the manner of a man confronted with a pleasant task, in which duty ran neck and neck with profit. He had been primed by Lord Bleakmoor, and was obviously at full-cock and ready to go off with ample smell of burning powder. That nobleman walked by Beau Morris, an ugly gleam of triumph in his cold eyes, and with them was John Sheldon, his grim, crafty face boding no good to the subject of his thoughts. Almost at the latter's elbow was Captain Barclay. Behind, in their train, were members of the committee, purse-proud, socially inflated, and ruffled like so many fowl disturbed over peaceful and desultory preoccupations by some unusual beast of prey. There were great lords and minor aristocrats, the full and round, the long and thin, clucking in the manner of men, saying, " I told you so." Younger bucks followed in their wake, maliciously agog, eager to be in at the death and ready to witness and enjoy the humiliations of a bird of high feather who, in a meteor-like flight through town, had outplayed them at the game of being young, ornamental, and audacious. And tripping behind, discreetly, were pretty women—though some were old in fat or angular, ugliness—very excited, and come to listen to as much as modest ears may accept without turning too pink, and prepared to scuttle away, horribly but pleasantly shocked, if the situation grew sultry and threatened completely to incarnadine.

Nevinson, slightly pale, stood confronting them. He did not put the question on his lips. There was no time. Beau Morris had made up his mind. The sacred call of duty, never more vicious than when it is applied socially, urged him forward. He was neither indirect nor nice in his manner. He stopped, ten yards from Nevinson, and the company, approaching with him, halted on his example. Beau Morris cleared his throat and looked ever so much like a blood-red turkey cock, secure in his weight, and one thought of fiercely wattled anger.

" Sir," he said, in his high-pitched voice, his chest swelling, " it has been reported to the committee of the Argyle Rooms that your conduct to-night in the company of gentlemen makes it no longer possible to receive you here."

"Who reports such flagrant lies of me?" Nicholas answered, his voice ringing with spirit.

"The committee of the Argyle Rooms does not explain. Its judgments are trusted," Beau Morris said, with profound dignity. "On behalf of the patrons the committee represents, I ask you to withdraw."

"And suppose I refuse the invitation and press my rights as a gentleman to insist on an explanation of this ill treatment—what then?" Nevinson asked, a mettlesome challenge in his voice and gesture.

"The explanation will be refused," answered Beau Morris, with brutal but polite directness. "You will be escorted to the door by the committee's servants."

Nicholas drew his sword. The weapon described a glittering circle, and swept the company back, those forward pressing with loss of dignity on the toes of others crowding behind. Beau Morris looked disturbed. Lord Bleakmoor edged a little out of the prominent centre of the group, as did Captain Barclay. The crowd of gentlemen began to murmur; a few ladies screamed, but, fascinated, would not run away.

Nicholas, standing there, saw red. A turbulent chaos of thought surged through his brain. For a moment he looked as if about to leap into this startled company of guinea-pigs and engage them, ruck and bulk. Then suddenly his brain cleared. An icy wave of reason steeled his nerves. Something we call courage in the last stage, when naked self-respect stands defenceless before the barbs of society linked in slander, came to his aid and gave him dignity.

"Let no man touch me," he said with flashing eye, "or, as God judges me, he'll lose his life the moment he attempts to further your powers to insult me. I have done you no ill, and meant you none; all the ill in me has come back to wither my poor self. But hark ye, gentlemen, I deny your right to judge me. You are a pack of cowards led by the nose by a foolish despot—Beau Morris; a liar, who is my Lord Bleakmoor; and a rascal, who is Captain Barclay."

His mind exulted as he thought of wounding phrases, and as he stood there, defying them, an odd picture fired his brain. He saw the gloomy night house, "The Finish," visualised the big, round, swarthy face of Steve Randall, and heard again his call to the life of the great North Road.

"Zounds, you wage a war on me, my bucks, and win," he went on, his words coming out in a whirl. "Take care of your well-kept skins, and look to it that I don't wage a war on you, and, first fooling you to my heart's content, trail the garment of your pride in the mud as you have trampled on mine. And I bid you a good-night, my gentlemen, having given you fair play, which is bonnie play, and more than you have offered to me."

He looked round on the startled company, his grey eyes shining like polished steel.

They met Peggy's face, its roundness dimpled; a sweet, encouraging laughter lighting every winsome line of it.

Nevinson raised his sword, kissed its hilt, and bowed, and the company thought it was to them he offered this ceremony, in fine irony. Only Peggy understood that once again a knight had pledged a world-old fealty to a lady. Nevinson laughed as he did so, recklessly, and the mocking light that had intimidated Sir Ladbroke Drake the morning before was in his eyes. Out of his own virile ego he had woven a mantle for his lost dignity, which was about him, protective as an armour, and holding his foes at bay.

"Now, gentlemen," he said, boldly moving towards them, with a flourish of his sword. "Divide and let me pass. Master or man, move one of you to my discomfort and that man will be carrion, stinking in body, and as offensive as his image is to my mind."

So compelling was his personality they all moved to his will, Beau Morris, connoisseur of deportment in difficult situations, open mouthed, as if he were in a trance. Nevinson passed between their ranks, a smile in his eyes, a sneer upon his lips. In the hall he slowly cloaked himself with the assistance of a porter, arranged his wig, and adjusted his feathered hat. He was as particular in his preparation for departure as if he were leaving on a pleasant journey, an honoured guest speeded by the whole company. The members of the Argyle Rooms, watching from the top of the great staircase, heard the heavy door clang behind him as he swaggered towards the street, and began furtively to look into each other's eyes as they awoke from the toils of a common spell.

CHAPTER VII

WHEN Nevinson, with a swagger, walked out of
the Argyle Rooms, his brain was on fire with the
bitterness of his humiliation. For some minutes he
walked very rapidly, without being conscious of his
own movements or having any definite objective. He
came more or less to himself and circumstances
as he turned into the Haymarket, which was still busy
and agog with the night life of London and the
traffic of the pleasure of the town.

In the narrower streets the roaring night houses
were open, and lights, which would have been a
welcome to him weeks ago, blazed in their windows.

Nicholas had neither the stomach nor the means
or the enjoyment of the later pleasures of the town.
He passed the open houses, whose lights seemed to
jeer at him, and sought the comparative quietness
of an inn devoted to the traffic of the highways.
It was a place of gables and latticed windows ; a
dark arch gave a vista of stables, and a great yard
where coaches and wagons were housed. A sleepy
ostler was just completing the equipment of a chaise
for the road.

The house itself was quiet, but, judging by the
lights in several rooms, the inn was open for the

reception of guests. Nicholas stalked in, his feet grating on the sanded flags of the passage. He found himself entering a tiny taproom, drawn there by a huge fire crackling in an open grate. Pulling a hanging bell-rope, he sat down near the blaze, on a much-used oak settle, and stretched out his legs to thaw himself in the heat. A waiter, with straws in his hair and signs of the stable about him, came in obedience to Nevinson's summons, and received an order for a bowl of punch in silence. When the reeking jorum was delivered, Nicholas paid for it with his last guinea.

"At all events," he chuckled, "I am fulfilling my intention. I am spending my last guinea on a toast for my dismal prospects."

He remained, sipping his liquor, in the deserted taproom, and as he did so panoramic pictures of his flight through town flitted through his mind—a whirl of gay phantoms not unpleasing to memory, though the reaping of their consequences must not have been very cheering.

Nicholas remembered his first journey to town with an ample portion to his credit. He retraced the steps by which all his possessions had been squandered, and saw himself, a reckless young man, courted and flattered by the well-dressed harpies who flocked round the gaming tables after midnight, playing high when fools like himself were heavy and stupid with wine. Nicholas saw the days trooping by, so many ghosts in his memory, the last similar to the one before, but perhaps wilder in the manner. And the ghosts of the vanished days trailed away, each with a slice of the young man's fortune. He saw Isaacs enriched; men such as Sir Ladbroke Drake and Captain Barclay plucking him with infinite zest, and finer gentlemen still, of the Lord Bleakmoor type, indirectly profiting as owners, or sleeping partners, in such hells. He cursed himself roundly as a fool, but he cursed the harpies who had preyed on him still more—by bell and book and candle.

As his thoughts turned from the past to the present and then threw out tendrils into the future, one picture would recur in Nevinson's mind. He saw again the grotesque, stout figure of Steve Randall, with the throaty voice of the night bird issuing from the depths of the many capes about his neck.

"What was it he said?" Nevinson asked himself, recalling the words the stranger had used. "'They skin you in town, and you wait for them and skin them in the country. It's fair, young master, ain't it?' Those were his words, and, by God, they sound fair enough to me now," Nicholas added.

The call of the North Road, for the first time put into his mind by a chance encounter at "The Finish," now worked persistently in his brain. Bankrupt in pocket, with no prospects; himself at war with a class who had squeezed him dry and flung him forth as an outcast, with every humiliation, the career sketched by Randall was being painted in detail by Fate. He had been a pigeon for the gentlemen of the town to pluck; why should he not be a hawk of the highway, plucking them in his turn?

And it should be remembered his day was a lawless period. Civil war had split the land from end to end, and much of the law in vogue was force. The second Charles held his throne with an unscrupulous heel upon a restless people. Some of the symbols of his kingly dignity were only maintained by the habits and actions of a freebooter. His example had vitiated the English love of law, order, and honour, and even in reputable circles definitions outlining "mine and thine" were hazy. The evil examples of lax government, maintained by immoral servants, had spread with the contagion of the Black Death. The very soldiers of the King, travelling the country, were little better than highwaymen. The rival factions in the civil war, subdued but growling, still recouped the losses of the feud by preying on each other. Every landowner living adjacent to great main roads, levied tolls legally and supplemented them with raids on travellers that were indefensible.

The minutes of the morning hour, between one and two, slowly ran out as Nicholas sat sipping his punch. As he plied his glass in the solitary room, the images in his mind grew from flitting shadows to fixed purposes. When the bowl was empty his position was clearly defined. He would answer the call of the gay North Road. Nevinson had walked into the house a ruined gentleman; he came out of it a highwayman, with the fortunes of the road before him. He had even gone so far as to tear the lining of his cloak for material to fashion into a rude mask, and when he sought the streets again, this, lightly rolled, was in his clenched hand.

The gods of chance elected to play a whimsical trick at that moment. Uncertain of his first steps towards a wilder series of adventure, Nevinson strolled down the Haymarket and stood at the corner of Pall Mall, in the shadow of a gabled house with an enormous frontage, which began with high walls round the out-buildings.

At that moment, in Regent Street, the disturbed gathering in the Argyle Rooms was separating. Linkboys, with lighted flares, swarmed about the doors. Private and public chairmen wrangled for precedence and the right of way. A few family coaches were lined up and lumbered towards the entrance as they were summoned by running footmen. The separation of the company within made a brave commotion without, as in groups of three or four the guests laughingly exchanged parting salutations, climbed into chairs or coaches, with their ladies, or rattled off afoot in groups—retaining each other's company as protection against the dangers of the streets.

Almost one of the last to depart from the Argyle Rooms was Beau Morris. He came forth from the scene of his nightly splendour with a noisy party of reeling young men who had stayed to crack several parting bottles. He stood for a moment or two bowing to them, chatting and smiling, his finery hidden under a great blue outer-garment, neither coat nor cloak, but combining the function and appearance of both. Then he turned to a gilded chair, with coats-of-arms painted on its panels and all sorts of flamboyant fancies, including cupids, and lavish floral garlands. His chairmen wore a wonderful livery of his own designing, and by their gilt braid and cocked hats were known as Beau Morris's men. There were three of these servants, and when they set off two carried and a paunchy third porter walked at the side of the chair, armed with a flaring torch. They all turned in the direction of St. James as the florid face of Beau Morris beamed through the open window and his fat hands waved final salutations to his friends.

By the aid of the flare Nevinson saw them coming. He recognised the cocked hats and the too lavish golden braid. His eyes gleamed in the dark and a smile broke upon his reckless face.

"The devil himself could not have planned it better," he said. "Here comes Beau Morris. I could not take to the road with more dignity than by making this old buck settle the score I have against him." He stepped back into the shadows, and rapidly adjusted his black mask.

The great street was deserted. The two o'clock watch had long since cried down the by-way. There was not a soul about in the black darkness but the three men advancing with the chair along a wall that formed an enclosure for one of the royal mews. On they came with sober dignity, befitting the progress of such a person as Beau Morris, until they arrived opposite to where Nevinson was standing in the shadow.

His sudden appearance in the light of the flare was sufficiently startling. For a moment the three chairmen saw a tall, cloaked man, with a black

mask stretched across his face. A voice cried
"Stop," with a ring of authority about it. The
chair came to the ground with a jolt that jarred
Beau Morris from head to heel and sent his hat
askew over his eyes, producing a total loss of the
dignity he tried to preserve with the sacredness of
life itself. Then all was darkness, for the fat link-
bearer, in his fright, clumsily let fall the light he
was bearing and the flames faded out in the gutter.

"Who goes there?" asked Nicholas, his voice
setting the servants' teeth a-chatter.

"His honour, Beau Morris, of the Argyle Rooms,"
a wavering voice replied.

Nicholas grasped the fat light bearer and shook
him until his brains rattled and the little sense in his
head flew out of it.

"Zithee, my rascal," Nevinson said, "I would
speak to his honour, Beau Morris. I charge you
fetch him out and hastily, or"—he prodded at
the man with his blade—"I will speed you up, and
that unpleasantly. As for you," he said, threatening
the other two, "stand at your chair and do not
move, or I will chase you to Covent Garden and back
at the point of the sword."

His manner was enough for the chairmen. They
simply waited, and two of them stood cowering in
their braided coats. The light bearer went forward
towards the door of the conveyance, obeying Nevinson's behest. He need not have embarked upon
this duty, for the window was lowered and the large,
florid face of Beau Morris looked out of it.

"What means this unmannerly interruption?" he

asked, his words sounding bold though his voice wavered.

"Come out, my little dancing master," Nevinson said, a grotesque sense of humour mounting in him. "Come forth at once, or stab me, I rout you out like a dog from under the table."

"In the name of God, what do you mean?" said the occupant of the chair, his fat voice whining abjectly.

"Just what I say. S'blood, I have a mind to have discourse with the finest gentleman in town, saving 'Old Rowley' himself. Rip and stab me for waiting on your coming—bestir yourself," commanded Nicholas.

"This is very unreasonable conduct," the Master of Ceremonies wailed. "A gentleman, even in wine, should content himself with the jest as far as it has gone."

"Well said," answered Nevinson; "but the jest is a merry one, and must go farther. Sink me, you are windy in your discourse and over slow of movement."

As he spoke Nicholas seized the chair, and pulling heavily on the vehicle, tilted it forward. The movement served to hasten Morris's progress into the street.

He was rather frightened and inclined to be angry as he landed upon his feet.

"By God, sir, if my rascals were not dolts and cowards, I'd call you to account for this pleasantry," Morris said, anger getting the better of fright and his voice rising.

"You should choose your company better,"

Nevinson answered; "who so able as Beau Morris to do that?"

"You know me," the Beau said, almost hopefully; for he could not imagine a gentleman of the town making his person an object of drunken pleasantry.

"Know you?" Nevinson answered, ironically. "Better than you know yourself, you purple-faced sinner. May not a gentleman of the road know the man whose word keeps in favour half the rascally pimps of the town?"

At these words Beau Morris for the first time realised he was not the butt of an intoxicated gentleman, but the prey of a highwayman, and glanced fearfully and vainly about for the prospect of assistance.

"Perhaps, now you have had converse with me, I may resume my journey home," he said, nervously pretending to keep up the farce that his stoppage was a jest.

"Most certainly," Nicholas assented. "I do not find your company inspiriting. First, I need a little help on a long journey. All you have upon you will be sufficient. Your purse, sir, and at once."

Beau Morris groaned aloud.

"Do you skulking rascals mean to see me robbed within sight of my own house?" he said; but the chairmen, intimidated by the voice and manner of Nicholas, still cowered about their vehicle.

"If they remain to look they will," Nicholas answered. "They'll see worse, if you do not hasten." He flourished his sword as he spoke.

Trembling, Beau Morris bent to search the low

pocket of his elaborate waistcoat. He produced, at length, a long knitted silken purse, heavy with gold, and handed it to Nevinson.

Jingling the coins in his hand, Nicholas curtly demanded his rings.

In stupefied silence Beau Morris drew his treasures, one by one, and slowly, from his fat fingers. He handed them with great reluctance to Nevinson, and that gentleman took the precious baubles—for Beau Morris was nice in his adornment—with a bow.

" I thank you," he said, with exaggerated courtesy. " I shall keep these little trinkets as memories of a night of somewhat mixed associations. I consider, so far as you may in kind, you have contributed with ample generosity to my maintenance."

"Then I may go?" Beau Morris asked, and he was for returning to the comparative security of the chair, vastly perturbed over his losses.

" Nay, by the jade of folly, no," Nicholas answered, laughing at his own conceit. " You have done much to repair my damaged fortunes, but sink me, I am still sore in my self-respect."

"What means your mirth?" Beau Morris asked. " You speak in unholy riddles."

" All the more pleasure in the guessing of them," Nicholas answered. " As a gentleman I once had the fortune to see you air your fine graces in the Argyle Rooms, where they have such a fitting setting. I have seen you blood your social power on gentlemen who could not resent it. Just as you make men dance to your tune in your world, I intend to make you dance to a tune I shall select, in mine."

"Surely you are not going to prolong this outrageous licence further?" Beau Morris asked, his wounded dignity getting the better of his scattered nerves.

"By the Lord, I am," Nicholas said, grimly. "I am going to whistle the tune, and you shall dance —dance, I tell you, as you do in the Argyle Rooms."

Nicholas began to whistle the slow movement of a minuet, but Beau Morris remained motionless.

"This is mad, preposterous folly," he said, fuming.

Nevinson ceased his whistling.

"It will be a tragedy if you do not dance. Dance, I tell you, or as sure as Old Rowley loves a pretty wench, I'll spur you to the movement, or spit you if you wince."

Dark as it was, there were the makings of a pretty sight on that pavement in Pall Mall. The chairmen, by the light of a moon struggling through the clouds, saw the stately master of social London compelled to air one of his lighter graces to a tune piped by a whistling highwayman. Nicholas, rendering a minuet through his teeth, made Beau Morris dance like a puppet, impelled by the point of his sword. If he did not bow with sufficient grace, or point his toe with a proper and stately dignity, the whistling ceased and the highwayman rated him with a torrent of contemptuous abuse. For five minutes he kept the Beau at his task, prancing foolishly to a piping whistle; then, the jest no longer appealing, Nevinson brought the strange scene to a close.

"I thank you for your courtesy," he said, with a fine air. "You may now bow to me, thrice, as you bow to good King Charles when he graces the Argyle Rooms."

Beau Morris hesitated, but a flourish of the sword in the moonlight set him bending, to the barely concealed delight of his chairmen. His face grew rosy to the point of apoplexy as he performed the repeated ceremony.

"Now, to conclude, you may say something socially pleasing," Nevinson finally suggested, with a further grim touch of humour. "Say, for instance: 'I have never realised the delight of your company until to-night.' You might add, 'I look forward to renewing our pleasant intercourse.'"

"The Lord forbid!" Beau Morris muttered.

"The Lord is neither here nor there. I want homage—lip service," Nicholas retorted, with an air of tranquil enjoyment. "Say it, man, say it, or, rip me, I'll set you dancing like a trained bear until the daylight."

Beau Morris repeated the words as if he were a child conning lessons.

"And now to your coach, my dancing master. Handle him tenderly," Nevinson said, mockingly, to the waiting chairmen, who were broadly smiling. "He is a precious vessel. His honour, Beau Morris, has now added to his experience of the art of pleasing gentlemen of the town, a knowledge of the manner of addressing a gentleman of the road."

With a bow, almost regal, Nicholas saluted the astonished Master of the Argyle Rooms, and humming a ballad, turned upon his heels and sauntered down the street.

CHAPTER VIII

ONCE away from Beau Morris, Nicholas pocketed the mask and went down the Strand feeling something of his former self—a gay gentleman of fortune with a pouch lined with gold images of merry King Charles.

He retraced his steps to the "Bull and Mouth," the rendezvous of much road traffic, and the inn he had left an hour before. The warm room was yet empty of travellers and the fire was still burning brightly, though the flames were lower. Nicholas had decided to toast himself during the few remaining hours before daylight and be about and out, making a bee-line for Barnet, with the breaking of the day.

Once back in the house, Nevinson found a place by the fire and called for a bottle of wine, served to him after a considerable interval by the sleepy waiter, who seemed to be the only man on duty. The house was wrapped in silence, for the time was no man's hour of the night. The "Bull and Mouth" was slumbering through the three empty hours which divided one busy day from another. Seldom did incoming travellers call for hospitality after the hour of two, while the traffic of those who had to adventure forth rarely brought any one about the inn before five o'clock in the morning.

The watch was calling the hour of three outside, and the shambling figure growled out the information that the morning was fine but misty. Nevinson, within, stirred as he heard the hour called, wrapped his cloak closer about him, sipped the red wine and was comfortable enough. He had counted the coins in Beau Morris's purse, and found that it discovered a neat pile numbering forty-five guineas. Afterwards he fell to dozing, and finally his head dropped forward on to his arms, outstretched upon the table, and the volume of his regular snoring proved how deeply he was asleep.

Nicholas might have been sleeping for more than an hour. He was aroused by the tramp of a man's feet, booted and spurred for the road, grinding the stone flooring. Nicholas did not stir, but remained in the dark room—for the fire had spent its energy and was dying down—listening and now fully awake, with his head resting on the pillow made by his outstretched arms.

Two men had entered the inn. Both stopped in the passage by the square wooden bar and called loudly for the tapster. Nicholas knew them at once by their voices, and smiled grimly as he listened.

" Well, all that is settled," one voice was saying, Buck Dowling's. " We might crack a bottle, drinking success to my mission and to the devil with the house of Stuart. You will have the comfort of knowing the stirrup-cup that sends me forth on the road, on a bitter morning, speeds you to bed and all the comfort of it in such raw weather."

" And damme! a good thing, too," a voice, surly with lack of sleep, answered—the voice of Captain Barclay.

" Hurry up, potman," the same voice added. " I have been abroad late for three days now and out with the cock-crow each morning. I feel that I could sleep like a dead man."

The waiter was routed out and set to the task of satisfying their needs, grumbling as he did so.

Nicholas heard the clinking of glasses. Judging from the crisp, surly tones of his reply to the toast, Captain Barclay was evidently bone-weary and not by any means in a cheerful temper.

" You positively know the instructions," he said, speaking hastily. " Out as quickly as you can to the Cock Tavern, in Bedford. There you wait for the messenger, as appointed. Once you have the dispatch, you hasten back. Sir Ladbroke expects you to make the journey within the day, allowing for a wait of an hour or two, more or less. You quite understand ?"

Buck Dowling laughed easily.

" That I do," he answered. " Sink me, I am not a child. I shall be in Bedford soon after noon. If our man is to time I ought to be making the return journey by nightfall, and back in town by the hour of eleven at the latest. Starlight will carry me easily ; he is the best roadster in London, I wager. They say he belonged to the great Du Vall himself, and knows the highways backwards. Plague take these road pirates!"

Captain Barclay's glass rang on the ledge of the oaken partition as he set it down.

"Then I'll leave you to your own resources," he said. "What time do you ride?"

"Within two hours," Buck Dowling answered. "Starlight is stabled here, and we shall be off before morning breaks, though the devil's own haunt the Holloway Road. I have no stomach for that part of the way in the dark."

"Adieu, then," Barclay answered, his tired voice still betraying his lack of interest. "I hope you have safe passage."

Nicholas listened to this desultory conversation. Dull as it was, he found food for amusement in it. When Barclay's footsteps died away out of the flagged passage, Nicholas heard Buck Dowling moving towards the room he occupied.

Quick as thought he pulled down the brim of his hat and adjusted the collar of his cloak. Then staggering as if under the influence of drink, he slouched to the door, rudely clashing against Dowling, who was coming in.

"Plague take your clumsy bones," Dowling shouted.

"And the devil take you for his own and sharpen your bat's eyes," Nicholas answered, drawling his words as if advanced in drink.

"You lout!" cried Dowling, angry and ready to quarrel.

The departing man did not stop. He snarled

back a volley of drunken oaths, verbal offal of street coinage, and passed out of the inn into the dark street, banging the door behind him.

Outside, Nevinson's gait steadied itself, and he walked sharply away through the narrow byways of Covent Garden in the direction of the city.

The hour was five o'clock when Starlight, a gallant chestnut with a white mark upon its forehead, was brought out of the stables and paraded underneath the arched entrance to the inn yard.

Buck Dowling, who had been yawning by the fire and was stupid through lack of rest, pulled his cloak closer and swung himself into the saddle, settling himself for a long, cold ride. The watch was crying the hour as he turned the spirited chestnut head towards the city and cantered along the dark and lonely Strand.

No need to follow him through the opening stages of his journey. In less than half an hour Starlight had put the city behind him and was cantering along the Goswell Road in the direction of Islington Green. A toll-keeper opened to Dowling after some slight delay, and he spurred onward along the Holloway Road, wider awake than he had been before.

Truth to tell, Holloway bore the worst of reputations as the haunt of footpads and Tobymen of the most lawless type. Dowling pressed on quickly, eager to be out of a notorious danger zone. As he reached the more open country his spirits rose, for the worst of the journey out of London was over. His manner relaxed unconsciously, and though the road was but ill going, Dowling set Starlight to a sharper canter with a touch of the spur, and with an added sense of security pushed rapidly forward to Finchley. The gallant horse responded readily enough, and the ring of his hoofs on the hard, frosty road struck sharp and clear in the still air of the quiet grey morning.

Just as the rider's sense of security had fully returned, Starlight suddenly swerved, nearly throwing his rider from the saddle. Caught by the bridle, the horse plunged and reared, held by a tall figure of a man, clad in a heavy cloak and masked, who had stepped from the roadside like a great, menacing shadow.

Dowling swore aloud and quickly recovered his seat. At once he lugged a huge pistol out of the holsters, levelled the weapon, and pulled on the trigger. The horse, nervous through the sudden stop, was at a standstill, every muscle of the beast quivering.

As Dowling's finger pressed on the trigger, the man in the road struck the weapon upwards. There was a flash of red flame in the darkness, a loud report, and the acrid odour of spent powder as the smoke drifted. The ball whistled overhead harmlessly enough, and the stranger still held on to the bridle and was pulling at the pistol in the near holster.

" Shrive me, for, by the Lord, that was a close call, and I was never nearer to the last need of a priest," laughed the man in the road. By this time he had possession of Dowling's second weapon, and was covering the rider of Starlight.

"By the living God," he said, threateningly, "you may thank your saints I am in great good temper this morn. I've plugged lead into many a man's bowels for a less close call than that. By Old Rowley, if you don't dismount I'll give you the answer to your bullet. Dismount, I tell you, or I'll plug holes into you."

Dowling spurred his horse and tried to canter away. The figure on the road clung to the bridle and covered the traveller menacingly with his own pistol.

"You gallows devil," Dowling cursed.

"Rip me, save your breath," said Nevinson, for it was the new highwayman. "Hard words break no bones," he added, flourishing the pistol. "I'll save you parley with the topster if you don't come off, I tell you."

Discretion played a great part in Dowling's make-up. Reluctantly, he climbed down and stood with teeth a-chatter in the roadway.

"What would you?" he asked, standing there.

"A pretty bit of blood you ride," Nevinson answered. "I need a horse to keep my engagements, and I have a fancy to try the paces of yours."

Suiting the action to the word, he put his foot into the vacant stirrup and leapt nimbly into the heavy saddle.

Nicholas looked on Dowling, standing in the highway—one of the men who had witnessed his humiliation in the Argyle Rooms without protest, a few short hours ago. His presence reminded Nevinson of his duty.

"A buck of your type should carry a purse heavy with guineas on a long journey. Hand it out," he ordered.

Slowly, Dowling began to fumble in his low pockets.

"Come, hurry, man—hurry," Nicholas prompted. "This is not the Argyle Rooms, and I have not the time for the ceremony of Beau Morris."

Dowling, shivering from head to foot, handed Nevinson a silk purse, neither heavy nor light with coin, but amply lined.

"And now, Master Buck Dowling, having paid your toll, you may go on in peace—back to London," Nevinson said, with a sneer. "You join the pimps who hunt together in gaming houses like pariahs in a meat market, and I'll keep the road against your like, and skin you as fast as you come this way. D'ye hear me, sirrah?"

At the mention of his name, Dowling started.

"You know me?" he asked, bewildered.

"By the Lord, I do that, well enough—and your business here. It bodes no good to Rowley," Nicholas sang out. "Shrive me, if I had the time, I'd find the purpose of your mission and hand you over to King Charles, myself, as a ripening traitor. For the moment I hold the highway against you. Begone, and the top of the morning to you. And mark you well, tell the man who sent you, Sir Ladbroke Drake, that if he comes upon the mission on which you have failed, he will find an enemy holds the road against him, too."

With a sweep of his hat Nevinson steadied Star-

light, and, splendidly mounted, put spurs to his
steed and clattered off in the direction of Barnet.

His destination was Steve Randall's, at the sign
of the "Lantern," for breakfast and a bed, but his
passage was not to be uninterrupted, and he was not
to arrive there without further adventure.

He was fully two miles from Barnet when Starlight again stumbled. The morning was breaking,
and the road, no longer dark, was faintly outlined,
while the world about shaped itself as it lightened
in the misty grey. In the pearly shadows, near
objects, somewhat ghostly, took shape. Nevinson
had no difficulty in making out a weird figure standing in the road with hands painfully outstretched.

The obstacle to his progress was a strange figure
enough. He was bent as if his back were broken,
and leered upwards as he glowered at Nicholas
through one eye, a patch concealing where should
have been the other. In truth he looked a ghastly
spectacle. His head was half hidden under an
enormous brimmed hat, but in addition to the one
eye, Nicholas could see an emaciated face, hollow
and clouded with shadows where the beginnings of
a beard had begun to crop out through lack of
shaving. The man's attitude of standing suggested
grave spinal deformity. He wore a woollen smock,
mud coloured, and breeches of the same material.
Stout legs, belying the enfeebled body, were encased
in grey, coarsely knitted stockings. He balanced
his ill-looking frame by holding on to a stout staff.
At first sight, Nicholas, reining up, took the in-
truder to be one of the common objects of the road,

a homeless cripple exhibiting his deformities for the pity of travellers.

"In the Lord's name," whined the distorted image of a man, "of your charity, kind sir, remember me. Paralysed I am, and no longer able; neither bite nor sup have I had these two days."

"You are abroad early," Nicholas said, feeling for Dowling's purse.

"It is the early bird, my master—you know the rest of a worn proverb," the beggar said, grinning slightly.

Nicholas opened the purse and flung three guineas from Buck Dowling's store to the man.

"These images of King Charles will lighten the road," he said, patronisingly.

"God save you, sir; you have good stores of wealth," the man said, stooping to pick up the coins.

"More—more of your charity," he called, as he finished the pleasant task with a speed surprising in one so handicapped, physically.

"Nay, for an early bird you have found the worms plentiful. Out of my way," Nicholas commanded.

"Where fare you so hastily, my gay gallant?" the beggar asked, his manner changing.

"What is that to you?" Nicholas answered, promptly. "It sounds ill for a beggar to be insolent with such a poor body to back his lack of manners."

Before Nicholas could get the words out of his mouth, a strange thing happened. The bent man rose to his full height, and Nicholas, in a flash, saw

that he cut no mean figure, and, straightened, discovered a pair of enormous shoulders. He was too
late in his knowledge, for the man sprang forward
with incredible speed, and the staff, whizzing in the
air, caught Nicholas a clout on the round of his
head that toppled him from the saddle. Surprised
as he was, Nicholas leapt to his feet and closed with
the man, and the two locked at once in a grim wrestle.

They fell into a hold which was peculiar to Cumberland and familiar to Nicholas, who tried to throw
the heavy man whose weight lay upon him.

The beggar, as he resisted and pressed on Nicholas,
grunted. " Ah—this—is—the game, my—swift—
lad," he sobbed, slowly, as he applied his great
strength. " Better than all your fights with the
toasting forks or the fireirons. Honest wrestling
is a mettlesome game for any man with sport in
his heart."

Nicholas, rather surprised at the turn of events
and the temper of the man, clung to his hold. He
had learnt his wrestling in the country sports of
Lancashire. They were placed in the Cumberland
style, and he found the other man was observing
its rules, throwing his weight into the clutch and attempting no use of the legs. Noting this, Nicholas
almost laughed with the humour of it, and went
into the fray with a better heart, and the old embrace
of a fine county was pushed home sturdily by both.
After a strained minute of heavy physical effort,
marked by the loud gasping exclamations of laboured
breathing, Nicholas, thinking his man was going
threw all his beef on to the beggar and tried to

swing him by sheer exercise of sinew. The consequence was they both fell to the ground together with a mighty crash.

Nicholas, on the alert, was swiftly in a sitting posture. He found the beggar had made the same movement almost as quickly as himself. For a second or two, they looked ruefully into each other's eyes, and the " paralysed " man rubbed his shin and suddenly broke into a guffaw.

" A dog fall," he said, springing to his feet.

" A dog fall it was," Nicholas answered. He, too, sprang to his feet and drew his sword.

" S'death—I'll spit you, you knave of a cripple whose bones are as good as mine," he said, advancing threateningly.

The other grasped his club, spitting on his hand as he did so.

" My club play is as good as anything you can do with the toasting fork," he said, and Nicholas noted that his emaciated face, a trick studied for effect, looked rounder, stern and hard.

The two men glared at each other. Then something in the beggar's face made Nicholas laugh. It was the quiet, impudent confidence of a man who was used to rough jousting.

" Damme, for a perpetual vagabond," said the big beggar man, " this is a meeting after my own heart. Sithee, lad, I like your face. We'll settle this in our own way. The Cumberland manner is dull and slow. Let us try a fall by the Lancashire method, all holds in, and with an honourable arrangement for the end of it."

"What do you propose, my precious rogue?" Nicholas asked, his eyes gleaming.

"Two shoulders on the ground win," the other answered, promptly. "If I throw you, I take the purse you flaunt, which is heavy enough for a mill, though lightish, as I see it."

"It holds good money for a vagrant. But what is there in such a game if I win?" Nicholas asked. "Do paralysed men who turn into giants possess money for wrestling bouts? Is the damned world suddenly gone mad?"

"Nay, nay, my lad," the other answered, "I've better than gold. Should you throw me, I give you a sign that means freedom along all the road from Holloway to York."

"What do you mean?" Nicholas asked. "That is preposterous. You give me the freedom of the road?"

"What I say, I mean," the vagrant answered. "My word, as you will find, carries along the North Road like a king's command."

"A strange manner of man are you," Nicholas suggested, clinging to his sword, but with rising curiosity that robbed his mood of temper. "Whom do I address? For, spit me, you are not as you seem."

"I am Nemo, the King of Beggars," the other answered. "After our bout I will explain. There is a strange honour amongst nomads that you may not understand."

Nicholas hesitated for a moment.

"How do I know this is not some clever thieves'

plan to advantage me," he asked, doubt uppermost in his mind.

The other nodded, as if he were admitting the justice of the question.

"You are as cautious as you are swift," he said, simply. "What is your name, since you ask mine? I like to know the man I beat."

"Nicholas Nevinson," he answered, promptly. "But first test me before the boasting. I have no reason to trust a rip like you, and still I hold advantage in my blade."

The padsman smiled amiably at this rejoinder.

"Sithee, Nick, lad, Swift Nick with the devil's speed. I'll trust you first," he suggested. "Doubt of a man's honour should not spoil sport. There is thieves' honesty, and you may set store by it."

As he spoke, Nemo threw his staff over the hedge-side, and stood alone, unarmed.

"A good wrestle," he said, "and an honourable understanding. See, I trust your face and the spirit for sport in your eyes. I am no longer armed. You may rip me, or play the game as you will. I'll take a risk for a clash with a game buck such as you are."

"By the Lord, I like your face, my beggar man," Nicholas answered, heartily. "I try you for a fall for the sheer fun of the thing. I know a trick in the catch as one may style, and I'll chance my luck on the value of your side of the stake."

He flung his sword full twenty yards away from him as he spoke, and the sturdy beggar smiled more heartily than ever.

" Then do you free yourself of that fancy cloak of yours," said the padsman, " and we'll see who is best man—here on my beat where my thews give me the right to rule."

" With all the pleasure in the world," Nicholas answered. " It is a treat to meet a sporting footpad."

CHAPTER IX

NICHOLAS stripped himself of his cloak and the coat and waistcoat underneath it. The beggar in the road followed his example. The woollen smock came off from over his head, and Nicholas, to his astonishment, discovered that underneath the mud-coloured garment the man wore a shirt of fine linen, of a quality surprising when considered in relation to the weather-beaten character of his external appearance. Stripped of his smock and standing upright, he appeared what he was—a toughened specimen of masculinity, and his trim, alert smartness was apparent, despite the cultivated disrepute of his face.

"Now, my young master," he said, stretching himself in the keen air of the early morning. "I am ready and willing to test what manner of buck fights me for the privilege of passing along the North Road."

"And I am ready for you, and willing too," Nicholas answered, with a laugh. "I'll test what manner of a rascal is the beggar man who challenges my progress. Did you say one fall and two shoulders to the ground, by the Lancashire method?"

"That is the game for me, my cock bird," the

other answered, boasting. "God help your guineas, if you are keen on holding them, for I need the coin sorely, this cold weather."

Without more ado the two men began to approach each other stealthily, as wrestlers do, each craftily watching for a useful grip. It was some minutes before they found a vulnerable point of attack. The first move came from Nemo, who sprang in, crouching low, and in a single move had Nevinson gripped by the waist with one hand and round the right knee with the other. He heaved on the leg with all his strength for a second ; Nicholas lost his balance, and the two men fell with a crash to the ground.

"How like you that ? " asked Nemo, immensely pleased with himself.

"A pretty move," Nevinson answered. "But finish it out, man—finish it, I say. There is no cause for the cock to crow yet awhile."

"To find a cause won't take me three wags of a dog's tale," Nemo said, with a breathless grin.

But it did. He was uppermost, with Nicholas lying underneath him, face downwards and arms spread out. Nemo tried to get a lock on the arm and some purchase by applying his other arm as a lever under his opponent's. He strained on Nicholas, minute after minute, his breath coming in gasping sobs, as he strove to maintain his advantage. But minute after minute went by and he had not moved Nicholas, though he had expended the full force of his strength on the task. Ten minutes might have passed thus purposelessly. Nemo's face was red through the exertion, and though the morning was cold, the perspiration beaded on his forehead and rolled in rivulets down the side of his cheek. In sheer disgust he got up at last and stood on guard against Nicholas, who crouched as he rose.

"Rest a minute," said Nevinson, his delight in the sporting situation conquering his keen desire to win. "All the work has been on your side, and I want no advantage from your loss of wind."

"To the devil with a tale like that," the other said, eagerly springing forward. His very eagerness made him careless. Crouching again, he tried the same trick, making a dive for the leg. He missed the hold by inches, and lurched forward, a trifle unsteadily. Nevinson, quick as a flash, caught him squarely, by neck and shoulder, and pinned him as tight as a rabbit in a steel trap. The padsman realised his mistake, and stiffened in every muscle to withstand the pressure. The wrestlers stood, bent about each other, locked and taut, strength against strength, the last to weaken being the more certain of winning. The advantage was with Nevinson. In that tight embrace he felt the steady heave of the man stooping under him quicken ; his shaking shoulders showed the increasing labour of his breathing. With fierce, but slowly applied pressure, and despite Nemo's grunting, Nevinson pressed his man's head downwards with the right arm, half strangling him, and, using his left arm, levered up the body. Against the tension Nemo stood firm for half a minute, during which he seemed to stop breathing. Nicholas, sure of his deadly hold, yet felt in those few seconds, through which the beggar's full strength resisted his aggressive pressure, as if he were trying to bend a stout, young oak. It seemed as if the man in his clutch would never break or bend.

The silent half-minute of effort finished with a softening of the resisting, upward movement of Nemo's neck. As he slackened, he drew a long breath, as if his lungs were bursting. Just when he did so, Nicholas strangled the respiration with a haul on the neck and shoulders backed by every ounce of his strength. The footpad's head went down and his body came up ; Nemo's skull crashed on the stones ; his torso, almost somersaulting as it followed the downward, curving drop of the head, fell with the dead weight of a sack of flour. The very sense of the man was shaken with the jolt he got as he toppled to the ground. His jarred mind did not give him the necessary impetus to take advantage of the priceless second and roll for safe purchase on the earth with arms spreadeagled. Before he could move Nicholas followed him, landed on the body, locked his man by both elbows, and, pressing with his full bulk and all the force of his tightened thews, pinned the padsman's shoulders to the ground, as flat as a piece of plaice lying at the bottom of a fishmonger's basket.

" My fall, I think," he said, with a gasp of triumph.

" Riddle me with shot or cast me to the topsman," a throaty voice shouted with a delighted roar. " If that don't beat cock fighting, sink me as lumber. As pretty a fall as ever I did see, so help me Rowley, and two shoulders on the ground as snug as a pancake on a plate."

Nicholas relaxed his hold and looked towards the voice of the new-comer.

From his position on the ground, he gazed into the eyes of a huge figure that seemed to tower upwards from his seat on the back of a wiry grey horse with a hard, nervous mouth. It did not take Nicholas a second to recognise the man, whose roguish eyes twinkled from their setting in a round, pock-marked face, as Steve Randall, the one-armed innkeeper, who had spoken to him at " The Finish."

As Nicholas rose, Nemo, recovering himself, sat up. His unkempt face was a study. There, surprise, discomfiture, and bewilderment struggled for expression. The noise he made as he sensed the situation was half a laugh and the other part a groan. The beggar rubbed the back of his head ruefully enough, and when he ceased to apply the hand and looked at that member thoughtfully, he found the fingers dyed with his own blood.

" Well, of all the popinjays who ever danced by me on horseback, you are the swiftest of the lot," he said, slowly. " S'death, you toppled me over as if I were a sack of malt."

" 'Twas a fair throw," Nicholas commented. " I had witness to it. Master Steve Randall, of the ' Lantern,' will say whether your shoulders were on the ground, or no."

" That I will," Randall answered. " On the ground and squarely there as ever shoulders were.

You've met your master, King of the Padsters though you be."

Randall roared with laughter as he spoke.

" I'm content enough with Steve's view," Nemo said, rising slowly, as if his bones were stiff and sore. " But, curse me, I knew myself that I was down and would have admitted it. I'm damned if it adds ease to my fallen pride to have old Randall see me floored. Not a fly-by-night Tobyman nor a peep-o'-day padster who travels by the ' Lantern ' will fail to hear of my beating at the good old game."

" And you with such repute at it," Randall laughed. " Be sure I'll tell the tale against you as long as you are in these parts."

" Well, there's no good growling over broken bottles," Nemo said. " You beat me fair and square, and that is good enough. You said your name was Nicholas Nevinson. I'll call you Swift Nick, for never did I see a man reach out quicker. I'll call you Swift Nick, and give you freedom of the road, whenever you travel, though it's bad business for the swagsmen to have you going scathless along the North highway and you so well laced with guineas and so free with them."

" Why, damme, I am one of you," Nick answered. " My stake of guineas came unwillingly enough from a gallant I stopped near Finchley."

" So, ho, my lad ! and that's the game ? " Randall roared. " By the Lord, I knew you as a coming roadster when I saw you last night at ' The Finish '; but Swift Nick you be, for I'm shrived if I thought to see you Tobyman by morning. I met your

5*

gallant footing it back to London before break of day. He fumed with anger, but bragged that he had bested you by withholding another purse of gold. He wanted to buy my horse for twenty guineas."

"And did you sell?" Nicholas asked, eyeing the grey horse Randall bestrode.

"There was no deal," Randall replied, simply. "I'm no Tobyman now with my one arm, but a winged pigeon tempted me, as I was advantaged by my mount, and I fell. I took his last twenty guineas."

"By force?" Nicholas asked, smiling at the thought.

"By gentle persuasion," Randall said, his bright eyes smiling with a reminiscent gleam. "I had to cudgel him a little, but only sufficient to stir his senses. I admonished him like a priest with a first, second, and thirdly for being dishonest to simple highwaymen; and I set him, without his guineas, face to London, and left him walking forward, cursing like a postboy who has driven into a pond. Where go you now?" he asked, curiously, and changing the subject.

"To the 'Lantern,' Barnet," Nicholas said, "in answer to your invitation. That reminds me— my new mount, acquired from my first collection on the road, is gone."

Nicholas looked along the highway for the chestnut, and the two men, following his glance, joined with searching eyes. Starlight was nowhere to be seen.

"Damme for a muddle-pated fellow," Nicholas said, swearing nimbly at his own folly in leaving

the horse free. " As good a roadster as ever a man
cocked a leg across. Starlight, a chestnut, and,
by hearsay, one of Du Vall's."

"With a white mark on its forehead," Randall
agreed, as if Nick's description were fixed on his
mind. " I know it for a gallant beast. Many's
the time he has nosed in my stables while Du Vall
tossed off his hot wine in my tap. A serious loss,
such a horse to a young Tobyman."

At Randall's words Nick fell to cursing more
glibly than ever.

The footpad shook Nevinson's elbow.

"Lithee, Swift Nick ; hold thy breath to cool
the jorum we'll have at the 'Lantern.' You do not
know me, and when you pledged your guineas on
a fall, you did not know the value of my brief to the
freedom of the North Road. I'll show you one
of its advantages now."

As he spoke, this strange man took from the folds
of his shirt a silver whistle hanging from a fine chain
concealed about his throat.

On this he blew once, and the call of the whistle
had a wavering, flute-like note, strangely penetrating
for so slight a sound.

" I was not as honest with you as you were with
me," Nemo said. "I took you for a gentleman of
the town."

" Zounds, am I not that ? " Nicholas asked, firing.

" God's luck, anything you like, lad, after the
bang you gave my poor pate. But a gentleman of
the road has a clearer title to our confidence. When
I tempted you to disarm by throwing my staff

aside, I really had you in my power. See for yourself," he concluded.

Somewhat ruefully Nicholas realised what the padster meant. Almost as soon as the sound of the whistle had ceased to echo, and at their very elbows, three men came dashing through the trees. A strange crew they were, similarly dressed to their leader in mud-coloured smocks. One short man, monkish in the roundness of his red face, was a blind vagrant, who could see—the shield for his eyes, a neglected symbol of sightlessness, hanging about his neck. A tall, lantern-jawed man had an arm swathed as if it were withered, but Nick guessed this limb was about as much crippled as Nemo's spine, and guessed correctly. The third man, almost a dwarf, presented no physical deformities. His mission on the highway was to appear simple, as Nicholas came to know when he had travelled the road many times. It was evident to Nevinson that the three, who were sturdy enough rascals underneath their mud-coloured clothing, had watched him measure his strength against Nemo, and would have been ready to intervene at their leader's call.

"Ah! there you are, Robin, Blind David, and Daft Harry," Nemo said, greeting them. "Allow me to introduce a new brother of the High Toby, a game fellow and a better wrestler than I am. From now on, he goes free between London and York. See to it that all the canters, beggars, mumpsters, chaunters, merry grigs, and padsmen between Holloway and Bedford know of his coming.

We journey to the ' Lantern,' where Swift Nick will carouse with the fraternity at the hour of ten and there receive the sign of his freedom and the symbols of luck. . . . Good Steve Randall here will prepare a feast fit for the tattered army, whose right it is to live well wherever they go. In the meantime, who saw the chestnut disappear ? "

" I did," Blind David answered, promptly. " He shied at your tuzzle on the road, and galloped off Barnet way, just as you began the wrestle."

Almost as he spoke the words, another man turned the bend of the road, leading a horse. He made a weird figure enough at first sight. Half of the creature was hidden by a long, white beard falling almost to the waist. A closer view showed the moustache and upper parts of the growth to be stained with tobacco to an amber colour ; but as the beard lengthened it grew into masses of silvery white, which sparkled in the frost. Under his arms the man carried two padded crutches, and, when he saw the group on the road, he hastily placed the pads in the armpits and began to hobble forward, his legs dangling horribly, though a second before he had been walking on them. Nick knew sufficient of the men he had to deal with to guess, shrewdly, that he was one of the crew, as physically able as the rest. His appearance was welcome, for the horse he led was Starlight.

" Ah, here comes the Scrivener," Nemo said, with a note of relief, as the man came in view. " He has caught Starlight on his way to Barnet."

The Scrivener came slowly towards them, and

it was evident that he had not realised the situation. As he hobbled up, a decrepit ruin of a man, he began to speak, singling out Nick as the owner of the horse.

"A guinea, gentleman, for my service," he said, with oily servility, but winking slyly at his friends. "But for my poor help your bit of blood would be through the town of Bedford by now."

Nemo and Randall laughed heartily.

"Nay, hold your tongue and close your paw," the King of the Beggars growled at the new-comer. "This is a friend of mine and all the fraternity on the highway. I frank him through, and to-night he becomes of us. Until then, he is entitled to the service of my subjects."

Nick laughed in his turn, but, all the same, dived into Dowling's purse and handed out two guineas to the Scrivener.

"'Tis little enough for the turn you have done me," he said, pleased to see his horse again. "You and these sturdy rascals may drink my health as you go."

Suddenly, all the men standing in the road became silent, listening. In the quiet morning the grinding of heavy wheels was heard and the ring of many hoofs.

"Cave, rascals," the Scrivener shouted. "'Tis the sheriff and his escort. I passed them baiting at the 'Red Lion' in the Barnet High Street. Cave, I say—cave."

Without further parley Nemo and his four attendants disappeared in the bushes.

"I'll see you, anon," Nemo called, as he walked

off after the Scrivener, whose crutches were again tucked beneath his arms.

Nick mounted his chestnut, and, side by side with Steve Randall, rode forward to Barnet. As they started, rounding the bend in the road came a heavy coach drawn by four horses. Half a dozen armed men rode in front and an equal number behind. Within the vehicle lolled a single man. Nicholas caught sight of his stern but loose and coarse face, the big fish-like eyes of which bulged inquiringly as the coach swept on. He had time to note the features, the set of the extravagant wig above the big rolling face, the chin of which was snuff-stained and soiled, and also the livery of the attendants who cantered in front and behind.

Steve Randall, when the coach had drawn past them and away, crossed himself, with a cynical gleam in his roguish eyes.

"From sheriffs, lawyers, judges, and topsmen, good Lord deliver us," he said, drawling the words as if he were praying.

"Is that the sheriff?" Nicholas asked, curiously.

"The very man himself, and a plaguy stiff nut, too," Steve answered, taking the reins from the pit of his empty coat sleeve into his good hand, and sawing on the wicked-looking mouth of his mount.

"Then Amen to your prayer," Nick replied with equal reverence; and the two men, at a swinging pace, followed the narrow road that opened out as they rode through Barnet, a sleepy wayside village, stirring once more in the early morning to the common round of the day.

CHAPTER X

THE " Lantern," Barnet, stood on the roadside, and was to be seen only after the traveller had passed through the village, journeying North. The inn lay away from the mansions, cottages, and church, and farther on than the great posting houses, the " Antelope " and the " Green Man," or the inns of lesser importance that lived by trafficking with passengers on public coaches and heavier road vehicles.

Half a mile before the road forks at Hadley Green—the spot where the fourth Edward put the Kingmaker's army to flight on the grim Easter day of 1471—stood the " Lantern." A low rambling structure, bigger than it looked from the outside, the inn was an old farmhouse that had turned from quieter ways to the entertainment of tavern company.

From the outside the " Lantern " did not invite the wayfarer of substance or position. There was something rather secretive about the exterior of the place, by day or night. The traveller scarcely saw the house before he was upon it, and rarely liked the looks of the building when he arrived opposite to it. The inn was a low, irregular structure with a heavy, projecting thatched roof. The windows were, in most cases, very small. The main door, often shut, was black, worn and studded with heavy nails —the sort of door one sometimes sees barring exit from a prison. The passage from the main entrance dropped two steps, was dark and narrow, winding a little, and by day or night a place of perpetual shadows. Inside, the rooms were irregular in shape, somewhat grimy and even darker than the passage. All the apartments were low and heavily timbered, and the fireplaces, built into the brick, had seats on either side of the chimney-corner type. Heavy, oaken benches shaped themselves to the sides of the rooms, the wood being polished with the friction caused by the rough suits of those who habitually sat rubbing shoulders and shins against the hard boards.

The " Lantern " took a great deal of its character from a big common room in the front of the house, on the north side of the door. Into this, wayfarers looked on entering, and timid people seldom went farther, for when the house was full the character of the company was to be seen at a glance, not always to the peace of mind of the visitor. The feature of this room was a great bay window, the angles of which provided seats, a heavy permanent chair occupying the centre. Outside, the framework of the window seemed to project fully a dozen feet in front of any other part of the inn. At night, lighted and seen suddenly, the bay window seemed to peer and pry into the gloom as if it were the eye of a dark lantern, the bulk being represented by the straggling house glowering in the gloom behind.

Secretive quietness by day, noise by night; a place of much coming and going and occasional scuffling, when patrons quarrelled and fought about the entrance, with fists or feet, with staff, drawn knife, or sword; a house avoided by the legitimate traffic of the road, yet always busy and sometimes thronged; with a horse ever at the door and stable hands gazing idly up and down the way to York—such was the "Lantern." There, Steve Randall, at home, stamped about in an atmosphere fumed with smoke and the odours of drink, the thick admixture of human savours being always heavy with kitchen smells—the reek of cooking long over, or just beginning.

To this house came Swift Nick with Steve Randall, about the hour of eight. Both men stiffly dismounted, and the ever-waiting stable hand took charge of the steeds.

The man smiled lavishly as he heard the instructions given for the stabling of the horses.

" The old star," he said, glancing with a grin from Starlight to his rider.

" Aye, the old star," Steve growled; " and see that he gets the same warm corner. And bestir yourself, and don't stand grinning there; see to it now."

Inside the inn, Nick found himself roughly but heartily welcomed.

" Rattle my bones, I little thought to see you in the ' Lantern ' so soon," Randall said; " but I knew you'd come. You arrive on the right horse, too. There's a might o' men between here and York will be glad to see the horse with the star on the road at night."

He bustled into the room with the big bay window, Nick following in his wake.

"Come you in and cower you down by the fire, lad," Randall continued. "I give you welcome. So long as you play the game, there's sanctuary here, silence, and a watch on both ends of the road. What say you to something hot to keep out the cold? The frost is in my marrow bones, and"—pointing to his sleeve—"the rheumatism shoots in my elbow as if the old arm were back again."

"A bed is more my business," Nick answered, yawning sleepily before the heat of a ruddy fire. "But I'll sample that mulled wine you bragged about in Covent Garden, before I go."

"That you shall, lad, and after that a hearty meal. Ho, there! is anybody alive in the 'Lantern'?" Randall called, smiting the benches with his one arm until they rattled again.

A stout, short country wench came at his summons and took his several orders. The "Lantern," in Steve's absence, was ruled by a sister of the innkeeper, Sarah Randall, a gaunt, silent woman, who ran her two domestics, the potmen, and the lads about the stable with the firm hand and crisp tongue of a captain of dragoons.

The hot wine soon mingled its warm bouquet with the colder savours of the heavy atmosphere.

"Here's to thee," said Steve Randall, toasting Nicholas, and holding out a long steaming glass of spiced red wine.

Nicholas, from a seat in the chimney corner, laughingly acknowledged the toast.

"Damn me," Randall went on, "I like you better when I see you in a proper setting for a good man. That's the seat to thaw in—the warmest corner in the room. By the heart, it has cheered up some of the warmest on the road. Du Vall himself sat there and tossed off his wine, the last time he came this way. That was the night he stopped the bishop, in his own coach, and blew the wig off him because he cursed in no manner fitting the cloth. All the bishop had Claude took, and left his episcopal nibs, bald-headed, with his traces cut and cursing like a drunken wagoner. A rare lad was Claude; as honest a Tobyman as ever came to a bad end. Too fond of the women and the wine was Du Vall—God rest his soul."

The hot wine was followed by huge rashers of fried ham, poached eggs, hot sausage meat, and a toast, to all of which hot spiced ale was served. After the night air, the thawing fire, the spiced wine, and the repletion which followed an attack on Randall's hospitality, Nick sat listening to the innkeeper, but scarcely hearing him. Indeed, so drowsy did the lad become that he rocked stupidly where he sat by the fire. Dull with sleep, he leaned forward and would have fallen into the flames but for Sarah, who, going her rounds in silence, saw everything. She seized Nick, shook him, and drew the tired man out of danger, rating Randall for keeping their guest up when he was road weary.

Prompted by the woman, Steve Randall piloted

Nick to a tiny room, aloft. Tired and stupid as
he was, Nevinson noted that the room was approached on either side by a flight of stairs, had
windows in three of the walls, a trap in the roof,
and a secret passage, explained by the landlord,
in the fireplace.

"Never a snugger pen for a Tobyman within
forty miles of London," said that worthy; "and I
can find you half a dozen more, nearly its equal,
between here and York." He winked, solemnly,
at Nick as he spoke; nodded, and then withdrew,
leaving his guest to tumble into a clean bed, partially dressed, where he slept almost as soon as his
head touched the pillow, so dead to the world he
might have been a log of wood.

The hours crept by, and outside the world awoke.
People of all conditions began to clatter up and
down the highway. The up-mail from Edinburgh
laboured by, on the last stage, the driver so beshawled that his nose and eyes only were visible.
Wagons grumbled and creaked. Now and again
their drivers, with a "Whoa" and a growled curse,
would halt before the "Lantern," leaving their
horses, eased from the strain, smoking outside.
Gallants on horseback appeared; then perhaps a
farmer with a woman pillioned behind. Smart
private chaises swiftly rolled by. Guarded family
coaches, housing nobility, bumped towards town.
Many men travelled afoot, walking slowly, but
pushing forward steadily as men do who are accustomed to pad the hoof over long distances. Pack-
men and pedlars called in to show their wares. A

company of horsed men of King Charles baited and remained to carouse, making the blustering clatter of travelling soldiers over their drink. Solitary wayfarers drifted in and out, some snatching sleep in the tap, while others, held by warmth and cheer, grew drunken and lingered on, to talk loudly, arguing, boasting and threatening by turns. The " Lantern " was about its business, for the North Road was alive. All the day Steve Randall passed about his house, watching the business of the inn, and during pauses in the round stood rubbing his good hand on the stump where the other arm had been, as he looked thoughtfully out of the bay window up or down the road. All day long, oblivious to the sound, Nicholas slept in the tiny room upstairs.

When Nevinson stirred in his sleep again many hours had passed. Indeed, a full day had gone. The hour was close on eight; the light had long disappeared; outside, the bay window glowed; inside, by the vague illumination of candles, the " Lantern " housed and entertained many guests. A curious company it was, roaring songs and calling weird toasts as big mugs passed from hand to hand and the warming liquor set tongues wagging.

As Nicholas, in some confusion, sat staring into the dark room, slowly comprehending, he heard the sound of footsteps ascending the creaking stairs, while a light shone through the chinks and keyhole of the door. Some one outside struck the door noisily three times, and Nick growled out a sleepy command.

"Come in!" he called. "Don't stand there knocking like Black Death upon the threshold."

The bedroom door swung slowly open. A candle in a dull brass stick pushed forward, and a man, with the upward gleams on his face, followed the unsteady light and peered in.

"Well, how now, my hearty buck?" the new-comer said, in friendly greeting.

Nick knew him by the voice.

"Why, Nemo, by the gods!" he ejaculated, sur-prised, as well he might be, for the Nemo of a cere-monial call was a vastly different fellow from the beggar he had met on the road.

His face was shaved, and showed, ruddy with health and bold of line, that odd geniality one seldom sees in men, but knows at a glance as going hand in hand with devil-me-care, rollicking reckless-ness. Nemo wore no wig. His own hair, long and curled, was caught in a bunch at the neck and fell in widening masses about the shoulders. He sported a plum-coloured ceremonial coat, with gold—real gold—buttons. A fine cravat, knotted gracefully, fell in ample folds over a salmon-coloured waist-coat. Much linen gleamed white about his slit coat sleeves. His stockings were of black silk, and his shoes glittered with silver buckles. At a first glance he might have passed for a gentleman, nobly born and facing the world, gracefully con-fident. Yet one look at his features destroyed the brief illusion. They were hard, brazen, and bold, clean cut like a pebble; the expression sug-gested a life of insecurity; even now, in repose, lawless purpose shone in the lighted eyes, and their very restlessness as they wandered, quickly and ceaselessly, hinted of the bird of prey, hunter and hunted always, and anticipating plunder or danger with every tick of changing time.

Nick, fully awake, looked on the buoyant, reckless figure of the man, admiringly.

" God ! " he said, " there must be precious picking on the road if its birds wear such fine feathers."

Nemo, placing the lighted candle, bowed.

" A king must rule," he answered, with grim humour. " The manner of a man is the chief secret of his power. I come to summon you to join our company. But first, I have a duty. I followed you direct to the ' Lantern ' to perform it, but found you asleep. We padsmen respect the slumber of the nightbird."

His eyes twinkled as he spoke. And, as he spoke, the man of the road took out a purse and counted out the number of guineas Nick had flung to him on the road at their first encounter.

" Yours—my master in the Lancashire manner," he said. " It's a poor pad that takes toll of an equal in the night life of the road and a superior at a chosen game."

Nick did not offer any argument. He did not attempt to press the coins flung at an abject beggar on to this reckless cavalier. Instead, he swept the guineas into his hand, and rising, pouched them in the purse he had taken from his enemy of the early morning.

" A study of manners provides separate lessons,"
he said. " This etiquette is new to me, but you
know more of the windings of the road than I do.
I am at your service."

" Then dress and come with me," said Nemo,
pleased his action had been taken for granted.
"My company await you."

So Nicholas dressed carefully. His neat green
coat was laboriously brushed. His linen, slightly
soiled, was turned. He performed a toilet as
nicely as if he had been going to the Argyle Rooms,
buckled on his sword, and, with a bow, offered Nemo
precedence out of the room and signified his readi-
ness to follow.

In the entrance passage of the inn the two men
met Steve Randall. He cocked his eye over Nick,
and seemed to approve of his neat, collected appearance and the confident nonchalance which had
come as the legacy of an uninterrupted slumber.

" Hearty, my buck," said Steve, clapping Nick
on the back. " Hearty, as all the world can see.
You meet strange company in the ' Lantern,' but
it is worth knowing. A greater honour than will
come to you was never paid to the dashing Du Vall
himself. Go forward, lad, and call for me if the
bottle lingers." With a push he impelled Nevinson, jovially, in the wake of Nemo, who was travelling
towards the bay-windowed room.

And what a company it was ! In our dull day
such a gathering is difficult to visualise. The old
bay-windowed room was tight packed with a hundred men, and was hot with their presence, tense

with their excitement, riotous with their reckless
geniality. A hundred men were there, packed
round tables closely. They had finished a big
repast of hot meat pies, hares cooked whole, legs
of mutton, and many other highly seasoned meats.
They had drunk deep, and were still drinking;
some were drunk and all were jolly. Men, they
were children; and yet, being children, were still
men, and the sense of responsibility about the
whole pack of them would not have lent dignity
to a magpie. Drunk they were, or coming drunk;
laughing, because it was their nature to laugh, or
growling because the stirred animalism on top
was of the jackal breed and found its expression
in the bared white tooth. No law was there amongst
them but that created for themselves; outlawed,
hunted, pestiferous, every man-jack of them para-
sites on a society in wild flux, they gloried in their
pariah estate, and, leagued together in their own
disorder, found reckless joy in pressing on the
social hand turned against them.

What were they? Who can tell? A mixed
company. Some there were, gay-clothed, in very
fashionable feather. You might have called them
gentlemen, only there was a cock of the eye about
the best that hinted of a life spent far from gentle
ways. Some looked wholly evil, and appeared
half blind, toothless, or maimed. Their deformities
were artificial and accentuated dramatically, in
most cases; where an eye or an arm was missing,
or a spine was misshapen, or some incipient madness
flared in a weak face, the departure from the normal

had been sedulously cultivated, until it was apparent, vivid, outrageously enormous, shrieking its call for pity, clamouring its physical awfulness. These men were either well favoured, making the most of their smartness, or ill formed, cultivating their physical abnormalities as marketable qualities. The smart preyed on the pleasure and confidence their appearances gave; the misshapen screamed for pity. The untidy crew, one by one, knew each other and had respect for the separate games played by every member upon the credulous travellers who frequented the highway. They appreciated each other in proportion to the power displayed, by abject wheedling or by blustering intimidation, in detaching contributions from the wayfaring peoples they met and bled as they travelled about the North Road.

When Nicholas entered the room, hot with these men, they broke into a sort of welcoming chant, and holding their glasses or mugs aloft, waved them at him in a disorderly toast. The Scrivener, with the immense white beard, a Druid in venerable appearance, but as drunk as a city tapster, unsteadily clutched a brown earthenware mug and clucked his delight, higher than the rest, in the same wild chant. His voice was full of falsetto notes, and against the growling masculinity of the roaring men about him, sounded, a bell-like feminine squeal.

"Here he is; see him, mumpsters, padsmen, chaunters. See him, the city sprig who welted Nemo's shoulders to the ground."

They laughed as his flute-like voice rang through

the baser sounds, and the Scrivener, pleased, went on.

" A pretty cock he is, who comes trapsing down the road to man-handle Nemo. Did you ever see braver doings ? He holds the eye like a petti-coat flaunted before sailors newly home. Rouse him, mumpsters, rouse him."

His call was a demand for greeting, and, still chaunting, the company rose in a body, battered on the table with their horns, cups, pannikins, and glasses and raised the roof with a three times three in cheers.

Nemo, who had taken the chairman's seat in the bay window, with Nick by his side, rose and hissed for silence as if he were an angry snake. His white hand, held aloft warningly, had its way. The unruly pack gave him best, through years of stern knowledge of his relentless purpose. The roaring welcome died away, as if a swinging, full tide, whipped by following gale, had turned back to the mighty deep through a peaceful, breathless evening. The room, by contrast, grew silent ; only a foolish man, half idiot and very drunk, beat with prehensile fingers on the table before him and whimpered a song that made him seem to be crying.

" Silence, dogs and whelps," Nemo cried, with an air theatrical but effective. He pointed to Nicholas as he commanded them.

" Here he is ! look at him."

With one accord they looked. Some wild freakish emotion made Nick stand up. He met their dog-like glare boldly, a challenge in his fine, reckless face. They were compelled to think of the highly bred amongst the mongrel pack.

" Lord Harry ! " screamed the Scrivener, " the light of the road freeman is on his face. Here's to him, wherever he is, and let him be ours wherever he goes."

The crowd sang with him until Nemo, with a superb gesture of command, brought them to heel in cowering silence.

" Mumpsters, beggar men, padsters," he called, " taletellers, chaunters, rufflers, Tobymen—here is the man who won from me the freedom of the road. Am I the king ? "

" You are, you are," they cried.

" Then see to it he gets good passage," Nemo shouted. " He is ours, of us, with us. He comes and goes, with the moon by night and the sun by day, and no man amongst us says him nay. All roadmen and beggar men serve him in his need ; fetch and carry for him ; fight with him in a crowd ; plot for him when he is endangered. I lay it upon you as a command. Do you accept ? "

" We do." " Aye, aye." " As often as he calls," they growled, in chorus.

" And he—he takes the pledge," Nemo said, grimly turning to Nick.

" As sure as death I do," Nick answered, readily enough. " What you ask me I promise."

Nemo went on as if he were speaking a ritual.

" You give the sign to them ; they give the sign to you. It is so." The beggar king made a swift pass with his hands. " You know it now ; they will recognise the sign everywhere between London and York. It will make your comings and goings easy and swift. And you must promise loyalty to them as they swear loyalty to you."

"I do," said Nick. "What is the code?"

"To be with them when you see them troubled," Nemo went on, speaking with grim force. "To take their risk against the forces of the road. To serve them as you command them. To honour the King if it cost nought; to honour the fraternity, whatever the cost may be. To war on the rich; to give to the poor; to spare the last penny with the brother who has not bite, nor sup, nor board. To see no padsman with empty pocket; to let no man of ours go bare or with an empty belly; not to leave a brother cold and sober at night, without a glass to clink or a can to rattle on the tavern's bench. Swear this, and you go with all the help that we can give and freedom for the fly-by-night from here to York."

"Right readily I swear," Nick answered, smiling. "I'm on the road and of the road. The rich plundered me in town, and I wait to skin them, one by one, as they pass through the country like rabbits from one warren to another."

"Good," said Nemo. "Now buy us liquor, and let us seal it."

The staff of the "Lantern" supplied the clamorous gathering. At a sign from Nemo, upstanding, with vessels in their hands, they heard his commands.

"By virtue of this sovereign liquor, with a damn for sheriffs, sergeants, catchpoles, and runners, I do install you freeman of the road and make you a denizen of our ragged regiment. So long as you recognise our rules, we take you into our protection and adopt you as a brother of our numerous society. Do we agree?"

They roared their assent in company, and above the din the Scrivener's bell-like voice was heard, swearing out, wholesomely, his desire to see all sheriffs in hell.

"And now," said Nemo, when something like quiet was restored, "the Golden Farmer, fool Tobyman and no friend of ours, keeps sheep by moonlight where the ways divide. What shall we do for Swift Nick when the Golden Farmer see-saws on the gallows and his bones hang rotting?"

They shouted out a recognition at the hint he gave them, and above the clamour the voice of the white-bearded Scrivener gave them impetus—nerved them to the weirdest and most superstitious orgy of the road.

"By God, on such a night as this," he screamed, "we'll light the Hand of Glory."

CHAPTER XI

HARD by the "Lantern" inn the road forks. One branch, by the right, runs away to the North, the other turns off by the left and rolls towards Holyhead. On the green which narrowed to a point and marked the parting of the ways, the Golden Farmer tended sheep by moonlight, while the tattered regiment caroused within the tavern kept by Steve Randall.

An eerie place, this spot upon the North Road. There was no immediate sign of human habitation, though a manor house nestled close by, hidden in its own grounds. By the clock the time was half the hour past eleven. The night was fine but wintry. Keen frost was in the air, and the powdered hoar sparkled in the grasses and on the road. Above, the crescent moon smiled in the cold sky, blue where it was clear, the mighty vault being alight with stars. A strong wind, keen and searching, drove along banks of scudding clouds above, and these pale shapes drew now and again across the moon and deepened the shadows falling upon the silent world. Below, the wind blustered, riotously rising and falling. Sometimes its rustle was just a quiet whisper stirring the grasses ; again, it would rise and scream a crescendo in the trees, which stiffly protested by creaking as their stark arms and sapless limbs bent before the blast. And when the breeze quickened a moving chain clanked and a hideous, flapping shape twisted slowly round, and loomed, grotesque and horrible, against the lighter sky.

In the foreground of the deserted, beshadowed landscape, lonely and sinister, a black framework reared itself. A rough, heavy post with a supporting cross-beam, its pattern told the purpose of the structure. No uncommon object on the road, this gallows-tree bore at once the fruit of the fear and the vengeance and warning threat of humanity. To travellers coming along the road the beams of wood stood up plainly in grisly silhouette against the sky. When the wind raged, above its scream was heard the clank of the rusty chain. Nearer still, the wayfarer saw a ghastly object depending. Turning, in the windy moonlight, was the figure of a man, the head rolling horribly; the torso, in its shredding clothes, hanging piteously, while the skirts of the long coat flapped. When the bank of clouds sailed clear of the moon the light fell, pale and cold, stealing to outline the hanging, swaying bundle of rotting flesh and bones; to set the honest wayfarer shivering with the lively horror that turns the quick from a contemplation of the dead, and to cast a chill foreboding stirring about the minds of those who hovered, batlike, in quest of plunder, about the favouring darkness.

There at the cross-roads swung all that was left

6

of the Golden Farmer, a warning to his kind. There the dead highwayman tended sheep by moonlight, as the roadsters put it in grim jest when they spoke of the death vengeance. There, on the road he had travelled in his heyday, the Golden Farmer had added the final horror to the terror of his presence. No longer might he spur up and, with horse sideways to the chaise, push a big pistol in at the window and demand tribute. Yet dead as he was, he haunted the highway, clamouring a reminder that those who pass upon the road of life must sooner or later pay the final penalty of all at the salute and command of Death, the greatest of the Tobymen, who reaps in lives and may not be bought off with all the gold that cumbers a rich man's progress.

Away back the inn gleamed like a beacon, and the bay window, that seemed like the eye of a dark lantern, peered curiously at the figure of the dead man swaying at the end of a clanking chain.

When the Scrivener, in bell-like tones, called a challenge to the company to light the Hand of Glory, his suggestion was met with a roar of approval. The company stamped their feet, rattled their mugs and pannikins on the tables, and joined in singing a wild song of death, dark roads, and violence by night, in terms a later century does not dare to recall. And group by group they tossed off their drink and walked into the narrow passage—some unsteadily enough—and so out on the gloomy highway leading to the warning horror of the Golden Farmer's presence. Outside, there was rude horseplay, and some of it was quarrelsome, ending in violent scuffles and hard knocks ; but the disorderly army quieted down when Nemo strutted out in all his finery, the last to leave the room, with Swift Nick on his arm.

The chorus, riotously sung inside the house, continued. Though the men were warm with drink and reckless to the point of madness, the blast of the chill, night air sobered them. The song remained upon their lips, but the spirit of the fierce music had changed. It was no longer a ribald chant, roared lustily with the spirit that fires ale-house mirth. From a rollicking expression of high spirits the song, despite its wicked rhymes, had become a wild hymn, hurled solemnly as a defiance to the mystery of night itself.

Truth to tell, wild as these fellows were—fearing little from the violence of living men—their actions were governed by a variety of superstitions, and the rite they had embarked upon, perhaps the most dreadful superstition of the road, proposed to ravish from a dead man's hand a charm they believed was a passport to success from the devil himself. To the terror of death they added, man by man, the separate terrors of superstitions that flitted through their minds. Their brains teemed with the gibbering horrors bred from a long period of superstitious belief, and the air brooded with the phantoms created within themselves. Each man amongst them had his own weird notions—scraps of religious teaching, folklore, tales of horror passing from mouth to mouth, the very legends of terrorised childhood, all materialised to chill their enthusiasm and alter the temper of their purpose. The men had less stomach for the adventure now that it was before them. Indeed, as their mood changed, some of them wavered, huddling close and sheeplike and looking enviously on the brightness of the tavern they had left. They waited for a lead, and would have preferred an order back to the warmth of the " Lantern " and its cheer.

The strutting Nemo looked over them, and he of all men knew what was passing in their minds. It was part of his complete mastery over this mixed company of desperadoes that he had no superstitions himself, or at least few that he confessed by his actions, and being free of them he was clever enough to see the value of keeping alive such ignorant fear in others. Although he cared not a jot for the Hand of Glory, nor any other but his own, he blew upon the spark set alight by the Scrivener.

" Now, then, tap-heroes all and pot-valiants, who reaches out for the dead hand ? " he called, and the mocking challenge in his reckless voice stung them to attention, as if it were a whip lash scourging their panic-stricken minds.

The song faded out of the voices of the tattered army, and followed a long, uneasy silence, men looking unsteadily at each other and edging outward, giving free place to all who chose the centre. As he saw them wavering, Swift Nick noted that his new friend's face grew more ironical. He himself had long since ceased to criticise the strange events of the day. Impressions had crowded so quickly as to stupefy his power to be surprised. To him the Hand of Glory had only been a rumour of the folklore type, and he waited, curiously enough, to see it emerge into this strange life of the road as a moving, vital expression of their ignorant superstition. As for Nemo, they had asked for the Hand of Glory and it was his business to see they found it. His contemptuous eyes swept the company, as if he could look behind the pale faces into the storm-ridden minds; and after the silence had endured for some seconds, the beggar king broke it again.

" What are we—children at the suckling age or grown men ? Do we drink milk or feed on pigeon's liver ? " he asked. " Who severs the dead hand and brings it as a lighted glory ? "

The Scrivener pushed himself forward. His great white beard made him look Druidical in the dark, a wild religious enthusiast; but the light in his eyes and the snap in his voice belied his venerable appearance.

" I'll get the hand," he shouted, in clear, bell-like tones. " Many are the hands these of mine have found and lit."

He held his prehensile fingers high above his venerable head.

" I'll bring down the Golden Farmer's paw if you will bear me company. It cannot be like the claws of York padsters—able to clutch after death. I dare to lead where others only follow. Damn my old man's beard, I'll show the way to you Johnnyraws, who get chilled marrow over a moonlight shepherd. Who follows the lead of the Scrivener, my merry mumpsters ? "

As he spoke, calling the words with a violence that made his hearers think of hounds before the blooding, he swung a lighted torch Steve Randall pressed into his hand.

The flaming mass, whirled above his head, lit up their pale faces, a fiery challenge, lurid in the night. Some of its glow fired their diminishing ardour, excited them, called and spurred the men on to action.

They all moved with one accord, a few, more timid, keeping to the rear, but as fearful of being left behind as they were of being thrust forward to go on alone in front. The man with the white beard, his glaring eyes burning fiercer than the light he carried, walked ahead, setting his face to where the roads forked, and going forward with the resolute manner of a patriarchal devil.

Swift Nick, immediately behind him, laughing; Nemo, strutting in the pride of his fine feathers, and all the rest of the odd crew, crowding and jostling, went down the road, and again they roared a song, as if to scare away the restless spirits of the eerie night.

So they went, until the framework at the forked roads stood clearly outlined, and as they neared it, instinctively the pace of the crowd grew slower. Only the Scrivener, with the lighted torch, went on, many yards in front and quickening his gait, with Swift Nick at his heels, still curious, and Nemo pushing forward, welcoming the moment as an opportunity of making a theatrical display of courage. Behind was the crowd, the song fading out, voice by voice, until it was no longer a song ; the shuffling footsteps growing slower still ; what speech there was dropping steadily until words they used to hearten each other were whispered.

The moon rode brave and clear. It seemed to pale the torch the Scrivener bore aloft. His beard was whiter in its cold light. The downpouring rays fell about the gibbet, until they even outlined the links in the frost-whitened chain. And those behind saw the white-bearded, malign figure with the torch cast it guttering to the earth and stop ; watched him swarm up the main shaft, and, holding there, saw him wait for the wind to turn the flapping bulk and enable him to clutch and pull on the dead man's hand.

As he did so, the Scrivener called to them. His summons seemed to be half a scream, expressing some latent madness, and part a squeal of dreadful triumph. He was waving something in his hand as he dropped to earth. Seizing his torch he whirled it round so that the draught might work on the waning fires.

As they saw him coming they parted, and he walked on rapidly between the assembled men. The crowd closed in his wake and swept on towards the " Lantern," the mood of every man changing as they pressed forward, half running in their eagerness to be back within the low rooms of the lighted inn. They called and swore and jostled each other; sang uproariously, and flourished weapons in their hands; front men, leading, turned round and called on others to follow; the really crippled hobbled laboriously to keep up with the speed of the new movement. And so, pell-mell; haunted, yet emerging from a shadow; eager, with fading spirit fires kindling and blazing; led by a tattered rascal with a venerable white beard and a flaring torch, they made the "Lantern" once again, and flooded forward into the room with the bay window.

In that room men's tongues babbled recklessly, because horror was freezing their very hearts. They herded together like so many fierce, wild animals. All were quickly drinking, for the potboy passed in and out, taking orders and delivering the tipple most to the fancy of each reckless palate. Standing, sitting, or sprawling, they clinked glasses or pannikins with the mad impulse that drives the half drunk forward to complete intoxication. Some hammered the tables with empty mugs. One man, stupid, sat with his head laid forward on the bench, half asleep, howling in a tearful monotone the dying speech of the Golden Farmer. Ratlike faces on one side of the room called to ratlike faces on the other, and such men, raising their mugs, leered out ribald toasts before burying their predatory noses in the vessels. Some danced riotously, others gravely. Little quarrels broke out, flaring into screaming oaths, hurled tumultuously and dying away into maudlin expressions of goodwill. Two ruffians, who had quarrelled noisily, fell into an embrace and kissed each other. One man, really deaf and dumb, whose irregular teeth gave a dog-like expression to his mouth, cried in his drink. As he could not speak the muddled grief in his mind, and could not hear the sounds he made, he mouthed horribly, and the inarticulate noises issuing from his lips ranged from piglike gutturals to screams in an uncontrolled falsetto—these last the horrible noises made by wild animals trapped and in pain. In this inferno, at a top table, Nemo sat sober enough and quietly restrained. His mien was one of conscious power; he looked much as a huntsman may do, controlling a pack of about-to-be-blooded hounds. Swift Nick sat at his side, flushed but self-controlled, and answered calls from every part of the room offering to drink his health. At the doorway stood burly Steve Randall, swarthy, merry, not ill pleased that so many fuddled away their money in his house. The only missing member of the party was the white-bearded Scrivener, who had not shown his face since the dead man's hand had been brought back to the inn by the wild procession.

An hour of this carousing went on, and the noise made the inn shake with reckless, evilly ex-pressed mirth, and the sound heard from without, if such gatherings often happened, must have accounted for the " Lantern's " sinister repute upon the road.

It was nearly one o'clock when Steve Randall whispered a message to Nemo, who, first taking a pull at his long-stemmed glass, stood and hammered on the table for silence.

6*

The pack were not so easily brought to heel, and long after he called for quiet the riot went on. Nemo, in a strident voice, had to name his men, and threaten in blood-curdling terms. The deaf and dumb beggar, growling and screaming, could not hear the command, and was the last to keep on making the room hideous with his noise. Nemo stopped him by the simple process of catching the crying fool by the nape of the neck and banging his head upon the rough table in front of him. The force of this reminder acted on them all. When they saw the deaf and dumb beggar slowly realise by the pain inflicted on his half-pulped face that Nemo commanded, more or less grudgingly they obeyed.

Standing up, obviously proud of his reign and power over his subjects, Nemo shouted above the waning din.

"Gentlemen of the road and mumpsters all—here is Swift Nick, our new brother. To-night the Scrivener will set blazing the Hand of Glory to lighten Nick's way and to make all his enterprises safe in the darkest places. Drink to him, mumpsters, the man whose way is lighted by the Hand of Glory, and then Randall will prepare the room."

They rose tumultuously at his call, and the rafters rang again with their shouted toasts. Then some resumed their seats, while others stood, but all, lower in key, subdued in tone, looked towards their chief.

Steve Randall passed amongst his motley company. One by one he snuffed the lighted candles. As each one went out before a pinch of his horny fingers, the room fell into deeper shadows. When the place was only lit by three small flames, there was darkness already—a faintly lit darkness, in which the varied faces glowered. All that one could see was the flame of a reckless eye or the working of darker patches which were nervously tremulous mouths. One by one the last three flames were extinguished, until the room of the " Lantern " was in total darkness. In the gloom, Nemo's voice sounded.

" Mumpsters—the Hand ! " he called, theatrically pointing to the door.

Dead silence fell upon that assembly—a stifled silence, that seemed to be rived by suppressed passions and the fear born of outrageous superstitions.

From the passage, into the room, came the Scrivener. He walked with a stoop, for he carried a tray. His white beard was illuminated by a ghostly light. A pungent smell preceded him. He droned a sing-song chant as he came forward, an old man, patriarch in appearance, performing a devil's rite. He walked with a shuffle, chanting his song, to the top of the room, and stood in front of Nemo and Swift Nick. Then, for the first time, the new roadster saw the lighted Hand of Glory.

On the tray was the stark, knotted hand of the Golden Farmer. Around each finger and thumb wicks had been twined, fatted to burn, and these had been set alight. Five tiny flames burned fitfully. They scarcely served to lighten the gloom. The points of flame blazed with a sickly, crackling noise, and flared blue. They played upon the face of the Scrivener, who kept up his chant, and no man there could tell the words he sang. It was a chant, horribly grotesque, and in one tuneless drone. It may have had no words at all. The sound just went on, rolled out by a senile voice; and when the monotonous song was varied in tone it was because the old man became breathless, and the thing he mouthed fell away into creaking groans.

Steve Randall stood in the doorway, his big face shadowed, watching phlegmatically. Behind peeped two scared serving wenches, their faces pallid. In disorderly circles, more or less clearly outlined—less as they stood from the centre and were jammed against the walls, more as they came nearer to Nemo's table and the light—were many faces. Every face—bold, handsome, and reckless, strong, weak, or merely vicious, and ranging through the ill types between these extremes—was intent on the waxing and waning of the lights on the dead man's hand. Some crossed themselves and others muttered, each his own superstitious jumble of prayer.

The Hand of Glory was alight.

As the five flares waned lower and lower, casting deeper shadows, and threatening to go out and leave the room in total darkness, Nemo again took the centre of the picture.

"Mumpsters and padsmen, lame rogues and merry rascals, salute the five flames. Here stands Swift Nick," he shouted. "He is one of us and ours. He travels quickly, with the way smoothed by our word. All his enterprises will be successful, for the devil has lit his way with the burning Hand of Glory; and when they are most in danger, the enemies of Swift Nick shall sleep, through the lasting, magic influences of the five flames lighting the dead man's claws."

As he finished the words, the dreadful blue light waxed suddenly, lit up their watching faces, and then guttered out, plunging the room into total darkness. The Scrivener stumbled away with the tray. A scared servant brought a lighted spill and touched the candles strewn about the place into life. The potboy staggered in with more drinks, quickly supplying the shouted orders. The company settled down to a night carouse and the "Lantern" roared with their wild conviviality. Early that morning, before the day broke, the "Lantern's" bull's-eyes still glowed. Inside, most of the company, drunken full, slept either in their seats or on the floor beneath the tables. But Nemo, the head of this fraternity, though he had drunk as deeply as any one, still remained upright, kinging it over the mob he ruled, and Swift Nick, with a mounting flush upon his face, sat in the chimney corner, taking his hot mulled wine in the chair so often occupied by Claude Du Vall. The Scrivener, venerable, his face somewhat drawn and his eyes wandering, was standing, singing to the company the farewell verses of the Golden Farmer. A few yards away from the inn, at the cross roads, in the mist of the early morning, all that was left of the Golden Farmer, save his right hand, turned slowly on the frost-whitened chain.

CHAPTER XII

THE first use Nick made of his new-found liberty of the road was to send Peggy Sheldon warning of his condition and news of his headquarters, with instructions plainly showing the means she should take to summon him.

The ramifications of Nemo's strange society were amazing. By a wonderfully organised, secret service, news travelled quickly between London and Barnet, in a manner no other system of communication could imitate, and the men employed at every stage were suited to the end in view. It was quite possible for Nick to give Peggy Sheldon a reputable receiving house for any message she might send, or to deliver into her hands, without exciting suspicion, any communication her lover desired to forward.

Within a week of the ceremony at the "Lantern," Nick had written twice, and with a certainty that commanded his respect for the system Nemo had placed at his disposal. In his turn, he had received two brief epistles from the woman who held an option on his services which confirmed him in the belief that all was going well with Peggy in London town.

But in London, affairs of moment, both to Peggy and Nevinson, were being discussed, and not totally unconcerned with their interest in each other.

A week after his duel with Nevinson, Sir Ladbroke Drake made the important decision of returning to the world from which he had been compelled to withdraw. For a full six days after the encounter he had been confined to his residence in Craven Street, through the painful nature of his wounds.

Each day Captain Barclay had come to him with news of the outer world, and had gone abroad about Sir Ladbroke's business, which was his own. On Barclay, Sir Ladbroke had depended for news of the doings of the town and the power to keep his fingers on the strings of the dubious life he lived and to pull them for his own profit. He had learnt details of the inquiry at Isaacs' rooms, and of the expulsion of Nicholas from the Argyle Assembly. He knew of the disappearance of Nevinson from accustomed, if not exclusive, haunts in town. This absence had troubled him. Vaguely he looked upon the young man as an enemy, and could not conceive that a gallant of such spirit would resist the temptation to try to trump the trick he had turned on him. He had set abroad inquiries for the purpose of determining where Nevinson had gone and what he was doing, without success. The absence of news of Nevinson was not the least of his preoccupations.

Of other news he had received his share. Buck Dowling had returned direct, to announce his failure to make Bedford and to refuse further attempt. He had recounted the substance of his experiences on the highway and had been roundly cursed for his pains. In addition, Sir Ladbroke had heard of the town talk about Beau Morris and the grotesque happenings in St. James's on the night when Nicholas had been publicly affronted at the Argyle Rooms, to his orders. The regular appearance of Captain Barclay, the comings and goings of other friends, dupes or conscious tools, kept Sir Ladbroke in touch with the strange world that staged the part he played in a life that joined the cream of the personalities of the town with some of its foulest undercurrents.

During the week, Sir Ladbroke's wounds had troubled him, but he had, in truth, kept his rooms, suffering rather from a sense of humiliation than from actual physical pain. He had chafed under the restraint of his confinement, but had wisely judged it best to keep away from accustomed haunts rather than challenge and set the tongues of the town wagging the faster for his presence. So a week had dragged on, slowly enough, and now, at the beginning of a second, Sir Ladbroke Drake, quite himself again, was contemplating coming out of his shell and making his reappearance in the town.

The gamester, on this Monday, rose at his accustomed hour. Breakfasting in his room, he made a slow and elaborate toilet, with all the care of a man of the world who sets great store by the value of appearances. By eleven o'clock, Sir Ladbroke walked with a swagger into the living room

that overlooked dingy Craven Street, in the Strand.
He stood for a minute or two, tying his cravat,
and shooting his laced sleeves negligently. He
turned afterwards to a mirror to admire the setting
of his perruque and the fall of the salmon-coloured
coat of ribbed silk that he had sported in Isaacs'
rooms, the night Nicholas had accused him of
cheating.

Satisfied that his appearance was equal to the
ordeal of close scrutiny which he knew awaited him
in town, Sir Ladbroke took to pacing the gloomy
room. His manner, stirred a little out of its wonted
calm by the relatively new prospect before him,
slowly became more normal. The sense of elation
at being about dropped from him; the features of
the man hardened; the air of studied repose,
habitually turned to his world, was willed back to
the expression in his eyes, the set of the thin, hard
mouth, the carriage of the head, and the slow swing
of the lithe body.

With jewelled hands clasped behind him, the
white linen at his wrists gleaming against the florid
silk; with head slightly bent forward and eyes
searching the floor, Sir Ladbroke paced the length
of his living room. He moved slowly. His slip-
pered feet slid over the carpet, dragging slightly
and making stealthy sounds. The shadows deepened
upon his face; the lines hardened about the man's
mouth; the crafty, astute eyes grew more concentrated in their intense preoccupation. Walking
there, up and down one side of the dark room, he
suggested by his manner one of the fiercer preying

animals, chafed by captivity, sweeping the ground with velvet paws, the hidden claws waiting the opportunity of sheathing themselves in their natural prey.

A quarter of an hour passed. The time was drawing close upon half-past eleven when a caller sounded an arrival at the street door. The progress of the new-comer was heralded by the swift ring of ascending footsteps on the stairway. When the door to Sir Ladbroke Drake's living room was thrown open, a manservant announced Captain Barclay, and that gentleman followed the statement in person, evidently assured of welcome.

Captain Barclay seemed a trifle surprised to find Sir Ladbroke fully attired for the outer world, but offered no comment. Instead, and with a bow, he congratulated his associate on his improved appearance.

Sir Ladbroke greeted his caller with a curt bow, and, still preoccupied, walked up and down the room with the same carefully measured, catlike tread. Suddenly stopping, he halted squarely before Captain Barclay.

"What news from Bedford?" he rapped out, curtly enough.

"None, on my life," Barclay answered. "Twice we have sent out for the expected docket from the North since Dowling returned. Twice we have failed."

"Failed!" sneered Sir Ladbroke. "What sort of men further my enterprises? 'Fore God, it's a pretty pass if London does not hold a needy adventurer who can be tempted by a handful of goldfinches to make Bedford. Is the devil in the road ? "

Captain Barclay scowled slightly.

"The devil is on the road," he answered. "Du Vall made the beat 'twixt Finchley and Barnet as hot as hell itself, when easy money was astir. But now the great Claude has skipped to native France another road-grig is levying toll, who makes the Frenchman seem an angel. From all accounts the new Tobyman is the very devil. He noses our men as keenly as a greyhound turns a hare. He's had both of 'em since Dowling failed, and has sent them back skinned."

"A white-livered pack they must be," Sir Ladbroke suggested, with a sneer. "After all, have we no firebrand good enough for one Tobyman ? "

"On my life, no," Captain Barclay answered. "He bags the lot."

Sir Ladbroke snapped his fingers.

"It's a milk-and-water stage we've come to if no one can get through, and some one must reach Bedford before the week is ended."

"I can send again," Captain Barclay answered, gloomily.

"And fail once more," suggested Sir Ladbroke, with a sneer. "No; I'll do better. I'll go myself. The man who stops me will need sit tight on his prad."

"Well, God save you on your errand, if you go," Captain Barclay answered. "And keep your eyes peeled for the Tobyman. I'd put a bullet through his middle before I parleyed with him."

"By God, I will," answered Drake. "Listen" —he began again earnestly—"I need money— big money. Pigeons will be scarce since the town has painted me so black."

"As for that——" began Captain Barclay, but his speech was broken off.

"Oh, damme, I know," said Sir Ladbroke. "I turned the trick on Nevinson, but the town will talk. I'm too old a bird not to realise that. Though I am whitewashed, the pigeons will be shy. They will see the rook's black feathers. Besides, the bolder game is the best game."

"And what is that?" asked Captain Barclay.

Sir Ladbroke looked at him keenly, as if wondering whether he might be trusted. The two men's glances met, testing each other, and apparently satisfied Sir Ladbroke unmasked himself.

"Hark ye, Barclay," he said, "there is big game afoot. I'm playing the city against the throne."

"You mean treason?" As he spoke Captain Barclay's voice wavered.

"Put it that way if you like," he agreed. "There's no earthly good in being mealy-mouthed about it. Rowley's a curse to himself and an infliction to the country. In the city, to a man, the moneybags are against him. They curse his knavish tricks with France, and want peace and trade with the Dutchmen. And they want to tinker with the Customs."

"Well, and suppose they do," smiled Captain Barclay. "I want the moon, but I do not get it.

I want the earth and all the rest of it ; but the duns are on me like jackals and threaten to bring me down. Let's get to the money, for I take it you don't run against the topsman and deal in treason against King Charles for the love of God, in the Puritan manner."

"S'blood, no," Sir Ladbroke answered. "There is a game, and the goldfinches might come home—will come home. The Puritans have the risen gorge against the King and his secret parleying with the Catholics, and will rise to a man in the North. The London cits, to a money-bag, are with them. There are ample funds for an army—enough to set the flame of revolt alight from here to Edinburgh, and the goldbags are blowing on the Protestant hatred of Rowley's flirtation with France and the Catholics. The money is against the King."

"Yes—that's very well," answered Captain Barclay. "I follow the money, of course. But I want to know how all this butters my parsnips."

Ladbroke paced up and down the room for some minutes in deep thought. Then he stopped his walk and once more confronted his henchman, Barclay.

"Zithee, my buck," he said ; "I'll let you into a game, better by far and richer in goldfinches than plucking barely fledged pigeons. I need money—badly. My gorge turns over the task of cooking the small fry of the town. Here is game—big game, and you and I may play it, free of fear of the topsman."

"My stomach is good for any game," Captain Barclay answered. "You set the guineas rolling, tell me where they are, and I'll help you to pick them up. I'm in for anything, from loaded dice to blackmail."

Sir Ladbroke Drake's face grew stern at the mention of the last word.

"This, by the Lord, is blackmail," he answered. "That damned old cit, John Sheldon, finds his parsnips buttered against the King. He deals with the Dutch, and the Customs are against him. He it is who is the centre of the new plot. That much I know, and I would know more. Those papers from Bedford, which I promised to bring to town in Sheldon's interest, would give him entirely into my hands—would confirm me in the power I hold over him, already great."

"And then—what then, by the Lord, what then?" asked Captain Barclay. "Do you ride against the King?"

Sir Ladbroke Drake shrugged his shoulders.

"That depends," he answered. "I'll weigh the chances first, and I'll come down on the buttered side, and you shall drop easily with me. But here's the point. I have Sheldon compromised even now. I can hold all the proof I need, if I get those reports from the North. Then, whether it's up or down with Old Rowley, it does not matter a pedlar's curse. We can stick to the revolt and share in the city plunder, or——"

Sir Ladbroke stopped in his speech and looked significantly on Captain Barclay.

The Captain slowly assented by an inclination of his head.

" 'Fore God, there's thousands of guineas in it," he said, slowly. " You bleed Sheldon white, if he fails ; or claim the price of silence before he succeeds ; is that it—eh ? " He laughed harshly as he spoke.

Sir Ladbroke's crafty face came as near as it could to a smile, the drawn mouth wrinkling like so much crumpled parchment.

" Rot me for a traitor, you have it," he said, his manner slightly excited. " You'll be with me in this—eh ? "

" Up to the hilt," answered Captain Barclay, with some show of confidence.

Again Sir Ladbroke paced the room. His eyes were lit with plotting fires. His nostrils were distended, as if, dog-like, he were scenting prey. The long white fingers, moving restlessly, snapped as though he were dispersing dangers or deriding them with his contempt.

" There's a fortune in it, whichever way the game goes," he said, at last. " We hold John Sheldon's head, and he has the gold pieces to pay stiffly if he decided to keep his graven image of a face on his damned shoulders. And more——"

He stopped again, thinking ; walked the length of the room and then spoke again, as if he had made up his mind.

" I play for two fortunes," he said, at last. " One we shall get from Sheldon, and the second I will secure by marriage with his niece."

Captain Barclay gazed on his chief admiringly.

" You mean, you'll work Sheldon to make her

go with you to the church?" he asked, struck with a new view of the game.

"If she prove unkind—yes, by Old Rowley, I will," answered Sir Ladbroke, with a sneer. "I'll try gentle persuasion first; force, if that fails. A wife, gold laced, would be of service to me, apart from the pleasure of holding the pride of this wench Sheldon."

"You will need force," Captain Barclay answered. "I did not know you had an eye for pretty Mistress Peggy and her snug fortune. Damme, I might have told you—you are second in the field, and the other has a good lead."

Sir Ladbroke scowled his anger at the suggestion. His figure stiffened, and for a moment he looked as if he were going to repay Barclay's suggestion by tearing out the man's tongue. He stood confronting Barclay, his eyes glittering spitefully, his hands working nervously.

"Curse you!" he shouted, his anger blazing into words. "What do you know of Peggy Sheldon? Out with it, man; out with it. If you've dared to look into her face, spit me, I'll see you drummed out of the town, so help me God, I will."

Captain Barclay stepped back amazed at the sudden display of anger, almost uneasy at the effect he had produced. All the same, affecting confidence of manner, and pretending to ignore the personal application of the outbreak, he threw back his head and laughed aloud.

"God save me," he said, "what a fire-eater you are! There's the ardour of youth in your love-making. As for me, looking on a woman with an eye to the church—s'blood! never. I'm well enough as I am. But, sink me, Sir Ladbroke, I only speak my mind; but it is the truth. There is already a gallant in the field."

Sir Ladbroke seized Captain Barclay by the arm. His face was red with anger. In his unconcealed rage he twisted the limb he held until Barclay writhed with pain.

"His name?" he shouted, straining on the arm, while Barclay's face grew pale. "His name? By all the furies, unmask him. I'll hound him from the town or pick a quarrel and spit him before the day is out. His name, I say?"

"God's mercy," Captain Barclay answered, with a nervous laugh. "Have a care, man—have a care. That is my arm you drag upon, and not a pump-handle."

"His name? curse you," commanded Sir Ladbroke, growing fiercer in manner as the other delayed.

"S'death, you should steady yourself," replied the other. "You are no callow youth, jealous as a green girl. I'll give you his name with all the freedom in the world if you will cease sawing on my arm. The man who is before you, who holds her warm regard already, if my eyes have not deceived me, is—Nicholas Nevinson."

Sir Ladbroke Drake started at the name, as if he had received a blow. For a moment or two he stood before Barclay, in a silence so tense that the second man himself grew pale. Sir Ladbroke seemed to have aged; the fire in his crafty eyes faded out; the carriage of his head, arrogant as he had outlined his plot, altered in a way that suggested he was weaker. When he began to pace the floor once more, his lithe body had lost its steely spring.

"God's life," he said, at last and aloud. "Nevinson—always Nevinson."

"He is not the devil," the other mocked, recovering his composure.

The words were a challenge, and the stiffening manner of Sir Ladbroke was the answer.

He resumed his steady beat along the side of the room, with returning composure, for many minutes. The crafty, self-contained, secretive, but dominant manner of the man returned. Catlike, he walked the apartment, and as his command of self came back to him, an ugly, purposeful concentration threatened in every line of his crabbed, thin, and lined features.

"Fair or foul, I'll put this popinjay down," he growled at length. "And if he plays for the girl, there'll be all the more pleasure in possession, if I wound him by flaunting her before the town."

Captain Barclay watched his leader, mirth uppermost, prompted by the revelation of the unexpectedly human character of Sir Ladbroke's aspirations.

At length, Sir Ladbroke lapsed into his normal self. Stepping before the mirror, he looked closely at the details of his attire and settled their shortcomings, one by one. Satisfied with his appearance, he turned to Captain Barclay.

"Bear me company," Sir Ladbroke said. "I'll make the tour of the town and brave the gossips."

The other laughed his sympathy.

"God's life," he said; "you wear a face that would intimidate the devil himself."

The two men spoke no more until they were together walking along Craven Street to the Strand, with mincing gait and ostentatious self-possession.

Sir Ladbroke broke a long silence by drawing close to Captain Barclay and leaning on his arm as he spoke.

"Your knowledge settles my hesitation," he said, more to himself. "To-night, I will open on Sheldon, and Peggy shall be a part of the reckoning he shall pay for retaining his head and dodging the axe kept by the King for traitors."

He did not further pursue this chain of thought aloud. The two men had passed through the Strand and were indeed turning into Covent Garden before Sir Ladbroke spoke again.

"Nevinson," he said, speaking his thoughts aloud. "Damme! must this man Nevinson dog my fortunes as if he were the devil himself?"

Captain Barclay, looking much like a middle-aged raven, smiled grimly.

CHAPTER XIII

SIR LADBROKE DRAKE spent the evening of his
first day in the town, after Nicholas Nevinson had
interrupted his routine, by dining with Mr. John
Sheldon at the mansion in Tavistock Place.

In a solid, heavy, city manner, John Sheldon lived
in state in his Bloomsbury house. Outside, viewed
from the dingy thoroughfare, the place looked dour
enough, and the front door, patterned with bars
of iron, might have guarded a prison. Indeed, a
little iron grille of a trap in the door itself could
be opened, and it was characteristic of the house
that when a stranger pulled on the heavy bell-handle,
a retainer, stationed in the hall, looked suspiciously
on the new-comer from the grille before affording
him the hospitality of the open door.

Inside, in a ponderous manner, the house was
luxuriously appointed. Sheldon cherished his
possessions with a purse-proud sense of style. His
taste in furniture ran to florid carving, and every
piece of oak in his entertaining rooms was tooled
and shaped into all manner of distorted patterns.
Great tapestries hung upon the wall, flamboyant
in a continental style. A candlestick upon the
table was of no account if it were not of gold,

heavily ornamented, and brackets on the walls
were richly gilt. Ornaments of cut glass, carvings
of ivory, India ware, gold plate in various show-
places, accentuated John Sheldon's pride in the
power of money and its display. The liveried
menials were gold-laced, paunchy fellows, whose
red-veined faces suggested good living and a
standard of nourishment carried to the bursting
point. John Sheldon, though a man of spare, mean
habit himself, was of the newly risen class of
wealthy citizens, and his home displayed evidences
of his riches on every hand. He believed in the
power of the wealth of the city to the point of
arrogance, and everything about him symbolised
his desire to maintain the estate of the caste in
which he moved—the then aspiring race of merchant
princes.

To this house came Sir Ladbroke Drake. The
hour was seven o'clock, and dinner had been
served—served with the prodigality of the merchant's estate. The Sheldon gold plate had appeared upon the table. A heavy meal of several
courses had been dished up by the gold-laced
servitors, under the direction of a proud but
apoplectic butler, who breathed hard as he bent
to carve, and seemed to be threatened at every
moment of his life with a rush of blood, or old
port, to the brain. Peggy Sheldon had dined with
her uncle and his guest, light of heart and gay of
speech, paying but little attention to either man,
but to rally them when they spoke to her and to
ignore the pointed attentions forced upon her,

through meaning glances and studied table services, by Sir Ladbroke Drake, as the dinner progressed. When the servants had placed a choice dessert and handed round a fine old port of the fruity vintage beloved by the prosperous of the city, she had risen to retire to the drawing-room and to leave the two men to talk over their wine.

The dinner over, John Sheldon leaned his shoulders against the stiff, high-backed chair, sinking lower to better stretch his spidery legs under the heavy table. He had dined sparingly, and the glass of port he had filled for himself was all the wine he had taken. Sheldon's face was white, and its expression did not relax. He showed none of the easier manners of average men softened by dining. Lounging back, he fingered the stem of his wineglass, and with a slight frown on his forehead bent his attention on his guest, whom he fixed with a concentrated, vigilant gleam of his crafty, piglike eyes.

Sir Ladbroke Drake was in fine feather. His progress through the town had not presented the difficulties he had anticipated. His world had been tolerantly disposed. At table, Sir Ladbroke, after the strain of the day, had unbent and exerted himself to please the lady, Mistress Peggy Sheldon, in an unmistakable manner. He had eaten liberally, and the bottle had not gone unpunished. Indeed, Sir Ladbroke had dined well, and now sat, in a glow of reflection, seeing life through a halo of self-confidence that made all things appear quite possible.

They fell to talking, first casually, of the affairs

of the town, and then intimately of matters of import to themselves.

In a grim, sour manner Mr. Sheldon had complimented Sir Ladbroke on his recovery, and their talk had skirted the duel and finally bent itself on the expulsion of Nicholas from the Argyle Rooms.

" A dangerous man, this Nevinson," Sheldon said, pursing his puckered, hanging lips. " Where has the young rumpad gone ? " he added, with intent curiosity.

" That I do not know," Sir Ladbroke answered, easily enough. " Since Beau Morris dealt with him, he has disappeared from all his haunts, and no man has seen him."

" I suppose he is somewhere, travelling to the devil, in the way such a gallows-bird must go," Sheldon suggested, with asperity.

" I know not, nor do I care overmuch," Sir Ladbroke answered. " I owe him a score, and regret he has quit the town so hastily. But, I take it, he will come back."

" God forbid," Sheldon said, an ugly gleam belying the pious expression. " I found him running Mistress Peggy pretty close, and his disappearance saves me the trouble of warning off a hang-dog adventurer."

A silence fell between the two men, and in it they eyed each other, closely.

Suddenly, Sir Ladbroke filled his glass, and, standing, drank off a bumper.

" To the fair Peggy Sheldon," he said, somewhat boisterously, " and to the prettiest eyes in London."

The other acknowledged the toast, wryly enough. Almost as if he knew what was passing in Sir Ladbroke's mind, as soon as his guest had seated himself he returned to the subject.

"I have other views for Peggy," he said, acidly. "I'll see no penniless adventurer intervene. A wealthy city match is best for a young woman of fortune. There's nothing like cementing money with what young blood calls love—eh ? "

Sir Ladbroke shrugged his shoulders and gulped his wine again. Then he laughed, recklessly.

"The lady may have a mind of her own," he dared.

John Sheldon smiled again, but there was no mirth in any line of it.

"There is only one mind in this house," he said, with grim arrogance. "It is mine. I am her guardian until marriage, with full power, and she must remain here under my control or marry according to my wishes—just as I will."

Sir Ladbroke Drake eyed the speaker closely, and then raising his glass, looked through the red fluid at a lighted candle, with one eye closed.

"Suppose," he said, speaking calmly, though the effort cost him something—"suppose I asked for the privilege of Peggy ? She is a wife-old woman and I have sown my wild oats."

"You mean——" Sheldon stopped with the query unspoken.

"Marriage, as I have hinted before," said the other. "S'blood, what else ? "

Something like anger smouldered in Sheldon's

narrow eyes, but an effort of will chased the rising fire away.

" 'Tis little enough you ask—tut ! tut ! " he said, ironically.

" But if I ask ? " Sir Ladbroke insisted.

" I shall refuse," Sheldon said, decisively, and there was a rasp in his voice as he brought his hand down on the table, emphatically. " We have spoken of this before."

Sir Ladbroke drank off his wine and filled another glass. The rare old port warmed and fired him.

" Think," he said, fingering his wineglass and looking on Sheldon, with a challenge in his furtive eyes. " Think again."

" Twice and thrice I might think," the other snapped. " The answer would be the same." Sheldon spoke with obvious heat. .

Sir Ladbroke stiffened in his chair and pushed his glass farther away, with a brisk action that suggested he had made up his mind. After a brief interval he broke the silence, and there was a steely quality in his voice.

" In view of what you say, I ask formally for the hand of Miss Peggy Sheldon." As he spoke he fixed Sheldon's angry glare, and met the glance firmly, with a deliberate purpose showing through his still suave manner.

" I would still——" John Sheldon began positively, but the definite refusal hung fire. He hesitated, and slowly his sunken eyes fired as he realised the other's purpose. He stood gazing at Sir Ladbroke as if he were a snake who had suddenly struck at him with poisoned fang. His pale face grew a shade more pallid.

' "You threaten me ?" he asked, in a tense whisper.

The other laughed unpleasantly.

"No, no !" Sir Ladbroke said. "I ask you a civil question, and"—he paused a moment, weighing his words—"there are good reasons why you should consider the possibility of giving me a civil answer."

Sheldon's crafty face looked still more startled at the turn the conversation had taken. The nature of the threat had not been spoken, but he knew the underlying meaning. In a crooked game he had had to trust some one, and the adventurer before him, highly paid, had seemed the likeliest tool. There were great stakes in the project he had afoot, and in his purse-proud way John Sheldon had felt certain of being able to outbid any other purchaser of the fashionable gambler's allegiance. That Sir Ladbroke should fly off the track, he, Sheldon, had mapped out, unnerved him.

He stood up, pushing back his chair, and for an instant looked as if he were going to dash the wine-glass in Sir Ladbroke's face and openly insult him.

"Damn you for a viper," he began, angrily enough, and speaking at the top of his voice.

"Tush, man," the other broke in, "have a care. You are old enough, and I should regret to make you pay the penalty of your wrath. But I am no man to trifle with, if you value safety."

Sheldon stopped in his violent speech. His manner changed suddenly, and the man's mind groped back to a more powerful weapon he was accustomed to use, and seldom in vain.

" Come, come," he said. " Is it money—a gentlemanly blackmail you put upon me ? You are a man of the world and have doubtless your price."

So engrossed were they in this duel of words, neither Sir Ladbroke nor Sheldon heard the door softly open. Peggy had come from the drawing-room and was upon her way to a heavy sideboard, intent on retrieving a volume she had left there.

" My loyalty is worth buying," Sir Ladbroke was saying as she entered, and speaking the words distinctly. " My price is the hand——"

" Hist ! Silence," whispered Sheldon, alarm on his face as he gazed across the room. " Something too much of this now ; let it be anon."

The other followed Sheldon's glance, and, slightly discomfited, did not speak further of the matter upon his lips.

" Come, Sheldon," he said. " Let us not entirely neglect beauty in our discussions. Miss Sheldon will not overlook our absence."

He turned to follow Peggy out of the room.

Sheldon, astounded at the turn of events, sat lingering at his own table some minutes after Sir Ladbroke had passed on to the drawing-room.

A pretty comedy to watch, was the next hour of that night. When Sheldon joined them, a few minutes later, he found Sir Ladbroke and Peggy engaged in a rapid interchange of light raillery. The girl, for a reason known to herself, was mighty civil to a man who had inflicted havoc on her lover, and replied pleasantly enough to all he said. Sir Ladbroke found for the first time that she received his advances with better grace. He had dared to make but thinly disguised love to the girl before, and had been frozen with the chilly methods of repulse so much a part of Peggy's armour. He made the most of the brief sunshine, and did so with all the keener zest because the light undercurrent of banter in an obvious flirtation challenged John Sheldon, again and again, in his own house and to his face. So enraged did the latter become that, almost incoherent with temper, he left the room on the plea of attending to his affairs. Then Sir Ladbroke made a mistake, which brought his house of cards tumbling about his head.

Sir Ladbroke had drunk freely and was excited. He had played his hand boldly, and knew that he held the trick on Peggy's guardian, however unwillingly he might consent. So well had the game gone, he decided to go farther and follow the motto of the gambler by at once pushing home an advantage.

The idea in his mind became an obsession. Now, while the matter was warm, he would propose to Peggy, carry her by storm, and with the girl's consent would play his trump card before John Sheldon, ere he left the house.

Sir Ladbroke found himself, with infinite cunning, aping the young lover. Trying to seize the girl's hand, in the quiet room, he began to pour out a stream of florid nonsense, that only sounds convincing when the ears drinking it in desire to hear the words, and wait, with a sigh and a rapid beating of the heart, upon every syllable. Sir Ladbroke even knelt, as he poured out his passion, simulated in the main, and real only so far as it was prompted by greed. He likened her, in the manner of his day, to the sun; her eyes became the stars; her hair so many fine-spun golden wires holding his heart. Much of this kind of speech he uttered, and Peggy listened, perturbed, but concealing the fact, and even for her own purposes seeming to be interested and fascinated by his proposal. She heard Sir Ladbroke out, until he had offered her his hand with a glowing tribute to the passion in his heart. Sir Ladbroke, who lived a rapid life, skating over thin ice, had made his lover's address almost convincing to himself, by talking on and on and with great rapidity, imagination spurring him to take fence after fence, as if speed would carry him quicker to the goal. But when he ended, the fire died out of his eyes and voice, and his manner, as he waited for her answer, was as insincere as that of the well-graced player who has merely mouthed the words of another man's passion.

At the end of Sir Ladbroke's heroics, the silence in the room grew deadly, and chilled his very senses.

"Speak, my life," he said, looking upwards at Peggy standing before him, the shimmering silk of her robe reflecting the candlelight.

"La!" she said, archly; "you offer me your hand, Sir Ladbroke; you speak of marriage?"

"It is the nearest thing to my heart," he answered.

The girl broke off into one long peal of exquisite laughter.

" My uncle's port is talking," she said, her voice cutting him as if it were a whip lash ; " it is counted a good wine amongst the bibbers from the city. Rise, Sir Ladbroke, and come from the fire into this cooler corner. You will be better, if you talk no more until the haze of the wine passes and leaves your mind unclouded."

Sir Ladbroke Drake rose, stiffly enough, for the girl's manner had brought him face to face with realities.

" I speak but what is in my heart," he said. " If I am drunk, it is with love of you," he added.

He leered at Peggy as he spoke, and drew closer to her.

At his action, her face grew stern, and she fell back, shrinking from the horror of his near contact.

" Hear me," she said, decisively. " Enough of this heartless comedy. The answer is ' No.' No, no, no ; a thousand times and a thousand more than that, if need be. You, tricked out to speak fair words to women, with a glow on your lying face, made it charitable of me to put the manner of your speech down to the lively action of my uncle's wine. If it were not speaking, then you insult me with words coined for a baser purpose. I know you, Sir Ladbroke, through an honest man's word, as a liar and a cheat."

As she spoke quickly, decisively, with a note that gave no hope of appeal, Sir Ladbroke steadied himself before the torrent of her anger. He swung away from his conception of the pleasing arts by which fair ladies are wooed, and in his sinister face the implacable purposes of his presence there glowered and were shadowed forth in all their ugly, sordid greed.

" Damn you for a sharp-tongued jade!" he said. " I'll make you eat your words."

" You'll make me do nothing against my will," Peggy said, and the pride of her womanhood stood before his craft and cunning, challenging it, and seeming even to him invincible.

He seized her hand and drew her to him.

" 'Fore God, I'll kiss your insolent mouth as a foretaste of the way I'll break your spirit," he said, his voice husky with passion.

" And before the same God, if you do not unhand me and let me go free of your evil presence, I'll call my uncle."

They swayed together, the girl struggling to be free.

" Call on your uncle; call and command him as you command me. See for yourself where my power begins and where yours may end," Sir Ladbroke said, brutally.

Peggy struggled for a moment or two more, then bending her head she bit savagely at the detaining hand.

Sir Ladbroke, surprised, growled an oath at the top of his voice and set Peggy free, his face grimacing with pain.

At the moment, John Sheldon entered the room. His ugly, receding, piglike eyes wavered as he glanced, understandingly, from Sir Ladbroke to his niece. He looked older, and seemed to have shrunk. There was something meanly inadequate about the poise of his spidery physique and the droop of his narrow shoulders.

" Uncle, uncle! " the outraged girl said, appealingly. " This man has insulted me under your own roof. If you have one shred of respect for my father's memory, you will order him forth, and will not permit him to cross our threshold again."

Sheldon still remained irresolute, staring at the distraught girl and the man before him.

Sir Ladbroke's face lit with an evil sneer. With the superb aplomb of the habitual gambler, he threw his hand of cards upon the table and dared everything.

" Order me forth," he said, ironically. " Ask again, my pretty one. There is a limit to Sheldon's power. He dare not act as other than a friend, and must further my enterprise. Ask him, you spit-fire, and see for yourself."

Peggy looked directly at her uncle. He showed no sign of offering her his protection. Indeed, Sheldon, grey and bent, seemed to be impotent.

" Is this man's word true ? " she asked, her voice quivering with scorn, and he could not ignore her question.

" You have been unreasonable in making a scene," was all Sheldon answered, in a whisper. " Go to your room."

Without a word Peggy left them, holding her skirts as if she were tripping through a muddy byway ; her pretty head tilted ; disdain about the girl as if it were an ice-cold, protecting mantle.

The two men remained confronting each other

for some seconds in angry silence. The merchant's glance was the first to waver.

"You fool!" Sheldon said, at last. "You fool, to challenge me in this manner. You have more than my impotence to ride over—easy as that may be. You now have to break down Peggy's pride."

"I'll do that, with your goodwill upon the adventure," Sir Ladbroke said, a triumphant note in his manner, that rankled even with John Sheldon.

"Leave the matter now," the latter urged, weakly. "We'll talk this question out to-morrow."

"As you please," Sir Ladbroke answered. "Your good offices are the price of my silence."

With a profound bow he saluted John Sheldon, the city magnate whose purse strings had betrayed him, and walked towards the great hall. There, the liveried servant behind the grille waited upon him, and ushered Sir Ladbroke, an honoured guest, forth into the night world outside.

7*

CHAPTER XIV

THE conference between Sir Ladbroke Drake and John Sheldon upon the following morning was a brief affair, and confirmed the attitude the former had taken.

John Sheldon had slept upon Sir Ladbroke's proposals, and a nightmare passage he had enjoyed. The city magnate spent the hours of retirement in an uneasy waking dream, and through his overwrought brain phantom shapes strutted in a mighty unreasonable frame of mind. Peggy became an awful figure of defiance. Sir Ladbroke preyed upon him as a friend and ally, changing like a set of dissolving pictures into several sorts of devils. King Charles came into Sheldon's dream as an avenger who knew his most secret thoughts before he had time to form them. He saw revolt flaming in the North, flying armies, bloodshed, failure, and panic. All these maddening impressions beat a restless tattoo in his mind and had the knack of turning, at intervals, into the most dread spectre, haunting his waking thoughts—himself a prisoner, his gold bags endowed with life and fleeing away from him; and afar off, in the grey dawn, a figure wearing

a crape mask—the headsman waiting for the fruit
of treason in the form of his own ripe head.

After supping full of such horrors, with the coming of the light of morning John Sheldon was more
amenable. When Sir Ladbroke called, he found
his patron had reconsidered his attitude and was
ready to meet him at all costs.

The interview did not take many seconds. Sir
Ladbroke stuck out for the whole of his demands
—Peggy's hand and fortune in marriage, with force
applied by her guardian if necessary. For this
he undertook to keep silence, and to throw in his lot
with Sheldon, with unquestioning loyalty, taking
a greater share in the work of organising the rebellion on which Sheldon's heart and soul were centred.

The alternative was betrayal by a word here and
a hint there; by a letter shown to this or that
officer of state, or by the forwarding of documents
already in his possession to the friends of the
King.

In the end, Sheldon capitulated: there was no
other way. He even assented to an early marriage,
and Sir Ladbroke grinned amiably at the thought
of it. "Unquestioning loyalty" meant to him the
right to sell John Sheldon to the highest bidder,
should occasion serve, on the completion of his
marriage.

After consenting, Sheldon paced his room in some
excitement. A load still burdened his mind.

Sir Ladbroke, in a high good temper, anticipated
all his host's personal troubles, and smoothed the
way with suspicious geniality.

" As for Mistress Peggy," he said, voicing their thoughts aloud, " we are grown men, I believe, and of the world. Our withers may not be wrung by a young girl's vapours and whimsies."

Sheldon, pursing his loose lips, nodded uncomfortably.

" You are the wooer," he answered. " My influence goes with your desires, but I expect to see you make things easy for me. Miss Sheldon's fortune is not less than £20,000 in her own right, and it is well worth your while to exert yourself so that you may acquire it without savour of scandal."

" S'blood," returned Sir Ladbroke, " you may trust me for that. Already I have planned a way. I think, with your goodwill, we may easily make the lady more amenable."

" How do you propose to do that ? " Sheldon asked, his mean face souring still more before the prospect.

" At three o'clock this afternoon, I ride for Bedford, on your errand. Why not await me at your country residence, the Chequers. Hitchin is on my way back, and I could be there, with average luck, by noon or evening to-morrow. Make a stay at your Hitchin mansion and take the fair Peggy with you. Away from her friends, your influence and mine will easily turn a girl's purpose, and we can pursue our plans against the King with all the greater ease at the same time. What say you ? "

John Sheldon thought awhile, and his face lightened as he pondered the problem.

" I will do exactly as you suggest," he said, at length. " Tuts ! there are more reasons than one why I am better away from town at this moment. Do you go on to Bedford as you suggest and leave me to follow to Hitchin this evening. I shall expect you at the Chequers during Wednesday."

The other man bowed.

" Good," he said. " Until then, adieu."

He started towards the door, with a little triumphant swagger in his manner which he could not suppress. Suddenly, he halted and turned to Sheldon.

" I'd travel light if I were you," he said, giving his host a warning. " There's a new fly-by-night on Du Vall's beat—a harpy worse than a leech, they say."

Sheldon looked up, only half interested.

" Who is the fellow ? " he asked, with scant curiosity.

" Swift Nick, by all account, if that is any illumination," Drake answered. " He has made many appearances on the road this week, by night and day. I'd keep a look-out for him about Barnet. Indeed, I am anxious on my own account," Sir Ladbroke answered, " and shall do the same."

" Be sure of that," Sheldon said, burying his head in his papers. " I shall travel under escort, in any case. The road through Barnet is never safe."

" Well, so long as you take good care—so ! Adieu," Sir Ladbroke added. " And freedom from the attentions of the new Tobyman."

A few minutes later, Sheldon was confronting

his ward. He had gone to her boudoir almost as soon as Sir Ladbroke Drake left the house.

Briefly he told the girl of his intention to move their residence on to Hitchin, and in a manner that was a veiled command asked her to be ready for the evening journey.

John Sheldon watched the girl closely as he stated his intentions, and was relieved to find her manner did not change when he announced the new plans. He had expected, at least, an outburst of suspicious resentment. That Peggy did not change colour, nor show any trace of temper, was a good sign and a matter for self-congratulation.

He would not have been so self-satisfied over the favourable reception of his news if he could have looked into the workings of his niece's mind. Peggy was alarmed, and had been much preoccupied since the scene of the night before, but she did not choose to show her feelings. She had placed a complete trust in the adroitness of her lover, Nicholas Nevinson, and believed she could rely on substantial help in the moment of stress, if it came. The news that the Chequers was to be their residence at once, instead of disturbing the girl as her uncle had expected, was really a source of joy to her, and did much to restore her self-confidence. Somewhere, Nevinson pursued his fortunes, in a manner he had not made explicit, on the highway near Barnet, and—Barnet was near Hitchin; so near indeed that she might easily see her lover and tell him her latest fears. John Sheldon's news was of such a character that she could hardly refrain from betraying her joy, but with feminine intuition she recognised the necessity of concealing her feelings and maintained an attitude of distinct reserve.

"We ride at five o'clock," her uncle said, in concluding his instructions. "I have sent messages forward, and we should arrive at the Chequers for dinner. I trust my plans suit you," he added.

"Why—yes," she answered. "At all events the change will free me from the attentions of that odious man, Sir Ladbroke Drake, since you cannot protect me in your own house."

John Sheldon's returning confidence was rudely jarred by her words.

"Ah!" he said; "I omitted to tell you. I and Sir Ladbroke have business together. He will be our guest at the Chequers for some time now. He rides for Bedford this afternoon and will stay with us on his return."

If Sheldon had told Peggy that Sir Ladbroke was coming to stay under their roof in Bloomsbury she would have been seriously perturbed, and there would have been a scene there and then. But something in the heart of the girl told her their move nearer to Barnet was a step towards a solution of the threatening troubles and her best guarantee of safety. Peggy felt that the challenge now being forced upon her would be brought to an issue at the Chequers, and her heart beat more rapidly, be it said, when she learnt that the plottings against her peace of mind were to be pushed forward in an area easily accessible to Nicholas.

At the same time she did not show what was

passing in her thoughts. Instead, she stopped her uncle, who was making his way to the door of her apartment.

" Just one moment, uncle," she said, a flush which might have meant anger slowly mantling her cheeks. " Do I understand that you propose to bring Sir Ladbroke to the Chequers in the face of the incidents of last night, and force him on my company ? "

" The matter is arranged," he said, with a shrug of the shoulders.

" Am I to be protected from the kind of thing to which I objected ? " the girl asked, her round voice rising, and her dark oval face showing contempt.

Sheldon's manner displayed some signs of embarrassment.

" Odds, girl," he answered, " why make a mountain of a molehill ? Sir Ladbroke is a gentleman of position, and his attentions are an honour to any lady. Why harp on the fact that he was over-ardent ? A man may be excused if he is fired by a pretty face, after dinner. It is not an uncommon happening."

Peggy shrugged her round shoulders, and then deliberately scanned her own features in the mirror, considering deeply as she did so. When she again turned to Sheldon there was an odd air of decision in her manner. Her round voice had lightened and was alive with laughter when she spoke, but the girl's message was direct, and John Sheldon knew he had her final opinion neatly sugar-coated with good temper.

"Lud, uncle," she said, "I am no ninny! I have been admired before, and—I rather like it." She laughed as she spoke, and then suddenly her manner changed. "But this man insulted me and —you."

"In what way?" Sheldon blustered.

"He made the distinct threat that you dare not but sanction his overtures," she said, pointedly.

"Tut, tut, child!—a misunderstanding. I approve of his proposals," Sheldon returned.

"Since when?" she asked.

His silence proved how unready her uncle was for the cross-examination.

"Since last night," Peggy answered for him; "and since last night only. You are not a free agent in the matter, and he has the power to coerce you, though I know not how. And now you calmly propose to take me into the country, where I shall have only you and this man to deal with. Do you purpose forcing this marriage on me?"

He did not meet the glance of his ward's frank eyes.

"No, no," he said, at last. "You jump too swiftly to conclusions. My business takes me to the country. That Sir Ladbroke comes is only an accident. And besides, what have you against him?"

The girl laughed scornfully.

"First, I do not like his manner," she began, ticking off her objections on her fingers, one by one. "Second, I do not like his looks. Third, I hate his method of love making. Again, he is a liar, and I hate liars. Worse, he is a cheat—that much I know from Nevinson. Five points I have against him." She held up her arm as she spoke and waved the count represented by the fingers and thumb on her dimpled hand in Sheldon's face.

"And if that is not enough, I have more," Peggy added. "His part in the life of the town is known well enough."

"Sheer nonsense," Sheldon blustered. "A maid's fancies born of the tittle-tattle of the town gossips."

His niece laughed recklessly in his face.

"Well, uncle, we differ on this apparently. I'll be frank with you," she went on. "I'll go to the country with you. I'll be the obedient little ward. I'll be civil to this man—*not* cordial, but civil."

John Sheldon looked his relief before her light raillery.

"I'll go," she said, and now her voice rang with a crisp threat as she spoke. "But we may as well understand each other at once and avoid collision in the future. I'll go to the Chequers, but if you try to influence me in this man's direction, I shall refuse to stop in the same rooms he occupies; and if you permit him to address me in the terms he used last night, I shall insult him and leave the house."

John Sheldon stood before her, his mind at war with himself. He would have liked to have blustered forth the designs he and Sir Ladbroke Drake held in common, and to have rated her there and then and commanded the girl's obedience. Wiser counsels prevailed, and he made a fine pretence of smiling.

"You have an utterly wrong notion of our intentions," he said, starting again for the door, "and time will disabuse your mind of that."

"We shall see," said Peggy, lightly; "and if I am right, you will find a bundle of trouble dancing about your plot for my future happiness. Two foolish men! you think you are dealing with a chit of a girl. Take heed you do not find me a woman and stir the shrew in me, for if you do, Chequers will be possessed of devils."

Sheldon held no further parley with his ward, but walked out of the room, closing the door behind him. Standing outside, thinking deeply of the plan he had in mind, and its chance of miscarrying, he thought he heard Peggy laughing. He clucked his loose lips grimly as he listened, and his expression boded no good for his niece.

"Chequers is a good place for the cure of tantrums and scolds," he said, and walked on through the passage to the staircase and so to his own room, smiling the thin, sour smile that puckered his loose lips when he displayed amusement.

Peggy, in her boudoir, sat brooding over the interview. Then she started to dress for the outer world. First the hat with its heavy brim and great sweep of feather, and then the blue coat with the fur lining that Nicholas had viewed with so much pleasure. Singing to herself, Peggy adjusted her rings, poured scent upon her laced kerchief, and before the mirror applied just the tiniest tinge of rouge and clearly defined her eyebrows with a dark pencil.

"La!" she sighed, laughingly standing back,

her eyes glowing; " now I may go abroad looking a person of quality."

She seized a bell rope and pulled on it heavily.

A domestic came in answer to the summons.

" Get me a chair," said Peggy, " and tell me when it is round. Also present my compliments to Mr. Sheldon, and inform him I am gone shopping for the country and will be back by one."

When the maid had left the room a new thought struck Peggy. Going hastily to an inlaid desk she took paper and a quill pen, writing hastily, with many blots and smears. After writing, she read the epistle over, threw sand across it, and then folded and sealed the sheet of paper with the ring that was her mother's, worn on her third finger.

By the time this duty was accomplished, the door opened again and the same domestic returned.

" The chair is at the door, my lady," she said.

Peggy followed, and soon tripped down the steps of the spacious mansion into the murky air of a frosty morning. She was quickly bestowed in the vehicle, and a minute after two beefy chairmen in livery bore the girl through the noisy streets towards the West End.

Peggy looked in at her dressmaker's, hard by Covent Garden, and gossiped there; took the air in St. James's and drank warm milk direct from the cow; after, she turned towards the Strand and went in and out of more shops, finally halting near Villiers Street.

There she left the chair to call in at the bookseller's, and from his place under the swinging sign walked to the corner of Villiers Street, upon the narrow causeway. At the end of the street, where it joined the Strand, a blind man, a regular object of charity, stood with a dog at his feet and a plate held out in his hand. He was a short, thin man, much wrapped up in wool about the neck, his eyes shielded by a green shade, his hands mittened, the blue thumbs showing about the plate he held. At intervals the man cried aloud words that sounded like a prayer. "Of your charity, kind friends, pity the poor blind," he shouted over and over again.

Peggy dropped a gold coin on the plate and the blind man thanked her religiously, calling down fulsome blessings after the manner of the professional takers of charity. Loud, so that all might hear, he hoped that the dear Lord would shower blessings on one so fair and beautiful, and bespoke divine regard for the girl's whole future, relations, and descendants.

"Fie," she said, with a laugh. "Look at me, Blind Tom."

He did not appear to look, continuing his exhortations, but he did see her, and Peggy made a sign and whispered to the man as he slowly ended his stock of blessings.

"Nemo commands—obey," were the words used by the girl.

The beggar made no movement, but stood there with his plate outstretched, looking at nothing with his shielded eyes.

Peggy dropped her sealed note on his plate.

" As quick as the roads will permit, and as fast as men can go," she urged.

He blessed her again loudly, as if he were still taking alms, calling again on God to pour down His bounty on an angel of light. But his free mittened hands, with the blue fingers, came down upon the note, covering it, and from the plate it quickly went to a pocket in his heavy overalls.

" I see it is the ' Lantern,' miss," the blind man said, for, at a glance as quick as an eagle's, he had read Peggy's sprawling, generous hand.

" There will be no mistake," Peggy insisted, " and no delay."

" Bless your bright eyes, no," the blind man answered.

As he spoke he turned to go, the dog leading him along the kerb, the man tapping the stones with his stick and crying out his well-known phrase, " Pity the poor blind; of your charity, pity the poor blind," over and over again. People made way for him and left the road free until he had crossed the street, when he disappeared into an alley and was lost to sight, his familiar cry ending with the turn he took.

As he left the corner of Villiers Street, another man, displaying stumps of arms, took the beggar's place. He made no sign of recognition, and Peggy paid no attention to his cry for alms; but when their eyes met, accidentally, both the girl and the armless man smiled.

As for Peggy, so smiling, she tripped back to her chair, and after an interval, in which the beefiest of the bearers had to be routed out of a tavern by his fellow, resumed her journey. She was jolted by a motion that seemed like a steady curtsey across Covent Garden, into Holborn, through Bloomsbury, and so home.

CHAPTER XV

THE hour was four o'clock ; the day, Tuesday ; the place the "Lantern" at Barnet. The inn was quiet enough, and two men only were in the bay of the big room that looked with unswerving vigilance on the road that leads from Barnet to Hadley Cross.

Outside the light was just beginning to fade. All day long the sun had struggled fitfully to warm the wintry grey sky. Now, sulkily, it had hidden itself in a bank of clouds in the west, and the pearl-grey mists, hovering over the road and turning the stark trees into distorted, fantastic shapes, were deepening in the dusky twilight, awaiting the rising of the moon.

Steve Randall left the bay window and went over to the fire burning in the deep, open hearth. This he kicked vigorously with his heavy boots, until the logs roared and crackled again, a flight of sparks careering up the chimney. The leaping flames served not only to light the room, but flickered on the landlord's swarthy face, and, playing upon his series of double chins, made him look as jovial as the features of an old Toby-jug.

Gratified with the combustion and pleased with the warmth, he sat himself in the chimney corner.

There he was joined by the second man—Swift Nick.

In the short space of a week Nevinson had altered. He was finer drawn, and his face, lean and hard, was roughened, as if it had cleaved much bleak weather. The softer airs of the buck about town had left him ; there was a ring about the way his top boots ground the stone floor, setting the stirrups jingling ; the carriage of his body had the stiff swagger that comes naturally to a man who spends much of his time on horseback. His straight mouth was firm, though a smile showed the saving grace of humour had not left him. The grey eyes of the man were bolder and a hard light blazed in them—the glint that comes of robust living, perfect health, and the taking of chances. His voice was deeper, and the gutturals rasped out the sounds one expects to hear in the speech of those who suffer many hours of exposure. About him was a subtle suggestion of recklessness born of the necessity to move, take chances, and to fight for one's own hand against the law-abiding world.

Swift Nick was dressed for the road. Less of the dandy about him, he was neatly clad. He wore a tight-fitting blue coat with ample skirts, the front double-breasted, and the sleeves turned back into a sort of gauntlet. A neat cravat of white lace showed at the opening about the neck. He had sacrificed the elaborate breech of his day and wore a tight-fitting trouser which ended in heavy riding boots, on which great spurs with big rowels were held by silver chains in the military manner. A light dress sword was buckled to his waist. Two heavy pistols lay upon the table, with a pair of leather gloves and a three-cornered hat caught with a loop of gold braid. The change from his town dandyism was accentuated by the fact that he sported no wig. His own hair, almost black, was worn crisp and short, and gave the set of his head something of the alert intelligence of a high-bred terrier.

Steve Randall warmed two glasses of spiced ale, by the simple process of stirring them with red-hot pokers, and pushed his pock-marked nose gratefully into one of the vessels of purling foam.

" And zithee, lad," he was saying. " You play the Tobyman well, and never a better lad than you ever climbed down from his nag to click his heels in my passage. I like your ways and I like your style. A Tobyman should be a gentleman, rob the rich, give to the poor, keep his tongue still, and remain sober when abroad. A wagging tongue and a love of drinking in strange company made an end of the Golden Farmer."

" As for that, I've no desire to imitate the Golden Farmer," Nicholas said. " A good coup or two and I shall lie low and go back and ruffle it in London."

" Shucks, lad," the other said. " You are safer lying hereabouts. At all events I would not risk the Barnet Road too much if I were you. It's getting too hot for any highwayman. No night-rider ever held so many travellers up in a week as you have done—not even Du Vall—and already the traps are getting keen."

" Damn the traps," said Nicholas, surlily. " Old Starlight can run anything off the road if need be, and there are many more ways than one of approaching the 'Lantern.'"

The other took another pull on his spiced ale.

" Well, youth will be served," Steve Randall said, reflectively. " I mind I was your way once. But no good ever came of being reckless, and never will. A man gets careless. I like your company, and value my best customer since Du Vall went off the road, and I'm not going to see the topsman make carrion of you for the sake of a word of warning. Take my advice; hold off for a week or two and live at your ease."

" Why should I ? " Nicholas asked, with a laugh. " I'm bitten with the challenge of the road. I've got the fever of the fly-by-night. The excitement of the hold-up; the pace of it; the hide and seek by day—all are in my blood. And what's the odds, so long as you are happy ? and devil take the long, dull life when one may live the short and merry one."

" Drink the mulled ale, lad, and get easier thoughts in your mind," Steve Randall said, sagaciously. " S'death, there's only one thing better than the short and merry life; that's a long one and a merrier. And there's reason in what I say. The reward has gone up. There's two hundred guineas on ye. And, hark ye, next week at this pace it will be three hundred, and it's good-bye to ye in these parts, for a man with three hundred guineas on his head will set all the traps agog, nosing about like prize ferrets.

Lie up, I tell you; or if you must go on at this gait, work another road, and get nearer to Doncaster and the cattlemen."

Swift Nick did not answer, but looked gloomily into the fire. He sat idly clinking the sheathed end of his scabbard on the polished boots.

"What's the odds?" he said, at length. "I'm in it now, and I'm going for the goldfinches. A man cannot be a gentleman if he work the road by night and hide by day. I'm going for the big packet, and then it's good-bye to the road and all forgotten, and I hope forgiven."

Steve Randall wagged his big head over these melancholy reflections.

"Girl?" he asked, curiously. "These wenches rattle the best of the Tobymen."

Nicholas shrugged his shoulders and relapsed again into silence.

"I don't know your business," Steve said, querulously; "but if it's a wench, all the more need for caution," he argued, with growing force. "A live loony is worth more than a dead hero to a woman who has got her eye filled with the prospect of mating. Hark ye to my advice and lie low for a week or two. And don't take the road to-night."

Swift Nick looked sulkily at his host for a minute or two.

"All right," he growled. "A bonnie patron of Tobymen you are to turn me chicken-hearted. However, I'll keep dark for a day or two, if that will please you."

The other man stood up and collected the glasses.

"I was young once," he said, "and I know. I'm ag'in the Government, which bleeds poor folk cruel. I'm ag'in the King and the vermin swarming round him. I'm ag'in the army and tax collectors, thieftakers, catchpoles, runners, and traps in general. And it gladdens me to see you take your crack at them and grow fat on their guineas. But I like you, lad, and have done from the night I saw you at the 'Finish,' and I'm damned if I wish to see you come to any harm except by a knock or two in a fair rough and tumble. But now, since there's sense in that reckless poll of yours, let's have another stiff glass of mulled ale, and I'll put you up to some fun that will keep you out of mischief."

He walked off heavily enough after putting the heating irons in the fire, and soon returned with the approved liquor. As the two men sat about the fire, horse hoofs were heard clattering, and a rapidly driven nag came up at a smart canter and was pulled up sharply on the stones before the door.

A man swung off the horse and entered the inn passage. The new-comer was coated and shawled, and his hat was pulled well down over his eyes. He walked stiffly, as if he were half frozen from the ride. For a moment the stranger looked about the house, and finally walked into the room where the two men were sitting.

"Landlord in?" he asked, looking at Steve and speaking throatily.

"That's me," said Steve.

"Letter, addressed 'Hand o' Glory, Lantern,'" he whispered, bending over Steve.

"That's your pippin," said Steve, pointing to Nicholas. "Have something hot?"

"S'blood, yes," the man grunted, hoarsely. "That tipple you are making, laced with brandy, would about thaw me."

He strode to Nick and handed to him a sealed note, which the latter broke open and read.

"Any reply?" asked the laconic stranger.

"None," Nicholas answered. "Any fee for the carriage?"

"No; Nemo calls," the rider replied, hoarsely.

"Well, here's a couple of guineas to drink my health," suggested Nick; "and one is ready for you any time you make the sign."

The other nodded stiffly and took the proffered coins, spun them one by one and put them in an inner pocket.

Randall offered him a hot pewter of mulled ale, laced as he had bespoken.

"You are a stranger to me; whose name shall I give if I am asked?" Steve questioned.

"Silent Harry—Finchley," the messenger replied, wasting no words and taking the steaming pot. Though it seemed scalding hot and reeked of the spices, the man raised it to his lips, swallowed the jorum without taking breath, gulped hard, and then said "Ha!" with a gasp that might have been his voice thawing into a sigh. He held out the empty pot and two flakes of foam dripped to the floor. Then he pulled his coat about him and backed to the door. There he raised his right hand with two fingers pointing upwards.

" Rumpad's blessing," he said. " Good-night and brave pickings."

Nick and the landlord made the same salute, and ere they had done so Silent Harry had disappeared into the passage, was astride his horse, and rattling back again towards London.

" By the Lord, Swift Nick," said Steve, " he's almost as quick as you are. The silent men cover the ground same as I've been telling you. With a still tongue, the Golden Farmer would never have turned night shepherd."

Nick was not heeding him. He began swiftly to withdraw the charges in his pistol and to set them again, being mighty particular with the powder, the packing, and the ball. To the astonishment of the landlord, he drew his sword and made several swift passes at the lighted candle on the table.

His manner had changed. A flush was mounting his cheek; a reckless glitter brightened in his eye; the curl of his lip was a laugh and a threat and a challenge all in one.

" Order round Starlight, Randall," he said, with a crisp suggestion of command in his voice.

Randall's jaw dropped.

" And I had your promise," he said, protestingly.

" And what, in the name of Heaven, is a promise between men against a promise to a woman ? " Nick answered. " Once a Tobyman, always a Tobyman.

I've got the clear call for big game; and if there is a trap to every milestone and a company of catchpoles at every turnpike, sink me for a chicken-livered pantaloon in slippers if I stop and toast my shins by your fire to-night."

"You are going?" gasped Steve, half in anger, for he had made certain of a warm evening with the dice.

"Going," said Nicholas, whirling his three-cornered hat wildly to the ceiling. "By the Hand of Glory—yes. Going to such a game as never a rumpad played before. Heat me some brandy and give me a stirrup cup; it will be strong indeed if it makes my heart beat to a merrier tune. They skinned me in town, old cock-bird," Nicholas said, seizing Randall and dancing him with wild energy about his own parlour, "and, 'fore God, I'll skin them at the cross-roads, as you said. For such a night as this I'd freely give my life and join the Golden Farmer as night shepherd on the forked highway."

"Steady, lad, steady," said Steve. "Take a leaf out of Silent Harry's book."

Nicholas stopped in his wild career and stood in the centre of the room, his dare-devil mouth set firm, his self-control in marked contrast to the turbulent spirits of his previous manner.

"Right, Steve, my buck," he said, grimly. "None so sober as I am from here to Charing Cross. Be easy, and keep a fire going, with a light in the window."

After a look over his horse, standing in the growing darkness, pricking its ears and pawing the stone flags, Nicholas rode off into the gloom.

"Now there's a lad for you,' said, Steve Randall, reflectively looking after him. "He has the makings of the finest roadster of them all. But he's like your true gentleman. He makes a pleasure of the business. I should not be surprised if he shot some one for nothing to-night, just out of sheer kind-heartedness."

Nicholas, on Starlight, flew down the road at a gallop, and was by Whetsone before he drew rein. The road narrowed here, and not a soul was stirring. A group of elms, with thickened trunks, stood in the frosty haze, and their naked branches weaved a spirited pattern against the sky, lightening now with the rising of the moon. They stood some ten yards from the rough highway, and Nick made for them, reining in Starlight between two of the giant trees. There he sat, in the saddle, the horse never moving so much as to paw the dead leaves of last year stirring about its hoofs. Motionless, masked, Nick stood sentinel, as one who was party to a tryst. Minute after minute sped by, and still the man and horse, as if carved out in stone, waited. A rumbling coach rattled out of the gloom and went on. Then silence, and only the murmur of wind about the limbs of the elm. A labourer, with bent head beside a pack-horse, crawled north towards Barnet. And silence again, with the faint breeze still whispering. Followed, the clatter of hoofs, and a chaise, with lighted lamps and one postilion outside, dashed forward.

8

Nick rode out swiftly, and Starlight turned her haunches on the harnessed horses, stopping them suddenly, the postboy cursing, with a pistol at his ear.

An elderly lady looked out, saw the masked figure and screamed.

Nick, looking on her face, raised his hat, noting swiftly that a second woman was the only other occupant.

"Good lady, my mistake," Nick said, bowing. "I give you the right of way as ladies of gentle birth. Drive on, postboy; you are safe as far as Hitchin, the road I warden from Finchley."

The postboy, scarcely believing his ears, tugged on the reins, and, impelled by whip and spur, the horses hauled on the traces and drew away, quickly increasing their pace.

As their lights disappeared, Nick and Starlight again sought the shadow of the elms and waited, the minutes dragging along one by one, and the wind singing a low melody in the swaying branches.

The silence was unbroken save for the night noises of a blanketed world. Low in the sky the moon gathered courage and threw deeper shadows from the trees. Stars above grew clearly defined, as if they were eyes filled to bursting with the comedy of life and set a-twinkling. A wisp of a cloud straggled here and there, mottling the grey sky, and slowly drifting. The baying of a dog sounded miles away; and, closer, the twit-too-hoo of an owl, the most lonesome of night sounds apart from those made by the creeping things that snap twigs or make whirring noises at one's very feet. And then, along the North Road, the clip-clap, clip-clap, clip-clap-clap, of an approaching horse, far off, travelling at the canter, the sound impeded by rising ground for a moment or two, and then coming on, each beat of the hoof ringing with startling clearness as the animal drew nearer. Out of the gloom it came until one could see the shape and the form of a rider, and could even hear the latter curse and coax as his mount stumbled. As the new-comer swept forward at the hand gallop, Swift Nick rode out, a touch of the spur prompting Starlight to a well-studied rush—a trick of the road taught by Du Vall—which brought his haunches into the flanks of the other horse, causing it to falter and then to stop trembling in its course.

The traveller was Sir Ladbroke Drake, and it shows the readiness of the man's resource that, despite the sudden discomfiture of his steed, he lost no time in making his defence.

Without a second of hesitation, he drew a pistol out of his holster and covered Nick, who sat almost opposite to him, his horse facing the way the traveller had come.

" What damned game is this? " Sir Ladbroke asked, roaring hoarsely.

" The same old game," Swift Nick answered, easily. " The pleasure of your company until you have paid toll through Barnet."

" You are the new collector, are you? " shouted Sir Ladbroke Drake, a threat in his voice. " Then, by the Lord Harry, I'll plug lead into you without further parley."

Sir Ladbroke suited the action to the word. He raised the heavy pistol and covered Nick. His action was so sudden that his opponent was at his mercy. For a second the highwayman's life hung in the balance. In that second Sir Ladbroke pulled the trigger. There was a click. With a gasp of relief, Nick saw no responsive flame nor heard the crash of the explosion. The flint of the weapon had failed to give off its spark. Quick as thought Nick caught Sir Ladbroke's hand, and with a twist and a jerk sent the pistol flying out of his grasp. At the same moment, he covered Sir Ladbroke with his own pistol, and that rider looked along its shining barrel into a pair of resolute grey eyes gleaming angrily through openings in a mask.

Swift Nick laughed recklessly.

"So, ho!" he said; "you'd make carrion of me with short shrift, would you? Dismount, and keep your hand off the other holster, or I'll give you as much lead as you meant to give me, and there'll be no slip 'twixt cup and lip, or between your mangy body and my bullet. Down, I say—down!"

Nicholas held the man at his mercy, and Sir Ladbroke had no other option but to obey the command.

When he stood on the ground, the other towered above him.

"It's your money I want, and, rip me, you are lucky if I give you the alternative of life," Nick said, sternly. "Turn out your pockets, or, 'fore God, I'll let a bullet into your gullet and rid the world of a rascal."

"And curse you for having the luck of the devil, for man to man I'd be your equal or better," Sir Ladbroke growled, "and not a damned guinea of mine would you see."

"Better or equal, I know not for the moment. Turn out your pockets and let's see how many gold-finches they nest."

Sir Ladbroke began sulkily to obey, and handed out a purse which bulked heavily in Nick's hand.

Nevinson was not content with this. He insisted on Sir Ladbroke turning out every one of his pockets, and sure enough his precaution was justified. As the inside of the third pocket was revealed, Nick saw a purse fall to the ground, bulkier and heavier than the first, and heard the cheerful chink of the gold within it.

Still covering his man, Nick wiped him down with his tongue.

"Do you cheat at every game you play?" Nick asked, scornfully. "You have ill repute at cards or dice, and now you would cheat an honest Toby-man. Sir Ladbroke Drake, you are a damned worse rogue than I am."

At the mention of his name, Sir Ladbroke looked up.

"You know me?" he asked. "Who, in the devil's name, are you?"

"One whom you do not know, but who knew you in the old days. And, sirrah! I have an old score to pick with you. You talk of being my equal or better. May I ask if you have any choice of weapons ?''

'' On equal terms I'll undertake to bring you to your marrows with the sword,'' Sir Ladbroke answered, eagerly.

'' Then, rip me, you shall try it,'' Nick volunteered.

Nevinson started to dismount. As he did so, Sir Ladbroke pulled on the holster of his own horse, and freeing a second pistol presented it at Swift Nick. The latter, when he turned round, looked into its menacing barrel. For a second Swift Nick again thought life was all up for him. His opponent wasted no words, but pulled on the trigger, and the weapon crashed and spouted a stream of flame. The ball whistled harmlessly high above Nick's head, for at that moment a man had stepped from the hedge and knocked the weapon up with a blow of a stout cudgel.

'' A damned, dirty trick !'' a voice Nicholas knew well enough said aloud. '' Fair play is bonnie play, and I'm here to see it. Shall I spit the knave ? ''

'' Nemo ! '' ejaculated Nevinson, with something like glee. The King of Beggars, tattered as Nick had first seen him, stood revealed. '' I owe you thanks. Your coming is an advance on account from the Hand of Glory. But don't misuse the cur,'' he said. '' I've a mind to test his sword play, of which he brags so freely, for your entertainment.''

Sir Ladbroke Drake was almost beside himself with anger at the opportunity so unexpectedly turned against him.

" Damme, you roadsters have had my gold. What more do you want ? " he asked, urgently.

" The privilege of testing your play with the blade," Nick answered. " I give you my word of honour you shall go free if our encounter end to your advantage. Draw, and let's see you make good your boast."

Sir Ladbroke's spirit leaped at the challenge. Not for nothing had he a reputation for swordsmanship. It would be ill work if he could not disarm a roadster, who would be unskilled in the finer arts of the game. With a quick movement he drew his blade and put himself upon guard to meet the shock of the man pressing on to him.

Sir Ladbroke met the onslaught, and with confidence became the aggressor. He had not the slightest doubt of the issue. But almost as soon as he felt the counter of his unknown opponent, his confidence evaporated. He knew from the " touch " of the other blade that the foeman was worthy of his steel. He tried his favourite lunge, the counter to which was known only to a few notorious swordsmen. As in his duel with Nevinson, a week before, he found a blade as firm as a wall of iron. It held his for a moment ; the weight and power of the man behind bore heavily on his own weapon ; an upward heave forced the sword out of his hand and it fell with a metallic rattle into the road.

Nick laughed aloud and pressed the point of his sword to Sir Ladbroke's throat.

" Who is master, I say ? " he asked, mockingly. "Who is equal or superior ? Rip me, out with it, man, or I'll press my advantage with the point at your throat."

Nemo, the beggar, laughed in sympathy.

"By the gods, you are the prince of Tobymen," he said. "As neat a preparation for pigsticking as ever I did see."

"Who is the kingpin at your game, Sir Ladbroke? Out with it, man," Nick insisted.

Sir Ladbroke Drake moistened his white lips and bowed grudgingly.

"You have the honour, whoever you are," he said, his voice dull with anger and humiliation.

"Then go your ways," Nick said, "and tell of your encounter. It will be pretty news for your friends to know you were stripped and disarmed on equal terms by a common Tobyman, before a laughing beggar."

The other slowly mounted his horse, and, leaving the two, highwayman and beggar, rode off towards Barnet.

As he drew away, Sir Ladbroke ground his teeth and shook his fist at the moon.

"As I live, I know that parry," he said to himself, hot with anger. "Only once have I met that counter in this country, and by the same hand. Swift Nick is none other than my old pigeon, Nicholas Nevinson, Esquire. It is news that will bear keeping, and Master Nevinson shall have occasion to remember the day he turned the trick on me for the second time."

Swift Nick had committed his first indiscretion as a Tobyman.

CHAPTER XVI

NICHOLAS watched Sir Ladbroke Drake mount his horse and clatter down the highway towards Bedford. Then he turned to Nemo, who stood, a sinister figure enough in his beggar's attire, grinning at the turn of events.

Swift Nick thanked his new friend cordially for his timely intervention.

"By the Lord, Nemo, you were in the game at the right time. Another second and he would have blown off the roof of my pate. I put your interference down as a working of the Hand of Glory. I can hear the whistle of that ball yet."

"A close call, sure enough," Nemo answered. "But a miss is as good as a mile. Where fares my merry rumpad now? Zounds, you play the Tobyman as no fly-by-night has ever dared in my time."

"Yes; and there's better game afoot," Swift Nick laughed, stroking Starlight's nose.

Very briefly he told Nemo of his plans. In her note, for Peggy had written to Nick, she had informed him both of Sir Ladbroke Drake's and her uncle's journey north. She had told of their proposed residence at the Chequers, the time of their start, and had begged Nick to communicate as quickly as possible on her arrival.

It was Nick's intention to do more than this. He planned to give the girl greeting on the highway as she went towards Hitchin, despite the fact that his lady was burdened with the presence of her guardian—John Sheldon—and his escort.

All this he explained to Nemo, whose eyes glittered at the comedy of the situation, for the beggar king had a taste for the grotesque.

Together, they estimated that the Sheldon coach, with its escort, would travel slowly and would not be due anywhere near Barnet for the best part of two hours. They accordingly designed to leave the highway for an hour of ease and shelter, and piloted by Nemo they went circuitously back to the "Lantern," for the beggar had no difficulty in making a mount materialise in the wilds of the country about them. There they spent an hour, maturing their plans, over hot grog supplied by Steve Randall.

The roads seemed deserted to Swift Nick and his friend, but at the "Lantern," Barnet, they came upon members of the beggars' fraternity, who told them the village was agog with the arrival of Sir Ladbroke, and that the traps had broken out and were chasing Nick, pell-mell, in the direction of London.

Steve Randall was openly concerned about their activities. Strangers had been in the house during the day, and he had heard whispered talk of the reward. Indeed, Nick found his presence as warden of the North Road an increasing peril as his activities widened and the toll of his exploits lengthened. He still fancied he had preserved the secret of his identity and that no one but the society of the "Lantern" knew the nature of his associations. As for Steve Randall, he begged again that Nick should pay heed to the danger and lie low, but he got but little satisfaction for his pains.

An hour later, Nick set out, after spending a merry interval at the "Lantern," Nemo accompanying him. For his new purpose Nick had pressed the beggar king and four of his associates into service, to balance the escort he knew would travel with John Sheldon. As they were unmounted the four sturdy beggars had gone on before, with instructions to stay at the elms which had shielded Swift Nick at the moment when he halted Sir Ladbroke Drake.

Punctual to the minute, Nick and Nemo clattered up the road and backed their horses between the clump of great trees. Almost as soon as they had come to a standstill, four dark figures slowly emerged from the shadows of the trees, and proved to be their associates in the enterprise.

They had hardly an interval in which to make their greetings and to pass their plans under rapid review, when sounds of an approaching vehicle were heard. By this time the moon had fully risen. Although the air was misty still, the road, whitened by the frost, stood clearly defined both up and down, though in the clump of trees neither Nicholas nor one of the five mumpsters could be seen by passengers who kept to the rough track.

The approach of the coach was heralded by the sound of many horses' hoofs and the steady, grinding rumble of the heavy wheels. The Sheldon party were travelling slowly at not more than six miles an hour, as the men in hiding could estimate by the fact that the horses were not going faster than the trot. Impatiently they waited until the headlights of the coach gleamed a few hundred yards away, when the vehicle drew clear of a bend in the road. From where they watched, the coach could be seen looming up, with its great box seat on which sat the coachman so swathed in coats and shawls that he could hardly move. Two men rode in front of the coach, while four more of the escort trotted behind. All were travelling comfortably enough, their numbers having communicated a sense of security. The party came on towards the sinister elms, where the road narrowed, until they were nearly opposite, when above the roar of the grinding wheels and the clatter of horses a sharp voice, sounding crisp and clear in the frosty air, called out the one word " Halt ! "

The coachman was typical of his class. He had no stomach for the night ambush, and believed the command would be followed by a bullet directed at his head. He pulled heavily on the team, until he had the two leaders round, while the horses behind were hauled up, short, their flanks quivering, on the front wheels of the coach. As the coachman stopped a crabbed, angry face appeared at the window, and a voice cursed him roundly for responding to the challenge. The escort, six in number, halted irregularly and peered anxiously towards the side of the road.

"Throw down your arms or we fire," the same voice shouted, and, as he spoke, the five men with Nick yelled and cheered lustily. The noise they made in the listening silence seemed enough to wake the dead. To the escort, peering nervously from the road, the volume of the six voices was magnified until it appeared to them as if a small army were concealed in the trees.

The voice of John Sheldon could be heard, loudly rating his escort.

"Spit me," he said, "what have I brought you here for, men—for a picinc with pixies and fairies in the wood? Have at the rascals and fill them with lead. That's what you are come for, and not to see me made to stand and deliver on the call of the first cutpurse who bleats the word 'Halt'!"

"But there are many of them," the leader of the escort said aloud, and his voice sounded like a whimper. "They have cover, too. We shall be riddled."

"And a damned good job," the traveller in the coach answered, "if that's the stuff ye are made on. Hark ye! at them, I say."

The escort wavered and made some pretence of closing up and acting according to their duty. Just as they did so a figure came from the shadow of the elms and rode clear into the moonlight. He was masked, and sat his horse like a statue; but all noticed he carried a pistol levelled directly at the wavering group. With little heart or

stomach for the job, the escort began to raise their
weapons.

" Stand ! " said the ringing voice of the solitary
man on horseback. " Stand, I tell you, while your
heads are on. We have double your number in
the wood, and, by the Lord, if a single shot is fired,
you are all dead men."

As he spoke, again arose the cry of the hidden
men, at once a derisive cheer and a threat, and
sounding appallingly like the presence of a great
crowd.

" Throw down your arms without further parley,"
commanded Swift Nick, " or your blood be on your
own heads."

The leader of the escort, a stout middle-aged
man in the service of the city magnate, turned
white to the gills. He lowered his weapon and
looked to his friends.

" Force is force," he said, nervously ; " we don't
want to fight an army."

His suggestion was received with silent approval.
One by one the men lowered their carbines.

" That's right, my men," jeered Swift Nick's
laughing voice. " Now ride on slowly, and remember you are being watched as you go. The coach
will catch you up at Barnet."

" Damn you for a lot of chicken-hearted scum,"
roared John Sheldon, angrily. " If you won't fight,
by the Lord, I will."

As he spoke, he thrust out his arm and pointed
a pistol at Swift Nick. The moment he did so
there was a blaze of shots from the elm-trees, and

the bullets whistled, startling most of the horses. This was too much for the escort, who saw the blaze of firearms and heard the whiz of the ball amongst them. They gave rein to their horses, and fled down the highway towards Barnet.

John Sheldon, hot with anger at being deserted, would have pulled on the trigger, but a feminine voice in the carriage spoke to him, and some one lugged on his elbow.

"For Heaven's sake don't shoot, uncle," she said. "They'll fall on us like wolves, and worse ill will come upon all if you fire. Parley with the man and see what he wants."

Swift Nick heard Peggy Sheldon's voice. He rode up to the carriage window, poked a big pistol into the face of John Sheldon, and peered into the carriage through the slits in his black mask.

"Stand, I tell you, and deliver," he said, sternly. "The lady speaks the words of wisdom. Stand, or I'll blow the teeth out of your head."

John Sheldon put up his pistol.

"What would you have of me?" he asked, in an altered tone.

"That's a more civil manner," Swift Nick laughed. "I came to greet you on the road, and give you pleasant passage."

"Well, in Heaven's name let my man get on. That's the pleasantest passage you can give me," Sheldon rasped out.

The coachman sat huddled upon his box, looking, as a man who had no part in the altercation, on the highwayman.

"Softly, friend; softly," Nick returned, gaily. "You must pay the toll. Deliver up, and you'll have smooth passage enough after."

John Sheldon drew out a heavy purse.

"Here, take this," he said, unwillingly, "and be gone. And may every guinea hurry you on the road to hell."

"I thank you for a prettily spoken gentleman," said Nick, taking the grudgingly offered purse. "Your manners are almost as pretty as your companion."

"You give my coachman the word," Sheldon blustered. "You've had your toll, devil take you; what more do you want?"

"I see you do not like my company," Swift Nick returned. "Take it for granted, I do not keep you here for the pleasure of yours. I covet the necklace the lady has about her throat and the rings upon her fair fingers."

Swift Nick could just see the face of the girl outlined in the far corner of the coach in the dim light of a carriage lamp. It was the face he had longed to see for many days, and he noticed with admiration that the cheeks had not blanched, nor was there a tremor in her voice.

"Why, sir," she said, in an even voice that carried an appeal, "you would not rob me of my poor trinkets. You have had your pound of flesh of my good uncle here."

"Aye, his purse is heavy enough," Nick answered. "These wealthy cits, for I judge him to be one of them, go well lined; and since you put my gallantry to the test you shall keep your jewels at a price."

"And what may the price be ? " she asked, and her dark eyes shot him a cold challenge.

"A kiss," he answered, boldly. "The price of nearly all the geegaws in the world."

"But not the price of these," Peggy answered, with heat. "I kiss no fly-by-night who uses his power to insult a woman."

As she spoke Peggy tore off a necklace from underneath the collar of her coat, and drew some rings from her fingers.

"Here," she said ; "take them and be gone." As she spoke she thrust the jewels into Nick's hands.

"Hoity, toity!" he replied ; "our Mistress Disdain is very proud, and values her kisses highly."

"Higher than I value your company," she retorted, with spirit.

"Gad! a lass after my own heart," Nick returned, and there was something youthful in his accompanying laugh.

John Sheldon scowled on the highwayman.

"Now you have despoiled the lady," he said, "perhaps we may go. We can cut out the rest of the foolery, for plucked pigeons are no good to those who live by the feathers."

"Easy, sir ; easy," Nick replied. "A civil tongue never palls in the wagging, just as kind words never die. I'm no despoiler of ladies, and would make a proposal to your fair companion. List to me. lady," Nick said, addressing himself to Peggy,

" I'll hand you back your geegaws if you will step out and dance a measure with me, on the road."

She laughed aloud.

" A pretty figure I should cut," she replied. " I do not fancy catching my death of cold over such an adventure, much as I would like to keep my possessions. Besides, there is no music."

" As for that, Nemo shall whistle—Nemo, who is king of the road and is always obeyed—while we dance," Nick said.

Peggy started as she heard the words. The spoken phrase had been much in her mind and ears for many days.

" A measure is little enough for my jewels," she said, with promptness. " If my uncle will await, I'll dance to Nemo's music."

Swift Nick laughed loudly.

" It is mighty pleasant of you," he replied. " Be sure your uncle will wait. I hold the road, and all who travel hang upon my word. What ho, there, Nemo !"

Nick's hail was quickly answered by the appearance of a man on horseback—the grotesque figure of the King of the Road, who, though he wore peasant garb and a make-up that made him appear an emaciated wreck, rode as smartly as a trooper.

" What is the trick of the game ? " he asked, coming up at a gallop.

" Do you hold my horse and keep guard on this city bug in the coach. The lady will dance with me," Nick said.

" A merry sight, in good sooth," said Nemo,

jovially. "A fitting pleasantry for a happy meeting."

Nick quickly dismounted and handed the reins to his friend. As he did so, Peggy came to the door of the coach. There was something like laughter in her eyes and about her oval face; her manner was strangely assured and confident.

"I'm ready to dance for my jewels," she said, almost merrily.

"But this is nonsense," Sheldon glowered. "Let the man take the trinkets and be gone. We have suffered sufficient humiliation."

"La, uncle! a dance is worth the while if I save my mother's necklace," she answered. "I am at your service," she added, looking at Nicholas with brightening eyes.

Nicholas held out his hand with a flourish and a bow. A warm, eager ungloved hand was pressed within his own. With a light jump Peggy Sheldon leapt from the high coach, despite the further protests of her guardian, and was caught by Nicholas, standing on the road.

A faint blush mantled Peggy's face as her eyes met those glancing with laughing tenderness from behind the black mask.

"Faith, my gallant," the girl said, "it is ill footing a measure without music."

"I had forgotten, my lady," Nick answered, pressing her hand. "Nemo, my buck, can you whistle?"

"Like the thrush," he answered. "And always better on a cold night after good pickings."

"Then throw a stave or two of a minuet while the lady gives me the honour of a dance. And keep that Jack-in-the-box in the coach quiet. He growls like a damned Roundhead over a pleasant diversion. If the killjoy interferes I give you leave to strangle him, so long as you keep on whistling and do not spoil the dance."

And so John Sheldon, angry to the point of madness, had to look upon a sight that made his purse-proud soul wince. There on the frost-whitened road stood the coach, the driver huddled up and taking no part in the altercation, and himself a prisoner deserted by his escort; the door held by a hideous, emaciated, but truculent rascal, who piped with the gaiety of a lark flying skyward on a summer's day, as he reined in his own horse and Nick's. Coming from the shadow of the trees, four other figures, creeping closer for their own amusement—the last humiliation of all, for Sheldon had believed with his men that the force was double the strength of his escort. In the moonlight Peggy, catching up her skirt and the folds of the heavy fur travelling cloak, was dancing with zest, and appeared intermittently as Sheldon dodged to view the scene from the coach window, half blocked as it was by Nemo, whose position showed qualities of design rather than accident.

Sheldon would have been still more discomfited could he have known that the dancing figures were talking and what they said.

As they made stately bows preliminary to the dance, Peggy gasped out her delight.

" Nick—you dear, of all men," she whispered.

" Peggy—you darling, of all women," he said, and his voice stirred her with its strong emotion.

" You dared this, for me ? " she said.

" This and much more," he answered. " Were you afraid ? "

" La, no ! " she answered. " I was delighted. I knew your voice almost as soon as you spoke, and was confirmed in my guess when you spoke of Nemo."

They whirled together to Nemo's piping, and Nick thrilled to the contact of her warm, lithe dancing figure.

" Nick, I am in danger," she murmured, swaying on his arm, her breath coming short and clipping the words. " Watch over me at the Chequers. They take me there to force a marriage upon me with Sir Ladbroke Drake."

" I'll see you do not go unprotected a single hour," he replied, stepping back, bowing, and resuming the dance according to its figures.

" I would not have come, but I felt it safer to be near you," Peggy sighed.

" There is no power they can use that I cannot break, so long as they stop near the road. To-morrow I will find a way for you to tell me all that happens."

They were whirling somewhere behind the coach and out of view of Sheldon.

Nick drew her, unresisting, closer to him, and kissed her unprotesting lips.

" You make me very happy, master—er—Swift

Nick," she said, and she hung close and warm in his embrace.

"And I am happier still," he answered, and kissed Peggy again and again.

They might have forgotten the coach, the frosty road, Nemo and his men standing sentinel, and Sheldon fuming. But suddenly Nemo's piping melody stopped and their dance ended.

"Horses on the road," he called. "Damn us for a lot of fops in a ballroom. End it, Nick, and let's ride hell-for-leather, or we greet the topsmen and dance at the end of a length of hemp in the frosty morning."

Nick led Peggy to the coach with much ceremony, the two walking as if they were leaving the floor of the Argyle Rooms.

"I thank you, sir," he said to John Sheldon, helping Peggy to the coach. "A lady of charming breeding and nicely trained in the dance."

Peggy was in the coach, John Sheldon sulkily making way.

"Permit me to offer you a souvenir," Nick said, lightly, and handing Peggy her trinkets with a gallant flourish.

"La, Mr. Highwayman!" she said; "you are most kind."

"He is a damned gallows bird," Sheldon said. "I hope to hear of his hanging by morning."

Nicholas banged the door in Sheldon's angry face.

Away in the north the sound of rapidly driven horses was growing more audible; the speed of their approach almost indicated the impulse driving them forward.

" Take care, my buck," said Nick, mounting his horse and firing a parting shot at Sheldon. " 'Tis not only the fly-by-night who meets the topsman. Lady, I salute you with many thanks for your charming company."

He could not see Peggy's face, but the movement of her head showed that she had bowed.

" Hoicks, lads, away !" Nick commanded peremptorily, turning rapidly to Nemo.

With a sweep of his hat to the now moving coach, Swift Nick spurred his horse to the gallop, in the wake of Nemo travelling south, the other padsmen having scattered and taken to cover in the woods. John Sheldon, fuming in his coach, rode northwards to meet the traps, nor did he see in his anger that Peggy was smiling as she kissed the rings upon her round white fingers, or he would have been more angry still.

CHAPTER XVII

ON the day following Swift Nick's encounter with Sir Ladbroke Drake, the latter arrived at the Chequers late in the afternoon. He was greeted grimly enough by John Sheldon, but by Peggy with unconstrained cordiality.

The dinner party of three, that night, was friendly. The chatter was light as the courses were served. None would have thought that Peggy Sheldon, her uncle and guardian, John Sheldon, and Sir Ladbroke Drake represented three varying, clashing wills, at war with each other and wholly irreconcilable.

So free was the atmosphere and so easily did they seem to mingle that Sir Ladbroke Drake considered his plans were approaching fulfilment as easily and naturally as fruit ripens on the fertile branches swaying in the summer sun. He did not know, and indeed could not, that the first morning after her arrival Peggy had met Nicholas Nevinson, and had laid the understanding between her uncle and Sir Ladbroke Drake, as she knew it, before her lover.

The Chequers was a fine mansion, standing just outside Hitchin in its own grounds, and away from the high road. The old hall was a building of grey stone, low and squat, with many windows looking on a terrace that fronted well-kept lawns. From the highway a spacious carriage drive ran for a mile between an avenue of chestnut trees. It led directly to the main entrance, a door with a stone canopy built out for shelter, under which carriages drew to deposit their burdens on the steps that led to the hall.

The Chequers was a family residence of the finer type of country house, which had passed through vicissitudes during the banishment of the Stuarts and had come to John Sheldon by intrigue with Roundhead usurpers, into whose hands the mansion had fallen.

Although John Sheldon's purpose was clear, he had put no constraint on Peggy. He was content to believe that away from London she was in his power and would be amenable as soon as pressure had to be used to force the girl in the direction of his desires. The knowledge withheld from Sir Ladbroke Drake was also withheld from her treacherous guardian. He, too, did not know Peggy had that very day seen her lover in the arbour, and had poured out her misgivings. Nor was he aware that Swift Nick had allayed Peggy's fears with much lover-like talk and some substantial proofs of his power to aid her. When Peggy left Swift Nick, after a tender meeting, she had been provided with a line of communication as infallible as the system devised for her use in London.

During the first two days of her stay at Chequers

Court, Peggy had no complaint to make of the attitude of the two men. They treated her with profound respect when they all met about the house. Sometimes, looking at the calculating face of her guardian, Peggy would find his ugly eyes fixed upon her, speculatively. Again, when Sir Ladbroke, at their quiet dinners, took more wine than was good for his discretion, he would make covert allusions to his proposals with a familiarity bordering on the intolerable. Both men, however, appeared content with the seeming impregnability of their position and were apparently prepared to bide their time. As for Peggy, she made the most of her awkward situation. Her nonchalant civility in meeting Sir Ladbroke subtly encouraged him to believe his plans were maturing without trouble ; while avoidance of any scene between Peggy and her uncle left John Sheldon easier of mind and firmly convinced that his wishes in the matter of the proposed marriage would not be actively opposed.

The two men were much together. They spent hours examining bulky packages of papers and reading messages arriving almost daily on horseback. When Peggy approached them suddenly, she would find the pair in absorbed conclave, but the substance of their conversation would be broken off as soon as they were aware of her proximity. Their preoccupation was obvious. There was something furtive about their movements ; something sinister about the conversations so often clipped off in the middle of a sentence as she approached ; something uneasy in the comings and goings of the many messengers, who rode up to the great hall door, were admitted, delivered their statements, and then were shown out, to ride or drive rapidly away. John Sheldon, when the house was uninterrupted, spent many hours each day in his study, and there Sir Ladbroke remained closeted with him for the major part of the mornings and the afternoons. The Chequers ran smoothly in every detail of its routine, save for the constant coming and going of travel-soiled strangers; but the silent house seemed to be quiet, with the kind of calm that presages the bursting of a storm. About the mansion a mystery was brooding, itself part of the strange happenings Peggy had noted in the Bloomsbury residence of John Sheldon without being able to pierce the secret.

Left to herself, Peggy spent much time in exploring the Chequers. The great rambling house was almost new to her, for she had only stayed there once before, and that for only a few days in passing on a visit north. There were many interesting features about the house, and not a few mysteries. Peggy had been allotted a suite of rooms on the second floor. From the corridor, a door led into her boudoir, and through this room, and only to be entered that way, was her bedroom. One of the curious discoveries she made was connected with this inner bedroom. Both boudoir and bedroom were large, sombre apartments, heavily panelled, and the carved oak that covered the walls seemed as solid as rock itself.

On the Wednesday after her arrival, Peggy had

remained in her apartment all the afternoon, sitting reading before a great fire. She had thrown her book carelessly aside when the light had begun to fail, and had sat, reflectively watching the glow of the fire, until the firelight had turned to darkness. A lantern clock bracketed on the wall had struck the hour of six and brought Peggy out of her reverie with a start. It was time to dress for dinner and the evening. She rose, intending to call her maid and procure lights. Peggy pulled on the bell-rope in her boudoir, and waited some minutes without receiving an answer. Repeating the summons, the outcome was again abortive. Fancying the bell was out of order, she had groped her way into the bedroom, and in the dark had felt for the other bell-rope, which hung on the right side of the fireplace. In groping round the space, in the gloom, she had stumbled. To save herself from falling, the girl had put out her hands. One, her right, fell upon a solid panel and steadied her. The pressure of the left hand was not resisted. The panel she had touched gave way.

The bell, once found, brought the necessary servant with the lights, and as soon as she had withdrawn Peggy went back to the bedroom to examine the woodwork that had given under her pressure.

She found one panel had opened, and looking closer, discovered it swung on a fine hinge like a trap-door. Peggy placed her hand through the opening, and feeling round, discovered a bolt. This she drew and then applied the weight of her young shoulders against the oak. A huge section of the wall gave way before her—sufficient to allow any one to pass through the woodwork. Raising her candle, Peggy found that she had undoubtedly discovered a secret door. Looking through the aperture, she saw an empty space behind the walls, leading to narrow steps that went down into a gloom her candle would not dispel.

Peggy's curiosity was stirred by the discovery, but her maid was due. Quickly she dragged the big section of the panel back into position, pushed the bolt home, and pulled the trap-door into its place. The girl's curiosity was stirred by the discovery, but she deferred further inquiry to a more favourable moment, and some instinct told her to keep the knowledge of the sliding panels to herself.

Friday came at the Chequers. The week had dragged on uneventfully, and the routine had not been altered. Peggy had dined with her uncle and Sir Ladbroke. Both men had been talking as she entered the dining-room, and both, greeting her with a bow, stopped the conversation as if it had been cut with a knife.

After dinner the two men spent an hour with Peggy. Sir Ladbroke, who had taken much wine, paid her many fulsome compliments, a smile meant to be winning on his flushed and crafty face. He had even hinted at a possible reconsideration of his proposal, and without concealing her distaste for the subject she had curtly turned the reference.

Sir Ladbroke Drake did not pursue the matter, but smiled meaningly across at his host.

John Sheldon rose stiffly on his spare limbs.

"I shall be obliged if you will give me your company in the library," he said, walking towards the door.

"What, and leave the most divine of women!" Sir Ladbroke answered, breaking into a smile that was a leer.

"With your permission, gentlemen," Peggy said, "I will retire. I was up and out over-early this morning and am fatigued."

Her uncle turned and bowed to the girl as he continued to walk from the room.

Peggy went towards the door in his wake, and Sir Ladbroke Drake, stepping aside, offered his hand with a bow, which she took with a curtsey, and gave her precedence.

Peggy reached her boudoir, where her maid was waiting, and passed into the inner bedroom. A fire was blazing on the open hearth. Three candles were lighted. The room looked very cosy. With the assistance of her tiring-woman Peggy disrobed, and then enfolded herself in a heavily quilted dressing-gown. The maid pulled a chair before the fire and stood waiting expectantly. Peggy sank into the seat, took up a book, stretched her limbs towards the blaze, and yawned slightly.

"Place the candle near me," she said to the waiting girl.

Martha obeyed, quietly.

"You may go now, Martha," Peggy said, sleepily. "I shall not want you again."

"Good-night, milady," the maid answered.

Peggy sat before the fire, heard the door pulled

to, and listened until her maid's pattering feet had died away along the corridor. Then throwing off the assumed sleepiness, she sprang up, cast the volume on the bed, went through the boudoir and locked the outer door.

" And now to see the mystery of the secret door," she said, glancing once more in the softly lighted bedroom and staring intently at the panelled oak, her heart beating rapidly.

Within, the house was silent as the grave. Once she heard a door bang on the floor below; else there was no other sound of life in the gloomy mansion. Outside, the wind moaned slightly and the driving rain beat on the leaded panes. The noise without served but to accentuate the silence within the rambling old house. Peggy shivered as she drew her wraps closely about her shapely frame.

She pressed on the panel, and the square of wood gave way. A pull on the bolt liberated the whole section and left open the space down which she had looked for the first time a day or two before. The passage amid the stonework looked gloomy enough, and a cold, earthy taint rose to greet her in a way that repelled. Peggy, holding a lighted candle, the fine edge of her courage gone, still pressed on, and found herself walking down the stone steps. The steps evidently led to the ground floor below, and in the mysterious darkness, only half dispelled by the candlelight, Peggy began to trace the secret passage. To the girl's excited fancy there seemed miles of it. The passage wound about, making awkward angles, and Peggy, turning the corners, expecting to find the end, would be confronted with another mysterious-looking section. After many minutes, however, she found the passage ended abruptly, and, looking closely, the wall that barred her passage proved to be another section of panelling. By the candlelight the girl noted that the construction of the panelling was the same. A rusty bolt, inside the passage, when drawn, opened the false door towards her, and the girl, creeping out, found herself at the end of the corridor leading straight through the house from the entrance hall to the door that opened on the gardens in the rear of the Chequers.

The place was in darkness as she looked out, and Peggy did not stay for more than a second or two. Then, hastily pulling the panel back, she again stood in the secret passage, ready to make the return journey.

Peggy found herself breathless with the excitement of a strange adventure, and perhaps slightly chilled, but the girl's face brightened as she thought over the details of the unusual quest. The knowledge she had gained pleased her. At least she had a line of retreat from the rooms if anything untoward happened, was her first thought ; her second was to wonder if any of the household, most of all her uncle, knew of this secret exit. Speculating over her adventure, Peggy began to retrace her steps back to the bedroom.

The silence of the dark passages had excited the girl, and made her nervously sensitive. She began to imagine the presence of some one else, either in front or behind, and saw ghosts in the shadows cast by her candle. Once, a rat, squeaking, pattered away in front of her, and set her heart beating rapidly. Peggy had traversed half of the passage back, every sense alert, and was quickening her pace, when she heard the sound of a human voice. It seemed so distinct that, for a moment, the girl thought the speaker was in the passage, at her elbow, and halted. As she did so, the voice was raised again, and in a flash Peggy recognised the thin, acid monotones of Sir Ladbroke Drake. She guessed at once that the passage had brought her on the other side of the panelling of the library used as a study by her uncle.

" And so it is all complete," Sir Ladbroke was saying distinctly, his voice as clear as if she were sitting in the room opposite to him. " You say the city will march out at your bidding."

" Sufficient for our purpose, when I say the word," answered the crabbed voice of John Sheldon.

" Then let us make it a fortnight to-day," Sir Ladbroke said. " Rowley will be at York, on his journey south. If your men come out, a thousand strong, we shall gather an army as we go. Bedford is right. Sir John Lechmore will take the field with five hundred men. And so it is, in every village and town from here to Grantham and Doncaster. The country is seething, and you have only to put your men on the road, and from every village fifty men will ride against the King, and from every town anything from a hundred to five. I tell you the thing is safe. The Protestants are mad with

9

hate of him, first because of the taxes, and second because of the rumour he has turned Catholic and is drawing subsidies from France."

Peggy, listening, heard the voice going on in a confident, unwavering monotone. Quietly she tip-toed twenty yards down the corridor and placed her candle on the floor. Then she returned in the dark-ness, until the sound of voices told the girl she was back again beside the library wall.

Peggy felt the stone wall, and found that it ended for a space that made a doorway and was just such another opening as the one formed by the swinging panels of her room. In the dark a gleam of light showed. A knot in the wood had been displaced, and left a hole through which she could command the room. Looking, she saw Sir Ladbroke Drake, sitting in a high chair opposite a table, a glass of wine before him. Opposite, with chair drawn to a table littered with papers, sat John Sheldon, his piglike eyes contracted as he listened to Sir Lad-broke, the colour of his thin face resembling more than ever a piece of yellow parchment wrinkled with age.

" And you say it is safe," he said, at last.

" S'death—as safe as human chances can be," Sir Ladbroke Drake said, smiling. " A Hampden would set the country alight from one end to the other ; another Cromwell would break the King himself. Have them here, I say. Lechmere of Bedford ; Barrington of Grantham ; Nichols of Retford ; and all the little squires in between. Let them meet your city friends and see you are in earnest. Then give the word, and, by the Lord, you'll set England ablaze from here to York. You'll break this fool who struts in England as King!"

John Sheldon rose slowly and gnawed a quill pen reflectively. For a moment or two, he paced the apartment in deep reflection, calculation writ large on his thin cheeks, in which the nerves were dancing with excitement.

"To break the King!" he said, at last. "Yes —that's the cry. To break the King and make the city. There will be rich pickings if we have peace with the Dutch, and red guineas will run freely in London."

The other, watching him, smiled grimly to himself. He had John Sheldon in his power, and knew it. However went the game in which passions were used as a motive, and flesh and blood were to serve as pawns, his well-being was assured. He flicked the linen at his wrists, delicately; caught up his glass of red wine with his slim, white fingers, and sitting back, drinking there and looking on his dupe, seemed more like a sinister bird of prey than ever.

John Sheldon stopped in his nervous, crouching walk about the room.

"Zounds!" he said, at last; "I'll do it. To-day is Friday. Assemble them here for dinner on Tuesday next. We'll have a dance and make the gathering a county merrymaking. And, by the gods, while the women and young folk are dancing, we'll set a train that will blaze through England. And more, by God—we'll break the King."

The other shifted slightly in his seat.

" And my reward ? " he said, the voice hungry with the greed of the calling bird of prey.

" Peggy," said John Sheldon, " and Peggy's fortune. If you are minded that way, the marriage shall be when you choose."

" You shall announce it at the dance," said the other, " if Peggy wills it that way."

" If this marriage be my will, it shall be my ward's," the older man said, grimly.

Sir Ladbroke drank his wine slowly, as a man might do who has concluded a good deal.

" We have no points of difference," he said, rising at length.

" None," said John Sheldon. " Your aims are mine, and our policy demands that the girl should be yours."

Sir Ladbroke laughed easily.

" Then, since you are assured, I will withdraw," he said. " Permit me to say ' Good-night ! ' "

John Sheldon returned the salutation as his guest left the room.

Peggy, in the secret passage, saw him go ; then groped towards her candle. Within a few minutes she was back in her room. The secret door was replaced. Peggy, no longer shivering, climbed into the great four-poster bed ; set the candle near it, and took up her book again, this time to read herself to sleep. The girl's manner was a trifle excited. Her eyes were glowing. The florid dressing-gown about her breast rose and fell. A rebellious smile lurked around her full lips.

" La ! " she said to herself, cuddling beneath

the blankets. " So uncle is to break the house of Stuart, and I'm to be a burnt-offering, on the altar of Sir Ladbroke Drake, to the new dynasty."

Peggy looked at the candle reflectively; then burst into a richly gurgling laugh. .

" I wonder what Nick will say when he hears the news," she sighed. " I fancy he will find it vastly entertaining."

Peggy turned to her book with the relief of one who puts the preoccupations of life aside, having solved a problem.

CHAPTER XVIII

THE assembly at the Chequers, at which John Sheldon intended to announce his intentions, made brave comings and goings upon the highway, and involved vast preparations in the house itself. Sheldon's city adherents and friends were duly invited, and certain trusted leaders were called from the country, chiefly wealthy landowners whose estates drew near to the York Road and were easily accessible. Nominally a dinner and a dance, to which all concerned brought their ladies, the chief male guests were drawn from a circle of gentlemen whom Sheldon had sounded, either directly or through his representatives.

These people were arriving through the greater part of Tuesday. Some from the farthest distances were guests at the Chequers, and the gloomy rooms had to be prepared for their reception. Others were billeted at Hitchin, and made the most of the accommodation in the inns there. A few from the south intended staying overnight at Barnet, at the two great coaching houses. Many from the city were prepared to start away as soon as the ball was over, and journey back to London by road without making more extended stay.

On the morning of the ball the guests began to arrive from the hour of noon, and John Sheldon, as host, and his ward had ample duty in receiving them. As they came there was much talk of the perils of the road, but most made the journey safely. Their very numbers made their exploitation by daylight a matter of difficulty for the highwaymen.

Of the people from the city, two only complained of misfortune.

Lord Bleakmoor, alone, arrived at the hour of four on horseback. It was evident that his lordship was in no pleasant frame of mind. He scowled grimly when Sheldon and Sir Ladbroke met him in the hall, and complained that he had been stopped just before entering Barnet.

The story of his humiliations, told to the company, proved commonplace enough. Lord Bleakmoor admitted that he had been waylaid by a mounted horseman, and had had to part with a purse containing twenty guineas and a brace of gold-mounted pistols. He contrived to mention that he had proved an ugly customer until overpowered, and inferred that he had given the highwayman cause to remember the encounter to the extent of a bullet in the Tobyman's shoulder.

. Captain Barclay arrived an hour later, afoot. There was little need for him to tell his story. Barclay's dishevelled appearance plainly betrayed his discomfiture. He had been dismounted almost within two miles of the Chequers, and in the struggle had been rolled on the dusty road. The bridge of his nose was bleeding; his cloak was torn; his arms and money had gone. He admitted that besides being robbed he had been given the choice of a duel on the highway with the masked man who had stopped him, or, as an alternative, a horse-whipping. In the engagement with the swords he had been disarmed in the first minute and compelled at the point to make a journey in the woods, where he had been forced to dance before a camp of tattered rascals, one of whom had piped a jig for his accompaniment.

Captain Barclay was much comforted by the warmth of his greeting and the condolences of his friends, and, cheered in mind, walked stiffly off to his room.

The halls were busy and crowded, and John Sheldon and his niece had but little time to do more than welcome their guests. From London had come, besides Lord Bleakmoor and Captain Barclay, half a dozen of the wealthier city merchants, each in ornate coach and under armed escort. From the North, landowners, smarting through the uproar of the country, the tyranny of the King's collectors, the anger of the population at the royal betrayal, and eager to loosen the coils about them, came some forty strong. They were mostly smaller squires who had followed Cromwell and profited by the association. They looked to playing a similar part against the second King Charles for the sake of getting immediate ease from his extravagant government and perhaps ultimate profit.

Sir Ladbroke Drake went slowly to Captain Barclay's room about the hour of six. He found that gallant making the last touches of his toilet by candlelight, sitting in a high-backed chair before a mirror as he did so.

The two men wasted no time in the cordialities of small talk.

"Well, how goes the conspiracy?" Barclay asked, looking up. "And what's the justification for bringing me on an evil journey from snug quarters in town to this bleak monastery of a place?"

"Tut, tut!" answered Sir Ladbroke, a grim smile playing about his thin lips. "The game is very much alive and well worth a little discomfort. The rising is assured, and seems more than likely to be successful. The pickings will be on our side. To-day I have news of an errand after your own heart. Negotiations are going on between the King and France. A messenger with the King's undertaking rides from York on Friday. We have made an engagement to have him stopped on Sunday, and those papers are to come here, if I choose."

"Why, 'if you choose'?" asked Captain Barclay, curiously.

"They might be valuable elsewhere," Sir Ladbroke said, lowering his voice. "The Dutch, for instance, should be curious, and they have their agents in London."

Captain Barclay nodded slowly and his restless eyes gleamed.

"I want you to find that out," Sir Ladbroke continued; "but we will talk further of that to-morrow. Meanwhile, there is the ball—the dance of the conspirators. The safe squires are to meet the

city at a council, and Sheldon will outline the plans.
Between us we may have useful knowledge from the
meeting, if our interests should swerve in the direction
of the King. And to-night I hope to induce Sheldon
to announce my engagement with his ward, before
the company breaks up."

Captain Barclay raised his eyebrows.

"You are riding a cracking pace," was his comment. "Take care you do not come a purler."

Sir Ladbroke Drake snapped his fingers at the
imaginary ghosts the other's words had called up.

"Pish! Whichever way the see-saw goes, we
are on the safe end. And mark me, I have more
news. Would you like to know who humiliated
you on the road, this afternoon?"

Captain Barclay's face flushed scarlet.

"By God, I would! I'd give my ears to ride him
down. But I do know him, in a sort of way. He
was undoubtedly the new roadster—Swift Nick."

"And what good is that knowledge to you?"
asked Sir Ladbroke. "You need more explicit
information. Who, think you, is Swift Nick?"

Captain Barclay shrugged his shoulders.

"The devil, I should say," he growled. "Who
is he, since you know?"

"An old friend of yours; an old friend of mine.
A man who stands in my path. A man who owes
me a turn or two in the game. A man I hate, since
many times of late he has come into my way. Swift
Nick is Nicholas Nevinson—I recognised him by
the trick of the sword when he disarmed me on the
road."

Captain Barclay whistled his astonishment.

"The devil in very truth!" he answered. "Why, I take it, you'll hunt him like a rat—eh?" he grinned. "A second card to play against Mistress Peggy, should she prove unkind!"

"And a card I'll play freely enough, in any case," Sir Ladbroke said, decisively, the words rasping out a threat. "All in good time. I'll hunt him when the moment is favourable and lay him by the heels. I'll teach him the man does not live who plays fast and loose with Sir Ladbroke Drake. Whether Mistress Peggy is unkind or no, it will be the same. I'll make the North Road a red hell, and much too hot to hold the upstart popinjay. 'Fore God, I will!"

"Have you moved towards bringing him to the gibbet?" Captain Barclay asked, curiously.

Sir Ladbroke, into whose voice anger had crept at the very mention of Nick's name, frowned.

"No," he said, after an interval. "Swift Nick will keep, and be all the better game for playing on a longer rope. I have more precious fish to fry. When the time comes, hark ye! we'll hunt him down; for he is fluttering like a moth 'twixt here and Barnet."

The two men remained in earnest conclave as Captain Barclay dressed. The hour drew on until the time when a huge gong in the hall announced that dinner was being served in the great dining-hall. Together they went down, and found it crowded with gaily dressed women and richly apparelled men. The place was brilliantly lighted.

A touch of profusion was lent by the uniformed servitors. Menu, service, surroundings, were all pressed into the business of impressing John Sheldon's guests. As the courses were served a harpist played in the musicians' box above the head of the table. The banquet was a rich feast of rare viands and still rarer vintages. The guests were in gala attire, though the city people, by their finer habit, could be distinguished from the country gentlemen in more sober clothing. The ladies present, richly gowned, in the eccentricities of the costumiers of that day, prattled gaily enough, and accepted compliments levelled across the long tables. For the most part they were ignorant of the nature of the summons that called their lords from home. The men kept up an elaborate pretence of enjoying the passing hour, but many were preoccupied, and, despite the air of festivity, frequent lulls in the conversation betrayed the presence of some skeleton at the feast. Enjoyment seemed uppermost at the rich man's table, playing, as the host was, for a big stake; but the same undercurrent of mystery that had been about the house, brooding there for a week, seemed to be intensified until it dominated the very atmosphere. The gathering, despite its seeming gaiety, was tense, nervous, electrical. One felt as if drifting clouds, presaging thunder, had come together, crowding each other in glowering masses and rumbling ceaselessly during the tense moments that herald the breaking of a storm.

The dinner did not come to an end without a preliminary flash of lightning.

Before the ladies retired, John Sheldon rose to propose a customary toast.

Rising from his chair, exceedingly pale, nerves working in his thin cheeks, his hands shaking, he held up his long-stemmed glass.

"Ladies and gentlemen—The King!" he said, in a voice that shook under the strain.

The men about the table hesitated. Some rose to drink the toast with elaborate ceremony; others retained their seats, and with sneers upon their faces tacitly ignored the health.

John Sheldon looked them over, as if to appraise the loyalty of those about him.

"Come, gentlemen all, let us be united in the matter for once. The King!" he called again.

"God bless him!" Mistress Peggy Sheldon cried, a challenge in her eye, her oval face flaming scarlet.

There was something electric in the round notes of her youthful voice.

Every man stood up and drank the toast. Peggy had changed the very tone of that gathering with a phrase; had shamed the disloyal and galvanised them into life.

Sir Ladbroke Drake's eye caught John Sheldon's, and, as their glances met, the latter scowled. The incident was trivial enough, but in an indefinably subtle way Peggy's intervention had carried conviction.

As the ladies left the dining-hall, Sir Ladbroke leant across the table and whispered to Sheldon.

"It is as I say," he said, urgently. "You can see it for yourself. The sooner the better."

Sheldon, frowning at his long-stemmed glass, inclined his head, an ugly scowl wrinkling his close-set eyes and puckering his lips.

An hour later the ball was at its height. Mistress Peggy, by virtue of her youth and beauty, had become its belle. In the crowded room, hot with scents, gay with movement, tense with the mingled purposes of many minds, she looked as radiant as a queen. She danced in minuet and all the round dances with the company, but in the waltz favoured largely one gallant whom no one seemed to know. He was dressed ultra-fashionably in pale blue, with a close-fitting wig and a neatly trimmed beard. His face was darkened with exposure. The thought that he adventured on the sea was borne out by the fact that to all whom he was introduced, the name given was Captain Hampden, of the good ship, *Pioneer*, newly home from the Spanish Main. The captain became a favourite, especially with the ladies. He had about him a ready alertness, an assured poise of manner expressed in the carriage of his head and the swing of his shoulders, a genial but reckless buoyancy in the glance of his bold, challenging, grey eyes, that all combined to suggest the man of action and adventure. Mistress Peggy's attraction for him was obvious ; he scarcely made any pretence to hide his youthful joy in her company ; he followed in her train, alert, well poised, gallant, with an alacrity that betrayed the lover.

Sir Ladbroke Drake, passing in and out of the ballroom and refused dances by his young hostess twice on account of the stranger, was the last to note the gallant's surrender to the fascinations of John Sheldon's ward. When the gossip of the room reached him, he eyed the man closely, and bit his thin lips irritably as he measured Hampden's success.

" Who is the coxcomb with the seaman's beard ? " he asked Captain Barclay.

" Truth, I know not," the gambler answered. " They say he is new from the sea after a good run, and with a pocket full of guineas. I am marking him down for an hour in the card-room, when the night is older."

He turned away to seek his partner.

The stranger was just leading out Mistress Peggy to a dance. The girl was leaning heavily on his arm, and tapping it, in pleased raillery, with her fan. There was a light in her eyes that Sir Ladbroke had never seen before.

" Curses on the popinjay," he said to himself, and then still more irritably scrutinised his rival. " Upon my soul, I must inquire into him ! I thought I knew by name and station every gallant invited here to-night."

He would have set about his task at once, but the meeting claimed him. In the library, some twenty men sat closeted for an hour. At the head of the table was John Sheldon, nervously chewing a goose-quill pen. On his right, was Lord Bleakmoor. By the left, sat Sir Ladbroke Drake, looking more like a bird of prey than ever ; near him his henchman, Barclay, who had dined and

wined and was visibly satisfied, pluming himself
with obvious pleasure before the company; his
hooked nose, on which was a slight abrasion, high
in the air; his manner studiously appraising. The
company assembled was made up of half a dozen
pompous city magnates, for the most part fat and
florid, and the remainder of those round the table
were of the country squirehood; some lean and
hard, others robust and inclined to portliness, all
high coloured from contact with the open air.

Sir Ladbroke Drake explained his purposes and
the secret activities of many weeks. As he spoke,
in a thin, harsh voice, one forgot his words. The
substance of what he had to say proved that the
hovering spirit of war flapped sable wings above
the sleeping world. He pledged his word to set two
thousand men marching towards the North to meet
the forces of the King, on his return from York.
His power to do so was guaranteed by the city representatives. The room was hushed, tense, nervously expectant when the statement of the city
interests had been made.

Then, one by one, the squirehood pledged themselves. The substance of their speeches was the
same—the gentlemen of influence they could persuade, the number of men-at-arms they could
place upon the road. The toll of Sheldon's army
grew as they spoke, one by one. The date was
arranged; the day stipulated by Sir Ladbroke
Drake. Times of meeting on the Great North
Road were appointed for those who had thrown in
their lot with the gathering army. The con-

spirators sat the round of the clock, and when they
rose, the dream of Sheldon's life—the breaking of
the monarchy, freedom for the crippled trade of the
predatory city interests—had become a very solid
and sinister fact. Outside, in the corridor, the less
trusted guests and a host of pretty women laughed
and flirted or danced in the crowded ballroom.
Only Peggy and her favoured gallant were absent
during the time the conclave was sitting in Sheldon's quiet library.

When the conspirators returned to the ballroom
or the card-tables, pledged to the intentions of
John Sheldon, three men remained with their
host in the library—Sir Ladbroke Drake, Lord
Bleakmoor, and Captain Barclay.

The conversation was carried a step forward, for
Sir Ladbroke claimed, as his reward for the success
of the meeting, the announcement of his engagement to Mistress Peggy Sheldon.

"I press you now," he was saying, speaking the
words coercingly, as the four men stood before the
huge fireplace. "Both Lord Bleakmoor and Captain Barclay, who have taken no mean part in your
movement, are in my confidence and agree. The
time is ripe to-night. The announcement of the
engagement will strengthen my prestige in the
remaining negotiations. My association with you
in such a close personal matter will convince
some of the waverers unsecured. I ask you to
do this now," he concluded, and his voice grew
threatening; "I ask it as a right you cannot
refuse."

"I agree," Lord Bleakmoor said, as if speaking to a brief; "the moment is most opportune."

"There is the girl to consider," John Sheldon urged weakly, and with an obvious lack of decision.

"A chit of a woman!" interjected Captain Barclay. "Damme, our purposes should not be weighed in the balance against a girl's whimsies."

John Sheldon, his face furrowed, looked from one man to the other. He had schemed for power and profit, and had bought it by placing the secret of his ambitions in the custody of three men he now knew to be more unscrupulous than himself.

Without further word he went to the bell-rope and pulled upon it; he seemed to have made up his mind.

A servant came in answer to the summons.

"Call Mistress Peggy," he said, grimly. "Tell her I would speak to her in the library."

"Gentlemen," he said, when the servant had gone, "step aside into the adjoining room. I will tell you the substance of the interview, and trust I shall be able to make my ward amenable to our plans."

Sir Ladbroke looked, with an ugly smile that flared his triumph over every line of his calculating face, upon his two friends.

"Come, my lord, and you, Barclay. We can safely predict the outcome of our honest friend Sheldon's domestic efforts."

With a smirk of sinister satisfaction he led the way from the library into the adjoining room.

CHAPTER XIX

MISTRESS SHELDON, whom her uncle's messenger sought, was standing in one of the several ante-rooms leading from the ballroom.

The music of the dance stole softly through the curtained doorway. The swirl and patter of feet sounded on the polished boards. Above the gay clamour, one heard a man laugh recklessly, or the light ripple of mirth tinkling from the lips of some dancing woman. The very odour of the crowded room, with that hot, exhausted, scented atmosphere that grows out of human revelry, drifted to Peggy's nostrils. Though the air was warm —even hot to the point of sickliness—it chilled her. It carried to her heart a sharp contrast, a feeling of loneliness, that always seems to sweep over those who stand aloof when others make merry as the hour goes on towards twelve.

Peggy did not stand alone many minutes. The curtain parted, and the favoured gallant of the evening looked in, saw his hostess, and came eagerly forward.

He seized Peggy's hands and began to see-saw them gently backwards and forwards.

" Ah, there you are ! " he said, smiling as his eyes

looked gaily into her troubled face. " I've danced
with Lady Bletchmore as you told me, though it's
a devilish thing to ask a man to prance with a set of
shoulders full of salt-cellars, when the best of fair
women is nigh. But I've done it—yes, I've danced
with Lady Bletchmore, and she thinks Captain
Hampden is the choicest spirit here. Now I claim
my reward."

The sailor guest looked round as he spoke. The
room was quite deserted. Unresisting, he drew
Mistress Peggy to him and kissed her, the girl
lying quietly in his arms, her breath coming and
going, her frame slightly shivering.

" Oh, Nick, dear mad Nick Nevinson," she said,
suddenly freeing herself; " how you rattle! You
dance as gaily as if all the world were a garden of
roses, and yet I know you are putting your neck in
a noose for me."

" Ha, my pretty one," he said, and the light of
gaiety did not leave his brave, grey eyes as he kissed
his hand to her. " The bravest dance I ever footed
is this, though you nearly made my heart go breaking by fobbing me off on Lady Bletchmore. I
think I ought to claim my reward again."

Playfully, he attempted to inveigle Peggy into
another embrace.

" No, no," she said; " not now. I made you
dance with that dear old frump, for there is danger.
Already they are talking and observing us too
closely. Oh! why did I bring you here, Mad Nick,
into so much danger ? "

" Lud ! " he returned; " into so much delight.

Your secret passage is the way to heaven—or heaven enough for me. Already I have danced with you eight times. And I have held your hand and heard your voice. And I have looked into your eyes. Surely, I have no cause to complain."

Mistress Peggy stamped her foot.

"Be sane, you madman," she urged. "Must you always laugh at danger? You have heard what is going on in the library?"

"Aye, every word," he said. "You gave me good vantage ground. I'm for the King—God bless him!—in the worst of his follies; and upon my soul, Peg, it's better to be a loyalist highwayman than a disloyal gambler. Lord save us, if they dare announce your engagement, I'll challenge the whole roomful, and s'death! that mangy city pimp, Sir Ladbroke, won't be first to come on if he know the buck he's meeting!"

Peggy put her hand forward as if to stifle the light, reckless words upon his lips.

"Don't, don't, don't!" she said. "Lord! why did I bring you unnecessarily to hear just that last part? I know you'll no more leave now than you will become virtuous. Do listen to my reasoning and go."

"Listen and go!" Nick said. "Listen will I and freely, but I'll stop this rout out as the gay Captain Hampden. Why, my love, I might dance with you six times more, and, i'faith, I am keen to hear that announcement of your impending marriage."

Peggy almost tore her fan in her emotion.

"Promise me, for the love you bear me, you'll commit no mad folly and hear it all in silence. Promise me——"

She broke off suddenly. Some one had parted the curtains and entered the room. A servant came towards her.

"Mr. Sheldon would speak to you in the library, Mistress Peggy," he said.

The girl's face paled, but she did not flinch.

"I will be with him almost at once," she answered. "Go—tell him that."

The man withdrew.

The reckless gaiety fell from Nick's manner as if it were a cloak.

"God's life, my dear one!" he said; "I would I could go with you now and affront these rascals one by one. And faith, when I look on you, I gain the nerve to do it."

"No! Go, go!" she answered. "Through the boudoir and by the way you entered. I can face this out alone, and if there is real danger for me I can summon you at my will and need. There'll be no happiness for me if ill comes to you through this mad prank."

Nick Nevinson was no longer smiling.

"Promise me, woman to man, now in the hour I need the hope of you, and for the sake of the coming days when my service may be better than your shame, you will not yield!"

Peggy drew herself up proudly.

"There is no man for me but you," she said, simply. "Now let us go."

" I am content," he said ; " and, remember, though we are not the least honest in an indifferently honourable age, the service of the road is loyal. Hard by your gate, by night or day, our messenger stands sentinel."

Quietly, and in curious contrast to his previous gaiety of manner, Nick drew Peggy to him and kissed her, tenderly.

With brightening eye she took his offered arm, and he, seemingly more light-hearted than ever, walked with her across the ballroom floor before the many guests, accompanying his mistress to the library door through the lively corridors.

John Sheldon turned from the position he occupied as the door closed behind her. He had been standing motionless before the big open fireplace, pursuing his mind's uneasy quest in the flames. In the room adjoining, three men sat round a little table, and Captain Barclay was shuffling a pack of cards as the other two laughed cynically at one of his not too nicely turned jests. As Peggy Sheldon entered, her uncle walked across the room and closed the door.

Sheldon offered his niece a seat, and then stood, slightly hesitating, before her. His mean face was bent forward ; his mouth was working slightly ; he moved his bony hands unceasingly, as if he were cracking the joints one by one. Long and spidery he looked in his plain black habit, though the length of his legs, which slightly bent at the knees, made him appear to be crouching and taking the shape of some vicious-minded stork about to strike.

"I have sent for you——". he began, and then halted.

"I am sufficiently intelligent to grasp that," Peggy said, and her manner was rich with the insolent expression of her contempt. "Perhaps you will tell me why?"

"I have decided to announce your engagement to Sir Ladbroke Drake," he said.

"I know that," she answered.

John Sheldon started and frowned uneasily. "How do you know that? The decision was only reached a few minutes ago. It has suddenly become necessary to our plans."

Peggy laughed in his face. Her teeth gleamed as her full lips parted, scornfully. Her breath came rapidly. The expression in her eyes was a defiance, and showed no traces of fear.

"How do I know?" she said, and forthwith began to prevaricate. "Perhaps a pretty bird whispered it to me, for surely it's a pretty tale. Or, maybe, the walls have ears for such a gentle story. Or, again, the ceiling may have liked to look on. But save yourself uneasiness—I guessed it. A woman's intuition, you might say; or, one of my whimsies. You need not look so scared."

John Sheldon's narrow eyes seemed to draw closer together as they hinted of the anger his niece was stirring by her raillery.

"Go on, my uncle; go on!" she laughed, scornfully. "You are better than the gipsies and the hag women who read fortunes. Since you have settled my future, tell me more of it: the when of the announcement, the where of my marriage, with perhaps a glimpse of my estate, and a word-picture or two of my possibilities of happiness."

She was fighting the crafty city-man with her tongue and goading him to indiscretion, and she knew it. Even in the moment of risk, Peggy was swept away by her anger and took a cruel delight in seeing each word, barbed as it was, wing its way accurately to stab and spur her uncle's mind into growing irritation.

By an effort John Sheldon controlled himself.

"I like not your manner," he said, sternly.

"Nor do I like your methods," she answered. "We may yet see whether you will stand more of my manner than I shall bear of your conduct. Tell me, when is this precious engagement to be announced?" she asked.

"To-night, before the company at supper," John Sheldon said, with a grim note of authority.

"And the marriage will take place—when?" she asked, her face flushing and dyeing still further the fashionable coating of rouge upon her cheek.

"That will depend upon Sir Ladbroke and the way other affairs, of which you know naught, unfold."

Mistress Peggy rose from her seat, clutching at the table with her round, white arm and jewelled fingers. They stood, one on each side of the table, confronting and testing each other by their silence. The glint in Sheldon's crafty, sunken eyes and the answering defiance in the girl's, seemed to meet and clash as if they were blades of steel. For many seconds they stood there, until, through tension, Sheldon's steady gaze wavered.

"And if I resist?" she asked, her round voice vibrating.

"It matters not," John Sheldon answered, coldly.

"And if I stand before the company and give you all the lie to your faces when you make the announcement—what then?"

Peggy pushed the questions home resolutely, as if, a duellist in words, each one were a thrust testing the weakness or strength of an opponent.

"Unless you are amenable, you will not hear the announcement," he said, frigidly.

"Do you purpose to govern my personal liberty and actions and to say where I shall be from now?" she asked, her voice rising.

"Yes," he answered, finally.

They stood again, facing each other, in a silence, broken only by the buzz of conversation in the next room.

Peggy was the first to speak again.

She rapped her fingers, emphatically, upon the table until her rings made dents in its highly polished surface.

"And, despite that, I say 'No.'" Peggy was speaking resolutely. "If you make this announcement before me, I shall deny it as soon as you have spoken. If you insist that I am not to be present, I shall refuse to go from the room. I'll make you use force to have me sent back to my room, and all the time I'll rage like a village scold, and create such a scene, in each crowded corridor through which we have to pass, as will shame you before every guest assembled here to be impressed by your manner and estate."

Her lip curled scornfully.

" A pretty baggage I shall look, hauled by force, about your corridors, as if I were a drab of the streets, and a grand finale the sight will be for your elaborate entertainment ! "

John Sheldon paled before the scornful flow of the girl's opinion. He was standing on the side of the table farthest from the door. As Peggy spoke, he moved with a sidling motion towards the door. His ugly eyes were fixed on the girl, and before he spoke the man moistened his dry lips, furtively, with his tongue.

" I have thought of that too," he said, at length. " I had some reason to suspect you would not see reason quietly. Your father was an unreasonable man, of hot head and reckless manners. But there will be no outrageous scene."

By the time John Sheldon finished speaking, he had sidled to the door, the one exit from the room, saving the entrance to the apartment in which his associates were laughing and talking. He stood there, an evil smile on his pale face, rubbing one hand upon the other in such a way that the bony joints seemed to crack.

" Until our guests go I shall ask you to remain in this room," he said slowly, a note of malignant triumph in his voice.

" And if I refuse to stay ? " Mistress Peggy

asked urgently, a deeper flush on her face, her fine lips curving more defiantly than ever.

" Then I shall take steps to compel you."

John Sheldon spoke the words slowly and deliberately; they had all the finality of a judge's sentence.

The girl had turned to face him as he stood with his back to the door. They remained, uncle and niece, confronting each other in silence, the girl trembling with indignation. For a moment she was nonplussed, then revolt surged through all her young being. Quickly she turned to the table and seized a heavy, upright gold candlestick, with a still heavier square base. The candle itself fell to the ground as she clutched and swung the metal holder. Peggy had no idea of what she meant to do, but surging through the girl's mind was the necessity of doing something at once. With blazing eyes and heaving breast, she turned to her uncle and strode towards him. In such a moment he noted the formidable strength of her round figure and the threatening force of her white shoulders.

" So, my uncle, it is to be war," Peggy said, her deep voice rising with passion. " Then I'll have the first blow and make part of the promised scene now—before your guests."

In a flash Peggy had made up her mind. She would carry the door by storm and go along the corridor, if necessary calling a protest before the assembled guests. Almost as if he were reading her mind, John Sheldon guessed his ward's intentions. He backed towards the door as if to lock it, but the girl was upon him before he could carry out his design. With one hand on the door handle and the other used to fend off the angry woman who came towards him, he called to his friends.

" Drake, Barclay, here, at once ! " he yelled.

Thwarted of her desire to reach the door, Peggy, struggling with her uncle, swung the candlestick. She meant to beat upon the panels and cry for help, but the first swing caught Sheldon on the forehead and stretched him on the floor, his body lying across the door.

The three men in the other room answered to his call almost at once. Captain Barclay, a laugh on his bold face ; Sir Ladbroke Drake, grim and curious, came together. Lord Bleakmoor, smiling cynically, followed his two associates. They ceased to smile when they entered and saw Sheldon lying upon the floor, his crafty face white and drawn, a thin stream of blood oozing from his cracked pate.

Mistress Peggy stood trying to pull the recumbent form away from the door, but in her excitement she could not move it.

The three new-comers strode towards the girl, and Sir Ladbroke Drake attempted to seize her, his eyes sparkling with a sinister leer as he did so. The moment he put out his slim gambler's hand, prehensile like a claw, Peggy smashed it down with a blow of her improvised weapon, the candlestick descending with a sharp crack on the knuckles.

As he fell away, Captain Barclay and Lord

Bleakmoor clutched the girl roughly. She struggled with the fierce, wild madness of some game, healthy young animal caught in a trap. One arm, emerged from the *mêlée*, white and bare, for the drapery had been stripped away in the struggle. Exerting all her strength, Mistress Peggy hammered on the panels of the door and called loudly for help. For a few seconds she held her own, but the force of the men prevailed and she was dragged away. At that moment, the heavy door, which she had failed to carry by assault, swung slowly on its hinges.

Captain Hampden, the guest whose unfamiliarity had puzzled Sir Ladbroke Drake, stepped quietly into the room.

Sir Ladbroke Drake stopped nursing his painful knuckles. In sheer shame, Captain Barclay and Lord Bleakmoor fell back and set the girl free. Peggy paled underneath the rouge, for here was the greatest danger of all—the one she most feared.

Peggy rushed towards Swift Nick.

" Captain Hampden," she said, urgently. " Please withdraw. This is a mere domestic matter, and it is almost settled."

" I have no desire to interrupt," Captain Hampden said, easily. " I gathered the impression that I heard a lady call for help."

As he spoke, he measured the three men with his eyes.

Sheldon, on the floor, stirred and sat up, rubbing his forehead in some bewilderment, his wig and linen dishevelled.

" Then," said Sir Ladbroke, " if you do not desire to interrupt, kindly withdraw. Your presence unsought in these private apartments is an intrusion."

" Damme !—an unwarrantable intrusion," echoed Captain Barclay.

The so-called Captain Hampden looked the other men over. He raised a fine, white hand and snapped his fingers airily in their faces.

" Pouf ! " he said; " by your manner my coming must have been very untimely. I go no more hurriedly for your commands, my bucks. If I have made a mistake I apologise—to the lady." Swift Nick smiled as he spoke. " As for you three rascals and the old fool on the floor, I like neither your looks nor your manners; and were I free to act and sure of my ground, I'd challenge you one by one."

Sir Ladbroke Drake walked up to him.

" You coxcomb, whoever you are, have a care with your saucy tongue. I have watched you all the evening, Captain Hampden, and doubt your right to be here at all. I should not wonder if you were a spy," he said, glowering at Nick.

Nick again laughed insolently in his face.

" Go, go, Captain Hampden ! " Peggy urged.

" I go at your command," he answered.

" Yes, go, before I clip your insolent ears," Sir Ladbroke Drake said, thrusting his face forward.

It was too much for Swift Nick.

He struck the gambler with the back of his hand.

"Take those evil features away from mine," he said. "I like not your evil face at all; I will not have it too close."

The enraged Sir Ladbroke leapt at the man who had assaulted him. There was a brief struggle, each man gripping the other where he could. In a second, however, Nick sent Sir Ladbroke Drake back, and, striking him with his fist, toppled him over on to the carpet. But as Sir Ladbroke Drake freed himself, the beard fell from Nick's face in the *mêlée*.

The four men stared at him, astounded.

"Oh, Nick, Nick!" Peggy called, anguish in her voice. "I knew what the end of this mad adventure would be."

"Faith, it is only the beginning!" Nick answered, airily.

"Nicholas Nevinson, as I live!" said John Sheldon, rising from the floor.

"Aye! Nicholas Nevinson it is, at your service, and in no way afraid to answer for his intrusion," Swift Nick answered. "Come, Sir Ladbroke! if you need satisfaction, you shall be first. We have met before; once to your disadvantage."

"Twice," snapped Sir Ladbroke. "Once on the road. I know you as Nevinson, but better still I know you as Swift Nick. There is a shorter way of dealing with you. Gentlemen, I call on you to arrest this man as the notorious highwayman."

For a moment the recognition was a thunderclap to Swift Nick, but he displayed no sign of his alarm. Plucking out a pistol concealed in his tunic, as the three men drew their swords, and John Sheldon walked towards the bell, he levelled its shining barrel at the whole party.

"Halt!" he said, sternly, to Sheldon. "The whole four of you hear me. The one to move dies with the first step. Mistress Peggy, 'tis more sultry than it seemed. Remember, I am yours to command. In the meantime a live highwayman is better than a dangling night shepherd."

"Yes, go, Nick, and go quickly," she urged. "You cannot serve me here."

The four men stood as if petrified, rooted to their places in the centre of the room. They still looked on Swift Nick and down the barrel of his heavy pistol, but their instinct held them still.

"I go, Mistress Peggy," he said, his voice ringing. "As for you, rascals, remember that from to-night you are watched by a hundred eyes. Take care that your house of cards does not come toppling to the ground, through the single breath of a high-wayman."

Backing slowly to the door, stern in his defiance, gay almost to recklessness in his courage, Swift Nick bowed to Peggy. He stood there a second or two, covering the nonplussed conspirators, then quickly left the room and banged the door behind him.

"After him, quick—after him!" Sheldon urged.

He ran, followed by the others, raising the halloo, out into the passage.

They were in time to see Swift Nick dive up the first corridor and turn into the grand staircase.

10

"God! he's going up the stairs," Sheldon shrieked. "We have him treed!"

The whole house joined in the pursuit of the highwayman, pell-mell. A startled chambermaid was the last to see him. She was of opinion that Nick had bolted into Peggy's chamber, but was too confused to be sure.

When Sheldon and a crowd of his guests came, fully armed, and stormed that chamber, it was empty of human presence other than their own.

Swift Nick had escaped by the secret panel, along the passage he had traversed, guided by Peggy, as Captain Hampden, dressed out for the conspirators' ball.

The announcement of the engagement was not made that night.

Sheldon, Sir Ladbroke Drake, Captain Barclay, Lord Bleakmoor, and other guests stayed up rather late, wondering how Swift Nick had got away from the Chequers, and debating the meaning of his final threat.

Peggy, the gayest dancer in the crowded ballroom, smiled as she listened absent-mindedly to the chatter of the gallants who fluttered in her train.

CHAPTER XX

IN the evening of the fourth day after the scene at Chequers Court, a man sat moodily stirring the fire in the big general room of the " Lantern " inn.

The flames, waxing and waning as the wood twisted and crackled, lit up his face, and at a first glance one who knew the " Lantern " would have put the man down as a casual wayfarer from the nondescript army who drifted past the doors of the inn.

His face was partially concealed by a ragged, disorderly beard. A deep, red scar almost across one cheek covered up much of the facial expression. Long hair, unkempt, straggled over the forehead and massed in unruly curls about the neck. The man wore, as his outer garments, a dirty mustard-coloured jerkin and breeches of the same material. His calves were covered by grey, worsted stockings, and these ended in heavy boots, apparently dusty and travel-stained. Few who knew Nicholas Nevinson would have recognised the tattered and battered lounger as the smart cavalier of the town, a few short weeks ago, nor would those who had seen him mounted on Starlight recognise him as the highwayman who had made the London end of the North Road notorious—Swift Nick.

Steve Randall bustled in from the tap, but Swift Nick, in his disguise, took no heed of him. He went on stirring the fire and prodding the wood until the flames roared in the chimney and the sparks flew upwards in a golden stream.

The "Lantern" was comparatively deserted. A drover or two and several farm hands lingered in the tap, noisy in their drink, and were the only patrons of the house.

"Damn their rattle!" said Swift Nick, looking up, sulkily.

"Nay!" answered Steve Randall, the landlord; "bless 'em as honest topers. The more rattle they make, the more grist comes to the mill."

"Then damn the mill, too!" Nick answered, sullenly enough.

Steve Randall cocked his eye and shot a humoursome glance at his guest. A smile slowly mantled his broad, oddly genial features.

"Perhaps while you are at it," he said, "you would like to damn the miller into the bargain," he suggested, jocosely.

The other slightly changed his note.

"Nay, old Steve," he answered. "As a miller you are well enough, and you must not take too much account of my churlish humour."

He jabbed the fire viciously as he spoke.

"Oh, I know fine and well enough what is ailing you," Steve said, his voice meant to exert a cheering influence. "But even a prime blade of your dashing habit must have his dull times."

"Well, these be dull enough in all conscience,"

Swift Nick answered. " Damme, I feel as stupid as a watchman."

" Bide your time, lad," Randall answered. " Even if you have to keep house you lack nothing, and are more than passing safe. You've a roof over your head, the good victualling of the " Lantern," and enough of the rosy mouth-wash as a man need have who does not want to woo gout or the drunkard's madness."

" That is all well enough," admitted Swift Nick, grudgingly.

" And other things are better," Randall went on. " You've got the traps on the wrong scent. Your journey Doncaster way, and your game of cat amongst the pigeons with the cattlemen, has sent them helter-skelter up the road to York, and here you are, having doubled back, as snug as a bug in a rug, while they nose round the wrong spinney. What more can a man of your parts want ? "

" I want the right to be abroad," Nick answered, still surly. " I'm sick to death of cowering here like an old wife with the snivels, these two days. I miss the road, the movement, the life ; and if I were to tell the truth, I'd like to take another hand in the game at the Chequers."

" What good would that do you ? " Randall asked. " You know all that is going on, and that Mistress Peggy is safe. Nemo's men watch all who come and go, and nothing can happen in the way of a wedding there without you getting a chance of dancing at it within the hour."

" All the same, I'm a devilish dull dog, and I'd

like to slip the painter and take a hand in the game," Nick answered.

" And faith ! what would a lad like you be doing ? None of the game is afoot, and you would only be running your neck into a halter for nothing until the hue and cry is over."

" There's one thing I could do," Nick said, his manner brightening. As he spoke, he brought his hand down sharply on the table.

" And what might that be ? " the landlord asked, curiously.

" I could ride to York," Swift Nick said, his voice ringing. " Yes, damme, instead of playing the old woman, warming my shins here, I could ride to York and warn the King."

" By the Lord, you could," Randall answered, holding to his point. " You could and all that. You could ride to the King and run into every hungry trap hounding Swift Nick along the highway. God save us, Nick, lad, Old Rowley isn't worth it—sink me if he is. Lie low, and let the pretty kettle of fish simmer down a bit, say I. Time enough for you to risk your neck when the game is on the move again."

The landlord took Swift Nick's silence for assent and bustled out about his business. Nevinson, left to himself, turned again to the fire and jabbed it fiercely. Then he sat listlessly watching the flying sparks, lapsing slowly into his former moodiness.

The truth of the situation was that after the excitement following his exit from town, two days of enforced inaction had grown irksome to Swift

Nick. Since his recognition by the quartette at the Chequers, Sir Ladbroke Drake had raised the hue and cry, and the York Road swarmed with eager runners and traps anxious to bag Nick and take the reward on his head.

Nick had been compelled to obliterate himself. On the night of his escape through Peggy's secret passage, Nick, by an inspiration, had mounted Starlight and flown in the direction of Grantham. With an inspiration, equally valuable, he had stopped and plundered the cattlemen by day and night, and had even committed the sacrilege of holding up a bishop. That dignitary had only parted with his money after Nick had threatened to blow his wig off. He had boasted before the bishop that he was travelling north, and his victim going south, had hastened up those who followed the hue and cry.

For a day he had ranged the road, making little or no concealment of his identity ; indeed, challenging recognition, until the way was alive with gossip of his presence and signs of his activity. When the uproar on the road was at its height, Swift Nick had quietly doubled, and by little frequented roads had retraced his steps and taken shelter in the "Lantern." The ruse had served its purpose, for away in the North, greedy traps, mouths watering for the reward, were scouring the land for Swift Nick, who seemed to have faded away somewhere on the fringe of Yorkshire, just when they appeared to be hot on his heels.

The Chequers had been watched by members of Nemo's band in his absence, and a steady stream of messages had filtered through. Since Peggy's determined stand, the matter of the forced engagement had gone no farther. After the scene, the company dispersed. Lord Bleakmoor and Captain Barclay returned to town the following day. John Sheldon and Sir Ladbroke Drake remained at the Chequers, and again began the coming and going of many messengers. The plot against the King continued almost openly.

Peggy's notes, brief as they were, proved encouraging. If things were not going well with her, at least nothing ill was happening. So far as the part arranged for the girl at the Chequers was concerned, the drama was at a standstill. Very wisely Peggy had decided to remain and watch the plot as it unfolded itself. Both she and Nevinson, without being aware of the fact, felt that their whole future turned on swift knowledge of the immediate happenings at the hall.

The "Lantern" grew quieter as the night travelled on towards nine o'clock. Vehicles of the heavier sort drew up before the door, and the carriers, stiff with cold, came in to thaw in the tap for a while before resuming their journeys towards the town. Now and again a horseman rode up and dismounted for rest and refreshment. For the most part callers were afoot, and several men of the road, noisily quarrelsome or genial as the case might be, drifted in and out. But as time wore on the traffic abroad began to dry up, callers grew fewer in number, while those in the house, drinking up and departing, began to empty the rooms as other wayfarers did not fill their places. The house was very quiet by nine o'clock, and only the muttered conversation of two or three sleepy voices in the tap drifted to Swift Nick's ears, as he sat crouching in the empty room.

While he remained moodily staring into the flames, a horse, rapidly driven on the road outside, was pulled up at the door. As soon as its rider dismounted, the animal was quietly taken off to the stable yard. Nick looked up curiously, for only friends stabled their horses at the " Lantern," and almost as soon as he recognised the fact, the solitary arrival entered the inn and strode into the room where Nicholas was seated.

" Nemo, by all that's beautiful," Nick said, eagerly looking up.

The beggar king walked quickly forward. He had dispensed with his mean disguise and was dressed for the road, heavily cloaked, booted, and spurred. As he threw off his plumed hat, Nick saw his keen, eager, devil-me-care face was flushed with excitement, and perhaps the reaction of coming into the warmth, suddenly, after a cold ride outside. His eyes were bright and sparkled with the glitter of the bird of prey hunting its game. The man's manner was quick, as if his purposes were being hurried.

Nemo rapped on the oak table with the butt end of a riding crop.

" Ho, there, Master Steve, mulled wine for a frozen night bird," he called jovially, and as Randall went out he turned quickly to Nick.

10*

"Hark ye, Nick, the game's begun. I'm just from the Chequers," he began, wasting no time.

"And Mistress Peggy—how fares it with her?" Nick asked eagerly.

"Well, as things go," Nemo answered. "We have a servant in the house who saw her this morning—bright and gay as a May morning, and in pleasant contrast to the raw wintry days we are having now. But that is only part of my news. Sir Ladbroke Drake rides to keep an appointment somewhere between here and London."

"Where?" asked Nick, and underneath his disguise one could see the jaw stiffen and the grey eyes gleam dangerously.

"That I know not," Nemo answered. "But I got the sign that he had started, and I saw him safely on the London road to Hitchin. I estimate I am about half an hour ahead of him. He is jogging along under a small escort, and will be going through Barnet in thirty minutes. A runner of mine will warn us of his approach."

"You do not know his errand?" Nick asked.

"No; we must hug him close and see how his game develops. Meanwhile you ought to be ready for the road. Starlight is in good trim, I hope. You'll want him before—— Hist!"

Nemo broke off in the middle of his sentence, and without a moment's hesitation walked to the other side of the room and threw himself down on a settle. At that moment, Steve Randall came in with the steaming drink the beggar king had ordered. Outside, the sound of a horse advancing had been heard by his keen ears, and by Nick himself. The ridden animal came up at the trot, and was pulled up on the cobbles at the "Lantern" door. A voice was heard giving instructions to the stable boy waiting outside. In a moment the footsteps of the rider, his spurs jingling, rang in the passage of the tavern. The open doorway was filled with a man's bulk; a traveller, heavily cloaked, who pulled off leather riding gloves as he walked, entered the room and looked carefully about him.

Nemo, glancing sideways, recognised the new-comer as Captain Barclay.

At the moment of his entry, Nemo, with the aplomb of a fabulously wealthy man, was throwing down a guinea.

"There, landlord, take my shot out of that," he said, insolently gracious. "You keep a clean, orderly house, and are a civil fellow, but I like not the looks of that rough creature by the fire."

Steve Randall, with never a change in his manner, bowed with unusual servility.

"As for that, sir, he is well enough," he answered. "He has been here a good hour, thawing himself by my fire, and is a civil spoken fellow. Still, if your honour objects, I'll rout him out to the tap—that's a fitter place for the likes of him."

As he spoke, Steve went straight to Nevinson, seized him by the shoulder, and shook him roughly.

"Here, you," he said, rudely. "Stir yourself; you've had enough warmth for one set of lazy bones out of my fire. Rouse yourself, man, and don't sit between the fire and nobility. The tap's the place for you."

Nick rose sleepily enough and scarcely seemed to comprehend the landlord's meaning.

Steve cursed him, easily and fluently.

Nick growled something indistinct, as if partly angry, but sulkily rose, yawned, stretched himself, and glowered at the landlord.

"All right, Boniface," he said at last, his voice stupid with slumber and drink. "I know my place; none better."

Nick lurched towards the door.

"Now, order my horse round," commanded Nemo, making for the fire and raising his glass as if drinking to it.

Captain Barclay; who had hesitated a moment and stood in the centre of the room, eyed the three curiously, but was apparently satisfied.

He took a seat near the chimney corner, pulled his hat farther down over his face, and, as if desiring to avoid observation, kept his cloak wrapped well about him.

Nemo drank his wine, scarcely noticing the newcomer, and with much deliberation began slowly to pull on his gloves as he heard a horse being led from the yard to the front of the house. Picking up his change, he walked with an air of extreme boredom to the door and prepared to ride away.

Outside, on the cobbles, Nick waited, and as he helped Nemo to the saddle whispered to him.

"Barclay," he said, in a low voice.

The other nodded.

" I saw him at the Chequers," Nemo said.

" He's here to meet Drake; you may stake your last goldfinch on it," Nick urged. " It is luck indeed they should choose our house."

Nick's friend agreed by a sign.

" I'll be back in ten minutes," Nemo whispered, eagerly. Rapidly mounting his horse, he threw down a coin which jingled on the stones, and with a loud " Thank you, my man," rode off in the direction of Barnet village.

Ten minutes later, Nemo, afoot, might have been seen entering the " Lantern " door, and quickly rejoined Nevinson, who was impatiently seated in his bedroom, waiting the beggar's return. The two men sat talking in the darkness until Steve Randall came up and explained to them the mysteries of the passage behind a section of the panelling.

Half an hour went by, or perhaps a little less, when, on the dark road outside, the sound of horses' hoofs and the grinding of wheels was heard. When the vehicle stopped before the " Lantern," it proved to be a chaise drawn by a pair of horses driven by an outrider, with three of John Sheldon's retainers travelling on horseback behind. Only one man alighted from the chaise, Sir Ladbroke Drake, and he, after giving some instructions to the retainers, walked into the " Lantern," while the escort with him took turn and turn about in keeping an eye on the horses and resorting to the warmth of the tap.

Sir Ladbroke Drake walked into Steve Randall's big room, preceded by the landlord, and in the dim-lit interior glanced round with the anticipation of a man who appears to keep an appointment. Nor was his quest in vain, for as soon as Sir Ladbroke entered Captain Barclay rose from his corner and came forward to meet his leader.

The two men talked commonplaces for a few minutes as Steve Randall bustled in and out about their needs, but when he had departed, having placed a bottle of port wine and two glasses between them, they sat in the shadows cast by the fire, with heads close together, in earnest consultation. Nick and the beggar king, behind the panelling, were within a foot of the two conspirators, and could hear every word of the whispered conversation.

" And what about the Dutch in London ? " asked Sir Ladbroke.

" I have made full inquiries," Captain Barclay said. " It is a ticklish business, but there is a market for the King's reply to France. They will not take a copy on trust, but must see the document itself."

" Pest take them ! " Sir Ladbroke said, his hands playing with the stem of his wineglass. " Sheldon insists on having the script as it is written. But we can get over that. What is the offer worth ? "

" On proof that it is genuine, they will pay one thousand English guineas for a sight of the screed and a copy."

" Do they know whom it is coming from ? " Sir Ladbroke Drake asked.

" Yes; I had to tell them that—these Dutchmen

are keen. They say they must interview the King's messenger who brings it south as proof."

Sir Ladbroke Drake shrugged his shoulders.

"The price is fairly generous for such news, but the conditions are dangerous. Where is the address of the Dutch negotiator?" he asked.

"'Tis a house in Wine Office Court, off the Fleet —a narrow place, and a small house, though several men are there always, and desperate fellows they seem."

Sir Ladbroke knitted his brows, carefully considering the proposition, which evidently presented some knotty points for solution.

"I hardly like that clause about the messenger," he said, at last. "It means so much delay. We have ample warning that he will be through Barnet to-morrow, and some description of the nature of the man. He is a Captain Forest, and will wear a cockade of silver ribbon tied to his hat. He travels alone, but only by day, and we have arranged to have him stopped by the Hadley Woods, about the hour of three to-morrow. Instead of knocking him on the head and leaving him there, we shall have to take him alive and carry him to town. Plague take these Dutchmen! And we shall have to travel home quickly, for I must put the paper in John Sheldon's hands without any delay that would arouse his suspicions."

Captain Barclay, looking furtive as he drank his wine, the shadows playing on the bold, hawklike face, watched his patron, but offered no suggestions. The other sat in silence for many minutes, a frown on his face, as if he were piecing together some puzzle in his mind. At last he seemed to see his way clear, and his crafty face grew less thoughtful. With an intaking of his breath, he looked closely at Barclay.

"We must have that thousand guineas," he said, at last; "come what may."

"Well, what's the office?" Barclay returned. "My hands itch to handle a few gold pieces too. I'm prepared to do my share and introduce you to the right parties, besides taking my half of the risk."

"Hark ye well," Sir Ladbroke answered. "You go forthwith to town and await me there. It will be dark by five o'clock to-morrow. I'll drive into Fleet Street by that hour at the latest, and you may await my coming with at least two men. The rest you may leave to me. I'll superintend the stoppage and the capture of the messenger, Forest, myself. Do you ride at once?"

"No," answered Barclay. "I'll sup and sleep in Barnet and travel with the sunrise."

"And I'll return to the Chequers," Sir Ladbroke said, rising. "Be careful of my instructions, and be particular to await my coming at the hour of five with two muscular bravoes, in case Forest proves difficult to handle in the city street. You understand?"

"Quite," returned Captain Barclay. "You may rely on me to the letter."

Sir Ladbroke Drake, standing, drew his cloak about him, bowed almost imperceptibly to his companion rook, and strode out of the inn.

After his carriage had drawn away, Captain Barclay remained on in the " Lantern's" silent room, drinking his red wine.

Upstairs, Swift Nick and Nemo sat together in the bedroom by candlelight.

" Sink me," said Nick, red with laughter, " what a game!"

" Of the very best," Nemo answered, grinning. " I have notions on the way it should be played."

" And so have I," Nick said. " Let us compare ideas on the subject."

They remained talking together until far on in the night, while unconscious of their plottings, Sir Ladbroke Drake drove back to the Chequers.

CHAPTER XXI

By Hadley Wood the road was always very quiet, and on Sunday afternoon, about the hour of three, the way was almost deserted. Indeed, a stranger going along by the wood about that hour—and there was only one—might have been forgiven for imagining himself alone.

So thought Captain Forest—the man answering to the description already in the possession of Sir Ladbroke Drake—of the King's Messengers, who, mightily content with himself after a substantial lunch at Hatfield, was riding his horse easily at the trot. Figure him as a soldierly person, in the prevailing habit of his time, a wallet strapped to his shoulders, going easily forward and twisting his moustachios contentedly after the manner of military men the world over and through all ages.

So he approached the Hadley Wood, self-satisfied and apparently anticipating no danger. Just as the road grew dark in the shadow of the elms on one side of it, six men came from their hiding-places beneath the trees, and, spreading out in the road, bade him to stop.

Captain Forest—for proof of his presence was apparent in the cockade of silver ribbon tied to his hat—when challenged by such formidable numbers, quickly reined in his horse.

For a man so upstanding, with moustachios that bristled of war, and a pointed beard of distinctly martial character, he was extremely amicable. When Sir Ladbroke Drake rode out to join his henchmen—for the seeming footpads were serving him—Captain Forest at once became the essence of sweet reasonableness.

"What want ye of me?" he asked Sir Ladbroke, jocularly. "I yield to any superior force. Faith, I'm not so mad with the love of Old Rowley that I risk my precious skin to the odds of seven to one."

Sir Ladbroke, pleased with the easiness of the man, reined in his steed.

"You are Captain Forest of the King's Messengers," he said.

"Well, and if I am, what of it?" the other asked, twirling his moustachios.

"I want your presence for a drive to London," Sir Ladbroke Drake said, pleasantly for him.

"And if I refuse?" the other suggested mildly, his manner showing he had no stomach for altercation.

"You go in that case as a dead man, instead of in comfort as a much alive gentleman," Sir Ladbroke returned, grimly. "Come, my brave gallant, you are playing with desperate men and are easily outnumbered. It will pay you to be reasonable. You cannot hope to make headway against my little army."

The messenger raised his hat and bowed profoundly.

" I give way to two things," he said, with a laugh
and a leer that suggested disloyalty. " To the will
of God, or the force of men."

" I have the latter," Sir Ladbroke said, slowly,
and the disloyal glance of the messenger started a
sympathetic gleam in his own eyes.

" But what would you of me ? " Forest asked.
" I have but little money and less property."

" You carry a message for France," Sir Ladbroke
answered. " I want that for a suitable market, and
I need your presence with it."

The messenger looked Sir Ladbroke in the eyes, and
the leer on his face grew more clearly defined.

" Is there money in your market ? " he asked,
amicably.

" There is money to the extent of fifty guineas
if you are complaisant," Sir Ladbroke Drake answered, readily enough.

" And if I resist ? " the messenger asked.

" We knock you on the head," Sir Ladbroke
returned, with an ugly grin.

" Ah ! I see," Captain Forest said. " A man
after my own heart, I fancy. Believe me, I'd sooner
be a live soldier of fortune with fifty of the best
than a dead messenger with nothing but the broken
head that caused my funeral."

Sir Ladbroke Drake laughed loudly. The adventure was turning out nicely to his taste. The
messenger, who might have shown fight, was as disloyal a rascal as himself and willing to be bought.

" I see," he said, at last. " The wind lies that
way, does it ? Well, meet me in my needs, and the

fifty guineas are yours. 'Twill be easier for you and more pleasant for me. An easy journey to London, and fifty guineas, eh? What do you say?"

Captain Forest laughed, easily.

"That will suit me so far as it goes," he said, grinning at Sir Ladbroke, "but I have a face to be saved."

"What more would you have?" Sir Ladbroke asked.

"Safe conduct back to Finchley," Forest answered, glibly. "Then, when I have my fifty guineas, you will bind me and otherwise show I have been mis-used, and see that I am discovered in sore straits by credible witnesses."

Sir Ladbroke Drake, more than charmed with the sweet reasonableness of his capture, agreed to the unexpectedly favourable conditions. With Forest, Sir Ladbroke and the six henchmen he had gathered turned off through a path in the wood and came to where a coach was concealed in a lane leading to the main road. The two clambered into the vehicle, and side by side, with three of the six men as escort, set off to London.

His companion proved a rascal after his own heart. Confessedly open for plunder, he met the conspirator at his own game. So lively was his readiness to grant Sir Ladbroke's wishes in the matter that the latter, measuring the man's readi-ness to sell his honour by his own, outlined the plot that he and Captain Barclay had matured. Not only did Captain Forest hand over the papers and consent to play the part of unwilling prisoner before the Dutchmen, but five miles short of London he submitted to being bound, and even allowed his clothes and facial appearance to be so dishevelled as to suggest signs of a tiresome struggle.

The coach dragged on, without interruption, to London. So pleased was Sir Ladbroke Drake that at Islington he dismissed his escort and bade them return. With the bound man in the coach, he made the rest of the journey to the city. Five o'clock was striking as he reached the Ludgate, and already the streets were dark and lent every aid to his designs. Captain Barclay stood awaiting his leader in the shadows of the gate, with two assembled bravoes. Sir Ladbroke briefly explained the situation to him. Together, the prisoner making no sign of resistance, they went along the Fleet to the dark passage which Captain Barclay indicated, and after knocking on the big heavy door of a narrow gloomy house were admitted.

Never was a plot more successful. The prisoner was a born actor. In the presence of the three Dutchmen he comported himself as a man brought there by force and suffering from grievous wrong. He would not answer questions nor explain anything. To every question put to him in broken English, he replied with a volley of angry oaths. He violently resisted an effort to search him, the successful result of which was to reveal proofs of his identity. He was so morose, and so mulish, that a stranger to the circumstances could not have guessed that he had a part in the designs of Sir Ladbroke Drake.

The negotiations were long, for there was suspicion

on both sides, but the story told by the three convinced the Dutchmen. The oldest of them, a grave man clad in sober clerkly habit, after puckering his brows over the document Sir Ladbroke delivered, nodded his head slowly. Forthwith he began to make a fair copy of the letter, which was all the more valuable to him as it was favourable to the Dutch and apparently put an end to the designs of France. Then in a dull, heavy, business-like way he paid Sir Ladbroke Drake, in little bags of English gold, the thousand guineas for which Captain Barclay had bargained. He did so with some show of disgust, for though the Dutchman was steeped in political intrigue, he played the game according to his lights—which were as honest as political intrigue would allow—and had no respect for traitors.

" Now, go," he said, at last, after counting out the payment. " In my country, for what you do men are shot," he added, with heavy cynicism.

" In my country men are hanged for the same thing," Sir Ladbroke replied, brazenly. " That is," he added, " if they are found out."

" Take care of your prisoner," the elderly Dutchman said, " and see that he does not unmask you."

" As for that," said Captain Barclay, who was enjoying the joke, " he'll give us no trouble. A knock on the head in a dark alley will settle his hash. Dead men tell no tales."

Captain Forest fumed all the more. His indignation at this threat was not the least pleasing part of the comedy to Sir Ladbroke Drake and Captain Barclay.

The latter held out his hand to the Dutch secret agent.

" Adieu," he said ; but the other made no motion to take his hand.

" Adieu," answered the stolid foreigner, and then shrugged his shoulders. " I do not intend to take your hand."

" S'death, you mean to insult me ? " Captain Barclay shouted, while Sir Ladbroke's face crimsoned.

" One cannot insult traitors," the Dutchman answered simply, turning to his companions. The words spoken to his associates were evidently meant to set them on their guard against any action the two English men might take.

The anger in the hearts of Sir Ladbroke Drake and Captain Barclay was visible on their glowering faces, but the manner of the three Dutchmen was inflexible. Swallowing their rage they motioned to their prisoner, and were soon outside the door and in the narrow street.

" Where now ? " said Captain Barclay, looking at Sir Ladbroke.

" To the Chequers, Hitchin ; I want you there," he answered.

" And the prisoner ? " Captain Barclay asked.

Sir Ladbroke smiled.

" He goes with us to Finchley. I think we may dispense with the escort. He is one of us," he added.

Within the hour they were going at a round

canter north, and London was well behind them.
The three men had stopped talking, for speech was
difficult through the noise and vibration of the coach
on the rough road. Captain Barclay and Sir Ladbroke Drake sat side by side, looking to the front
of the coach. Captain Forest, freed from his bind-
ings and huddled up, seemed to be half asleep.
The night was dark, with no moon, and there was
a faint drizzle in the air. By seven o'clock they
were well past the Highgate.

As they went through Finchley, Sir Ladbroke
stirred Captain Forest with his boot.

" Where shall we put you down ? " he asked that
bravo.

" Oh, half way across the common, by the roadside," the other answered, readily enough.

Sir Ladbroke Drake nodded.

In the fitful light of the carriage, he drew out
one of the bags of money and counted out fifty of
the gold pieces. These he handed to Forest, who
counted them over again, carefully, before putting
them in his pocket.

They travelled in silence together, Forest looking
out of the window. There was not much to be seen,
for the place was one unrelieved black waste, and
looked dour and grim from the coach window.
Very suddenly, however, the man seemed to make
up his mind.

" Here, by God! it looks lonesome enough to
rob even a King's Messenger," he said. " I'll get
down here, if you'll pull up your driver."

Sir Ladbroke, with his face outside the window

of the coach, called to the coachman, and the great, lumbering vehicle pulled up.

"I must thank you for a heartening adventure," Captain Forest said.

"Pish! you played a useful part," Sir Ladbroke answered, with a grin.

"Aye, and a bonnie one," agreed Captain Barclay.

"I have a still prettier part to play," the messenger said. "God send you like it as well."

The two men opposite looked at him, somewhat startled.

"What mean you?" asked Sir Ladbroke, laughing to hide his uneasiness.

"I want the full price of my disloyalty—the rest of the golden guineas," the messenger said, sharply.

"What mad notion is this?" growled Captain Barclay.

"There is no madness about it," Forest said. "You stand and deliver, in the good old way, or one of you will find a chunk of lead in his skull."

Before they could change their positions Sir Ladbroke Drake and Captain Barclay were gazing into the barrels of a great pistol, and two mocking eyes looked at them over the sights.

"Trapped, by God!" shouted Sir Ladbroke.

"No, by the messenger," the stranger returned. "Do you deliver, or must I persuade you with an honest bit of lead in your ugly pate?"

The three confronted each other in silence for a brief space of time in the dimly lighted, stationary coach.

" My advice is pay," said Captain Barclay, whose face had whitened.

Forest smiled at him, mockingly.

As he did so Sir Ladbroke Drake realised the second's advantage of the man's divided attention. With a leap he sprang upon the messenger, one hand clutching the arm that raised the pistol and forcing it upwards, the other grabbing the man's throat. The weapon went off with a roar and the ball crashed through the carriage window, adding to the explosion the noise of the fall of broken glass. Captain Barclay had dived, as he saw the pistol waving in the air, but now that he knew he was safe he followed the example of his leader and threw himself on Sir Ladbroke's prisoner.

The struggling figure they held became quiet, and they allowed him to raise himself. In the scuffle the huge military moustachios had apparently disappeared. The face they looked upon was clean shaven.

" Zounds ! " said Sir Ladbroke, triumphantly ; " it's Nevinson—our dear old friend, Swift Nick. What a turn in the luck ! We have him like a rat in a corner, and we'll drive him into Barnet, where they'll teach another road rascal to keep sheep by moonlight."

Swift Nick laughed in their faces.

" Who are the rats ? " he yelled. " Look to yourselves, for the trap is better baited than you think."

His confident manner sobered them in their triumph, and involuntarily they glanced about the carriage.

"By the Lord, Sir Ladbroke, look you there," Captain Barclay shouted, and his face blanched.

In at the broken window peered a masked face, and an arm with a pistol was thrust through the opening, covering them.

At the same moment, and as Sir Ladbroke turned to make a dive for the other door, the second window was smashed and the shattered glass made way for another pistol, which threatened in the wavering light.

"Ho, there! Nick, lad," shouted the first man who had shown himself, a masked figure on horseback. "Shall I blow out one of these rascals' brains?"

The voice was Nemo's, who, judging from his words, was expecting Nick.

"No, by the Lord, no!" answered Nick. "They've got a thousand goldfinches. Bag the swag and let them cumber the earth for a while longer. Pull them out on the road and go through their pockets."

No sooner said than done. In a trice Nemo and his three men were hauling the wayfarers out of the coach, and as each startled man was pulled from the vehicle, his pockets were searched.

The bulk of the booty was found upon Sir Ladbroke Drake, but there were rich pickings on the person of Captain Barclay. In less than three minutes, all the property had been transferred. The four highwaymen mounted their horses, and Nick bestrode Starlight, which had been led to the scene.

The two conspirators stood shivering on the road in the misty rain.

Nick and Nemo, pulling in their steeds, which were slightly restive, looked on their victims.

" They've evidence to hang you," Nemo said, still wearing his mask. " What say you, if we knock the beauties on the head ? The dead cannot raise the hue and cry."

Nick glanced contemptuously on his enemies.

" Nay, let them go," he said. " This is not our last meeting, and there are still bigger scores between us to be paid in full."

Sir Ladbroke Drake's keen, crafty eyes were fixed on Nick, and he followed their conversation closely.

" I take it we may go," he said, his voice sullen and heavy with anger.

" Thanks to Swift Nick, you may," Nevinson answered. " And take care, you who raise the hue and cry. You may have evidence to hang me, but be assured first that I have not evidence to hang you. Many of your plans I know, but you are only guessing at the least of mine."

Sir Ladbroke Drake, followed by Captain Barclay, slowly climbed into the coach. The evil in his heart was glowering in the former's sinister face. He spoke no word to Nick and made no sign of his intentions, but beat upon the panels of the coach and ordered his half-paralysed driver onwards into the night, in the direction of Barnet. Silent, white with anger, baffled, he crouched in the corner of the rumbling coach, while Swift Nick and his companions, ironically saluting, watched the coachman saw upon his reins and urge the horses forward along the North Road.

CHAPTER XXII

As Swift Nick, mounted side by side with Nemo and his followers, saw the coach bearing Sir Ladbroke Drake disappear, he burst into peal after peal of hilarious laughter, in which the beggar king joined him.

It is needless to say that by the simplest of all means they had forestalled Sir Ladbroke Drake on that Sunday morning. The roadsters, who worked a perfect secret service for Nemo, had easily found Captain Forest and advised Nick and his companion of the messenger's approach. They had waylaid him ten miles before the bogus messenger was spoken by Sir Ladbroke and warned him of the danger. Captain Forest had appreciated this warning by giving Nick a glance at the way the royal letter was made up. The document Sir Ladbroke Drake had sold in London was a clever forgery contrived by one of Nemo's men. A disguise was easily within the resources of Swift Nick, and the appearance of the highwayman in the place of the real Forest followed as a matter of course. The messenger of the King went forward through bypaths and completed his journey in safety, so far as Nicholas could judge.

Nick was recalled from his hilarious appreciation

of the jest by the facts of his own position, and his manner at once grew more serious.

" Where shall we make for now ? " Nemo asked Nick, for he was in fine feather over the big haul. " Shall we to the ' Lantern ' and share out the booty ? "

Nick suddenly saw the situation in another light. He remained in deep thought for some seconds. Then, as if making up his mind, he rode forward slowly, with Nemo by his side.

" I have already made up my mind," he said. " You will go to the ' Lantern,' and my share of the spoil can be handed on to Steve Randall. But if I return to the inn it will become a prison again. S'death, I've done the trick this time."

Nemo, for a moment, did not follow his train of thought, and rode on in silence. Suddenly his eyes brightened.

" God, Nick! you're right," he said, earnestly.

" That I am, my buck," Nick returned. " Both Sir Ladbroke and Barclay recognised me. Together, their word is good enough, for a summary hanging, if the traps run me down. And you may take it as certain they'll raise the hue and cry at once, and hunt me from pillar to post."

" And what do you propose ? " Nemo asked. " I know of a snug place for a Tobyman in the city, where a man might lie low and spend his guineas royally if he were so minded."

" Aye ! " said Nick ironically. " I could do that at the ' Lantern,' and be out of the way while those two devils in front complete their dirty work.

No; I know a better trick than that," Nick added, earnestly.

"Listen," he went on, as Nemo looked at him curiously. "You can watch the Chequers night and day."

"By the Lord, I can," Nemo said, confidently, "both inside and outside of the house. Nothing of moment, neither comings nor goings, can escape me. Our eyes never close on Sheldon's headquarters."

"Then I can trust you to see that Mistress Sheldon is safe?" Nick asked.

"Implicitly," the other returned, decisively. "No harm can befall her—rest assured of that."

"Then my game does not consist in lying low but in being abroad, playing a bolder part. I'll make an alibi."

Nemo's eyes gleamed, and he nodded his head as they trotted side by side.

"I'll ride like the whirlwind all the night and put such a distance between me and Finchley that no one will believe I could have stopped Sir Ladbroke at the hour he states. I'll ride hundreds of miles."

"Which way will you head?" asked Nemo.

"By the North Road," Nick answered. He slapped his thigh appreciatively, and his face lit up as he thought over a sudden idea. "By God, Nemo, that's the order of the going. I'll ride to York and be there for breakfast. I know an innkeeper who will swear I slept in his house overnight. And I'll see the King or one of his advisers and recount what I know of the plot from Chequers Court. And, faith, if I'm run to earth on this recognition, I'll call the King himself, or one of his own servants, to witness my alibi."

Nemo agreed with this startling proposal. It was a plan conceived on the bold and spectacular lines he loved.

"Good, my buck," he said. "And luck be with you. If aught happens at the Chequers, I'll keep our messengers forward. You can pick up any information from me on the way back at the usual places. You'll find all the horses you need on the road if you make the sign."

Off the main road, the party beat their way in the direction of Barnet, and at Elstree, which lies west of the "Lantern," they parted at the cross-roads. Nemo and his companions, who had been unrecognised, could safely show up in Barnet. Nick shrewdly guessed the new hue and cry would be already raised, and that he must make the best pace possible across country to get ahead of it, avoiding the highway until he had well passed Hitchin.

Nemo and his men took the turning to the right, shouting their adieux. Nick waved his hat as he swung off along the lonely byway, and by eight-thirty he had set out on his journey north. The night was dark; a drizzling rain beat down; the roads were soft, and, in some places, veritable quagmires. Starlight, a game steed, stumbled about in the gloom, and Nick prayed for the time when he could get off the sidetracks in the deserted country and, once on the highway, make a better speed over his hurried flight to York.

Starlight, gallant roadster, capable of going his fifteen miles an hour on a fair road, made slow pace in the direction of Hitchin through the narrow, foul, and heavy country lanes. The journey Nick had set out to accomplish was, measuring from London, close on the two hundred miles. From Barnet the distance into York was all of one hundred and eighty-eight miles, while the detour Nick was making added a good ten miles to the length of the journey. The country through which he was journeying was as quiet as the grave. Only once in the run to Hitchin did he pass a vehicle, the lumbering van of a carrier making through the night in the direction of London. At Starlight's full pace at one time ; again at a walk, for thirty minutes together, as the horse scrambled along the frightful roads, Nick pushed on through the night—by tiny hamlets and past straggling thatched cottages that showed no lights and gave no sign of life beyond the occasional barking of a dog. The hour was well on to eleven o'clock before he came to the byways upon the outskirts of Hitchin, and found his way to the " Running Hart," a tavern like a hole in the wall, built in the shadow of the church. Starlight was done up, and Nick would not ask his steed for more. Instead, he reined up outside the silent inn, and with the point of his sword tapped, in the darkness, on the latticed window panes.

A sleepy, frowsy head was pushed forward when

the pane was opened. So far as Nick could see from the round face, the man was angry. A surly voice asked what the devil was meant by dragging an honest fellow out of his bed in the middle of the night.

"A horse, a horse—the best you've got," Nick commanded in a whisper.

"A horse be damned!" the surly voice answered. "This isn't a posting-house; it's a lawful tavern. We keep no horses for fly-by-nights."

Swift Nick looked up, angrily.

"At the name of Nemo, you old fool," he said, raising his voice slightly.

"Make the sign," the innkeeper replied, changing his manner at once.

With a wave of his hand, Swift Nick did so.

Without further parley the head vanished from the window. In an incredibly short time the man appeared at the rear door, the sound of the lock being shot back making an angry echo. Speaking no word, the old fellow opened the stable and came back, leading a big high-standing bay by the halter. Both Nick and the old landlord of the " Running Hart " made haste to transfer Starlight's trappings to the bay, and Starlight, as if he knew the way, slowly dragged himself into the stable.

Nick swung into the saddle.

"Good-night, old Dave Sidcup, and good pickings," he said, in farewell.

The other saluted with the sign Nick had seen first used by Nemo's messenger coming to the " Lantern."

"Have ye heard any hue and cry?" Nick asked, as he settled in the saddle.

"Nothing have I heard these two hours," the innkeeper answered.

"Then sleep well, old worm," Nick returned, gaily. "It's evident I'm first here, and that's a fact. The devils will have to make good running if they get the news past me and up the road before I fly through. And it won't work up to Doncaster, this side of the dawn, I'll wager. Pleasant dreams, Sidcup," he added; "and when they rout you out you have seen nought and know nothing."

"Aye, aye, my fly-by-night," the old man answered.

Nick touched the willing bay with the spurs, and was off on the straight route for York, leaving the innkeeper to gaze after him until he disappeared.

Two miles from Hitchin Nick stopped. A new sound had been added to the rustling darkness and the drizzle of the cloud of fine rain. Booming away across the country stretching to Nicholas from the south, was the slow, menacing challenge of a heavy bell. The town call was pealing sonorously and slowly, and each clap of the hammer reached Swift Nick, sitting his horse, alert on the deserted highway.

"They are at Hitchin in good time," he said, cynically, and his spirits rose at the challenge of the bell. "They are hot after me on the highway, and raising hell itself. I am only started in time, but the road is free. And swift and silent must be the race for sanctuary."

From here Nick made fast progress forward.
The road was quiet, and the surface of the trunk
highway better. The bay, willing and eager,
soon began to stretch himself. The beat of his
flying hoofs was muffled by the soft going, but
the bay went forward, helter-skelter, not faltering
once in five miles. Henlow was well behind him,
and Nick had flown through, avoiding the centre
of the village and the sign of his presence that
would have been given by the ring of his horse's
hoofs on the hamlet's cobbled pavement.

In little more than half an hour he was descending to the Ivel and running along by the
oustkirts of Biggleswade. The clock in the church
was striking the hour of midnight as Nick eased his
horse and stole quietly through the sleepy village.

In fancy we may follow him on that pelting
journey through the night and the rain and along
the muddy roads. Yoho! what a ride! Mist and
more rain came as the horse and its rider, the bay
nigh spent and often faltering, left Biggleswade
behind and reached out for Buckden. Rider and
steed were half blinded by the water that dribbled
down Nick's cheeks and the horse's nozzle. As
the bay faltered over the bad parts, Swift Nick
would ease him ; when the going was good, the
horse, almost of its own accord, made a great effort
to gallop into the next village. Nick, with the brim
of his hat well down, would chirrup to the
animal and tell it aloud, as if it were human, the
few more miles it had to go. Yoho! and onward
through the darkness. The road, better metalled,

was hardening—a sure sign of their approach to the next village. A few lights were winking cheerily on the high ground, but the main street was enveloped in shadows black as pitch. Into Buckden at fifteen miles an hour—good going, but the spent bay was making its last game effort—and so on to the " George," an inn of fair repute, whose night ostler trafficked secretly with the roadsters and answered to the command of Nemo's name.

It was nearly half-past one as Nick drew out of the sleeping town and set his fresh horse to climb the Alconbury Hill, with a brave heart and a gluttonous notion of the work. But Nick pressed on too eagerly. The new steed went lame after making the descent from Alconbury. The horse had been going all out, on a fair road, a full sixteen miles to the hour, but from Sawtry, into Stilton, the pace was painfully slow, and Nick, swearing in his irritation, was walking his steed over the last mile of the approach. Stilton was abed and time was lost in rousing the " Pigeons " for a new mount. At Stilton, the fresh mount was a raw-mouthed roan which had flown the road on towards Doncaster all its nights. It made the fifteen miles into Stamford in the hour, and took the turnpike gate at the Wansford Bridge at a flying leap. So on through the night. The big roan seemed to love the work. Nick rode forward, swinging as if in a cradle. Sometimes he would seem to be asleep in the saddle for minutes at a time, his mind wandering strangely over the rapid sequence of events since he had been cast from the town. From this partial sleeping state he would awaken stupid, stiff, leg-weary, to find the ugly but useful roan stepping out with monotonous gameness and making the best pace of any horse he used that night.

Yoho! Grantham ahead. The rain had ceased to drizzle down. The air was clearing, and above, stars shone in a moonless sky. The trees curtseyed by like big dark ghosts, waving stark arms as they passed. Now and again Nick would see the gleam of a lantern carried unsteadily—some hind going early to the stables on the high land. With the dry atmosphere, as Nick drew further north, came stinging frost, and two heavy jets of steam issued from the roan's nozzle and marked its laboured breathing. The sharp, early morning frost stiffened Nick's wet garments on him and rasped his face until the very flesh seemed rigid. His hands grew so numb that he could scarcely feel the reins he held between his fingers.

Signs of life, heralding the breaking of the day, began to appear as he rode into the town. Dishevelled potboys were opening wayside taverns. Wagons were pouring out of the inn yards. The mail lumbered away in the gloom, the guard sounding his bugle to clear the road as the four horses plunged in the dark streets. Out of Grantham, on a new horse, went Nick, the hour after four. More wagons crept forward, their drivers half asleep. Sometimes he had to halt, as cattlemen, travelling towards Doncaster in the early morning, drove their disorderly herds slowly and let them straggle and choke up the highway. At Newark, the eastern sky was lighting. The castle loomed up gauntly on the high hill. Cocks were beginning to crow; kine lowed in the shippons. Fires could be seen alight in the thatched cottages; carriers' carts were stopping in front of the taverns. It was almost daylight when Nick rode through Retford. The life of the road was moving, and fresh horses were easy to find, for innkeepers or ostlers had not to be roused.

Yoho! away along the road, faster and faster yet, as Nick's spirits fell with the cold of the bleak dawn. Yoho! at such a speed that cottage children, now about, looked with astonishment at the flying figure beating its way to York. By hamlet and village, by castle and hovel; nigh awakening farms; up hill down dale, and with the light at a steady fifteen miles an hour, Swift Nick won his way to York. In that cathedral town, stirring busily to the general habit of its day, by side streets little used, and soon after the clocks had gone the half-hour after ten, a man and a horse might have been seen going at the trot towards the Shambles. He picked his way amongst the street traffic, the herdsmen, and the soldiery, rolling in his saddle like a drunken man and sawing on the smoking horse's mouth to keep it on its lagging feet. The last willing steed trembled in every muscle and nerve as Nick halted before a quiet inn used by drovers, and it seemed fully half a minute before the rider could stir in his saddle and dismount.

By the roaring fire, in the market room at the " Red Lion," Nick sat slowly thawing, a strong glass of reeking hot spirits in his hand

Jerry Ambler, the landlord, a ruddy middle-aged man with merry-looking face, stopped before him on his rounds.

"A good ride and fine pickings, Captain?" he asked, with a grin, but dropping his voice.

"Faith! I ride through the night?" said Nick, looking him straight in the eyes and making an almost imperceptible sign. "Why, I've just risen from one of your comfortable beds and have overslept in the warmth of it. I'm now away to breakfast. These are my chops sizzling now, and there's the breath of life in the scent of 'em on a frosty morning."

The other looked with equal fixity on Swift Nick's face.

"You slept here overnight," he said, slowly, but with a twinkle in his eye. "Humph! I must have let you in myself."

Swift Nick nodded, pointedly.

"I'll go and enter you in the books. My fools are lazy of nights and keep their beds. They may not have heard of your coming," the landlord said, waddling off with a grin on his ample face.

Swift Nick's appetite was not the worse for the adventure, and a drover, who had been drinking overnight and was toying with his food, watched the highwayman's attack upon the chops with an astonishment so profound that it ceased to be polite.

CHAPTER XXIII

TWELVE o'clock had struck when Swift Nick set out in the direction of the castle, after showing himself freely about the town of York. The adventurer was there to secure an audience with the second King Charles, but he did not find it easy to become a courtier at a moment's notice. It is never, at the best of times, a simple matter to secure audience of kings, even when one is something socially better than a highwayman; though all the world may know it as a fact that those who plunder in the grand manner and play the High Toby in the superlative degree over whole empires, have at all times had direct access to the royal ear.

At York, they kept Nick waiting in the great entrance hall to the castle while minor functionaries, arrogant in their offices, tried to pump him about his business there. Courtiers, coming and going, looked on the travel-stained young man superciliously and passed on with an irritating suggestion of languid contempt that made his ears burn. The women of the court, mincing by, gazed on his faded finery and handsome face with warm, glancing eyes that set Nick's blood afire. Lacqueys, who judged his social importance by the fact that he was left

326

to kick his heels in the great corridor, pointed Nick
out amongst themselves. With sneer and jeer
they made merry at his expense, until Nicholas,
mad with rage, would fain have run amuck amongst
them.

Swift Nick had asked to see the King on urgent
business from the south, and had been roundly
laughed at for his pains. Seeing how hopeless the
position was, he had craved an interview with Lord
Shaftesbury, the King's confidant and Chancellor.
He was roundly begged to state his business by a
dozen jack-a-napes in office, who came and went
from the castle chambers. In great despair at ever
being successful in his quest, Swift Nick had an
inspiration. He took paper and pen and inscribed
his business on the former as "respecting a city
plot and rising against the King"; sealed the paper
with a wafer and again sent a message forward.

Then it was the luck turned in Nick's direction.
A slim gallant came along one of the dark corridors
and loitered in the entrance hall, apparently asking
a man-at-arms for some one. Nick saw himself
pointed out and looked eagerly over to the new-comer.
Recognition, in each case, was simultaneous. The
much bewigged, languid courtier threw off his
studied grace of demeanour and rushed toward Nick,
heartily slapping him on the shoulder.

"Why, mad Nick Nevinson, the fire-eater, how
do you here and what brings you? Faith, it's good
for the rheum in the eye to see you."

"Taunton, by the grace of God!" Nick said,
fervently. "Well, here's a start, if ever there were

one. Since when did you dance attendance on Rowley ? ''

Their greetings were cordial and lavish. It took both men some time to get to their affairs. Taunton wanted news of town and the gay company he had left behind him almost as soon as Nick had departed. He minded the duel with Sir Ladbroke, the fracas in Isaacs' night house, the affront in the Argyle Rooms, and the earlier incidents of their association. He seemed delighted with the encounter ; was vastly amiable and set great store on his friend's appearance.

" And what's the game ? " Taunton asked, at last. " What brings you here ? Have you found Eldorado yet ? I mind you made a glorious but impecunious exit on a golden quest."

" I am a gentleman of fortune," Nick said, a grim smile on his bold face.

" With pockets full of guineas, I hope ? " Taunton added.

" I am so-so, with the goldfinches," Nevinson answered with a grin. " And yourself ? You fare well, of course, if you dally in palaces and with kings."

" I serve the Lord Shaftesbury," Taunton answered, " and Old Rowley in some small degree by proxy. It is vastly amusing business, and there never was a merrier company nor a swifter service. But there is but little money in Old Rowley's train, and the little we do get vanishes each night at the dice. I'm this minute looking for a man who wants to frighten Rowley with some tale of a rising. That booby of an officer says that you are the latest fool

with the bogy story. Surely, Nick, you don't
deal in secret plottings against His Merry Majesty?
Every day brings such a wasps' nest about our ears,
yet nothing happens but the buzz of it."

Nick saw his opportunity and took it.

"Faith, Taunton," he said, speaking quickly
and seriously, "I'm begging audience of the
King, but the Chancellor will serve. I have news
of great moment. Take me to the Lord Shaftesbury, I beg of you. It will be to your advantage
and mine. I deal in plots for the moment—
s'death, I do; but there is a sting in my wasps'
nest, if the King and his counsellors do not smoke
it at once."

Briefly, Nick recounted the outline of his story,
and Taunton, listening eagerly, out of his experience
of such messages saw the significance of all Nick
had to say.

"Shaftesbury is the devil," he said, at last;
"but he's an amiable little devil. He has a body as
small as a rabbit's and a brain as bright as a newly
cut diamond. He has the temper of a saint and
the soul of a satyr. Nor does he suffer fools gladly.
Faith, he'll flay you with his wit, if you fail to interest him. But I'll risk my influence here by intro-
ducing you to an audience with him. Follow me,
and we shall soon see whether anything can be done
toward bringing you face to face."

On the first floor, George Taunton bade Nicholas
wait in an anteroom while he went forward into
the reception room used by Shaftesbury, then in
the zenith of his power. Many minutes passed, and

Nicholas was growing restive as he waited under the close scrutiny of the men-at-arms. Suddenly, after some fifteen minutes, half of the large folding doors was opened and Taunton stood beckoning Swift Nick forward.

The apartment into which Nick strode was stately enough, though there was but little furniture save a desk and a few elaborately carved chairs. Along one side were four high windows looking upon a lawn, and through them the noonday sun streamed vividly, lighting the apartment with pitiless clarity.

Two men were in that room. One was a tall man of forty. He sat with his back to Nicholas. Three spaniels sprawled about the floor in eager pursuit of a coloured ball he kept tossing along the carpet, and, each time they returned to him with their treasure, the dogs were caressed and fondled and set off again in quest of the same object.

Though sitting in a low chair and clapping his slim hands with the gusto of a boy, Nick saw this man was of good presence and about forty years of age. His face was swarthy and somewhat harsh, the nose long and saturnine, the top lip slightly moustached, the lower lip heavy. He had a restless, lively eye which seemed to be lit with a humour, cruel and quizzical, and very personal to himself. His big wig was superbly dressed and fell upon his shoulders ; his coat was of black velvet ; a vivid ribbon across his waistcoat indicated rank ; he was dressed for walking, and there were no spurs upon his buckled shoes. When he rose, lazily, and, in contrast with his indulgent manner, snapped a harsh command to his dogs, Nick knew that he stood in the presence of the King himself.

The second figure—the Chancellor—was not impressive at the first glance. He sat at the desk and had evidently been talking. Lord Shaftesbury was small, undersized, and fragile looking. His slight body, clad in black, with fur collar and cuffs instead of ruffles and lace, scarcely seemed strong enough to bear the proud head of the man. That head was his remarkable feature, and, looking into the face, one forgot the pigmy body. Big eyes, glowing, showed the energy burnt up by the unwearying brain behind them. They seemed to read personal secrets at a glance and plumb human motives. They were crafty, selfish eyes, quick to see the trick of a game and turn it to personal account. And, withal, they were humorous eyes, and gave the light of laughter to the face, hiding at the same time the workings of a brain that plotted, schemed, and intrigued for wholly ignoble ends. The Chancellor was a man of fifty, and his lean, mobile, almost handsome face showed a mixed jumble of moods, amongst which craft, humour, unscrupulousness, and urbanity strove for pride of place. Such was Ashley Cooper, Lord Shaftesbury, Chancellor and favourite of the King, a few years before his fall.

The Chancellor did not rise to greet the newcomer, but sat at his desk, closely observing every detail of Swift Nick's personality. The King, after shooting a swift, ironical, humorous glance at Nevinson, turned to one of the windows and began to wave his long, white hand at three ladies crossing the lawn. When they had tripped away his manner changed to settled melancholy, and he appeared to be brooding absent-mindedly, taking, apparently, no account of the conversation, though in truth he was listening to every word.

" And you, sir," said the smiling Lord Shaftesbury—"your name is Nevinson, I hear ? "

" Nicholas Nevinson, sir."

" Of what estate ? " he snapped.

" Gentleman," returned Nicholas.

" Of means and possessions—eh ? " this with a sneer.

" Of fortune," Nick answered, grimly.

A smile flickered round the Chancellor's lips.

" What brought you here ? " he asked.

" To serve the King."

" For money—fortune—eh ? "

" If my lord wills it—yes," Nick answered. " I need money."

" We all do," said the Chancellor. " And if there be no money, will you still be anxious to serve us—eh ? "

" Yes," Nick said, firmly.

" Out of sheer loyalty ? " asked the Chancellor, mockingly.

" I would prefer the money," Nick said ; " but I am satisfied to be loyal."

" Aha ! aha ! " A cynical burst of laughter rattled through the room. It was almost a croak, and coming from King Charles reminded one of a regal raven. "Encourage this young blade, Shaftesbury, encourage him. There are not many men loyal to our person for love. Even you, my dear Chancellor, are always harping on pelf."

The Chancellor's eyes gleamed, sympathetically.

"Tell your story, Mr. — er — Nevinson," he said.

Nick, without further ado, told the story of the rising fanned by John Sheldon. At the mention of the latter's name, the eyes of Lord Shaftesbury ceased to smile. The ready geniality of the man suddenly disappeared. His lean face stiffened and his firm mouth seemed to set cruelly, as if it were a steel trap. And from the window a harsh voice croaked—"Sheldon, by the saints! Sheldon, the purse-proud cit—aha, aha!" as if the matter were a joke smelling of the charnel-house. Nick told his story to the end—of his love for Peggy, at which both King and Chancellor smiled; of the knowledge she had gained; of the conversation he had heard on the night of the ball. He gave the names, taking care to place Sir Ladbroke's first, the numbers of men promised, the places of assembly, and the date of the rising.

"And that is all," said Nick.

The Chancellor, seated low in his chair, his chin buried in the fur collar about his coat, looked grim, and seemed for the space of a minute buried in thought. He roused himself at last and looked at Nick as if he were reading his soul.

"And that is all—eh?" he asked.

" Yes, my lord, that is all, as I know it," Nick returned.

The harsh voice of the kingly raven was heard.

"All—aha, aha! By God, all, Shaftesbury! By the sacred heart, it is enough—and more than that. All—aha! aha!—all. Why, Shaftesbury, this threatens our person."

" Sire, it does," Shaftesbury agreed, with more gravity. " The news this man Nevinson carries supports messages that have reached me these two days. It is for your Majesty to say what shall be done ; but in my opinion this is important, and we should act at once."

King Charles came from the window, where he had been pondering deeply, apparently lost in thought. He stood in the centre of the room before the Chancellor and Swift Nick. For a moment he remained there, smiling sardonically. Then, stooping, he picked up the coloured ball and flung it far across the long chamber. The spaniels leaped to their feet and ran to follow it, but, quarrelling amongst themselves, forgot the ball. They came back, sniffing and irritable, to the feet of the King, and Charles, intensely irritated, cuffed them until they squealed.

His swarthy face, with the prominent nether lip, was clouded ; the humour had vanished ; his expression was a long, curt snarl.

" I train my dogs to obey," he said, at last. " Sometimes they fumble. They forget me and quarrel amongst themselves. Then I must beat them and bring them to heel."

" And what shall be done with this John Sheldon and his rising ? " insisted the Lord Shaftesbury.

The King took up the coloured ball and threw it along the chamber floor. The spaniels raced after it. One brought the bauble back, and, almost abject, laid it at the royal feet.

" Beat them," said his Majesty. " Beat them and bring them to heel. They must fetch and carry according to our will ; nor quarrel amongst themselves or challenge our authority."

He stood silent in the vivid sunlight streaming through one long window. The dogs were tumbling about his feet. They looked at him, abject, imploring, their liquid eyes supplicating, and Charles, stooping down, patted and fondled them.

" You have heard, sire," Shaftesbury said. " And what shall be our answer ? "

The King threw the ball again, and fondled the dogs when they raced back with the toy.

There was no humour in his face ; none of the supercilious nonchalance that was his armour ; only pride and the sense of power ; and behind, hatred of those who thwarted him.

" This is our will," he said to Shaftesbury, the long, lower lip jutting threateningly. " Break them ; crush them ; bring them to heel—the dogs place. Then we may play with them, when the temper is better—eh, Shaftesbury ? "

As he spoke the last words, his cynical face lit up with laughter. He was King Charles again, whimsical, undisturbed, assured.

" See to it, Shaftesbury ; see to it," he said,

after another pause. " See that they bring the ball back to our feet. They have been badly trained. We'll ride to-night and take them, village and town, by surprise, bringing our royal wrath about their ears."

His Majesty paced the room for a few moments, Shaftesbury watching him, closely.

" We ride to-night," he said, at length. " Give the word now, Shaftesbury."

The Chancellor pulled on the bell.

The Honourable George Taunton answered the summons, instantaneously.

" The King commands we ride to-night towards London," Shaftesbury said. " Give the order in my name."

The progress of Taunton, leaving the room for the crowded corridors, seemed to set the whole castle in motion. A bugle sounded. The court-yards, lazily quiet, became thronged. The soldiery in the town appeared, hurrying back. And about the corridors servants began to go backwards and forwards in every manner of eager questing.

" So," said Charles, looking on the Lord Shaftesbury, " we are indebted to this gentleman —Mr.—er—er——"

He flicked his fingers, as if he would pick the name out of the thin air.

" Nevinson, sire," said Nick.

" We shall not be ungrateful," the King said, a smile upon his sallow face.

Nicholas grew bold, basking in the brief glow of royal favour.

"If I might crave advantage of your Majesty," he said, "it is that you remember I was here at this hour."

"Surely, surely," the King replied. "That costs us little, Shaftesbury—eh?"

The Chancellor smiled at the King's characteristic, sardonic humour.

"And if I might ask one more favour," Nick began, haltingly.

"Aha! aha!" the King rejoined, laughing and looking more and more like a handsome raven. "Aha! Shaftesbury. Trust them; trust them; all who advantage us attack our purse."

The Lord Shaftesbury lay back in his chair, laughing heartily.

Nick flushed under the royal insolence, but pulled himself together, determined to push home his claim on the King's clemency.

"I ask no financial vantage," he said, humbly. "But if it should be necessary for me to sue for it, sire, I bespeak your royal clemency."

"Clemency, by God!" the King said, and he threw back his head, laughing loudly. "Clemency, Shaftesbury, as I live. All that he asks for such a service is our clemency. And, by the rood, he shall have that when it is wanted. Our clemency is not a costly ware."

Lord Shaftesbury's face was puckered by a further studied smile.

"It costs so little, sire, that for such a service, Mr.—er—Nevinson ought to have all the clemency he requires," the Chancellor said. " I take it, Mr. Nevinson, you are a damned rascal."

Nicholas shrugged his shoulders, emboldened by their levity.

" I have only stopped short of being a courtier," he answered, with a grim smile that stirred the King again to humour.

The audience was at an end and Nicholas stood ready to go.

The King motioned him forward and held out his hand. Nevinson, kneeling, kissed it respectfully.

" Believe us, Mr. Nevinson," said His Majesty, " you will find we are not ungrateful—in the matter of—ah !—clemency. Adieu, my gentleman of fortune, until you ask our royal favour."

Nicholas left the castle and went back to his inn. At three o'clock, he started his return journey to Barnet and the "Lantern."

By midnight he was passing through Stilton, a town wholly asleep. He routed out the ostler of the "Cock" Tavern for a fresh horse, and tossing the drowsy man a guinea, mounted and was riding out of the inn yard.

A figure emerged from the shadow of the porch and laid his hand upon the bridle, pulling the new horse up in its own length.

Nick was about to curse him roundly, when the new-comer made a sign.

" Nemo commands," he muttered, and thrust into Nick's hand a sealed docket.

By the light of the ostler's lamp, after tearing

it open, Nick read the message that had arrived by road.

" Come without delay to Barnet," were the words scrawled in a well-known hand, and the brief message was signed by the familiar flourish of the beggar king.

CHAPTER XXIV

To account for the happenings after Swift Nick set out on his overnight journey to York, we must return to follow the fortunes of Sir Ladbroke Drake and Captain Barclay.

The two drove from the scene of their humiliation on Finchley Common, so madly enraged that scarcely a word was spoken between them for a full half-hour. Indeed, it was not until the vehicle in which they travelled was lumbering into Barnet that Sir Ladbroke Drake broke the silence. For mile after mile of that journey he had sat chewing the cud of his bitterness, scarcely able to trust himself to speak. Swift Nick had triumphed all along the line since they had first crossed swords, and his threat of further interference, more significant in view of his past successes, ate like a corrosive into Drake's mind and made him for the first time uncertain of his own judgment and the successful issue of his plans.

"Curse this popinjay!" he said, at last, as the coach rattled through Barnet. "Every time he crosses my path, my plans miscarry. He seems to have the devil's own luck."

"Aye, and the devil's own ubiquity," growled Captain Barclay.

They rolled on for a few minutes, when Sir Ladbroke again broke the silence.

"It comes to this, Barclay," he said, at last. "Before another hour goes we must set about the task of breaking this Tobyman. Now, between us, we have the evidence to hang him."

"Yes," agreed Barclay. "All we need is the young devil's body."

"And that we must find, alive or dead, ere another day go by," Sir Ladbroke Drake suggested.

With this end in view, the two halted their coach at Barnet and there set alive the hue and cry which, fanned by the offer of a reward of £200, in addition to the amount placed upon Nick's head by the outraged forces of the law, set in motion all the machinery for the chasing down of desperadoes. Captain Barclay himself led the party of men who started out on Nick's track, going south to London, and Sir Ladbroke urged on the men who rode for the North, intending to set every village up to York anxiously agog for Swift Nick's appearance.

Satisfied that as far as human incitement could ensure it, the North Road was being rendered too hot to hold Swift Nick in safety, Sir Ladbroke, still consumed with anger, though his rage was now under better control, journeyed alone to the Chequers, at Hitchin, where he arrived about the hour of eleven.

Peggy Sheldon had gone to her room an hour before, and Sir Ladbroke's arrival was evidently expected, for John Sheldon, poring over his papers, sat at the big table in his gloomy library. Peggy, in her chamber, heard the arrival of Sir Ladbroke, and locking her doors, once again made use of the secret passage and pried into the secrets of the two men.

Sir Ladbroke Drake, glowering with rage, came into the library in no pleasant temper, as Peggy well could see. He threw himself into a deep-seated chair and surlily returned John Sheldon's greeting. Truth to tell, he could only tell a portion of his adventure. He was not supposed to have trafficked in the papers stolen from the king's messenger, and laid these before Sheldon without telling him of the misadventure that had befallen them and himself. Sheldon looked the papers over, and, as far as his parchment-like face could show pleasure, it did so. The news was entirely favourable to his city interests, for even if the rising on which he was risking his reputation did not succeed, at least the rupture with France and a possibility of better relations with the Dutch, agreed with the policy of the commercial speculations in which he was engaged.

Peggy began to find her vigil intolerably dull as Sheldon bent with wry face and intent eyes over the paper, but the next words surprised her out of her boredom.

" Well," said Sheldon, eyeing Sir Ladbroke closely, " how goes the game ? You seem in ill humour."

" Ill humour ! " sneered the other. " I am accursed ; haunted by a damned spectre of a fly-by-night. I was hauled up and robbed on the road, with Captain Barclay, by the gallows bird, Swift Nick."

John Sheldon looked up, with some anger showing upon his crafty face.

"Damn the young upstart!" he said. "He seems always to be cutting in upon our tracks. We must lay him by the heels. There is some leakage here at the Chequers," he added, reflectively. "He gets too closely on to our plans. To-day, I am having the whole of the approaches watched."

Sir Ladbroke's scowl deepened.

"I've put the traps upon him again," he said, at last. "Captain Barclay is scouring the road to London, while we have set the hue and cry going along the road to York. He will be a slippery customer if he gets away to-night, and I have evidence enough, with my coachman and Captain Barclay, to set him swinging. But zounds, Sheldon, I am convinced of one thing. Mistress Peggy is in league with him, and has some method of communicating. He used threats to-night and suggested he knew more of our plans."

Sheldon sat frowning in silence, and turning recent events over in his mind.

"It's the jade," he said at last, as if making up his mind. "We made a mistake in dragging her into our affairs, or in opening up our projects until we were ready to force them to an issue."

The tone of his comment suggested that he was weakening in the matter of the contract relating to Peggy. The truth was John Sheldon had begun to see his way out of the wood. Their plot matured on the Friday, when the promised rising took place. He was developing the idea that if he delayed the issue, and the rising he had planned were successful, he would be able to snap his fingers at Sir Ladbroke Drake. At least, he saw clearly now that the only risk he ran was failure. If the rising inflicted defeat on the King's army, he could dictate his own terms. In the event of failure, he would still have to pay for the silence of Sir Ladbroke Drake. But one thing was clear, delay in carrying out his pledge would be to his advantage until the end of the week.

He reckoned without the acumen of his fellow plotter. All that he thought, Sir Ladbroke had foreseen as he had driven silently through the night, after he and Captain Barclay had separated at Barnet. And thinking quickly in his wrath, he had realised other possible turns of their association. Nick's threat had set his mind at work. His words, if they had meant anything, conveyed the threat that not only were their plans known, but that they would miscarry. He feared three things: Sheldon's success and the weakening of his hold on Peggy's guardian; Swift Nick's power to convey Peggy to safety from under his nose; and his own possible identification with the Puritan plot, a fact likely to weaken his grasp on Sheldon by compelling him to flee the country. Shrewd schemer as he was, he had made his decision, and that was to secure Peggy at once, leaving himself free to cover up his tracks and take no further part in the uprising. He proceeded now, as he saw John Sheldon hesitating, to compel the city magnate to his purposes. When the latter spoke of Peggy and the mistake they had made in forcing her to their wishes before they were ready to take action, he jumped at once to the main issue, as if he knew the very thoughts passing through Sheldon's mind.

"God!" he said, at last; "I'm sick of this shilly-shallying over a young girl's fancies. We must take the affair in hand resolutely. This man Nevinson has the luck of the devil. He may interfere again at any minute if he get out of the ring I have set about him, and spirit Peggy off under our very noses. I have made up my mind; the marriage must take place at once."

Sheldon looked up suddenly, and his face paled. An ugly frown settled about his long lean features. This was the last proposal he had expected to hear; the one he desired the least.

"Zounds!" he returned. "I'll have none of that. We'll wait until after the great rising. We'll wait and see what Friday brings forth."

Sir Ladbroke Drake brought his fist down on the table, urgently.

"We'll wait no longer," he said, passionately. "I've waited too long, and I have given too many chances already. To-morrow, I insist, we ride, and Peggy goes with us to town."

"I tell you," said the other, "I'll have none of it. To-morrow we have Bleakmoor to meet, and the two delegates from Bedfordshire. We cannot move away from here on Monday."

"Tuesday will serve, admirably," Sir Ladbroke answered, as one making a concession.

"No," Sheldon said, his voice rising. "I will not move so quickly. I insist—you must wait until after this momentous week in our affairs is over."

"And I insist," Sir Ladbroke answered, his voice rising too. "We wait no longer. Tuesday at the latest."

John Sheldon scowled.

"I will not move from here," he retorted, shouting the words.

"You will move at my bidding, and do as I say," Sir Ladbroke threatened. "I call the tune."

"Damn you! I will not dance to it," Sheldon returned, angrily. "I refuse, absolutely."

They eyed each other, passion rising on either side.

Sir Ladbroke smiled evilly, and the ugly expression on his face boded no good for Sheldon.

"You will do as I say—or——" He stopped, leaving the sentence unfinished.

"Or what?" asked Sheldon, with increasing anger. "You threaten me again?"

"Yes, by the Lord! I do," Sir Ladbroke said, speaking the words slowly. "I fear this man, Nevinson. I fear the risk of delay with you. I want my payment according to our compact, and I must have it—Mistress Peggy and her fortune. Either you ride on Tuesday with your niece or I ride alone to York."

"You mean——?" John Sheldon paled in his anger as he realised the other's suggestion.

"Yes—that," Sir Ladbroke answered. "Refuse at your peril, and if you do, I ride to York and warn the King."

The other sat in silence, cowed by the threat.

"You are in my power, Sheldon, and you must serve my interest," Sir Ladbroke said, an evil suggestion of triumph in his manner. "Next week I might be in yours, and I am not going to risk it. All is fair in love and war, and I intend to collect your debt to me at once, while the trick of the game gives me the power."

Sheldon sat staring moodily into the big fire, but puzzle at the tangle how he might, he saw no other way out. Sir Ladbroke held the strong card, weakening with the passage of time; he held the weak cards, which grew stronger with the flight of the days. Down in his secret heart he had always held other plans for the disposal of Peggy and her fortune, and would have welcomed any method of postponing the marriage. He cudgelled his brains for an excuse, but could find no reason for delay. At all costs he must prevent the leakage of any direct information towards the King, likely to set his Majesty and the army marching before his own army moved along the road. He sat frowning and chewing the end of his pen, his mind seeking a way out and failing in its search, while Sir Ladbroke Drake remained, a smile upon his cold, hard features, as one who waits, certain of his power and confident of the issue.

The clock had ticked away a full five minutes before he broke the silence again.

" Well ? " Sir Ladbroke asked, at last. " Is it the King or Peggy ? Do I ride south with you and your ward, or north alone ? "

" South," John Sheldon said, slowly. " Let it be Tuesday."

He spoke the words, as if each syllable were forced from between his clenched teeth.

With a politeness so studied that it amounted almost to insolence, Drake swaggered out of the room. Peggy, from the secret passage, went to her bed, hugging further additions to her secret. John Sheldon sat alone in the gloomy library until far into the night.

Monday came, and, by noon, Captain Barclay. He was obliged to confess that Swift Nick had run clean out of the hue and cry and gone to earth. South, there were no traces of him ; north, there were rumours of a solitary figure flying through the night ; but all the evidence differed in details, and none of it seemed likely to be helpful.

John Sheldon, Sir Ladbroke, and Captain Barclay discussed this at long length, and during the day were much together. Peggy went about her personal affairs in the house, apparently light of heart, awaiting the development of the plot. Although they had not unfolded their intentions, she had warned Nemo, and had no doubt her message was speeding with certainty along the North Road.

Morning dragged on, and brought Lord Bleakmoor

to lunch. Afternoon came, and with it hurried visits from the city and neighbouring squires. The light waned outside, and the big rooms seemed to grow more threatening with the oncoming of the darkness. Peggy, in her chamber, looked out of the leaded windows as the light failed. The clear frost of weeks had gone for two days, and Peggy gazed into a cheerless world of mist and drizzling rain, through which the stark trees in the park could be seen tossing their naked branches, threateningly. She began to wonder if her message had reached its mark, and as the darkness came, grew more and more anxious.

Peggy had decided in her own mind to consent to the plot to take her away by force, and trust to rescue on the road. Now, torn with doubt, she was wondering whether to avail herself of her line of retreat and make use of the secret passage, escape into the night, and, with such aid as she could summon, seek Nicholas along the highway. A great unrest had fallen upon the girl, who now stood torn by two impulses: one, to wait and trust to the resources of her lover and Nemo; the other to take immediate action, and fly. The girl's oval face grew more and more troubled as she looked out on the gathering night, and she shivered as she turned away to dress for dinner.

The evening meal was a taciturn affair. Peggy was nervous and uneasy. Her lips trembled, and her hand shook as it conveyed the food to her mouth. She tried to keep up some show of gaiety in her manner, but failed entirely to conceal the strain on her nerves. The girl's voice, even as it rose in raillery, would carry a note of hysteria and grow excited, though every effort of Peggy's mind was concentrated on keeping her self-control.

John Sheldon, at the head of the table, glowered as he sat absently following his own preoccupations, his gaze sometimes turned uneasily on Sir Ladbroke and sometimes on his niece. Drake was silent too, reserving himself for the scene he thought must come; but whereas Sheldon passed many dishes, he ate a liberal meal. Captain Barclay seemed satisfied with his world. He ate much and drank liberally, until his hawklike face grew flushed and his bold eyes sparkled with evil sensuality.

No reference was made to the morrow, and Peggy, somewhat reassured by the fact that she had not had to face a scene with the three men, returned to her rooms.

The hour was eleven and she was retiring, when John Sheldon, walking slowly, came along the corridor and knocked unsteadily on the door. Hastily she threw a dressing-gown about herself, and opened to him. He came, with great deliberation, into the boudoir and stood confronting the girl.

" We ride to-morrow," he said, his voice hoarse, his manner direct and threatening.

" Where to ? " she asked, her lips quivering.

" To London," Sheldon answered.

" For what purpose ? " Peggy said, her voice rising.

"Sir Ladbroke claims your hand, and will not be gainsaid. I am in his power. The marriage will take place at noon."

She bowed her head, almost submissively.

"As you please," Peggy answered.

She did not say anything further. Sheldon looked at the girl, suspiciously. He did not like her unexpected calm; it seemed to him almost threatening.

"You will be ready to ride at nine—eh?" he asked.

"If you command—yes."

He was puzzled by her manner and nonplussed. In his next words he voiced his suspicions.

"You are watched, remember," he said, his voice rasping under the influence of his mean emotion. "During the last few hours we have discovered much."

"What have you discovered?" she asked, scornfully.

"That!" he snapped, and placed a slip of paper in her hands.

She turned it over and her face paled.

Written on the paper were the words—"All is well," signed with a bold initial letter, "N."

"We discovered the traitor this afternoon, bearing your message as he skulked in the grounds," Sheldon said, enjoying his triumph in a grim, crabbed manner. "You are well observed, and we shall ride to-morrow under ample escort, despite your friends. There will be no slip 'twixt cup and lip, this time."

She spoke no word, but pale, almost stupefied,

swayed before him. Sheldon stood for a moment in silence and then slowly walked from the room. As he pulled the door to, Peggy fainted.

The girl must have lain there for many minutes. Peggy was shivering with cold as she came to her senses and struggled to her feet. The room was in deep gloom. The candle had burned low. The only noise was made by the drift of rain against the window panes.

And something more—a scratching sound, against the panelling. It began carefully, as if some one were scraping with the point of a knife, continued for a few minutes, and then all was still.

With hope rising in her heart, Peggy staggered to the panel and threw it open. There, pinned on the woodwork with a tiny dagger, was a message scrawled on soiled paper, while from the gloomy space came the sound of retreating footsteps.

" Still all is well," were the words she read; and then, grandiloquently, " We have more than one ambassador.—Nemo."

CHAPTER XXV

REASSURED, Peggy slept soundly, and woke about the hour of seven o'clock to a world which was to be her wedding morning, if John Sheldon had his way.

Peggy, still anxious when her mind began to dwell upon her own preoccupations, made a careful toilet. Looking from her window, she noted that the day was showing signs of being radiantly fine ; the air was clear and the sun was slowly struggling through the clouds. By the hour of eight, she descended to breakfast and found Sheldon, Sir Ladbroke Drake, and Captain Barclay awaiting her. All three were in ceremonial attire, and Peggy realised, with evident disgust, that Sir Ladbroke, to make himself particularly pleasing, had taken unusual pains with his appearance. He wore the gay, salmon-coloured coat that marked his appearances in the social circles of London, and the long slim waistcoat of gold brocade. His linen was extraordinarily ample , his perruque unusually well dressed. He made pretence of being uproariously gay in manner, and greeted Mistress Peggy with stately, elaborate civilities, which made her gorge rise. It was characteristic of the three

353

conspirators that not one of them referred to the immediate purpose of their journey.

Breakfast was a dull affair, despite Sir Ladbroke's forced spirits. Sheldon was silent, immersed in his own affairs; Captain Barclay was dull, in the light of the early morning. Peggy vied with Sir Ladbroke in maintaining an air of unconcern, but once or twice she checked his elaborate, fulsome compliments with a pointed rudeness that made the gallant grind his teeth, and substituted discomfiture for the smile of confidence upon his face.

As the meal was ending a commotion was heard in the hall. Outside, the sound of horses, plunging about on the gravel, betrayed the arrival of several men, and after an interval some one knocked loudly upon the panel of the door.

For a period Peggy's face brightened. Her heart beat high, for at that moment she hoped Nick and his friends had come to carry the mansion by storm and bear her away by force. Sheldon was a prey to fears he could not explain. The noise of so many arrivals seemed to bode no good. Sir Ladbroke rose immediately to make inquiries. His face had paled, for he feared at the eleventh hour, some untoward incident had happened to upset his plans. Only Captain Barclay, dull after the wine of the previous night, maintained his composure and attended sulkily to the business of breakfast.

The clamour of the new arrivals set them all moving, and Peggy followed Sir Ladbroke and John Sheldon into the hall. There stood six uniformed men—officers to the sheriff—twirling their moustachios, while domestics peeped out from different corners of the house and regarded the new-comers with profound interest.

Sir Ladbroke Drake was the first to reach the hall, closely followed by Sheldon and Peggy.

" Well, sir," he said to the officer in charge, making a studied effort to appear nonchalant and unconcerned. " What brings you so early to the Chequers ? "

The man in uniform smiled, as one who had something to say likely to prove acceptable.

" We have ridden by night from Stilton," he said, pruning himself like a peacock. " About the hour of one, this morning, my men arrested Nicholas Nevinson, known as Swift Nick, on the outskirts of the town."

The fear in Sir Ladbroke's face vanished. Triumph, an evil pleasure giving inordinate satis-faction, was in his manner. This was a business after his own heart. He glanced at John Sheldon, who shared his emotion, and at Peggy, who, as she heard the words, seemed for a moment as if stunned. The sense of security buoying her up slipped away and left the girl hopeless, almost despairing. In the very hour of her trial, this, the worst, blow had fallen, leaving her no loophole of escape.

" We rode to warn Sir Ladbroke Drake," the officer said, " and Captain Barclay. Their evidence is necessary, and will be taken in the town of Stilton."

John Sheldon's face showed the dawning of a new hope. Here at least was cause for more delay, and he looked from the officer to his guest, eager to turn the incident to his purposes. Peggy, with beating heart, tried to believe the new misfortune would at least serve to postpone their departure and give time for a new arrangement of their plans. Sir Ladbroke would have none of it.

"Hark ye!" he said, to the officer. "Urgent business calls me to town, and I cannot ride to Stilton with you, to-day. To-morrow, by the hour of noon, I can promise you an appearance."

The sheriff's man shook his head.

"We must have some evidence," he said. "The prisoner is even now clamouring for release and denies his guilt, challenging us for proof."

"You must go, Drake," Sheldon urged, after a pause. "We must not let this upstart Tobyman slip through our hands."

Peggy listened to the altercation, hopefully.

"I ride to London on urgent matters," Sir Ladbroke continued, doggedly. "My friend Captain Barclay will attend. He will tell you all we both know. If his evidence is not sufficient, you must hold your prisoner until I reach Stilton at noon to-morrow."

Beyond this Sir Ladbroke would not go. Captain Barclay sulkily acquiesced in the proposal, and prepared to depart with the sheriff's officials. Sir Ladbroke stood whispering his instructions. Peggy, with a heart of lead, retired to her chamber, and found it occupied by domestics, whose mission was evidently not to leave her alone. Half an hour afterwards she heard the officers riding away, and looking out of the window, saw Captain Barclay swaggering at their head. Her thoughts were on Swift Nick, held in the little country town, waiting upon that man's word, while she, almost prisoner, was led away to London and to a fate worse in her eyes than the danger now threatening Nick. The girl's spirit was crushed. Pale, trembling, dejected, she cowered in her dressing-room, until the sound of the coach wheels, crunching the gravel in front of the house, told her of the nearness of their departure. In tears, almost hysterical in her despair, she deplored the weakness or trust that had prevented her from making an attempt to fly in the dead of night.

John Sheldon came to tell her that the coach was waiting. For the space of five minutes, the girl lost her head. Peggy raved, stormed, threatened, and refused to move. Sheldon, a grim smile upon his face, listened to her vapourings, but his purpose was inflexible. When his niece had exhausted herself, he turned to her, and with a threat in every word he uttered, spoke his mind.

"Time passes," he said, "and we must be in London by the half-hour after eleven. I give you a fair option—to walk to the carriage or to be taken there by force."

Peggy suddenly grew calm and ended her tirade. She was in his hands, and the servants about her were tied to his purposes. The girl choked down the passion in her mind and heart, and with a great effort after self-control, walked slowly down to the coach awaiting them at the main entrance.

12*

John Sheldon and Sir Ladbroke Drake had left nothing to chance. Sheldon had strengthened his escort to thirty men, some of whom were imported from the city, to ride against the King—bravoes who cared nothing for their cause so long as the pay was available. It was evident that John Sheldon and Sir Ladbroke did not intend their purpose should be thwarted by the intervention of any chance gang of highwaymen.

To the last day of her life, Peggy never forgot that journey. She sat in the coach like a bird in a cage, her warring soul beating against the bars. She had given up all hope of intervention with the knowledge that Nick had been trapped, and prayed only for some strange mischance that would set her free. In her bosom, she carried the dagger, used by Nemo's agent to pin the message to the panel, the night before; and in her young heart was the fixed determination to use it—either on herself or Sir Ladbroke Drake—rather than submit to dishonour. A young, wild creature of radiant beauty, she sat pale and still, speaking no word as the coach rolled on towards the city, her eye searching every object on the road in the hope that behind it lurked salvation. Sir Ladbroke lolled opposite to her, smiling evilly in the hour of his triumph, while John Sheldon, looking meaner than ever, fidgeted in his seat by her side.

Hitchin had long been left behind. They had gone through Barnet, and about the hour of ten the heavy vehicle, with its escort, was rolling through Finchley Common. Here, Peggy imagined was the last hope of intervention, but the progress of the party was not interrupted. From the common, the road went through an avenue of trees, which, though they were leafless, shut out much of the light. Once through Finchley, hope of any successful intervention was at an end. Through the avenue of trees they went until, almost at the end of it, they came upon a part of the road that opened out. The horses were doing their best, and the coach was swinging forward at fully ten miles an hour, each occupant being shaken bodily through the vibration caused by the uneven surface over which they were travelling.

As the coach and its escort drew near the open space, a single horseman rode towards them.

He was heavily cloaked, wore a plumed hat, and sat his horse like a travelling gentleman. The coachman paid but little heed to his presence, and the man cantered up until he was abreast of the team. Then, with extraordinary skill, he seized the bridles of the leaders, and with a wrench brought the whole four carriage horses to a standstill.

The coachman, with the suddenness of the stop, was nearly thrown off his seat. Inside, Sir Ladbroke was pitched bodily on to John Sheldon. With a volley of oaths, he recovered himself and reached for the window, out of which he thrust his head, storming angrily because the vehicle had been halted.

The figure on horseback now pranced away from the disordered, plunging team and sat his steed in the centre of the road, smiling mockingly at Sir Ladbroke.

The latter, looking into Nemo's face, even yet did not realise the nature of the stoppage. He regarded it as impossible that a solitary rider should bring them to halt for any other purpose than an unseemly jest. He took Nemo for a reckless gallant, for he bore none of the marks of the beggar about his person. He was superbly mounted, and, so far as his apparel could be seen, was attired after the manner of gentlemen of his day. Only his long, lean, predatory face—the face of the hunter and hunted in one person—belied the fact that he was a man of assured position.

Sir Ladbroke Drake shook his fist at the newcomer.

"Damn you for an insolent pup!" he yelled. "How dare you stop our progress?"

"As for that," Nemo said, easily enough, "it is a fine morning, and I am socially disposed. I thought amiable people of such fine habit would like to dally, and pass the time o' day."

At this insolence, Sir Ladbroke's face crimsoned.

"Have a care, my mad gallant," he said, threateningly; "take heed that I do not have you seized and whipped at the coach wheels."

The other threw back his head and laughed, and every note of his mirth was a challenge.

"Have a care!" he threatened, sitting his horse, with ever the mocking smile upon his face; "and take heed that I do not have you seized and hanged to the highest tree. They tell me you travel a lady with you. I desire to pay my respectful addresses. I desire, most of all, to ask if she travels willingly or approves of her escort."

Sir Ladbroke, for the first time, suspected the motive of the intervention, and his manner grew angrier than ever.

"I'll have you beaten and your ears clipped if you do not get out of the way and leave us free passage," he stormed.

"Hoho!" said the other. "I am not accustomed to bluster about free passages. I give them to my friends and levy toll upon those I dislike. My toll, in your case, is a word with the lady."

The effrontery of the man puzzled Sir Ladbroke. That one single person should have the nerve to hold John Sheldon's coach and escort up, was beyond his comprehension.

"Once for all, will you give way?" Sir Ladbroke asked, sternly.

"Once for all," said the other, wagging his head, jeeringly, "will you give me sight of the lady?"

Sir Ladbroke, fuming with impatience, looked towards his escort.

He spoke curtly to one hired ruffian—a dark-faced man, who sat his horse, a pistol in his holster.

"Seize this coxcomb, Austin," he said; "teach him a lesson with the horsewhip."

Austin, clutching the pistol, was riding forward to obey his leader's command. Nemo sat his horse, motionless, still smiling, now menacingly, unmoved at the prospect of having his head clubbed by the butt of Austin's weapon.

The servant approached, a trifle dashed by the unconcern of Nemo, and raised his hand, with the heavy pistol in it.

" Put it down," said Nemo, in stern command. " Put it down, I say ; you are a marked man." He was still smiling, but his eyes had a steely quality the bully did not like. He came on at the challenge, intending to deliver the blow, when just as he drew abreast of the solitary man who challenged their right of road, another pistol shot rang out, and Austin, throwing up both hands in a spasm of pain, crumpled in his saddle and rolled off to the ground.

Peggy had followed the altercation with heightening hopes. Through the coach windows she could see something of what was going on. The girl, in common with Sir Ladbroke Drake, had regarded the single man's intervention as mere suicidal recklessness. Her face blanched as she saw Austin ride on Nemo, but when the servant threw up his hands, she realised that he had been shot by another—that the solitary guardian of the road had not moved or flinched.

When Sir Ladbroke saw his man topple from the saddle, his crimson face, distorted with anger, suddenly paled. At once he saw the man in the road was no mere dare-devil adventurer, and that there was method in his intervention.

" Shoot the damned coxcomb!" he growled to the escort. " Shoot him down like a dog. Ten guineas for the man who brings him off his perch."

Nemo still laughed in his face.

"The first man who raises a firearm on me dies as sure as he makes the move," he said, his words crisp and threatening in their steely clearness.

The men about the coach hung back.

"Once again, I demand speech with the lady," Nemo commanded, and looking on him, Sir Ladbroke Drake realised that the game was going against him—though how, he could not see.

"I tell you, I'll see you damned!" he said. "Men, ride over the fool and drive on, coachman. If he interferes, shoot him down, I say."

"And, by God, if you want shooting you shall have it," Nemo said. "I hate to make a scene before so sweet a person as the fair Mistress Sheldon, but since you press me, by Rowley, you shall have it."

He took from his breast a silver whistle and blew on it—a fluted, birdlike call, clear but musical, and not very loud.

It seemed as if the road were suddenly filled with men, who came crashing from the trees—some on horseback, some afoot, some startlingly well clad, others apparently cripples or diseased mendicants —a ghastly looking rabble these last — but all armed.

They came into action silently, as if they were a trained army, and, at the sight of them, John Sheldon and Sir Ladbroke Drake knew the game was lost. The latter, in his anger, would not give way, but, motioning his men on, bid them ride through the crowd and protect the carriage, while Sheldon screamed to the coachman to drive on.

Nemo's arm went up as he pointed to the threatening escort.

"At them, boys!" he said, wheeling his horse from the side of the coach; and then Peggy saw a sight that surprised her. The whole heap of men were suddenly, it seemed to her, gone mad. A man, with an eye shielded, appeared at the window and clubbed Sir Ladbroke, sending him back into the carriage, the blood streaming down his face. The coachman made a brave attempt to whip up his horses as soon as he heard shots fired. Four nimble figures cut his traces and led the horses away, while another, mounting the coach from behind, seized the driver by the neck and threw him bodily to the ground. Almost frozen with fright, Peggy watched the *mêlée*, heard the occasional explosion of a pistol, saw a man on horseback torn down and clubbed, heard the grunts and curses of combatants, and now and again a wild scream of pain. John Sheldon sat cowering in the horseless coach, white to the lips. He saw, in the appearance of so many men, the intervention of perhaps the King's army. Sir Ladbroke, dabbing the blood from his face with a kerchief, now dyed red, leaned out of the window, urging the escort on towards resistance. He saw the mounted beggars, with pistol, sword, and club, ride into the escort, now surprised out of their senses and huddled together like sheep; heard the cries of wounded men, as Nemo's gang crashed into them; watched the huddled defenders waver, separate and break up, until all that were left mounted of the whole thirty, swearing in sheer hysteria, broke and rode away in the direction of London.

Long as it takes to tell, the scuffle did not last two full minutes, and suddenly the chaos became a quiet, orderly scene again, with only the groans of wounded men to suggest that there had been any disturbance. Out of the disorder came Nemo, gaily to the carriage window.

" I demand speech of Mistress Sheldon," he urged, coolly; but he no longer smiled. " If you resist, I'll blow your brains out and make carrion of that other hangdog knave cowering in the corner seat. Do you hear ? " he said, impatiently. " Bestir yourself, for we cannot hold the road all day."

Sir Ladbroke, baffled, speechless, helpless, moved from the window, and Nemo opened the carriage door.

His manner had scarcely altered since he had first pulled up the horses on the highway. He smiled as if he were greeting a lady at a fashionable rout.

" Good morning, mistress," he said. " I am to ask if you desire to go to London in your present company."

A bright smile crimsoned the girl's pale face.

" I am not in love with my escort or its project," she answered, primly.

" I am at your service, lady, and can carry you where you please, if you will ride pillion," Nemo said, gallantly.

" La, Master Nemo ! " Peggy said, rising to leave the coach, " you are most kind, although you have dealt harshly with our men, and I am sore concerned about all the broken heads.''

" They will mend, mistress," said Nemo, recklessly—" easier than broken hearts.''

One of his men helped her to a seat upon the pillion behind him.

" And now, Sir Ladbroke Drake,'' Nemo said, raising his hat, " I have to bid you adieu. I scarcely think we shall meet again. My desire, saving the lady's presence, was to riddle you with shot and truss you up to a tree like a common footpad, and the like I had in mind for that mangy, city hunk, John Sheldon. But I hear there is worse in store for you. The King left York on Monday, and is well upon the way South. I would not deprive his royal topsman of the task of hanging ye both.''

John Sheldon listened to the wild adventurer, and at the words his jaw dropped, and he looked with growing hatred at Sir Ladbroke Drake.

Clinging to the strange man who had come into her life so often, Peggy went at a trot that soon settled into a gallop, along the road towards York, behind Nemo.

One of the escort was dead; three others were binding their wounds. The rest had ridden for help. Nemo's army had withdrawn and the two men were left alone with the empty, unhorsed coach.

John Sheldon stood before Sir Ladbroke Drake, mad with anger, his piglike eyes blazing.

" Traitor! viper!'' he shouted, and then fell to cursing unintelligibly, in his overwhelming rage.

"You hound!" he said, clearly, at last, "you have sold me to the King."

"As I live," Sir Ladbroke answered, his eyes gleaming dangerously, "I know naught of what that hell hound threatened."

"Liar!" John Sheldon almost screamed.

Angry as he was, the gambler's mind suddenly cleared. He saw the game as it stood, just as he surveyed the situation when passions were high in the night houses of the West. The Sheldon party were down—hopelessly down. He would fly towards the King, inform, and make what terms he could. And here in the highway, he would silence Sheldon himself.

"No man calls me liar without paying the penalty," he said, significantly, and drew upon his sword.

Mad with anger, scarcely knowing what he did, with one thought only, to break the man he thought had betrayed him, Sheldon drew his own. No match for Sir Ladbroke, aroused and implacable as he was, their duel ended almost as soon as it began. Three swift passes, the clash of steel, a feint from Sheldon, and Drake's answering lunge disarmed the city man. John Sheldon did not ask for quarter. He knew his man now by the cold, purposeful ferocity gleaming in his merciless eyes.

Drake paused for the fraction of a second; then drew back and lunged again. Sheldon blindly tried to ward off the sword with his hands. The blade found a pathway through his heart, and Sheldon dropped convulsively, never speaking again.

"I call you to witness it was a fair duel," said Sir Ladbroke to the wounded attendants, who stood gazing with awe at this new horror.

Then Sir Ladbroke set himself towards York afoot, and went to meet his King. Nor did he look back again at the figure of John Sheldon, whose grey face, fixed in its last agony, stared through sightless eyes at the blue sky above.

CHAPTER XXVI

THE story of Swift Nick's discomfiture at the hands of the sheriff's officers is easily told. Anxious to get on towards Barnet, he quickened his pace between Stamford and Stilton, and was pushing a tired horse to its limits as he rode into the outskirts of the quiet old town.

The night was dark and the road silent, though all along he had received warning that the hue and cry was out and every man possessing a taste for man-hunting, with a fat reward behind the quarry, kept eyes peeled on the highway.

Once only had Nick met a likely patrol—outside Doncaster, in the early evening, an hour after dark set in. Something like a little army of riders, twenty in number, had approached. They had evidently been out all day, and liquoring freely in the town, for some were singing as they drew near. Nick found it easy to avoid them by reining in the scrub, and remaining there motionless. He saw the merry heads of the patrol bob along the road in a ragged cluster, and when the hoof-falls of their horses had died away, he had proceeded on his journey.

At Newark, later, he had called in a tavern, and as he sat in one room heard a party of men file out, with his name on their lips. Since then he had made good going, untroubled.

By one o'clock, he was travelling through a night blanketed with a mist that seemed to deaden all things. Almost feeling his way on a spent nag into Stilton, he ran full tilt into half a dozen men on horseback, who were holding the road; and, as he neared them, stood up sharply outlined as so many ghostly sentinels.

"Halt, there!" said a quick, gruff voice. "Halt, or we fire."

A hasty glance at the dark figures grouped together showed they were armed. The danger of retreating or going forward was about equal.

"Halt be damned!" Nick shouted insolently, as he pricked the sides of his spent mount and went dashing into and through the group of men.

Almost simultaneously, the six men fired on his retreating figure. Nick heard the balls whistling past his ears, but, sustaining no hurt, turned in the saddle and jeered at his pursuers, ironically waving his hat.

The patrol at once set off in his direction, and Nick, again pressing his spurs home, called for an extra turn of speed from the exhausted mare. To his dismay, the mare failed to respond, and instead of leaping forward, faltered. The fusillade had left Nick unhurt, but his mount had evidently received a ball. The mare staggered as if dead lame, and a further effort to pull her together only sent Nick's steed to the ground.

Nick had scarcely touched the earth when he

rolled clear of his horse and struggled to his feet. He was too late to make any effective resistance; the six riders of the patrol were upon him. Nick plucked out a pistol, but the first rider charged right atop of him, and, when the highwayman's piece exploded, the ball whistled away high over the heads of the sheriff's man. In a trice they were all upon him—one burly fellow clubbing Nick, while the rest speedily fell to clawing his struggling, resisting limbs.

"By God! I wager we've got him, my lads," said the leader, rising breathlessly after the sharp tussle on the ground.

"He's been astride one of the 'Cock' Tavern's horses," another husky but excited voice replied. "I know his old brown mare with the white fetlock. It comes from a house where they've always done a bit in the horsing of night riders."

"I arrest you, Swift Nick, in the name of the King," the leader said, his voice rising angrily, for his shins had been well barked in the tussle on the ground.

For reply, he got a burst of ironical laughter from Nick.

"Swift Nick, i' faith," laughed Nevinson, as if the joke were too good. "Shrive me, if you are not a gang of crazy pates unfit to guard your old wives' market baskets. I am a messenger of his very Majesty, in whose name you stop me. I charge you to beware of any delay your outrage may cause to my passage."

Nick's confident manner visibly shook his captors,

but, after wavering a minute or two, they seemed to make up their minds.

" Messenger, or Tobyman," the man who stood before him said, " we'll find out later. You are uncommonly like the gallows bird described, and you don't rush past our chance of the reward without further parley. You ride with us to Stilton, and we'll look at your credentials there."

To Stilton Nick had to go, a prisoner, and was cast into the tiny town gaol, a place of unsavoury odours and unpleasant rooms. He maintained a sturdy indifference to his captors on the road, and on arrival in Stilton, during a brief examination kept up his attitude and steadily denied his identity, vowing the vengeance of the King would fall on those who mishandled his messenger. His appearance, however, was so strictly in accord with the one sent down the road with the hue and cry, by Sir Ladbroke Drake, that the sheriff's officers would not accept his denial, though Nick was able to shake their confidence. The sheriff himself conducted a solemn examination of Nick, on the Tuesday morning, putting leading questions in a pursy, dogmatic way, and proving himself a very knowing fellow. He could not shake Nick, however, and grew cautious, for he was aware of the approach of the King. He decided to await both the coming of the royal procession and the arrival of Sir Ladbroke Drake and Captain Barclay, with their evidence of identification.

That day was the most humiliating experience of Nicholas Nevinson's life. The most interesting object on earth in Swift Nick's time was a captive highwayman. He became the very life and soul of the town and a desirable public spectacle. Nick's exploits, much magnified and largely mythical, had gone the rounds of the ballad-mongers—the true and the untrue being woven into a farrago of sentimental gush, hero worship, and pious moralisings. His exploits were familiar to all the good folk of Stilton, who came out to gloat over the bold-spirited, full-blooded adventurer; their interest heightened by the knowledge that the hero of the road was a promising candidate for a public hanging.

They crowded round the prison house all day, peering in through the barred opening in the heavy gate. Some were sympathetic and admiring; others openly jeered and reviled Nevinson; mothers held their babes up to look upon him as an evil example; little boys climbed up, peeped in, and then ran away squealing with fright. A few of the well-to-do paid the gaolers fees and entered the prison to converse with the highwayman. Two or three local gallants came and patronised him. A pretty, blushing damsel looked on Nick and sighed, leaving behind her a woollen comforter, though Heaven knows exactly what purpose she intended this to serve on the throat of a man who stood in the shadow of much more uncompromising neck-wear. A venerable man, of Puritan habit, appeared to inquire after Nick's immortal soul, and to point out, in salutary but vivid terms, the kind of hell yawning for highwaymen. Outside, the ballad-singers, almost as keen on the track of an execution as vultures are upon the ghastly fruit of war, were chanting the record of his deeds, with the metrical life-stories of other higher criminals, doing a ready sale of the broadsheets amongst the simple country-folk. One fellow, more enterprising than the rest, was already singing Nick's last dying confession, chanting the unsavoury horror in a monotonous, singsong, and raucous voice that set Nevinson's hands itching to strangle the words in his throat.

Only one gleam of comfort did Nick get. Eleven o'clock came, and then twelve—the hour of noon. The sunlight, stealing south, had crept round and began to flood the grim stone cell and slightly to warm it. The most of the crowd had gone to the midday meal, and Nick was left to his own bitter thoughts. He pictured many horrors arising out of his confinement, but the worst horror in his mind was Peggy, calling to him from the South along the road, and himself, laid by the heels, caught like a rat in a trap, unable to answer. His mind would dwell on these affairs to the exclusion of all other preoccupations ; they dwarfed even his own immediate danger. The thought of Peggy's danger constantly revolved in his mind, and he pictured every combination of horrors befalling the Mistress Sheldon, until his very fancies grew so real that they began to pass as actual pictures of what was happening, dancing with the heartless conviction of the mirage in the dark corners of his cell. And then, suddenly, in the gloom, he found himself thinking of nothing, while out of the world came the sound of a voice he knew. Wheezing, raucous, it sang the "Golden

Farmer's Last Farewell," sometimes breaking and wavering as if sound could be cracked and splintered into jagged silences. Slowly, as Nick heard that familiar voice, he listened more closely. It went over the verses one by one, with a quaint monotonous relish, and then, after a pause, sang them again. The second verse droned in the still air.

> " A gang of robbers then,
>   Myself did entertain ;
> Notorious, hardy, highwaymen,
>   Who did like ruffians reign.
> We'd rob, we'd laugh and joke,
>   And revel night and day ;
> But now the knot of us is broke,
>   'Tis I that lead the way."

The verses were being repeated for the second time, and Nick followed each word with a concentration that held every one of his senses strained. When the wavering chanter had finished the second verse for the second time, the voice suddenly broke off. An interval followed in which Nick heard the laughter and jeers of the idlers about the building ; then the wavering voice began with the second verse, over again.

Word by word, followed the lines of the ballad as the voice wavered, droned, and halted to the end, and, as the singer repeated the two last lines, Nick noted two facts—the voice was suddenly articulate, with a curious bell-like clarity, and the words had been slightly altered.

" But now the knot of us is broke," forming the last line but one, was followed by an altered line : " 'Tis Nemo leads the way."

There was no doubt about it. The message was there woven into the foolish ballad of the Golden Farmer. Nemo was speaking through the wavering, chanting voice of the Scrivener, and as if to make sure that his message was understood, that mysterious beggar repeated the whole ballad a third time, and the second verse was rendered twice, once correctly, and afterwards with the slightly altered line. After the Scrivener had reached the second verse and repeated it twice in the third recital, giving the two versions, Nick could hear his wavering voice die away as he trailed off along the streets.

At three o'clock, Captain Barclay rode into town, travel-stained after his long journey, and saw the sheriff at his house. In a few minutes, a party of servants followed the two to Nick's place of confinement.

Nick was pacing the cell, cheered by the brief message from the outer world, but still fretted by his confinement. The big door was suddenly opened, and the sheriff, Captain Barclay, and several attendants, walked inside. Nick stood in the dim light, still defiant, but at the sight of Barclay his spirits fell. For the first time, he saw the possibility of his life being sworn away before Nemo could have time to act or help.

"There's our man," the sheriff said, pursing his lips and blowing out his cheeks like a turkey-cock. "I, representing law, order, and His Majesty the King, say he is Swift Nick. The rascal says he is a messenger of the King I serve. You've seen the fly-by-night we want—who is this man?"

Captain Barclay looked with malignant triumph on the prisoner, and his bold eyes gleamed with the hate of a man who sees his enemy powerless.

"That is the man who waylaid and robbed us on Sunday night on the Finchley Common. He is Swift Nick Nevinson—one time Nicholas Nevinson, Esquire, a familiar at Isaacs' in Covent Garden and the Argyle Rooms."

"It's a lie, a damned lie!" Nick insisted, boldly. "I know this fellow. He is a gambler and a cheat. His word would not hang an unowned dog; let alone that it should swing a gentleman. I repeat, I am a messenger of King Charles, and demand the respect due to the royal service."

"And I say you are Swift Nick," shouted Barclay, his face flushing under Nick's insults, "and I can prove my words."

"Bah! your bare words would not carry weight with a dying tramp," Nick answered, contemptuously. "If this is your fancied evidence, Master Sheriff, you must set me free at once, or I bring the King about your ears, and in a royal, ugly humour; on my sacred oath, I do."

The sheriff, cautious man, was daunted. His personal predilection was a town trial and summary hanging; but one man's evidence was not sufficient for his careful mind, particularly when the prisoner claimed the protection of the King himself.

The sheriff's officer saw his hesitation.

"There was a second gentleman involved in the robbery, and plundered by the man Nevinson—

Sir Ladbroke Drake. He will be here at noon to-morrow."

The sheriff's face lightened.

"Messenger or Tobyman," the stout sheriff said, with heavy humour, "your neck does not bear the weight of your body, at least until to-morrow. I will see this Sir Ladbroke Drake first, and perhaps by that time the King himself. If the one calls you Nevinson and His Majesty disowns you, my pretty gallant, then I promise you just time for the shriving."

Captain Barclay looked angry as he heard the sheriff practically refuse his word.

"Shrive him!" he said, brutally. "I'd hang the dog to the nearest gibbet. Surely my word is to be taken before a common cut-throat's? String him up and put the responsibility on me."

"The responsibility is with the man who hangs me," Nick said, fiercely, his ringing voice carrying conviction to the timid sheriff. "God-a-mercy on the man responsible, whoever he be, if the King sees one of his gentlemen keeping sheep by moon-light. As sure as plague breeds sudden death, he'll set the sheriff swinging beside me."

This appalling threat, extravagantly couched, settled the sheriff's halting mind.

"At least," he said, blowing out his fat cheeks, "we may wait the coming of the King and this Sir Ladbroke Drake."

Scowling angrily, uneasy at the slip in his plans, Captain Barclay followed the sheriff out of the cell.

The afternoon wore away without incident, and

Nick sat despairing in his cell, the cheering influence of Nemo's message dying out of him with the passage of the hours. As the afternoon turned towards dusk, and the shadows deepened as the light gave out, the guard about the cell was changed and strengthened, the curious crowd thinned, and finally faded away and the place became quieter.

Nick was sitting morosely in the gloom, his only light a stray beam from a lantern hung outside upon the wall. His high spirits had fallen to the lowest depths of despair, when new voices were heard about the door.

"Ah! I may see this hangdog highwayman," a voice he knew well enough, said. " I have made good pickings from the ballad about his deeds, and I'll give two fair copies of the broadsheet for a sight of his ugly phiz."

" Aye, old mole," one gaoler answered, with surly humour. " Tip us the ballads and you may have sight of him."

A few moments after a torch lightened the room. It was held aloft by a gaunt, skinny hand. An old face, lined, gnarled, and twisted, with wild, peering eyes, appeared at the grating, and the upper part of a long white beard followed it. The light of the torch showed Nick plainly visible, glowering in the corner of his cell.

" And that's the merry dog, is it ? " the Scrivener said, in a thin, cackling voice. " A careless lad, I warrant, who failed to burn the Hand of Glory. What a life to shrive ! What a neck for the hanging ! What a body for the swinging ! "

The senile old beggar chuckled and cackled gloatingly.

"And that's Swift Nick, the bold highwayman —eh?" he continued. "An ugly rascal he do look, and a well-made gallows bird. I'll come, my lad, with a pair of silk stockings, to fit you for the topsman in the morn. A man who is to be turned off should be properly turned out, I say. I'll come and sing your last dying speech if they ever swing you up like the Golden Farmer. A merry lad he is, I'll warrant, who'll go gaily to the topsman if they send him there."

Cackling and chuckling in senile glee, the old beggar stood looking his fill on Swift Nick, as if he found him a rare spectacle; and when he had looked enough, sidled from the door with a blessing so blasphemous that even the watch outside was shocked.

Only Nick, who watched the old man closely, and guessed that mere idle curiosity had not brought him there, saw a tiny package dropped through the bars by the prehensile hand clutching at the iron work.

Nick, as quickly as possible, opened the package, to find a piece of paper and a phial with a few drops of liquid colour in it. The words, written in a rude, scrawling hand upon the paper, were six. The paper simply bore the message: "Paint blue spots on your face."

As Nick read the message, he cursed softly to himself. At first he was inclined to think the affair was some monstrous practical joke, and was sorely tempted to fling the phial and its contents to the stone floor. A minute's reflection, however, proved to his own mind there was method in the Scrivener's madness. In the strange underworld of the Ishmaels, he had learnt the existence of obscure ways of gaining not very obvious ends. The old man, if he could not help, would not be in the least likely to come and scoff at his fall. In the darkness, and as well as he could, Nick followed out the cryptic instructions. By rolling the paper into a fine spill and using it as a brush, he was able to dip into the colour. In the darkest corner of the cell, Nick was busily occupied in plentifully spotting his face.

The idea that he should be there, lying in the dark, painted like some clown at a fair, seemed so grotesque that Nick lay back laughing to himself for many minutes. But as the time dragged on, his curiosity to know the virtue of the blue spots became more than a jest; it haunted him as an ever-growing anxiety. About the hour of seven, he heard an aristocratic, cultured voice speaking to the guard in affected tones of patronage.

"This young blade, my son, is hankering to see the man you have laid by the heels," the voice drawled. "He has a morbid desire to speak with a cutpurse who is about to be hanged. As a matter of conduct, I do not approve, but I am prepared to humour him if you can admit us for a guinea."

"God bless your lordship, certainly," Nick heard the surly voice of the gaoler reply, hastily. "It's a proper taste for the young and virtuous to see them that's laid low through viciousness and sin. It improves their morals and elevates their minds. I'll show the rascal quick enough for a guinea," he concluded.

Nick heard the jingle of coins, saw the approach of a light, and heard the key turn in the lock. When the heavy door grated upon its hinges, Nemo walked forward—the beggar king in all his state finery, and the very gentleman to the life. With him was a younger man, of slight habit and mincing manner, ultra fashionable in dress, with a foppish wig falling over his narrow shoulders. He strutted behind the beggar king, his sword trailing on the stone floor, his spurred heels jingling. Nick, reviewing all the men he had known of Nemo's strange army, could not place him.

Nick's strange friend made no sign, and his companion, beyond sniffing the air, did not speak.

Instead, he insolently stirred Nick with a trim boot, and the latter, though confronted by four men, leapt up in anger and would have struck the buck.

The gaolers laughed heartily at their prisoner's humiliation, and Nemo joined them.

" A dangerous knave—eh ? " Nemo said, ironically. " A lusty cut-throat for the gibbet. Upon my soul, as a physician, I should like to study him at the hanging."

The new-comers all laughed heartily together, but Nick, guessing that his visitors had some purpose in deliberately insulting him, grew calmer, though he still simulated anger, and growled fiercely at them as they mocked him.

The elder gaoler, who had been spokesman, held up the light with a jocose laugh.

" Now, my pretty fellow, take a good look at this gallows face," he said. " I never saw a prettier face go to a hanging." His voice suddenly trailed into silence as the light struck full upon Nick's features.

" Good God ! " Nemo said, in great alarm, pitching his voice high and thrusting the younger man back. " Out, Stephen ! out, as quickly as you can."

The gaoler's faces turned pale as they saw the blue spots on Nick's face, and they stood, fascinated, glancing in terror from their prisoner to the visitor who had feed them.

" But, sir, I would ask him questions about his evil past," the young buck said, hesitating to obey the elder man's command.

" Out, I say ; out," Nemo repeated again, his obvious alarm increased as he crossed himself ostentatiously. " God-a-mercy ! this is the plague as sure as I live, and every breath we take may mean death to us as well as to this man's worthless carcase."

Nick stood there in the light, with the blue marks of death upon his face—death the most awful, in that it reached out from the stricken to corrupt the healthy and the quick. Every one in the cell stood in a panic-stricken silence before a man with the plague, doomed as he stood there, destined to give death to all who came within the influence of his tainted breath. And in his secret heart, Nick now knew the meaning of the Scrivener's foolish parcel, and thanked the gods that the grotesque instructions had been carried out. More, he did not laugh, but, with a groan, fell back, grovelling on the floor.

The panic-stricken silence was broken by the noise he made. The sight of the dreadful evil was too much for all. Nemo, familiar with the contagious influence of example, seized his so-called son and literally pushed him from the cell.

"Out of it, I tell you, my boy; out of it," he kept calling, urgently, as he forced on the younger man. "'Tis the shadow of death itself I see on that awful face."

With a shriek of horror, both gaolers scrambled towards the door after the visitors, one dropping his lantern with a clatter as he ran.

"The death! the plague!" they shouted, their terror-stricken voices fading out into whimpering gutturals and choking, breathless sobs; into the physical, inarticulate despair of living things suddenly face to face with some awful danger that seems to spell extinction.

Forthwith they ran pell-mell towards the town, and had gone some two hundred yards before they remembered their charge. Breathless, reluctant, they pulled up and gazed into each other's pallid faces. Recovering slowly, but with terror still in their voices and showing on their features, they went back to lock the prison door. They had not been gone half a minute, but in that brief period their prisoner had disappeared and they found it useless to fasten the door, for the cell was empty. Perhaps guessing the trick of it, they went clamouring back to the sheriff, who, frantic with dismay, rang the town bell, and once again set agog the wild clamour of the hue and cry.

CHAPTER XXVII

AT the cross-roads, outside Stilton, the three fugitives—Nemo, the young man who had masqueraded as his son, and Swift Nick—came to a halt after travelling helter-skelter out of the town and two good miles along the highway. Ringing in their ears still, was the warning of the town bell, raising once more the hue and cry.

Their horses needed a breathing badly, and as the three slowed up almost simultaneously, it occurred to all that they were flying the country lanes without any definite notion of what they desired to do.

"Phew!" said Nemo, "that was a near touch for you, Nick, old lad. You've got to thank the day you won my regard and the freedom of the road for coming out of Stilton with a whole neck to your shoulders."

"And that I do right heartily. We'll have a squaring of accounts, I hope, one of these days," Nick answered, warmly. "The point now is, where are we making for and what are we about? The Mistress Peggy Sheldon, how fares it with the lady?"

"Excellent, in truth," Nemo answered. "I

have her packed away safely in a disguise no man can penetrate.''

"Lead me there at once," Nick suggested, ardently. "I'll warrant I'll see through any disguise where Peggy is concerned."

"A monstrously pretty lass," said the foppish stripling bestriding a grey mare, which sidled restlessly as the two others talked, their horses going at a sober trot. "For one glance of the lady's eyes, I would even sacrifice my best friend."

Nick eyed the young lady-killer with rising indignation.

"I know not who you are," said Nick, irately; "it is sufficient that you have served me well and are a friend of Nemo's; but even gratitude does not give you claim to speak lightly of a lady whom I happen to respect."

Nemo grinned as he heard Nick's angry words.

"He's Master Gregory, a pigeon turned hawk, and in my favour," he said, pointing to the youth.

"Odds, man," the dandy said, jauntily, "I know not who you are; neither do I care. It's an ill day when a man may not sing the praises of a pretty wench. The Mistress Sheldon has a saucy eye and a pleasant smile for a comely gallant, I warrant you."

"You cock-a-hoop!" Nick stormed. "For two pins, or less, I'd make you think twice about what you say in the future, and eat the words you have already spoken."

"Gentlemen, gentlemen," Nemo urged, his teeth showing in the light of the rising moon.

" Let's put an end to this wrangling. It's an ill thing on both your parts to quarrel, with a road alive with traps behind and the King in front."

" So!" Nick answered, hotly. " But I ask leave to say the wrangle is not of my making. This popinjay, who stalks in the fine feathers, is too glib of tongue."

" Popinjay yourself," Master Gregory replied, with equal heat. " Because the lady smiled on you, 'tis no reason why she should not smile on me, as she did this fine morning."

" You saw her ? " Nick asked, astonished.

" In truth, I did," Gregory answered. " While you were cooped up like a woman brought to bed, I was out with Nemo, rendering her service. She was very grateful. Like all the rest of the jades, I warrant she is," he added. "Off with the old when he's in misfortune, and on with the new. A live buck of my parts is better than a dead highwayman of your style, Master Nick."

" You liar! you young tosspot! If you were more my size, I'd have you off the nag and spit you on the highway," Nick fumed, his wrath boiling over."

He was not prepared for the next incident.

" Liar yourself!" said the gallant riding at his side, swiftly drawing off his glove. Nick noted that the hand revealed, in common with all the youngster's limbs, was slender and dainty, and as he did so the glove whirled in the air, impelled by the same hand, and slashed him on the open mouth.

Nemo, for the moment, laughed almost uproariously, but Nick, in his rage, scarcely heard him. With a bound he was out of the saddle, and gripping Gregory as he trotted on, toppled him to the ground.

"Draw, you little whelp," he said, "and, Nemo, lend me your blade. I'll split the little fire-eater as a lesson in manners."

Gregory drew at once and placed himself on guard. Nemo, protesting, held out the hilt of his sword. Nick seized it and made towards the insolent dandy.

"On guard!" he said, and, saluting, went about his task of teaching the younger man manners.

No blade met his, however. To his astonishment the soft tenor voice that had already made him set Gregory down as effeminate burst into peal after peal of exquisite laughter, more feminine than ever.

"Who is this little prig with the spiteful tongue?" Nick asked, irately. "He is more like a woman than a fit subject for my steel."

The gallant figure in the road shook with laughter, and Nick, astonished beyond measure, listened until the outburst had finished.

"I am a woman, mad Nick Nevinson," a well known voice replied, and Nick turned all scarlet at the familiar use of the old endearment.

"Mistress Peggy," he said, surprised, delighted; and, after their long separation, the lovers fell into each other's arms, while Nemo affected to be caring for the horses.

It was a jovial party of three that mounted again and at the trot set off in the direction of Stamford.

13*

Peggy told of the happenings since the Sunday, the attempt at forcing her to marriage, the raid on the road, and Nemo's timely intervention and succeeding care. They had not learnt the end of the fracas with Sir Ladbroke and John Sheldon, but had pressed on towards Stilton, only stopping for satisfactory equipment and disguise.

Suddenly Nemo halted, and Peggy and her lover reined in their mounts.

"Where fare we now?" the first named asked seriously, "and for what purpose?"

"I ride to meet the King," Nevinson said, as if the matter had been decided. "I hold a promise of clemency from Old Rowley, and with all his faults, the King keeps his word. Behind, are Captain Barclay and all the sheriff's men. My business is to reach the King's ear first."

"And after that?" asked Nemo, his face changing from its habitual expression of devil-me-care recklessness.

"Why, after, should all come well of this journey, there is Mistress Peggy, and the 'Lantern' will know me no more."

Nemo sat his horse in silence. Suddenly from the road, and not very far behind, came the clatter of wildly driven horses, and the sound of voices calling to each other.

"The traps—the sheriff's gang from Stilton," Nemo said, all his attention on the sounds of the road. "It's a race now for Old Rowley, and I will see you there. After that our roads divide."

Swift Nick looked up, quickly.

" But surely," said Nick, " we do not part like
this after so many adventures ? My debt of gratitude does not end with a parting."

" Our debt will never be paid," Peggy said, her
sweet eyes glowing in the moonlight. " Bid him
to stay; make him stay," she urged. " Let us adventure onward together."

" 'Tis no use, sweet mistress," Nemo said, doggedly. " From now your ways and mine are different.
I have no favours to ask of the King. As yet, I
am not even suspect. The road is in my blood, and
I am tied to it by habit and inclination. The
King cannot grant me anything I value. I have
no use for the easy, adventureless life of the towns.
With you it is different ; with me it will be the
great North Road to the end."

Nick tried to stop him, but Nemo held on to his
purpose.

" It is better as it is, Nick, lad," he said, soberly.
" I'll miss you these moonlight nights, when I'm
abroad and about the snug houses where we have
lain low, so often, with glass and song and all the
cheer of both. But that's the truth of it—you'll
be wedded to Peggy and I'm wedded to the road.
With me it will be the North Road, as long as I can
sit a saddle or walk a mile. And now, press on, for
I know by the sound of them that the hounds behind are on our heels, baying their hearts out for
the reward."

The three wayfarers set their steeds going rapidly,
the hour being somewhere about eight. Behind
they could hear their pursuers. So wrapped up in their

own affairs had they been that the sheriff's men had been given full chance to make up the lost way, and as they flew forward now, both Nick Nevinson and Nemo realised that some of their pursuers at least were closer up than was comfortable. It seemed, too, that those behind had heard the sound of flying hoofs in front, and quickened up their gait.

The pursued and the pursuers sped on until the road turned into a straight mile. Looking back in the moonlight, Nick could see at least three figures riding at the gallop, and now not more than a few hundred yards behind.

Nemo swore softly. Nick leaned forward in his saddle to encourage Peggy. The girl sat her flying horse like a man, her eyes sparkling with the adventure, though her small teeth were set behind the straight, determined lines of her lips.

Away back on the road, apparently on faster horses, at least three of their pursuers were gaining.

The few hundreds of yards between became periously shorter: first, a hundred, then less than a hundred; the horses stretching themselves as if they were racing. In that mad, helter-skelter ride, Nemo's horse, deceived by the uneven road, stumbled, lost its footing, swerved, and fell. The two went plunging down together, through brief but valuable seconds, and then Nemo rose to his feet.

" Get on ; get on ! " he shouted ; " for the love of God. Don't wait for me."

" You go on, Peggy," Nick urged. " Follow the straight road."

" I stop with you," she answered, taking no heed of his command.

They stood waiting astride the sweating horses.

Fifty yards away, Nemo was mounting again. Nick turned back towards him. Behind Nemo, the nearest pursuer was in range.

" Stop, in the King's name," he called, hurrying forward with three other mounted men. Nick recognised his voice as that of Captain Barclay.

Nemo's answer was only a laugh and an insolent jeer as he pricked up his steed and strove to ride away.

Captain Barclay, flying forward, levelled a pistol at his disappearing figure. The weapon flashed in the night, its roar startled Nemo's horse forward, and the three fugitives, closing up, rode on towards Stamford. Nick, who was watching the other two, saw Peggy was unhurt, but Nemo's face had suddenly grown white; his body, instead of swinging easily in the saddle, grew lumpy and lifeless, and he began to sway and pitch as if about to fall. Nick closed on him.

" Steady, old fellow, steady," he said, holding Nemo as their horses galloped side by side.

" I'm done for, Nick," the beggar king said. " He's plugged me in the side. Leave me and get on with your lady. I'm only carrion now."

Nick still clung to Nemo's swaying body, but their pace was slower.

" Yoho ! " sounded Captain Barclay's voice, coming nearer. " We've hit one. Forward, and we have them."

Peggy had closed in, and, on the other side of Nemo, speaking no word, silent, determined, was supporting him in the saddle.

Nick turned round and saw Captain Barclay, eager, in full cry, the trumph of the chase in his face, plunging on to them behind, a pistol waving in his hand. Without a second's hesitation, Nick drew a weapon from his holsters, prayed that it would not fail, levelled the pistol, and fired point-blank at the oncoming gambler.

Through the smoke, he saw Barclay's horse galloping on alone, for Barclay had pitched forward out of the saddle, and was lying, with his contorted face turned towards the ground, his limbs working convulsively.

His fall stopped his two nearest companions, but behind, other figures on horseback were showing up. The only chance of the pursued was to ride and make the most of their temporary advantage.

Nick spurred forward, and the three, Nemo still swaying, galloped on side by side; but their gain was only temporary, for, in front, loomed dozens of horsemen, and in a matter of seconds they were riding into them. The new-comers, travelling South, were soldiers; and as the figures coming forward drew near, they levelled their flintlocks and, in a solid wall, barred further progress. As they halted, Nemo slipped in his saddle and nearly rolled off.

"Nick, lad," he whispered, leaning heavily on his friend. "It's sanctuary for you. They are soldiers of the King."

Nick, helped by the advance guard of the King's

army, lowered Nemo, and Peggy rapidly unloosed his tight waistcoat and cravat. The white linen of his shirt was dyed with blood. As they grouped themselves round him, the pursuers from behind came up, and the scene, as they stated their purpose, became somewhat confused. Indifferent to it, Peggy and Nick stood in the centre of a company of men as Nemo tried to rise.

" I have no favour to ask of the King," he gasped, as he struggled to a sitting posture. " My way is the road I rule, to the end."

The dying man coughed a little. His hand grew limp as Nick held it; his eyes glazed warningly. Then suddenly his limp hand contracted on his friend's in a final pressure.

" To the end, Nick," he said, making another effort. " This is the end. It's been a short reign and a merry one, but this is——"

He did not finish the sentence, but smiled, as if he realised he was losing the words, and saw how odd it seemed to others that he could not speak to them. Then his head fell forward with a laughing sigh. Nemo, King of the Road, had died.

The king is dead; long live the king. As one king passes from the stage, another takes his place and struts his hour. Soldiers were crowding up, and even as Nemo gasped out his life and Nick and Peggy, stupefied with horror, leaned forward to hear his last words, a great carriage lumbered up and short military commands cleared a way for it amongst the soldiery.

In the monolight, from the carriage window, a sallow, harshly humorous face, with wig falling forward, stared out on the strange scene—on Nick, holding his dead friend ; on Peggy, pale, apparently a gay gallant, crying as women will in the face of death ; on the soldiers, puzzled to pick up the threads of the matter ; on the pursuers, clamouring to explain and only making the confusion worse.

" Ah, ha ! " the King said, smiling as was his habit, " what have we here ? "

An officer went towards the royal coach.

" Some road row, your Majesty," he explained. " I cannot make top nor tail of it, and the more I listen the more confusion grows."

Nick stood up in the centre 'of the group and faced the King, who seemed to recognise him instantly.

" Part of your clemency I claim, your Majesty, for a dead friend," he said, urgently.

" It is granted," Charles replied, simply, crossing himself. " And amongst the living, who are you ? "

A group of officers, gaily equipped, jingled up and joined the crowd.

A gallant as nobly clad as any of the rest swept up with the latest new-comers, and his eyes fell on Nick and Peggy Sheldon. For a moment, he seemed surprised beyond measure, and then his manner changed to one of mean triumph.

" I am Nicholas Nevinson, your Majesty, fleeing from my enemies," he heard Nick say. " This young lady is in my charge, and is unwittingly involved in my dangers."

" Ah ! ha ! " said Charles, smiling sardonically. " A comely lass and a gallant of parts, but women are ill things in the breeches."

" If your Majesty will permit me to say so," the rider who had looked on Nick with so much interest said, forcing himself to the front, " he has not told you all."

As Nick heard the voice, he turned and looked into the sinister face of Sir Ladbroke Drake, who that afternoon had joined the King and had placed his knowledge of the uprising at the disposal of Charles and his Minister, as they travelled to quell the rebellion.

" What more is there to say ? " King Charles asked, his mocking eyes fixed on Sir Ladbroke Drake and Nick, alternately.

" Much that is worth hearing," Sir Ladbroke said, with vicious eagerness. " The man, Nick Nevinson, is the notorious highwayman, Swift Nick, wanted many times for ill use of your Majesty's subjects. That trollop in the gallant's clothes is Mistress Peggy Sheldon, niece of John Sheldon, who plotted against your Majesty's person and is now dead—killed by my own hand."

Nick would have leapt at Sir Ladbroke Drake's throat as he spoke the words, but Peggy and the men about him restrained his impulse.

" There is even more, your Majesty," Nevinson said, boldly. " The informer who is with you and of your company, is Sir Ladbroke Drake, a double traitor : traitor first to you and then to the man he says he killed—John Sheldon."

As Nicholas spoke Sir Ladbroke Drake paled, and the confidence expressed by his manner seemed to weaken. He was going to speak again, pressing eagerly forward, when the King checked him.

" An odd kettle of fish, this," he said, mockingly, and turning to Lord Shaftesbury in the carriage; " we cannot make out the right of it. What shall we do with these knaves ? "

" Bind the three of them," the Chancellor said. " Bind them and bring them all forward to Stilton and let us sift the story to its foundations at our leisure. We cannot hold conspiracy trials by the roadside."

" Excellent Chancellor," replied the King, his swarthy face alight as he looked out of the window again. " I charge you," he murmured to one of his escort, " these two roadsters are our prisoners, and also Sir Ladbroke Drake, the man who came to us this afternoon. I look to you to conduct them in our train and to make provision for the removal of the dead adventurer."

Charles crossed himself again as he referred to the dead, then made a sign and his coach drove on.

Peggy and Nick clasped hands as the royal coach travelled forward. In the girl's face was fear almost amounting to panic. In Nick's bold, reckless features were only signs of a grim, ferocious pleasure.

" Believe me, mistress," he said, kissing her hand before they were separated, " this is the better way."

"God grant it may be ; but to me it seems our troubles only crowd thicker upon us."

Sir Ladbroke Drake, in close custody, a yard or two in front, rode on in silence. Something in the hard, cold challenge of Swift Nick's fearless grey eyes filled his mind with vague uneasy fears, which grew into alarm as he travelled through the night in the wake of the King he had betrayed.

CHAPTER XXVIII

So we come to Stilton in the train of the so-called merry monarch, Charles the Second, about the hour of nine, with Swift Nick, a prisoner, returning to the town out of which he had escaped.

At Stilton, Charles and his suite were housed in the "Old Bell" over-night, for the King was making a ruthless, rapid progress, stamping the fires of rebellion under his heels as he marched. Perhaps that was why, immediately after His Majesty had supped with Shaftesbury, they began an inquiry into the statements made by the three prisoners brought from the road.

Only one scene need be offered to the reader who has followed the fortunes of our hero, thus far. Peggy had told her story, detail by detail, beginning with the plot at Chequers Court and Sir Ladbroke Drake's share in it. She outlined the attempt to force Sir Ladbroke's hand upon her, the journey towards London, the fight on the road, the intervention of Nemo, their ride to Stilton, and the rescue of Swift Nick. The sheriff had been examined as to the charges against the latter, and had admitted the only evidence of actual robbery rested on the word of Sir Ladbroke Drake and Captain Barclay, whose dead body had been brought into Stilton with Nemo's. Lord Shaftesbury had cleared the great dining-room, and now it was occupied by six men only—the King, his Chancellor, Swift Nick in the custody of the Honourable George Taunton, and Sir Ladbroke Drake in charge of a gentleman-at-arms.

King Charles stood in front of the open fireplace, toasting his royal limbs before the blazing, crackling wood. Two of the spaniels slept at his feet. He had supped generously, and the red wine was in his blood. There was a high colour in his cheeks; his heavy lips curled in the smile that almost habitually marked his harsh, humoursome face; his proud, implacable eyes veiled the thoughts rioting in his mind.

Lord Shaftesbury sat at the big dining-table, his great head bowed on his narrow shoulders, though his unwearying eyes peered as vigilantly and un-wearyingly into the papers before him as if the day were beginning rather than ending. The hour was nearing eleven.

"And so," said King Charles, flicking a speck of dust off his faultless ruffles, "that is the story—eh? A pleasing story, Shaftesbury, for our royal ears."

He puckered his swarthy face in deep thought, until his long nose looked more like a raven's beak than ever.

"It makes ye both a pair of precious rascals," the King said, at length. "You seem to have taken an even share in disturbing the welfare of our people. What have you to say—eh?"

As Charles spoke, he looked at Sir Ladbroke Drake, whose figure seemed to have shrunk and grown furtive under the royal scrutiny.

"Your Majesty," he said, his voice hoarse, rasping, and eager, "I claim that I should not be judged by the word of a common highwayman and a trollop who rides the country in such indiscreet habit."

The King's lower lip jutted out, half in anger.

"I think this trollop, as you call her, is the only one who comes out of the affair with clean hands," he said, for His Majesty had looked with kindly eyes on Peggy, and the odd, winsome, appealing figure she had cut in the clothes used as a disguise, when she gave her evidence, meeting every question of the Chancellor frankly, and fighting his inquiries step-by-step in the interests of her lover and herself. "Go on, man; go on."

"I claim, your Majesty, that I was at Chequers Court as a loyal servant of the Crown to hear more of the plot of which I was already aware. I claim that all my actions prove it. Directly the plot had matured, I risked death at the point of the sword; I slew the leader of this rising, and came in haste to lay my knowledge at your Majesty's disposal."

"Aha! aha!" laughed the King. "I take it the forced marriage of the Mistress Sheldon was a part of your plans for our royal happiness."

The shaft struck home. This was the one situation Sir Ladbroke could not explain—his journey by road, with Mistress Sheldon and her scheming uncle.

" I deny absolutely the whole story of the forced marriage," he said, his face flushing an angry red. " The whole of the evidence against me hangs on the word of this man Nevinson and the foolish girl who is under his influence."

There was a dead silence after Sir Ladbroke Drake had stopped speaking.

The King looked up, stifling a yawn.

" Go on," he said, at last ; " go on."

" That is all I have to say," Sir Ladbroke answered.

The King looked towards Nevinson.

" And you, my patriotic friend," he said, a sneer curling his sardonic upper lip.

" I set no store upon my patriotism, sire," Nick answered. " I claim the royal clemency."

King Charles threw back his head and laughed heartily.

" Hear him, hear him," he said to Shaftesbury ; " he claims our clemency."

" 'Tis not a heavy fee for what he has done in our service," the Chancellor replied, the ghost of a smile flickering about his face.

" The worst of the count against me," Nick said, boldly, as he heard the Chancellor's words, " is that I have levied toll upon the highway. Of that there is no satisfactory proof. No man has been brought forward to say 'twas I who stopped him, or even to prove I eased him of his gold. Against the mere suspicion, I set the service I have rendered, from whatever motive, to the State."

Again the King smiled. The insolence of this adventurer was born of a spirit after his own heart.

" Bravely spoken," he said, his croaking laughter lurking behind the words. " Take notice, Shaftesbury, he speaks in the manner of a courtier."

" But there is evidence," Lord Shaftesbury said, mildly. " This man, Sir Ladbroke, identifies him."

" The word of a traitor," Nick broke in, urgency in his manner and voice. " The word of a scoundrel, who, first a traitor to the King, turned round and sold the man who bought his allegiance from your Majesty."

" He stopped me in the highway through Finchley, on Sunday night," Sir Ladbroke said, hope flaring again in his shadowed mind.

" At what hour ? " asked the King.

" At the hour of eight, so near as I remember," Sir Ladbroke replied.

" And I can prove I slept in York on Sunday night, having ridden to see the King," Nick urged. " Your Majesty will remember I spoke you in the morning on matters of grave import."

" True," answered the King, decisively. " No man could have been by Finchley at night who saw us at York in the morning. The thing's impossible."

For the first time, Sir Ladbroke Drake's nerve gave way. This was the only intimation he had received that Nick had been in York and forestalled him with the King.

" He has an alibi, upon our royal word," the King said, turning to him, his face puckered in a whimsical smile.

" And even were that so, he robbed me on my first

journey to the Chequers, hard by Barnet," Sir Ladbroke exclaimed. " I recognised him though he was masked. We had a passage with the swords on the road, and there was a thrust peculiar to him which I knew. I am something of a swordsman, your Majesty."

" You mean that in the duel he has a personal style, even as he has by virtue of his insolent manners," the King asked, brightening.

" I say I know this man Nevinson," Sir Ladbroke clamoured, almost forgetting the presence of the King in his eagerness to destroy his enemy. " In town I met him as a gentleman, in the duel. He disarmed me with a thrust I have only seen employed by a master of the sword in Paris. I am something of a connoisseur, and I recall the incident because it was my first humiliation."

" I accused him of cheating in a gaming house," Nick said, his eyes gleaming. " Taunton, here, my Lord Shaftesbury's servant, will bear me out."

" Willingly, my lord," Taunton answered, grinning in his enjoyment of the scene. " Nick pinked him twice with the same pass. The encounter took place in the Green Park."

" You know this man—eh ? " asked the King.

" Only as a gentleman of nice spirit and of a fine sense of honour," Taunton replied. " I was his second."

" And once again the pass which disarmed me, an expert swordsman, was employed against me, a few days later on the highway. I recognised

Swift Nick, as Nevinson, the first night he stooped me, by his sword play."

Sir Ladbroke Drake spoke the words triumphantly, and his manner carried conviction.

" The word of a rascal, the word of a cheat, the word of a traitor," Nick answered, roundly. " 'Tis not sufficient to hang a dog upon."

The King stooped to toy with one of his spaniels. He seemed to have forgotten the inquiry and the men who played their parts before him. His face was wreathed in a kindly smile as he bent towards his dogs. When he straightened himself, after a long interval, his mind appeared to have travelled a long way from the point at issue.

" Tell me, Sir Ladbroke ; is this sword pass noticeably good ? " he asked, smiling.

" Once seen, it was sufficient evidence, when I came across it again, to prove to my satisfaction that the masked Swift Nick, highwayman, was the Nicholas Nevinson who affronted me in Isaacs' rooms."

" Ah ! " snarled the King, suddenly, the change in manner making his voice sound discordant and threatening ; his speech seeming to show that he had made up his mind. " Word against word, Shaftesbury. Two rogues, eh ? an amusing situation—and either of them liars ; perhaps both. The end is obvious : trial by battle—eh ? Sir Ladbroke shall make Swift Nick prove himself here now, and by his wonderful pass—eh, Shaftesbury ? There is something picturesque about the ancient customs, Shaftesbury, and here is an opportunity of employing them to our profit."

The King broke into peal after peal of laughter, the harshness of which chilled his hearers' blood.

The Chancellor rose slowly from his seat and faced the royal figure.

"There are times," he said, in his staccato, nervous, humorous manner, "when I believe in the divine wisdom of kings. Your idea is an inspiration. Let these knaves be their own executioners."

Even then, Sir Ladbroke Drake did not understand, but Nick had grasped the meaning of the King.

"Your Majesty, it is as you will," he said, slightly shrugging his shoulders. "If I show that pass, at the point of this man's sword, he will die."

Sir Ladbroke Drake paled before the thunderbolt the King had prepared for him. At Nick's words, the full meaning of the situation flooded his senses. A cold sweat broke upon his brow. There was terror in his eyes. He looked about the room fearfully, as if for a chance of escape.

"Your Majesty," he burst out, at bay, angry, and terror-ridden; "this is unworthy, unfair, unjust. I have ridden far to-day. I am not fit."

"It is our will," the King replied, an icy smile playing about his features. "Draw and be your own judges."

Taunton handed Nick his sword. His Irish eyes were dancing. Here, at last, was the situation he loved.

"Once again, Nick, my boy, I second you," he said. "The stakes to-night are life itself, and not a salve for wounded honour."

Sir Ladbroke Drake drew his sword. There was no other way. Caught in the toils he had spun for another, he stood, a grey, ashen figure in the lighted room, knowing his life hung on the prowess of his hand and the purpose of his brain. Hanging on the issue was the chance of life, and, as he knew in his secret heart, the probability of certain death.

The King leaned against the mantelpiece and stirred the spaniels with his foot. He stood pluming himself there as if he were gazing on a pretty girl dancing a minuet, scarcely looking at the two men as they disrobed. When they stood armed, in breeches and shirt, his mind seemed still fixed on his dogs.

Lord Shaftesbury clapped his hands, and suddenly the King turned his gaze on the two men, cruel humour in his lively, threatening eyes; his nether lip jutting out, excitedly; his attention strained, held, riveted by the prospect of combat.

" Are you ready, gentlemen ? " the Chancellor's voice cried, sounding, in the quiet room, cold and unconcerned.

" Yes," they answered, simultaneously.

" On guard," he answered, stood back, and the two blades clashed.

A gloomy room, lit by guttering candles. Six men there ; two fighting for their lives. A King, rubbing his palms, in childish excitement, on his breeches ; stirred out of himself, his nature, cruel to the core, expressed in a wolf-like smile. The Chancellor, calm, impassive, showing neither undue interest nor excitement. Steel clashing on steel ;

hungry blades catching the candlelight until they
seemed to live as streaks of warring fire ; the stamp
of feet, the lunge, the parry, the quick recovery.
One face deathly white, vindictive, yet despairing :
the face of a man with his back to the wall—Sir
Ladbroke Drake. The other, a typically English
face, the head courageous in its carriage, a scornful
curl on the lip, and a light in the cool, grey eyes that
came from love of combat. And all this only for
the space of two minutes, and in the last of them,
Sir Ladbroke lunging, missing, forced back by the
parry. Angered, he came again. The two blades
crossed, seemed to measure each other and test
strength of muscle, nerve, and eye. Then they
clashed, and the blades appeared to be locked. Sir
Ladbroke knew by the strain on his arm, as if every
taut muscle were being wrenched asunder, that for the
third time he had met the pass that twice before had
humiliated him. And even as the horror of the knowledge froze upon his face, and in wild despair he
tried to hold the fatal stroke, his weapon glanced
upwards out of his hands, and Nick's blade, impelled
by all the weight behind it, pierced his enemy's
heart. Sir Ladbroke spoke no word, but fell upon
the floor, face downwards, blood staining his white
shirt. Rapidly, as the life stream flooded outwards,
ran the sands of a traitor's life, while five men, one a
King, pale of face as they confronted death, watched
the end in a chilling, appalling silence.

" Dead," said Shaftesbury in a whisper, looking
down. " A neat trick with the sword that, and
Master Nick must teach it to me."

"So die all traitors to our person," the King replied, crossing himself sedately, and though his harsh face was pale, he still smiled.

Nevinson stood hesitating in the silent room, and looked towards His Majesty.

"It is true, as the dead man said. I was Swift Nick," he said, his voice wavering.

"Swift as the wrath of God," the King said, grimly, holding out his hand.

Nick knelt and kissed it.

"We passed our word, Swift Nick," King Charles said, the wintry smile still haunting his swarthy face. "You have our clemency. Withdraw, and sin no more against our lawful government."

As Nick turned to leave the room, the King became himself again, forgetting the ugly incident as if it had been turned over in his mind, like a leaf in a hastily read book.

"Clemency, Shaftesbury, clemency! 'Tis a royal virtue, and in this matter it cost us nothing," he croaked.

"And the service you bought, sire, saved your crown," the Chancellor said, significantly.

"To say nothing of the cost of an executioner," the King replied, his eyes fixed on his Chancellor.

Old Rowley and his Minister laughed as they left the room, without a glance at the dead man, lying, face downwards, on the floor.

. . . . . .

And that is the record of Swift Nick. The incidents happened a long time ago, but the ends of the story may be pieced together for those who like order in the routine of human lives. Peggy had her own fortune and inherited John Sheldon's. She married Nick a few weeks after their mad flight along the road. For the most part, they lived at the Chequers by Hitchin, and Nick became a good husband, a gentleman, and the founder of an honoured family, which blushingly bears a title these days, and is not too proud of its turbulent ancestor. All of which goes to prove nothing beyond the fact that great families, in common with all other great things, often spring from small beginnings. A long time afterwards, the "Lantern" kept its roaring company, and Steve Randall, rubbing his empty coat sleeve with the sound hand, would tell of two great men he knew, Claude Du Vall and Swift Nick Nevinson. Nemo's death split up the strange company of the Great North Road into warring factions. A few of the old gang clung together and assembled to drink, deep and heartily, at the "Lantern," and to roar ribald songs. Sometimes, fed up with too much happiness, as is the way of men who live the perfect domestic life, a person of consequence would come to the old inn. On such nights, there would be open house, free tap, and good cheer at the "Lantern." The old Adam does not die, and warmed by red wine, Squire Nevinson would talk of Nemo, the dead king, the call of the road, and the glorious qualities of a horse he called Starlight. And at his house, the Chequers, I am pleased to add, strange people used to call, a crippled, ragged, bob-tailed army; lame, halt, and blind, blasphemous in their speech, unlovely and unruly of habit. They made a sign which every servant about the Chequers knew and recognised. The pariah children of the North Road found it a coinage for rare hospitality, which Mistress Nevinson would honour with her own hands as a tribute to Nemo's memory. Long after the beggar king had been forgotten, the words, "Nemo commands," worked wonders at the Chequers. A kink in my nature bids me to add it matters little what a man may be, if, when he pays, all that he has to give, in sense and substance, goes freely to the underdog. As I grope amongst the shadows of the past, I like to think that this was freely said of Swift Nick Nevinson, when he became a gentleman of substance and honoured the claims of Nemo's tattered army, wandering by his door on an unending quest along the Great North Road.

THE END

Printed by Hazell, Watson & Viney, Ld., London and Aylesbury.

FICTION

THE MORNING POST says: " Mills & Boon seem to have acquired a monopoly in clever first novels."

SIX-SHILLING NOVELS.   Crown 8vo.

Happy Ever After		R. Allatini.
All Awry	*2nd Edition*	Maude Annesley.
Nights and Days		Maude Annesley.
The Sphinx in the Labyrinth		Maude Annesley.
Eve, Spinster		Anon.
Mastering Flame	*4th Edition*	Anon.
Middleground		Anon.
The Playground		Anon.
The Nursing Home		Arthur Applin.
Shop Girls		Arthur Applin.
The Seas of God		A. W. Armstrong.
The Romance of Palombris and Pallogris		G. P. Baker.
The Magic Tale of Harvanger and Yolande		G. P. Baker.
Cardillac	*5th Edition*	Robert Barr.
The Sword Maker	*3rd Edition*	Robert Barr.
The Story of Joan Greencroft		A. N. Bax.
Mrs. O'H		Harold Begbie.
The Good Ship Brompton Castle		Lady Bell.
Kiddies		J. J. Bell.
Jeremy's Love Story		B. Y. Benediall.
The Child Lover		B. Y. Benediall.
Blind Sight		B. Y. Benediall.
Golden Vanity		Maisie Bennett.
The Room in the Tower	*2nd Edition*	E. F. Benson.
Seven Keys to Baldpate		Earl Derr Biggers.
Mr. Lyndon at Liberty		Victor Bridges.
Jetsam		Victor Bridges.
The Man from Nowhere	*3rd Edition*	Victor Bridges.

1

"There is always a new Mills & Boon Novel"

Spray on the Windows	*3rd Edition*	J. E. Buckrose.
Gay Morning	*2nd Edition*	J. E. Buckrose.
Because of Jane	*2nd Edition*	J. E. Buckrose.
The Browns	*3rd Edition*	J. E. Buckrose.
A Bachelor's Comedy	*3rd Edition*	J. E. Buckrose.
A Golden Straw	*2nd Edition*	J. E. Buckrose.
The Pilgrimage of a Fool	*2nd Edition*	J. E. Buckrose.
Down Our Street	*6th Edition*	J. E. Buckrose.
Love in a Little Town	*4th Edition*	J. E. Buckrose.
Breadandbutterflies		Dion Clayton Calthrop.
Etcetera		Dion Clayton Calthrop.
The Fabulists		Bernard Capes.
The Enemy		G. R. & Lillian Chester.
The Borrowed Liner		Laurence Clarke.
The Prodigal Father	*4th Edition*	J. Storer Clouston.
Struggle (2s. net.)		Cassels Cobb.
Andrew and His Wife		Thomas Cobb.
Lady Sylvia's Impostor		Thomas Cobb.
The Transformation of Timothy		Thomas Cobb.
The Voice of Bethia		Thomas Cobb.
A Marriage of Inconvenience		Thomas Cobb.
Phillida		Thomas Cobb.
The Loitering Highway		Sophie Cole.
The House in Watchman's Alley		Sophie Cole.
Skirts of Straw		Sophie Cole.
Patience Tabernacle		Sophie Cole.
Penelope's Doors		Sophie Cole.
A Plain Woman's Portrait		Sophie Cole.
In Search of Each Other		Sophie Cole.
The Thornbush near the Door		Sophie Cole.
Blue-Grey Magic		Sophie Cole.
A Wardour Street Idyll		Sophie Cole.
Hester and I		Mrs. P. Ch. de Crespigny.
Mallory's Tryst		Mrs. P. Ch. de Crespigny.
The Valley of Achor		Mrs. P. Ch. de Crespigny.
The Mark		Mrs. P. Ch. de Crespigny.
Diane of the Green Van		Leona Dalrymple.
The Loom of Life		Edith Dart.
The Education of Jacqueline	*3rd Edition*	Claire de Pratz.
Elisabeth Davenay	*3rd Edition*	Claire de Pratz.
Little Faithful	*2nd Edition*	Beulah Marie Dix.
Traveller's Samples		Mrs. Henry Dudeney.
Honours of War		George Edgar.
Kent the Fighting Man		George Edgar.
The Pride of the Fancy		George Edgar.
The Red Colonel	*2nd Edition*	George Edgar.
Swift Nick of the York Road	*2nd Edition*	George Edgar.
The Blue Bird's-Eye	*3rd Edition*	George Edgar.
The Torchbearer		Dorothea Fairbridge.

Mills & Boon's Six-Shilling Novels

Piet of Italy	. . . .	Dorothea Fairbridge.
The Rock	. . . .	Mrs. Romilly Fedden.
The Man Hunt	. . . . . .	Tom Gallon.
The Diamond Trail	. . . . .	Tom Gallon.
The Man in Motley	. . . . .	Tom Gallon.
Olga Nazimov	. . . . . .	W. L. George.
The Witch Child	. . . . .	Louise Gerard.
Life's Shadow Show	. . . .	Louise Gerard.
The Virgin's Treasure	. . . .	Louise Gerard.
Flower-of-the-Moon	. . . .	Louise Gerard.
The Swimmer	. . . . .	Louise Gerard.
A Tropical Tangle	. . . 2nd Edition	Louise Gerard.
The Leech	. . . . . .	Mrs. Harold E. Gorst.
Sons of State	. . . . .	Winifred Graham.
Mary	. . . . . 4th Edition	Winifred Graham.
The Needlewoman	. . .	Winifred Graham.
The Kris Girl	. . . .	Beatrice Grimshaw.
Guinea Gold	. . . . 2nd Edition	Beatrice Grimshaw.
When the Red Gods Call	. 3rd Edition	Beatrice Grimshaw.
Edward Racedale's Will	. . . .	Mark Hardy.
Entertaining Jane	. . . .	Millicent Heathcote.
Clark's Field	. . . . .	Robert Herrick.
The Common Lot	. . . .	Robert Herrick.
His Great Adventure	. . . .	Robert Herrick.
The Web of Life	. . . .	Robert Herrick.
One Woman's Life	. . 2nd Edition	Robert Herrick.
The Progress of Prudence	. . .	W. F. Hewer.
The Old Road from Spain	. . .	Constance Holme.
Crump Folk Going Home	. . .	Constance Holme.
The Lonely Plough	. . . .	Constance Holme.
John Ward, M.D.	. . . .	Arthur Hooley.
Pollyooly	. . . . 2nd Edition	Edgar Jepson.
Arsène Lupin	. . . .	Jepson and Leblanc.
The Enlightenment of Ermyn	. .	Harry Jermyn.
The Adolescence of Aubrey	. .	Harry Jermyn.
High Stakes	. . . . .	Ruth Kauffman.
Jim—Unclassified	. . .	Robert J. Kelly.
Jehanne of the Golden Lips	. 3rd Edition	F. G. Knowles-Foster.
The Written Law	. . . .	F. G. Knowles-Foster.
The Net of Circumstance	. . .	Mr. & Mrs. O. L'Artsau.
The Confessions of Arsène Lupin	.	Maurice Leblanc.
813	. . . . . . 2nd Edition	Maurice Leblanc.
The Frontier	. . . . .	Maurice Leblanc.
The Lightkeeper	. . . . .	Anatole Le Braz.
The Little Lady of the Big House	.	Jack London.
The Night-Born (Stories)	. .	Jack London.
Lost Face	. . . . .	Jack London.
The Jacket (The Star Rover)	2nd Edition	Jack London.
The Mutiny of the Elsinore	3rd Edition	Jack London.

3

John Barleycorn	3rd Edition	Jack London.
The Valley of the Moon	6th Edition	Jack London.
South Sea Tales		Jack London.
Smoke Bellew	4th Edition	Jack London.
A Son of the Sun	3rd Edition	Jack London.
When God Laughs	2nd Edition	Jack London.
The Music Makers		Louise Mack.
The Marriage of Edward		Louise Mack.
Attraction		Louise Mack.
Outlaw's Luck		Dorothea Mackellar.
A Rich Man's Table		Ella MacMahon.
Grandpapa's Granddaughter		Mary E. Mann.
Through the Window		Mary E. Mann.
Men and Dreams	2nd Edition	Mary E. Mann.
The Yoke of Silence (5s.)		Amy McLaren.
The Prince		Thomas Metcalfe.
Second Bests		L. G. Moberly.
The Cost	2nd Edition	L. G. Moberly.
The Game of the Tangled Web		S. C. Nethersole.
Wilsam	2nd Edition	S. C. Nethersole.
Mary up at Gaffries	4th Edition	S. C. Nethersole.
Ripe Corn	2nd Edition	S. C. Nethersole.
Ruth, the Woman who Loved		Horace W. C. Newte.
Sidelights		Horace W. C. Newte.
The Sins of the Children	2nd Edition	Horace W. C. Newte.
The Ealing Miracle		Horace W. C. Newte.
The Unknown Mr. Kent		Roy Norton.
The Boomers		Roy Norton.
The Plunderer		Roy Norton.
Guppy Guyson		W. M. O'Kane.
With Poison and Sword		W. M. O'Kane.
Harm's Way		Lloyd Osbourne.
Stories without Tears	2nd Edition	Barry Pain.
Love the Magnet		Pan.
Wonderful Love		Pan.
White Heat	2nd Edition	Pan.
Scorched Souls		Pan.
The Adventures of Captain Jack	3rd Edition	Max Pemberton.
Lily Magic		Mary L. Pendered.
Phyllida Flouts Me		Mary L. Pendered.
Two Young Pigeons		Mrs. H. H. Penrose.
Something Impossible		Mrs. H. H. Penrose.
Burnt Flax		Mrs. H. H. Penrose.
Tales from Five Chimneys		Marmaduke Pickthall.
Miss Elizabeth Gibbs		Alicia Ramsey.
The Kingdom and the Wall		Mrs. Baillie Reynolds.
The Court Favourite		Mrs. Baillie Reynolds.
The Relations		Mrs. Baillie Reynolds.
The Swashbuckler		Mrs. Baillie Reynolds.
The Silence Broken	2nd Edition	Mrs. Baillie Reynolds.
Nigel Ferrard	2nd Edition	Mrs. Baillie Reynolds.
Long Furrows		Mrs. Fred Reynolds.
An Absent Hero		Mrs. Fred Reynolds.

4

Mills & Boon's Six-Shilling Novels

The Gondola		Rothay Reynolds.
The Valiants of Virginia	*2nd Edition*	Hallie Erminie Rives.
Her Last Appearance		A. Nugent Robertson.
Force Majeure		Patrick Rushden.
Mr. Sheringham and Others		Mrs. Alfred Sidgwick.
The Dividing Sword		Harold Spender.
The Flame of Daring		Harold Spender.
One Man Returns		Harold Spender.
The Call of the Siren	*2nd Edition*	Harold Spender.
Kicks and Ha'pence		Henry Stace.
—And What Happened		E. S. Stevens.
Allward	*2nd Edition*	E. S. Stevens.
Sarah Eden	*3rd Edition*	E. S. Stevens.
The Long Engagement	*3rd Edition*	E. S. Stevens.
The Veil	*7th Edition*	E. S. Stevens.
The Mountain of God	*4th Edition*	E. S. Stevens.
The Lure	*3rd Edition*	E. S. Stevens.
The Earthen Drum	*2nd Edition*	E. S. Stevens.
The Edge of Empire		Joan Sutherland.
Beyond the Shadow	*2nd Edition*	Joan Sutherland.
Cophetua's Son	*2nd Edition*	Joan Sutherland.
The Hidden Road	*3rd Edition*	Joan Sutherland.
The Monument		Tilk Tattingham
The Man who Stayed at Home		Beamish Tinker.
The Captain's Furniture		John Trevena.
Moyle Church-Town		John Trevena.
Love		W. B. Trites.
Stormlight		Lady Troubridge.
The Girl with the Blue Eyes		Lady Troubridge.
The Cheat		Lady Troubridge.
Salt of Life	*2nd Edition*	Mrs. G. de H. Vaizey.
Grizel Married		Mrs. G. de H. Vaizey.
The Adventures of Billie Belshaw		Mrs. G. de H. Vaizey.
An Unknown Lover		Mrs. G. de H. Vaizey.
Sport of Gods	*3rd Edition*	H. Vaughan-Sawyer.
The Lizard		H. Vaughan-Sawyer.
Mary Moreland		Marie van Vorst.
Big Tremaine	*2nd Edition*	Marie van Vorst.
His Love Story (5s.)		Marie van Vorst.
Mr. Perrin and Mr. Traill	*2nd Edition*	Hugh Walpole.
The Unknown Woman		Anne Warwick.
Toddie	*3rd Edition*	Gilbert Watson.
Ifs and Ans		H. B. Marriott Watson.
Tess of Ithaca		Grace Miller White.
The Wind among the Barley	*2nd Edition*	M. P. Willcocks.
The Friendly Enemy		T. P. Cameron Wilson.
The Court of the Gentiles		Mrs. Stanley Wrench.
Ruth of the Rowldrich		Mrs. Stanley Wrench.
Arm Chair Stories		I. A. R. Wylie.
Tristram Sahib		I. A. R. Wylie.
Happy Endings		I. A. R. Wylie.
The Temple of Dawn	*3rd Edition*	I. A. R. Wylie.
The Red Mirage	*4th Edition*	I. A. R. Wylie.
The Daughter of Brahma	*5th Edition*	I. A. R. Wylie.
The Rajah's People	*8th Edition*	I. A. R. Wylie.
Dividing Waters	*4th Edition*	I. A. R. Wylie.
In Different Keys		I. A. R. Wylie.

MILLS & BOON'S SHILLING NOVELS

Picture Covers.   Crown 8vo.   1s. net.

Ashes of Incense	The Author of "Mastering Flame."
Eve—Spinster	Anon.
The Nursing Home. The Particular Petticoat	Arthur Applin.
Shop Girls. Sister Susie—Spinster	Arthur Applin.
The Woman Who ——!	Arthur Applin.
The Girl who Saved His Honour	Arthur Applin.
The Rainy Day. A London Girl.	Harold Begbie.
*The Bill-Toppers	André Castaigne.
His First Offence. The Peer's Progress.	J. Storer Clouston.
The Prodigal Father	J. Storer Clouston.
Isobel in Wardour Street	Sophie Cole.
*Within the Law	M. Dana and E. Forest.
Peer Gynt	Melrod Danning.
*Romance	Acton Davies.
The Blue Bird's-Eye	George Edgar.
Swift Nick of the York Road	George Edgar.
The Last Challenge	Langley Edwards.
A Tropical Tangle	Louise Gerard.
The Bolster Book	Harry Graham.
The Love Story of a Mormon	Winifred Graham.
The Needlewoman	Winifred Graham.
Can a Man be True (Sons of State)	Winifred Graham.
The Rugmaker's Daughter	Martin Ingram.
Pollyooly	Edgar Jepson.
The Confessions of Arsène Lupin	Maurice Leblanc.
813 (A New Arsène Lupin Adventure)	Maurice Leblanc.
*Arsène Lupin	Edgar Jepson and Maurice Leblanc.
Paste	Bannister Merwin.
A Young Lady. Pansy Meares	Horace W. C. Newte.
The Square Mile. The Socialist Countess	Horace W. C. Newte.
The Sins of the Children	Horace W. C. Newte.
The Lonely Lovers	Horace W. C. Newte.
Sparrows: The Story of an Unprotected Girl	Horace W. C. Newte.
Lena Swallow: A Sister to "Sparrows"	Horace W. C. Newte.
Living Pictures	Horace W. C. Newte.
Scorched Souls. White Heat	Pan.
The Adventures of Captain Jack	Max Pemberton.
Beware of the Dog	Mrs. Baillie Reynolds.
*D'Arcy of the Guards	L. E. Shipman.
Santa Claus (The Fairy Story of the Play)	Harold Simpson.
*The Marriage Market. *The Dollar Princess	Harold Simpson.
*The Count of Luxembourg	Harold Simpson.
The Mountain of God. The Lure	E. S. Stevens.
*The Man Who Stayed at Home	Beamish Tinker.
The Price of a Soul	Paul Trent.
John Cave. Life	W. B. Trites.
The Cheat. The Woman who Forgot	Lady Troubridge.
Body and Soul	Lady Troubridge.
The White Hope	W. R. H. Trowbridge.
The Prelude to Adventure	Hugh Walpole.
Mr. Perrin and Mr. Traill	Hugh Walpole.
The Daughter of Brahma	I. A. R. Wylie.
Dividing Waters	I. A. R. Wylie.
For Church and Chieftain	May Wynne.

* Novel of the Play.

MILLS & BOON'S
Shilling Cloth Library

1s. net each volume (postage 3d.)

A London Girl. The Rainy Day	HAROLD BEGBIE.
Closed Doors	HAROLD BEGBIE.
The Room in the Tower	E. F. BENSON.
Mr. Lyndon at Liberty	VICTOR BRIDGES.
The Man from Nowhere	VICTOR BRIDGES.
Aunt Augusta in Egypt. (Entirely New)	J. E. BUCKROSE.
Because of Jane	J. E. BUCKROSE.
Down our Street	J. E. BUCKROSE.
Love in a Little Town	J. E. BUCKROSE.
In Search of Each Other	SOPHIE COLE.
Kent the Fighting Man	GEORGE EDGAR.
Guinea Gold	BEATRICE GRIMSHAW.
When the Red Gods Call	BEATRICE GRIMSHAW.
The Blindness of Virtue	COSMO HAMILTON.
The Frontier	MAURICE LEBLANC.
Twenty-Four Years of Cricket	A. A. LILLEY.
Lost Face. The Jacket	JACK LONDON.
Before Adam. A Son of the Sun	JACK LONDON.
An Odyssey of the North. Adventure	JACK LONDON.
John Barleycorn. Children of the Frost	JACK LONDON.
Love of Life. Smoke Bellew.	JACK LONDON.
South Sea Tales. The Cruise of the Dazzler	JACK LONDON.
The Cruise of the Snark. When God Laughs	JACK LONDON.
The God of his Fathers	JACK LONDON.
The House of Pride. (Entirely New)	JACK LONDON.
The Iron Heel. The Mutiny of the Elsinore	JACK LONDON.
The Scarlet Plague. (Entirely New)	JACK LONDON.
The Road. (Entirely New)	JACK LONDON.
The Valley of the Moon	ROY NORTON.
The Flame. The Mediator	ROY NORTON.
The Plunderer. The Boomers	SIR GILBERT PARKER.
Cumner's Son	EDEN PHILLPOTTS.
The Haven	WILLIAM LE QUEUX.
The Czar's Spy	WILLIAM LE QUEUX.
Who Giveth this Woman	HALLIE ERMINIE RIVES.
The Valiants of Virginia	H. DE VERE STACPOOLE.
The Order of Release	E. S. STEVENS.
The Veil. The Mountain of God	JOAN SUTHERLAND.
The Hidden Road	THORMANBY.
Sporting Stories	W. B. TRITES.
Life	MRS. G. DE HORNE VAIZEY.
An Unknown Lover	MRS. G. DE HORNE VAIZEY.
The Adventures of Billie Belshaw	MRS. G. DE HORNE VAIZEY.
Grizel Married	MRS. G. DE HORNE VAIZEY.
Salt of Life	MARIE VAN VORST.
Mary Moreland. Big Tremaine	MARIE VAN VORST.
The Girl from His Town	MARIE VAN VORST.
His Love Story	MARIE VAN VORST.
Her Heart's Desire	I. A. R. WYLIE.
The Rajah's People	I. A. R. WYLIE.
The Red Mirage. The Temple of Dawn	I. A. R. WYLIE.

MILLS & BOON'S
SIXPENNY NOVELS
Picture Covers. Demy 8vo.

MILLS & BOON are issuing a new series of Copyright Novels by the foremost Novelists of the day. They are printed from large type on good paper. The first volumes are:

Calico Jack. By HORACE W. C. NEWTE, Author of "Sparrows."
Globe.—"Calico Jack is no mere creature of invention, but the real thing."

The Sins of the Children. By HORACE W. C. NEWTE.
Globe.—"A strong convincing picture of life."

Lena Swallow. By HORACE W. C. NEWTE.

Living Pictures. By HORACE W. C. NEWTE.
Glasgow Herald.—"None of them is less than brilliant."

The Lonely Lovers. By HORACE W. C. NEWTE.
Daily Chronicle.—"A very vivid rendering of tense human passion and emotion."

The Summer Book. By MAX PEMBERTON.

The Adventures of Captain Jack. By MAX PEMBERTON, Author of "The Summer Book."
Punch.—"What he has to tell is so deftly told that I spent an excellent afternoon a-reading his volume (Mills & Boon)."

A Golden Straw. By J. E. BUCKROSE, Author of "Down Our Street."
Daily Graphic.—"A story of invincible freshness and charm."

The Pilgrimage of a Fool. By J. E. BUCKROSE.
Globe.—"Far and away above the ordinary novel."

Fame. By B. M. CROKER, Author of "Angel."
Scotsman.—"A clever workmanlike novel, always bright and entertaining."

The Quaker Girl. The Novel of the Play. By HAROLD SIMPSON.

The Education of Jacqueline. By CLAIRE DE PRATZ, Author of "Elisabeth Davenay."
Observer.—"Jacqueline is a darling."

The Silence Broken. By Mrs. BAILLIE REYNOLDS, Author of "Nigel Ferrard."
Freeman's Journal.—"A most suitable book for the summer holidays, filled from cover to cover with love and romance."

MILLS & BOON'S
MY YEAR SERIES

My Siberian Year. By M. A. CZAPLICKA. With 28 Full-page Illustrations. Demy 8vo. 10s. 6d. net.

An extremely interesting book, containing the record of a remarkable year in a woman's life.

My Japanese Year. By T. H. SANDERS. Illustrated. Demy 8vo. 10s. 6d. net.

Glasgow Herald.—"A valuable record, vivid and impressive pictures of the people in their homes and at their work."

Truth.—"An interesting book; an obviously fair and therefore a decidedly favourable impression of the Japanese."

Standard.—"Can be heartily recommended as a genuine record of an intelligent and unprejudiced witness."

My Italian Year. By RICHARD BAGOT. With 25 Illustrations. Demy 8vo. Second Edition. 10s. 6d. net.

The Observer.—"'My Italian Year' will tell the reader more about the real present-day go-ahead Italy than any other book that has come to our notice."

Daily Telegraph.—"A thoughtful, knowledgeful book."

Truth.—"The best-informed book which has appeared of late on Italy."

My Russian Year. By ROTHAY REYNOLDS. With 28 Illustrations. Demy 8vo. Second Edition. 10s. 6d. net. Also Popular Edition. 2s. 6d. net.

Times.—"Full of anecdote, sometimes indeed of gossip, but it is first-hand anecdote and the characteristic gossip which comes to the ears of a man who has lived in the country and understood its people. . . . Mr. Reynolds has succeeded in drawing a truthful and impartial picture of the ordinary Russian."

Truth.—"I have never read a book on Russia which gives such intimate and interesting, and at the same time vivid, pictures of social, domestic, political, and ecclesiastical life of Russia."

Punch.—"It is the best work of its kind I have seen for years."

Mills & Boon's My Year Series

My Cosmopolitan Year. By the Author of "Mastering Flame" and "Ashes of Incense." With 24 Illustrations. Demy 8vo. 10s. 6d. net.

Times.—"Here we have the fresh and breezy comments of one who has ' seen the cities and known the minds of many men.' "

Athenæum.—"Brightly written, admirably illustrated, should become a favourite with observant travellers."

My Parisian Year. By MAUDE ANNESLEY. With 16 Illustrations from Photographs and 1 in Colour. Demy 8vo. Second Edition. 10s. 6d. net.

Pall Mall Gazette.—"The 'joie de vivre' radiates from its pages . . . never dull or commonplace."

Observer.—"Lots of wrinkles . . . a sprightly book."

Evening Standard.—"What Max O'Rell did for our countrymen Maude Annesley does for his."

Scotsman.—"Convincing as well as highly entertaining."

My German Year. By I. A. R. WYLIE, Author of "The Rajah's People." With 2 Illustrations in Colour and 18 from Photographs. Demy 8vo. Second Edition. 10s. 6d. net.

Evening Standard.—"Should be read by every household. We have seldom read a more interesting book."

Westminster Gazette.—"A wise, well-informed, and very readable book, with some delightful fresh information and shrewd criticisms."

My Spanish Year. By Mrs. BERNARD WHISHAW. With 20 Illustrations from Photographs. Demy 8vo. 10s. 6d. net.

Westminster Gazette.—" A vivacious and charming record."

The Times.—"Has real value as an interpretation of Spain to English people."

Daily News.—" An admirable volume in an admirable series."

Mills & Boon's Rambles Series

Rambles with an American in Great Britain.

By CHRISTIAN TEARLE. With 21 Illustrations. Crown 8vo. 6s.

Liverpool Courier.—"An interesting and ingenious account of a literary pilgrimage, and in every place the author has something lively and original to say."

Daily Express.—"Good and wholesome reading."

Rambles in Ireland. By ROBERT LYND. With 5

Illustrations in Colour by JACK B. YEATS and 25 from Photographs. Crown 8vo. 6s.

Pall Mall Gazette.—"Mr. Lynd's delightful book, which he presents with beauty simple and unaffected."

Evening Standard.—"Mr. Lynd knows his Ireland and has written a charming book on it."

Daily News.—"This fascinating book."

Rambles in Florence. By G. E. TROUTBECK.

With 8 Illustrations in Colour by R. McANDREW and 32 from Photographs. Crown 8vo. 6s.

Guardian.—"The work of a real student of Dante."

Times.—"Full of information."

Dundee Advertiser.—"Written with an equal appreciation of artistic beauty and historic greatness, this book is one which will commend itself to every lover of Florence."

Rambles in Rome. By G. E. TROUTBECK. With

8 Illustrations in Colour by R. McANDREW and 32 from Photographs. Crown 8vo. 6s.

Rambles in Holland. By E. and M. S. GREW.

With 32 Illustrations and a Map. Crown 8vo. 6s.

Aberdeen Free Press.—"A delightful book about a delightful country. Altogether admirable."

Globe.—"A very charming and a very useful book."

Rambles in the North Yorkshire Dales. By

J. E. BUCKROSE. With 24 Illustrations in half-tone and 4 in colour. Crown 8vo. 3s. 6d. net.

Daily Chronicle.—"It is altogether a joysome time, with sunshine and merry episode to ensure success."

MILLS & BOON'S
VOLUMES OF REMINISCENCES

Sam Darling's Reminiscences. With 8 Photo-
gravures and 42 Half-Tone Illustrations. Demy 8vo.
21s. net. Large Paper Edition, limited to 75 copies,
signed by the Author. 52s. 6d. net.

Sporting Life.—"A most valuable addition to the literature of the Turf."
Scotsman.—"A very desirable addition to every sporting man's library."

What I Know. Reminiscences of Five Years' Personal
Attendance upon his late Majesty King Edward VII.
By C. W. STAMPER. With a Portrait in Colour, never
before published, by OLIVE SNELL. Third Edition.
Demy 8vo. 10s. 6d. net. Popular Edition. Crown 8vo.
2s. net.

The Times.—"What would the historian not give for such a book about
Queen Elizabeth or Louis Quatorze? . . . adds something to history."

Forty Years of a Sportsman's Life. By SIR
CLAUDE CHAMPION DE CRESPIGNY, Bart. With 18
Illustrations. Demy 8vo. 10s. 6d. net. Popular Edition.
Large Crown 8vo. 6s. .

Sporting Life.—"More enthralling than the most romantic novel."
Daily Mail.—"From cover to cover there is not a dull page."

From a Punjaub Pomegranate Grove. By C. C.
DYSON. With 14 Illustrations. Demy 8vo. 10s. 6d.
net.

Evening Standard.—"So pleasant and picturesque is Miss Dyson's style
that we would gladly welcome a second volume."

My Slav Friends. By ROTHAY REYNOLDS, Author
of "My Russian Year." Illustrated. Demy 8vo. 10s. 6d.
net.

In this new book, by the author of "My Russian Year," the author aims,
not merely to present his Russian friends of all sorts and conditions to
the reader, in the hope that they may interest or entertain him, but also
to help him to understand the way in which they look at life, and to
account to him for their behaviour. He writes of the people he has met,
of cities he has visited, of manor-houses and third-class railway carriages,
of shrines and playhouses, of servant-girls and politicians, of station-
masters and Polish countesses, of Jews and priests and dancing-girls, of
the Queen of Poland, of the jumble of people he has lingered with, or
jostled against, in going up and down the Russian Empire.

Forty Years in Brazil. By FRANK BENNETT.
With 24 Illustrations. Demy 8vo. 10*s*. 6*d*. net.

Standard.—" Can be recommended to the reading public generally, and it should command close attention from students of international politics, and from the business world."

Pall Mall.—" May be warmly recommended to all who are interested in a country that is steadily coming more and more to the front."

Sheffield Daily Telegraph.—" Intending residents in, and visitors to, South America will serve their own interests greatly by reading through this capitally written book."

Memories and Adventures. By MADAME HÉRITTE-VIARDOT. With 20 Illustrations. Demy 8vo. 10*s*. 6*d*. net.

Daily Telegraph.—" Full of the deepest interest for both laymen and musicians."

Sheffield Daily Telegraph.—" A mine of amusing anecdote."

Sixty-Eight Years on the Stage. By Mrs. CHARLES CALVERT. Popular Edition. Large Crown 8vo. 6*s*.

Morning Post.—" Agreeable and amusing."

Pall Mall Gazette.—" Charming."

Yvette Guilbert: Struggles and Victories. By YVETTE GUILBERT and HAROLD SIMPSON. Profusely illustrated with Caricatures, Portraits, Facsimiles of Letters, etc. Demy 8vo. 10*s*. 6*d*. net.

Daily Telegraph.—" The volume is a real delight all through."

Daily Chronicle.—" A fascinating book, and a remarkable one, because for the half of it you may read Yvette Guilbert's own French, and the translation of Mr. Simpson on the opposite page."

ROMANTIC HISTORY

The Hero of Brittany : Armand de Chateaubriand. Correspondent of the Princes between France and England, 1768—1809. By E. HERPIN. Translated by MRS. COLQUHOUN GRANT. With 8 Illustrations. Demy 8vo. 10s. 6d. net.

Armand de Chateaubriand was a cousin of the famous French author René de Chateaubriand. The book presents a very faithful and pathetic picture of Brittany during and after the great Revolution. Armand was a fine sportsman, and served with Condé's army; but he spent his days crossing the Channel, often in great peril, for the purpose of embarking the escaping emigrants, and bringing back such men as were assisting the return of the Bourbon princes.

The Man Who Saved Austria : The Life and Times of Baron Jellačić. By M. HARTLEY, Author of "A Sereshan." With 18 Illustrations and a Map. Demy 8vo. 10s. 6d. net.

Bookman.—"A capital account of the life and times of Jellačić. Exceedingly readable."

A Mystic on the Prussian Throne : Frederick-William II. By GILBERT STANHOPE. With 12 Illustrations. Demy 8vo. 10s. 6d. net.

Morning Post.—"We congratulate Mr. Stanhope on a very genuine piece of work."

The Life and Times of Arabella Stuart. By M. LEFUSE. With 12 Illustrations. Demy 8vo. 10s. 6d. net.

Globe.—"An extraordinarily interesting book."

Pall Mall Gazette.—"A vivid picture of a remarkable and unhappy woman and of the times in which she lived, loved, and suffered."

A Queen's Knight : The Life of Count Axel de Fersen. By MILDRED CARNEGY, Author of "Kings and Queens of France." With 12 Illustrations. Demy 8vo. 7s. 6d. net.

Liverpool Courier.—"Far greater than that of the ordinary novel is the interest in the story of his life as told in this book."

Roman Memories, in the Landscape seen from Capri. Narrated by THOMAS SPENCER JEROME. Illustrated by MORGAN HEISKELL. Demy 8vo. 7s. 6d. net.

To make the great historical suggestiveness which the country around and near the Bay of Naples possesses for the cultivated observer assume a more distinct form in the consciousness of visitors to these shores, is the purpose of this book. It begins with the old myths and continues down through the surprisingly large number of Roman events associated with this district to the end of classical times (476 A.D.), keeping the local episodes in their due relation to the general current of ancient history by giving an outline thereof, which makes it of value as a general sketch of Roman affairs.

Margherita of Savoy. By SIGNORA ZAMPINI SALAZAR. With a Preface by RICHARD BAGOT. Illustrated. Demy 8vo. 10s. 6d. net.

In the present volume the part played by Margherita di Savoia in encouraging every legitimate and practical effort to enlarge the sphere of feminine action in her country, and to employ feminine influence as an intellectual and civilising influence instead of confining it entirely within the walls of palaces and cottages, is described by Signora Zampini Salazar both accurately and faithfully.

In Cheyne Walk and Thereabout. By REGINALD BLUNT, Author of "Paradise Row." With 22 Illustrations. Demy 8vo. 10s. 6d. net.

To say that Cheyne Walk is the most interesting, historic, and delightful street in all England might strike a stranger to Chelsea as rather an extravagant claim, yet these pages go far to support it.

The English Court in Exile : James II. at St. Germain. By MARION and EDWIN SHARPE GREW. With 16 Illustrations. 15s. net.

Spectator.—"Should certainly be read by all students of the revolution ; an exceedingly interesting and readable book."

Athenæum.—"Not a single uninteresting page. We had no idea so good a book could be written on such a story.'

Truth.—"Excellent . . . picturesque and impartial."

The Court of William III. By EDWIN and MARION SHARPE GREW. With 16 Illustrations. Demy 8vo. 15s. net.

Morning Post.—"Done with fairness and thoroughness. . . . The book has many conspicuous merits."

The Romance of the Oxford Colleges. By
FRANCIS GRIBBLE. Popular Edition, with 12 Illustrations. 2s. 6d. net.

Westminster Gazette.—" Does not contain a dull page."

The Romance of the Cambridge Colleges.
By FRANCIS GRIBBLE. With 16 Illustrations. Crown
8vo. 6s. Popular Edition, 2s. 6d. net.

Times.—" May be cordially recommended."

Truth.—" The history of the colleges in a bright and readable form with
an abundance of anecdotes."

Aberdeen Free Press.—" Not a dull page."

The Romance of the Men of Devon. By
FRANCIS GRIBBLE, Author of "The Romance of the
Oxford Colleges," etc. With a Photogravure Frontispiece
and 16 Illustrations. Crown 8vo. 6s.

The Lady.—" A delightful volume."

Dundee Advertiser.—" Written with a charm and ease which are delightful."

The Story of the British Navy. By E. KEBLE
CHATTERTON. With a Frontispiece in Colour and 50
Illustrations from Photographs. Demy 8vo. 10s. 6d. net.

Naval and Military Record.—" Contains practically everything which the
average individual wishes to know."

Royal Love-Letters: A Batch of Human
Documents. Collected and Edited by E. KEBLE
CHATTERTON. With 12 Illustrations. Demy 8vo.
10s. 6d. net.

The Petticoat Commando: or, Boer Women
in Secret Service. By JOHANNA BRANDT. With
13 Illustrations and a Map. Second Edition. Crown 8vo.
6s.

Romances of the War. By E. S. GREW. Illus-
trated. 3s. 6d. net.

" Romances of the War " is a volume dealing, as the title denotes, with
many incidents, some tender, some pathetic, some romantic, and most of
all with the human side of War as it is in France at the present time.
The great charm of the book is that it proves how true is the well-known
saying, " What a small world we live in," and also perhaps that " Truth is
stranger than fiction."

17

FOR EVERYDAY LIFE

Stammering. By EDWIN L. ASH, M.D. (Lond.). 2s. 6d. net.

Nerve in War Time. By EDWIN L. ASH, M.D. (Lond.). Crown 8vo. 1s. net.

Nerves and the Nervous. By EDWIN L. ASH, M.D. (Lond.). New Edition. Crown 8vo. Cloth, 3s. 6d. net.

Daily Express.—"One of the most refreshing books published for some time. Dr. Ash not only probes into exactly what one feels when one is nervous or worried, but the treatment is so free from fads that it does even an unnervy person good."

Mental Self-Help. By EDWIN L. ASH, M.D. (Lond.), Assistant Physician Italian Hospital, London; Physician for Nervous Diseases to the Kensington and Fulham General Hospital. Author of "Nerves and the Nervous." Crown 8vo. 2s. 6d. net.

Athenæum.—"A lucid little book. His style is clear and convincing."

Can't Waiters; or How You Waste Your Energies. By EDWIN L. ASH, M.D. (Lond.). Crown 8vo. 1s. net.

How to Treat by Suggestion. By EDWIN L. ASH, M.D. (Lond.). 2s. 6d. net.

Life Without Servants; or, the Re-discovery of Domestic Happiness. By A SURVIVOR. 1s. net.

A Manual for Nurses. By SYDNEY WELHAM, M.R.C.S. (late Resident Medical Officer, Charing Cross Hospital). With Diagrams. Second Edition. Crown 8vo. 3s. 6d. net. Paper cover, 1s. net.

British Medical Journal.—"A useful reference work for nurses both early and late in their career."

Nursery Nurse's Companion. By HONNOR MORTEN. Crown 8vo. Paper 1s. net. Cloth 1s. 6d. net.

Household Accounts. By RUPERT DEAKIN, M.A., and P. J. HUMPHREYS, B.Sc. Fourth Edition. Crown 8vo. 6d. net.

Dog Lover's Companion. By an Expert. Crown 8vo. 2s. net.

Poultry Keeper's Companion. By A. T. JOHNSON. Crown 8vo. 2s. 6d. net.

SPORTS AND PASTIMES

England v. Australia. By P. F. WARNER. Popular Edition. Demy 8vo. 7s. 6d. net.

Sporting Life.—"The book is one that every cricketer should possess."

Twenty-four Years of Cricket. By ARTHUR A. LILLEY. Popular Edition. 1s. net.

All About Bowls. By G. T. BURROWS. 2s. 6d. net.

Switzerland in Winter. By WILL and CARINE CADBY. With 60 Photographs by the Authors. Crown 8vo. 5s. net.

Country Life.—"A little book, admirably written, and packed with useful information. Brings back a thousand memories to many thousand people."

The Motorist's Pocket Tip Book. By GEOFFREY OSBORN. With 13 Full-page Illustrations. Fcap. 8vo. Leather. 5s. net.

Scottish Field.—"Contains in the clearest, most condensed, and most practical form just the information one wants."

The Chauffeur's Companion. By "A FOUR-INCH DRIVER." With 4 Plates and 5 Diagrams. Waterproof Cloth. 2s. net.

The Lady Motorist's Companion. By "A FOUR-INCH DRIVER." With 7 Plates and 4 Diagrams. 2s. 6d. net.

British Mountain Climbs. By GEORGE D. ABRAHAM, Author of "The Complete Mountaineer." With 18 Illustrations and 21 Outline Drawings. Pocket size. Leather, 7s. 6d. net. Cloth, 5s. net.

Sportsman.—"Eminently a practical manual."

Swiss Mountain Climbs. By GEORGE D. ABRAHAM. With 24 Illustrations and 22 Outline Drawings of the principal peaks and their routes. Pocket size. Leather, 7s. 6d. net. Cloth, 5s. net.

Country Life.—"As essential as good climbing boots."

19

The Golfer's Pocket Tip Book. By G. D. FOX,
Part-Author of "The Six Handicap Golfer's Companion.
Fully Illustrated. Pott 8vo. Leather. 5s. net.

HARRY VARDON says :—"It is a very handy little book."

The Six Handicap Golfer's Companion. By
"TWO OF HIS KIND." With Chapters by H. S. COLT
and HAROLD H. HILTON. Illustrated with 15 Photographs of JACK WHITE (ex open champion). 2s. 6d. net.
Popular Edition. Paper cover, 1s. net.

Golf Illustrated.—"The author's aim is to teach inferior players how to
reduce their handicaps to at least six. There is a great deal of sound advice
in the book, and its value is greatly increased by two excellent chapters by
Mr. H. H. Hilton and Mr. H. S. Colt."

First Steps to Golf. By G. S. BROWN. With 94
Illustrations by G. P. ABRAHAM, F.R.P.S., and 9 Diagrams. Crown 8vo. 2s. 6d. net.

Daily Graphic.—"A most lucid guide for the benefit of the beginner."

Letters of a Modern Golfer to his Grandfather.
Arranged by HENRY LEACH. Crown 8vo. 6s.

Outlook.—"A book in which the human interest is as marked as the
practical instruction."

Club Bridge. By ARCHIBALD DUNN. Crown 8vo
Popular Edition. 3s. net.

Evening Standard.—"This is, in fact, 'THE BOOK.'"

Royal Spade Auction Bridge. By ARCHIBALD
DUNN. Second Edition. Crown 8vo. 2s. 6d. net.

Birmingham Post.—"An exhaustive discussion of the many debatable
points in connection with the systems of play at present in force. Mr.
Dunn's reasoning is logical and his suggestions valuable."

Auction Bridge. By ARCHIBALD DUNN. Crown
8vo. 3s. net.

The Rifleman's Companion. By L. R. TIPPINS.
With 6 Illustrations. 2s. 6d. net.

TRAVEL AND ADVENTURE

The Philippines Past and Present. By DEAN C. WORCESTER. With 128 Full-page Illustrations. 2 Vols. Demy 8vo. 30s. net.

Morning Post.—"Mr. Worcester's knowledge of the Philippines is un-surpassed."

The New Russia: From the White Sea to the Siberian Steppe. By ALAN LETHBRIDGE. With 95 Illustrations and 3 Maps. Demy 8vo. 16s. net.

Times.—"Page after page discloses a homely and intimate acquaintance with the habits and thoughts of Russians of every stock."

Pall Mall Gazette.—"Piquant impressions of the Russian disposition—the whole narrative is engaging to those who have a compartment of their minds devoted to the present and future of Russia."

Evening Standard.—"Mr. Lethbridge's cheery and glowing pages should have a great effect when the war is over in stimulating both the tourists and the merchandise of this country to enter Russia. Altogether an attractive book."

Voyaging in Wild Seas: or, A Woman among the Head Hunters. A narrative of the voyage of the *Snark* in the years 1907-1909. By CHARMIAN KITTREDGE LONDON (MRS. JACK LONDON). Demy 8vo. 15s. net. Illustrated.

Daily Graphic.—"Jack London has narrated the story of 'The Cruise of the *Snark*.' But his wife believes she can supplement that history with details likely to interest her husband's public. Hence the 'Voyaging in Wild Seas.' Whatever the incidents to be recorded, and they are countless in number and of thrilling variety, she describes them in a straightforward manner. Consequently there is not a dull page in the book. It is alive with human interest and high spirits all through. As may be inferred, this is in large part a biography of the novelist for the period it covers. But it is more; it presents an absorbing picture of the natives with whom the travellers came in contact."

The Cruise of the *Snark*. By JACK LONDON. Fcap. 8vo. 1s. net.

Scotsman.—"Makes a fresh and strong appeal to all those who love high adventure and good literature."

Daily Graphic.—"We have to thank Mills & Boon for publishing this remarkable world's cruise."

Two Years with the Natives in the Western Pacific. By DR. FELIX SPEISER. With 40 Illustrations. Demy 8vo. 10s. 6d. net.

Illustrated Sporting and Dramatic News.—"A really valuable book of travel."

Daily Chronicle.—"Supplies valuable material for a knowledge of races low down in the scale of culture in his detailed account of their social life, belief, and customs."

Experiences of a Woman Doctor in Serbia. Cr. 8vo. 5s. net. By DR. CAROLINE MATTHEWS.

The Wonderful Weald and the Quest of the Crock of Gold. By ARTHUR BECKETT, Author of "The Spirit of the Downs." With 20 Illustrations in Colour and 43 Initials by ERNEST MARILLIER. Popular Edition. Large Cr. 8vo. 6s.

Daily Telegraph.—"A charmingly discursive, gossipy volume."

Sunday Times.—"He adopts the quest in the Stevensonian manner, and creates the right atmosphere for the vivid presentment of the history and romance of the Weald. He knows the Weald so well, and can chat about it with such unobtrusive communicativeness, such a charm of literary allusion, and such whimsical humour, that we journey with him delightedly, and come to its end with regret."

Tramps through Tyrol. By F. W. STODDARD ("Dolomite"). With 20 Illustrations. Demy 8vo. Second Edition. 7s. 6d. net.

Standard.—"The outcome not of a mere holiday scamper, but of long residence. In his good company we explore the Dolomites, the Brenner Pass, cross the Fanes Alp, and make acquaintance with such delectable places as San Martino, Molveno, and Cortino—to say nothing of Innsbrück and Meran. He tells us a good deal about shooting and fishing and the delights of the swift ski. Altogether 'Tramps through Tyrol' is an alluring book. 'Try,' we say, therefore, 'Tyrol,' and take Mr. Stoddard's delightful 'Tramps' with you."

From Halifax to Vancouver. By B. PULLEN-BURRY. With 40 Illustrations. Demy 8vo. 12s. 6d. net.

Daily Chronicle.—"Well written, well arranged, full and complete."

BOOKS FOR CHILDREN

The Dolls' Day. By CARINE CADBY. With 29 Illustrations by WILL CADBY. Crown 8vo. 1s. 6d. net.

Daily Graphic.—"Wonderland through the Camera. Mrs. Carine Cadby has had the charming idea of telling in 'The Dolls' Day' exactly what a little girl who was very fond of dolls dreamed that her dolls did when they had a day off. Belinda the golden-haired, and Charles the chubby, and their baby doll disappeared from their cradles while their protectress Stella was dozing. They roamed through woods and pastures new; they nearly came to disaster with a strange cat; they found a friendly Brother Rabbit and a squirrel which showed them the way home. In short, they wandered through a child's homely fairyland and came back safely to be put to bed at night. It is a pretty phantasy, but it is given an unexpected air of reality by the very clever photographs with which Mr. Will Cadby points the moral and adorns the tale. In them the dolls are so cleverly posed that they look quite as lively and quite as much alive as little Stella thought them. The combination makes one of the most unusual and pretty gift-books of the season."

The Children's Story of Westminster Abbey.
By G. E. TROUTBECK. With 4 Photogravure Plates and 21 Illustrations from Photographs. Third Edition. Crown 8vo. 5s. net. Popular Edition, 1s. net.

Stories from Italian History Re-told for Children.
By G. E. TROUTBECK With 22 Illustrations from Photographs. Crown 8vo. 5s. net.

Tatler.—"These stories are so vivid and so interesting that they should be in every schoolroom."

Kings and Queens of France.
A Child's History of France. By MILDRED CARNEGY. With a Preface by the BISHOP OF HEREFORD. With a Map and 4 Full-page Illustrations. Crown 8vo. 3s. 6d.

Science and Magic.
By F. H. SHOOSMITH, B.Sc. With 54 Illustrations. Crown 8vo. 2s. 6d. Also School Edition. 1s.

A unique science book for boys on uncommonly interesting lines, containing a clearly written account of some of the many ways in which a knowledge of scientific principles has been utilised by magicians of all ages to deceive and astonish others. Magnetism and Electricity, Chemistry, Sound, Light, Pneumatics, and Surface Tension are laid under contribution, and the author, after carefully describing the tricks and the means by which they are performed, utilises them as so many illustrations of scientific laws and principles. The language employed throughout is as simple and untechnical as possible, and the interested reader—and what boy is not interested in conjuring?—is put in possession of the secrets of a number of capital tricks and astonishing feats, while absorbing a very considerable amount of scientific knowledge.

Queery Leary Nonsense. Being a Lear Nonsense Book, with a long Introduction and Notes by the EARL OF CROMER, and edited by LADY STRACHIE. With about 50 Illustrations in colour and line. 4to. 3s. 6d. net.

The Lear Coloured Bird Book for Children.

By EDWARD LEAR. With a Foreword by J. ST. LOE STRACHEY. 2s. 6d. net.

Francis Chantrey: Donkey Boy and Sculptor.

By HAROLD ARMITAGE, Author of "Chantrey Land," "Sorrelsykes," etc. Illustrated by CHARLES ASHMORE. 2s. 6d. Also School Edition, 1s.

A wholly delightful book, giving a sketch of the life and work of Sir Francis Chantrey, the milk boy who modelled the statue of the Duke of Wellington opposite the Royal Exchange, and the Sleeping Children in Lichfield Cathedral. He gives many romantic details about Chantrey's boyhood, and tales about him and his donkey that are particularly attractive to children. Scott, Wordsworth, and most of the famous men of his time, were modelled by Chantrey, and monuments by him are to be seen in London, Liverpool, Dublin, Edinburgh, Glasgow, etc. The clever pen-and-ink illustrations by Mr. Charles Ashmore are exactly in tune with their subjects.

The Duke of Wellington. By HAROLD ARMITAGE.

Illustrated. Crown 8vo. 2s. 6d. Also School Edition, 1s.

A book for boys of from 12 to 14. Mr. Armitage writes with spirit, and he is a master of vigorous phrase-making. The book will be of special interest in view of the Centenary of the Battle of Waterloo. The author's description of Wellington's amazing industry, of his unswerving loyalty, of his unbending devotion to duty cannot fail to impress all those who read this biography of Britain's hero.

A Little Girl's Cookery Book. By C. F. BENTON

and MARY F. HODGE. Crown 8vo. 2s. 6d. net. Paper, 1s. net.

Daily Telegraph.—"A capital idea. Hitherto the manufacture of toffy has represented the limit of nursery art in the direction indicated, but this volume contains excellent recipes for dishes which children will find quite easy to make, and their elders to eat without misgivings. Every father, mother, uncle, and aunt should make a point of presenting their child friends with a copy of this useful and practical book."

A Little Girl's Gardening Book. By SELINA

RANDOLPH. Crown 8vo. Cloth, 2s. 6d. net. Paper, 1s. net.

Aberdeen Free Press.—"A first-rate book."
Manchester Courier.—"All children love gardens. This book will make them genuine gardeners."

ON MATTERS THEATRICAL

A Century of Great Actors (1750-1850). By
CECIL FERARD ARMSTRONG, Author of "The
Dramatic Author's Companion," etc. With 16 Illustrations. Demy 8vo. 10s. 6d. net.

Standard.—"An interesting series of pithy biographies—concise and entertaining."

World.—"An interesting and useful book."

Bookman.—"Very alert, very scholarly, and entirely readable."

A Century of Famous Actresses (1750-1850).
By HAROLD SIMPSON, Author of "Yvette Guilbert,"
"A Century of Ballads," etc., and MRS. CHARLES
BRAUN. With 18 Illustrations. Demy 8vo. 10s. 6d.
net.

Illustrated London News.—"We have seen no book of bygone actors giving a better idea of their acting."

A Century of Ballads (1810-1910), Their Composers and Singers. By HAROLD SIMPSON. With 49 Illustrations. Demy 8vo. 10s. 6d. net.
Popular Edition. Large Crown 8vo. 6s.

Daily Express.—"Deals brightly with a most fascinating subject."

The Garden of Song. Edited by HAROLD SIMPSON.
Fcap. 8vo. 2s. 6d. net.

Scotsman.—"An excellent anthology of lyrics that have been set to music. They are, for the most part, songs that have enjoyed a wide popularity, and this collection of lyrical gems forms a very desirable little volume."

Shakespeare to Shaw. By CECIL FERARD ARMSTRONG, Author of "The Dramatic Author's Companion." Crown 8vo. 6s.

Athenæum.—"The dramatists—Shakespeare, Congreve, Sheridan, Robertson, Sir A. W. Pinero, and Mr. Shaw—have been selected as landmarks of English drama. The method adopted by the author is the separate examination of every play of his subjects with criticism of the qualities of each."

An Actor's Hamlet. With full notes by LOUIS
CALVERT. Crown 8vo. 2s. 6d. net.

Daily Chronicle.—"Full of illuminating insight."

The Dramatic Author's Companion. By CECIL
F. ARMSTRONG. With an Introduction by ARTHUR
BOURCHIER, M.A. Second Edition. Crown 8vo.
2s. 6d. net.

Times.—"This is a very useful book, and there seems little omitted which
will be of practical service to an aspiring playwright. All about different
kinds of plays and their production, contracts, placing MSS. (with an
excellent covering letter), facsimile MS., copyrights, etc."

Pall Mall Gazette.—"The best book of its kind we have seen. Its author
has not only a wide knowledge of plays, but a sound judgment both from
the artistic and popular standpoint. His advice is always practical."

The Amateur Actor's Companion. By VIOLET
M. METHLEY. With 8 Illustrations. Crown 8vo.
2s. 6d. net.

The aim of this book is to be a more complete and more up-to-date
handbook upon Amateur Theatricals than has yet appeared.

The Actor's Companion. By CECIL F. ARM-
STRONG. With an Introduction by ARTHUR BOUR-
CHIER, M.A. Crown 8vo. 2s. 6d. net.

Whilst having no pretensions to teaching the difficult art of acting, this
book will be found to contain many practical and useful hints to the
young actor. The author, associated as he has been for many years with
one of the larger West End theatres, has had exceptionally good
opportunities of studying the inner workings of a theatre, the technical
requirements of the actor, and the many considerations besides that of
mere talent necessary to ensure success on the stage. Two special chapters,
one dealing with Scientific Voice Production and the other with the Art
of Gesture, are contributed by well-known experts.

Peter Pan: The Fairy Story of the Play.
By G. D. DRENNAN. With a Photogravure of Miss
PAULINE CHASE as Peter Pan. Fcap. 8vo. Leather,
2s. 6d. net. Popular Edition, Crown 8vo. Paper, 6d.
School Reader Edition, with an Introduction by A. R.
PICKLES, M.A. Cloth, 6d.

Votes for Women. A Play in Three Acts. By
ELIZABETH ROBINS. Crown 8vo. 1s.

VOLUMES OF VERSE

Rhymes for Riper Years. By HARRY GRAHAM.
Fcap. 8vo. 3s. 6d. net. Illustrated by N. B.

Deportmental Ditties. By HARRY GRAHAM.
Profusely Illustrated by LEWIS BAUMER. Fcap. 8vo. Third Edition. 3s. 6d. net.

Daily Graphic.—"Harry Graham certainly has the knack."

Daily Chronicle.—"All clever, generally flippant, invariably amusing."

Canned Classics, and Other Verses. By
HARRY GRAHAM, Author of "Deportmental Ditties," "The Bolster Book," etc., etc. Profusely Illustrated by LEWIS BAUMER. Crown 4to. 3s. 6d. net. Also Fcap. 8vo. 3s. 6d. net.

Times.—"As fresh as ever."

Evening Standard.—"One long delight."

Founded on Fiction. By LADY SYBIL GRANT.
With 50 Illustrations and a Cover Design by GEORGE MORROW. Crown 4to. 3s. 6d. net.

T. P.'s Weekly.—"A book of chuckles."

Daily Chronicle.—"The vivacious offspring of a witty mind."

Times.—"Mr. Morrow's pictures fit the verses like a glove."

Poetry for Boys. Selected by S. MAXWELL, M.A.,
LL.B., F.R.A.S. Crown 8vo. Second Edition. 1s. 6d.

Schoolmaster.—"The sixty-three poems in this volume have been very carefully selected. Each is of high literary merit, and of such a kind as will especially appeal to boys and make them wish to know more of our heritage of English poetry."

Through the Loopholes of Retreat. By HANSARD WATT. With a Portrait of COWPER in Photogravure. Fcap. 8vo. 3s. 6d. net.

Daily Chronicle.—"Mr. Hansard Watt has hit upon the happy plan of placing poet and letter-writer side by side, so that the two voices may blend in unison. The volume has a select passage of prose and verse for every day in the year, and the whole is a pleasant and surpriseful storehouse of good things. Mr. Watt prints for the first time a letter from Cowper to his friend Joseph Hill: it is full of interest, and lends an additional charm to the volume."

FOR THE CONTEMPLATIVE MIND

Involution. By LORD ERNEST HAMILTON. Demy 8vo. 7s. 6d. net.

Daily Graphic.—"Extremely interesting, an honest and lofty endeavour to seek the truth."

St. Clare and Her Order: A Story of Seven Centuries. By the Author of "The Enclosed Nun." With 20 Illustrations. Demy 8vo. 7s. 6d. net.

Catholic Times.—"Fills a gap in our religious literature."

The Town of Morality: or, the Narrative of One who Lived Here for a Time. By C. H. R. Second Edition. Crown 8vo. 6s.

Daily Graphic.—"In short, C. H. R. has written a new 'Pilgrim's Progress,' a passionate, a profound, and stirring satire on the self-satisfied morality of Church and of Chapel."

The Book of This and That. By ROBERT LYND. Crown 8vo. 4s. 6d. net.

A collection of brilliant Essays by a talented Irishman.

Pall Mall Gazette.—"This delightful book. Mr. Lynd writes so wittily and pleasantly."
Manchester Guardian.—"His cleverness is amazing; fresh, amusing, suggestive."

The Enclosed Nun. Fcap. 8vo. New Edition. Cloth, 2s. 6d. net. Paper, 1s. net.

Pall Mall Gazette.—"A remarkably beautiful piece of devotional writing."

Unposted Letters. Crown 8vo. 6s.

Daily Express.—"Full of tender memories. There is something about them peculiarly touching and very human."
Morning Post.—"They have a style of their own which must attract every reader of taste."

A Little Book for those who Mourn. Compiled by MILDRED CARNEGY. A little volume for those in sorrow, chosen with care and sympathy. Pott 8vo. Cloth, 1s. 6d. net. Lambskin, 2s. 6d. net.

An Englishman's Farewell to his Church, 1s. net.

FOR POLITICIANS AND OTHER READERS

Joffre and His Army. By CHARLES DAWBARN. Crown 8vo. 2s. 6d. net.

France at Bay. By CHARLES DAWBARN. 5s. net. Popular Edition, 2s. 6d. net.

Makers of New France. By CHARLES DAWBARN. With 16 Illustrations. Demy 8vo. 10s. 6d. net. Popular Edition. Crown 8vo. 2s. 6d. net.

Pall Mall Gazette.—"Well worth setting alongside the best literature that we have on France from Bodley or the Philosophers, for the book is imbued with a profound and instructive sympathy expressed in admirable form."

Morning Post.—"A triumphant book which ought to be read by everybody who wishes to understand the new orientation of French mentality."

Liverpool Post.—"Mr. Dawbarn is a literary ambassador of the Entente."

Romany Life. By FRANK CUTTRISS. With an Illustration in 4 Colours and 46 in Monotone. 7s. 6d. net.

A charming book on Gipsy life, beautifully illustrated and quite the best thing of its kind that has been published. It is written by an expert whose knowledge of Gypsies is beyond question, and whose photographs are the real thing.

Home Life in Ireland. By ROBERT LYND. With 18 Illustrations. Third and Popular Edition, with a New Preface. Crown 8vo. 6s.

Spectator.—"An entertaining and informing book, the work of a close and interested observer."

Sidelights on Austrian Society. By X. Crown 8vo. 5s. net.

Music as she is Wrote. By SIR F. COWEN. 1s. 6d. cloth. 1s. paper.

Captive of the Kaiser in Belgium. By GEORGES LA BARRE. With 7 Illustrations by the Author. Paper Cover. 1s. net.

Military Mail.—"One of the best and most reliable personal narratives of the state of Belgium at the time of the German invasion."

Mills & Boon's Catalogue

Physical Training for Boy Scouts. By LIEUT.
A. G. A. STREET, R.N., Superintendent of Physical Training to the School Board of Glasgow, with a Foreword by SIR R. S. S. BADEN-POWELL, K.C.B. With 29 Diagrams. Paper Cover. 7d. net.

Morning Post.—"An excellent little Manual, it should be invaluable to Scout Masters."

The Italians of To-day. By RICHARD BAGOT,
Author of "My Italian Year." Crown 8vo. Third Edition. 2s. 6d. net. Popular and Revised Edition, 1s. net.

Scotsman.—"Shows the same intimate knowledge of Italian life and character as 'My Italian Year.'"

The German Spy System in France. Translated from the French of PAUL LANOIR. Crown 8vo. 5s. net. Paper Cover, 6d. net.

T.P.'s Weekly.—"A book that should awaken the public and the authorities to a condition of things that can only cease to be alarming if prompt action is taken."

The Pocket Gladstone : Selections from the Writings and Speeches of William Ewart Gladstone. Compiled by J. AUBREY REES, with an Introduction by the Rt. Hon. Sir ALGERNON WEST, P.C., G.C.B. Fcap. 8vo. Cloth, 2s. net. Paper, 1s. net.

The Pocket Disraeli. By J. B. LINDON, M.A. Fcap. 8vo. Cloth, 2s. net. Paper, 1s. net.

The Pocket Asquith. By E. E. MORTON. Fcap. 8vo. Cloth, 2s. net. Paper, 1s. net.

Spectator.—"Should be useful to the student of contemporary politics."

The Bolster Book. A Book for the Bedside. By HARRY GRAHAM, Author of "Deportmental Ditties." Frontispiece by LEWIS BAUMER. Fourth Edition. Fcap. 8vo. 3s. 6d. net. Popular Edition, 1s. net.

Daily Chronicle.—"Humorists are our benefactors, and Captain Graham being not only a humorist, but an inventor of humour, is dearer to me than that 'sweet Tuxedo Girl' of a famous song, who, 'though fond of fun,' is 'never rude.' I boldly assume that Biffin, like 'the Poet Budge' and Hosea Biglow, is a ventriloquist's doll—a doll more amusing than any figure likely to appear in the dreams of such dull persons as could be put to sleep by articulate laughter."

Daily Graphic.—"Most refreshingly and delightfully funny."

EDUCATIONAL BOOKS

Full particulars of these may be obtained from MILLS & BOON, LTD., 49, Rupert St., London, W. Heads of Schools are invited to write for specimen copies of books likely to prove suitable for Introduction as class books.

ENGLISH TEXTS

As You Like It. Edited by C. R. Gilbert, M.A. With Notes. 1s.
Henry V. Edited by C. R. Gilbert, M.A. 1s. Plain text, 6d. net.
The Tempest. Edited by Frank Jones, B.A. 1s. Plain text, 6d. net.
The Merchant of Venice. Edited by G. H. Ball and H. G. Smith. 1s. Plain text, 6d. net.
Maxwell's Poetry for Boys. 1s. 6d.
Smith & Ball's English Composition. 1s. **English Grammar.** 1s. 6d. 1 Vol. 2s.

FRENCH

Baron's Exercises in French Free Composition. 1s. 6d.
Barrère's Elementary French Course. 1s.
Barrère's Intermediate French Course. 2s.
Barrère's Précis of Comparative French Grammar. 3s. 6d.
Barrère's Récits Militaires. 3s.
Barrère's Short Passages for French Composition. 2s. 6d.
Bossut's French Word Book. 1s.
Bossut's French Phrase Book. 6d. net.
Shrive's First French Unseen Book. 6d. net.
Shrive's Second French Unseen Book. 1s. net.
Walters' Reform First French Book. Illustrated. 1s.

DIRECT METHOD FRENCH TEXTS

Edited by R. R. N. BARON, M.A., Cheltenham Grammar School.
Tristapatte et Goret. 1s.
Claretie's Pierrille. 1s. 6d.
Daudet's La Belle Nivernaise. 1s. 6d.
Merimée's Tamango and **José Maria le Brigand.** 1s.
Hugo's Bug Jargal. 2s.

MODERN FRENCH AUTHORS

With Introductions, Notes, Exercises for Retranslation, Vocabularies, etc.
Balzac—Ursule Mirouët. Without vocabulary, 2s.
Daudet.—La Belle Nivernaise. With vocabulary, 1s. 6d.
Gréville.—Le Moulin Frappier. With vocabulary, 2s. Without, 1s. 6d.
de Nerval.—La Main Enchantée. With vocabulary, 1s.
Toudouze.—Madame Lambelle. Without vocabulary, 2s.

GEOGRAPHY

Wetherill's New Preliminary Geography. 1s. 6d.
Bird's School Geography. 2s. 6d.

GERMAN

Walters' Reform First German Book. Illustrated. 3s. net.
Lange's Advanced German Reader. 2s.

DIRECT METHOD GERMAN TEXTS

Meister Martin. Edited by L. Hirsch, Ph.D. 1s. 6d.

31

EDUCATIONAL BOOKS—*continued*.

MODERN GERMAN AUTHORS

With Introductions, Notes, Vocabularies, Exercises for Retranslation, etc.

Auerbach.—Selections from Schwarzwälder Dorfgeschichten. With vocabulary, 2s. Without vocabulary, 1s. 6d.
Bechstein—Ausgewählte Märchen. With vocab., 1s. 6d. Without, 1s.
Benedix.—Doktor Wespe. With vocabulary, 2s. Without, 1s. 6d.
Ebers.—Eine Frage. Without vocabulary, 2s.
Freytag.—Die Journalisten. Without vocabulary, 2s.
Freytag.—Soll und Haben. Without vocabulary, 2s.
Heyse.—Hans Lange. Without vocabulary, 1s. 6d.
Hoffmann.—Meister Martin. Without vocabulary, 1s. 6d.
Hoffmann.—Schiller's Jugendjähre. Without vocabulary, 1s. 6d.
Moser.—Der Bibliothekar. With vocabulary, 2s. Without, 1s. 6d.
Scheffel's Selections from Ekkehard. Without vocabulary, 2s.

LATIN

Ball's Latin Extracts for Sight Translation. 1s.
Williamson's First Latin Unseen Book. 6d. net.

MATHEMATICS

Boon's Preparatory Arithmetic. With answers, 1s. 6d. Without, 1s. Answers only, 6d. net.
Boon's Arithmetic for Schools and Colleges. With answers, 4s. Without answers, 3s. 6d. Answers only, 6d. net.
Deakin's New School Geometry. 2s. 6d. Part I, 1s.; Part II, 1s. 6d.
Deakin's Rural Arithmetic. With answers, 1s. 6d. Without, 1s.
Deakin's Household Accounts. With or without answers. 6d. net.
Harrison's Practical Mathematics. With ans., 1s. 6d. Without, 1s. 3d.
Harrison's Practical Mathematics for Elementary Schools. 6d. net.
Stainer's Graphs in Arithmetic, Algebra, and Trigonometry. 2s. 6d.
Walker's Examples and Test Papers in Algebra. With or without answers, 2s. 6d. In 2 parts, each with answers, 1s. 6d. Without, 1s. 3d.

READERS

Peter Pan: The Fairy Story of the Play. Illustrated. 6d.
Francis Chantrey: Milkboy and Sculptor. Illustrated. 1s.
Armitage's The Duke of Wellington. Illustrated. 1s.
Cadbys' The Dolls' Day. Illustrated.
Shoosmith's Science and Magic. With 54 Illustrations. 1s.

SCIENCE

Goddard's First School Botany. With 207 diagrams. 2s. 6d.
Hood's Problems in Practical Chemistry. With 22 Illustrs. 5s.
Oldham's First School Chemistry. With 71 Illustrations. 2s. 6d.
Oldham's Elementary Quantitative Analysis. With 11 diagrams. 1s. 6d.
Norris' Experimental Mechanics and Physics. Illustrated. 1s. 6d.
Laws and Todd's Introduction to Heat. With 108 Illustrations. 2s. 6d.
Stanley's Outlines of Applied Physics. Illustrated. 2s. 6d.

SCRIPTURE

Gilbert's Notes on St. Matthew's Gospel. 1s.

Hazell, Watson & Viney, Ld., London and Aylesbury